Also by Heidi Swain

The Cherry Tree Café
Summer at Skylark Farm
Mince Pies and Mistletoe at the Christmas Market
Coming Home to Cuckoo Cottage
Sleigh Rides and Silver Bells at the Christmas Fair

Heidi Swain

Sunshine and Sweet Peas in Nightingale Square

SIMON &
SCHUSTER

London · New York · Sydney · Toronto · New Delhi

A CBS COMPANY

First published in Great Britain by Simon & Schuster UK Ltd, 2018
A CBS COMPANY

1 3 5 7 9 10 8 6 4 2

Simon & Schuster UK Ltd
1st Floor
222 Gray's Inn Road
London WC1X 8HB

Simon & Schuster Australia, Sydney
Simon & Schuster India, New Delhi

www.simonandschuster.co.uk
www.simonandschuster.com.au
www.simonandschuster.co.in

A CIP catalogue record for this book
is available from the British Library

Paperback ISBN: 978-1-4711-6487-3
eBook ISBN: 978-1-4711-6488-0
eAudio ISBN: 978-1-4711-7473-5

Typeset in the UK by M Rules
Printed and bound by CPI Group (UK) Ltd, Croydon, CR0 4YY

MIX
Paper from
responsible sources
FSC® C020471

Simon & Schuster UK Ltd are committed to sourcing paper that is made
from wood grown in sustainable forests and support the Forest Stewardship
Council, the leading international forest certification organisation. Our
books displaying the FSC logo are printed on FSC certified paper.

To
Grandad Herb
Who grew sweet peas in abundance

Prologue

'Are you sure you're all right, Kate?' David asked as our honeymoon flight finally touched down and I twisted in my seat to catch my first glimpse of an Italian sunrise. 'I know she said something to you.'

'Honestly,' I said, shaking my head and dismissing the harsh words my mother had used to warn me that my marriage would last six months, if I was lucky. 'I'm fine. It's nothing.'

'But you were late to the church,' David persisted in spite of my reassurance. 'Very late.'

'I've already told you,' I laughed, reaching for his hand and kissing it. 'That was down to Dad dithering about. He was more nervous than I was.'

David nodded.

'Did you think she'd finally got to me?' I asked, half-jokingly. 'I hope you didn't think she'd made me change my mind?'

'The thought did enter my head as the seconds began to tick by,' he admitted with a boyish grin.

'Then you're more deluded than she is,' I tutted. 'I love you, David and no amount of mithering from my mother could ever change that.'

It was true. I loved the man in the seat next to me body and soul. I had from the very first moment I laid eyes on him. Yes, he had a dubious relationship history but I knew he wasn't the same person any more. Unfortunately, my mother didn't share my belief, but had she paid half as much attention to the impeccable present as she did to the promiscuous past, she would have seen for herself just how well-suited we were.

David hadn't so much as looked at another woman since our relationship had turned from casual to serious and sitting on that flight, poised to explore Rome, Venice and beyond, I could see both my marriage and my career comfortingly stretching out ahead of me. David and I were to be partners both in our lives and our work in the antiques trade. Granted we had each chosen to make sacrifices to make our relation-ship work, but we were both equally determined to make a success of it all.

'She still doesn't know you like I do,' I said consolingly, 'but she will. In time.'

David didn't look convinced.

'I just wish I could make her see how much I love you, Mrs Kate Harper.' He burst out, more serious all of a sudden,

'I just want her to understand that I would never hurt you, that this old leopard really has changed his spots.'

'Hey,' I cut in, feeling giddy at the sound of my married name, 'less of the old, thank you very much! There aren't that many years between us.'

David was not to be distracted from making his heartfelt declaration.

'No,' he said, 'I mean this, Kate. You're the best thing that's ever happened to me. You've been a breath of fresh air since the first moment I clapped eyes on you and I would never, ever do, or say, anything that would hurt you or make you doubt me. I don't care what anyone else thinks of us, all I need to know is that you trust me with every bit of your heart.'

I closed my eyes as he tenderly cupped my face in his hands and brushed his lips lightly against mine. I had never felt so happy, so loved and cherished. I held tight to that moment and locked it away for safekeeping.

'I trust you,' I whispered, looking deep into his eyes.

Chapter 1

Eight years later

'What I don't understand is why you feel you have to go at all.'

This had been the initial reaction from David when I told him I was moving out of our house and leaving London for good, and he had been adding to his arguments to try and make me stay every day during the weeks that followed.

'There's absolutely no reason why you should go,' he had said when he realised I was actually serious about making a clean break and not playing some game of cat and mouse.

My days of playing at anything were well and truly over, but I had struggled to make him believe it. I had struggled to make myself believe it for a while. There had been times when his offers to start over had sounded almost appealing but in the end, I knew I couldn't live with a half-arsed happy ending. There was no way now that I could ever have what I had once been so content to forgo and what was left over simply wasn't enough. It was all a far cry from the promises we had made on our honeymoon eight years ago.

'I've left you alone, haven't I?' he now said reasonably.

He had. In fact, he had behaved impeccably throughout the proceedings and complied with every stipulation my legal team had suggested.

'I've moved out,' he continued, 'even told you that you can have this place, every last brick of it and that solicitor of yours has already screwed me for more than half of the business.'

'The business that we grew and developed together,' I gently reminded him.

'Yes,' he said, slumping down on the sofa, 'sorry. I know it's what you're entitled to. I just can't bear the thought of you being so far away and it's making me say stupid things.'

'I'm not going to be *that* far away,' I sighed, 'and besides, you lost all rights to keeping me close when you—'

I bit my tongue to stop the words tumbling out and reminded myself that it was my badgering which had triggered the ruinous chain of events in the first place.

'I know I did,' he said, shaking his head, 'I know, but there are only so many times I can say sorry without it losing its meaning.'

He sounded absolutely miserable and I cursed the naivety which had led me to think that I could bend him to my will once we'd settled companionably into married life. Had I respected the bargain we'd struck, his friends would still be marvelling at the fact that I'd somehow tamed 'the old rascal' with the dire reputation whom they all loved so much.

'Talking of the business,' he said, thankfully changing tack, 'Francesca Lucca was asking after you today. She wanted to know if you'd found anything for that new place of hers in Florence.'

I stopped packing and stood with my hands on my hips.

'Please don't tell me you haven't told her.'

'How can I?' David shrugged. 'She's a good Catholic woman. Divorce doesn't feature on her radar.'

'Well, it didn't feature on mine until you—' I stopped myself again and took another deep breath.

It was a miracle that our sniping had never escalated into anything really regrettable, but it was getting harder rather than easier. This move was happening just in the nick of time as we strove to keep our increasingly terse exchanges on the right side of civilised.

'Well, you'll just have to look after her yourself now, won't you?' I told him bluntly.

David and I had built up our bespoke business, travelling the world sourcing antiques, artefacts and curios which would delight our list of discerning clients, who were prepared to pay handsomely for the 'seeker' service we provided. Francesca Lucca was one of our wealthiest and fussiest and she had always preferred to work with me rather than 'that naughty boy'. At almost fifteen years older than me I couldn't see David as a boy, but she was spot on with the 'naughty' tag.

'Are you leaving all of these?' he asked, pointing at a little side table which was full of photographs.

'Yes,' I shrugged, averting my eyes and wondering if he'd noticed I was no longer wearing my wedding band. 'I have a head full of memories, David. I don't need photographs as well.'

There was one picture I had kept, though. It was taken the summer we met, just before my final year at university. I hadn't wanted to go home for the holidays, so needed to work to pay my rent. I had ventured into an antique shop after a particularly awful interview for a job in a fast-food chain, hoping to be appeased by looking at beautiful things.

Galleries and museums were my usual go-to soothers, but access to the shop was both conveniently close by and free. It belonged to a friend of David's and the man himself happened to be there bartering over the price of a small statue. They somehow roped me into their conversation and the shy, gauche twenty-year-old I was at the time fell hard for the sophisticated smart-talking man who paid over the odds for an art deco figure just because I said I liked it.

'Let me take you out to lunch,' he had said once we left the cool emporium and were outside in the heat of the midday sun. 'It'll soften the hit my bank balance has just taken.'

I insisted on paying and the only thing I could afford was burgers and chips which we ate outside under the shade of a tree in the park. It was a strange beginning, an unusual afternoon by any standard, but by the end of it I had a job to see me through the summer and a heart brimming with love that my housemates warned me was bound to end in heartbreak.

Heartbreak . . .

'You can keep them,' I said quickly, returning to my half-filled box. 'And the statue.'

'Oh, Kate,' said David, mournfully shaking his head. 'I can't believe this is happening.'

'Me neither,' I sniffed.

I had always assumed that when relationships came to a difficult end there was shouting and recriminations, drama and things being thrown and torn, but our untangling hadn't been like that at all.

'If only I could hate you,' I sighed, wishing that, in spite of everything, I wasn't still a little bit in love with him.

I had watched other people's relationships break down and they seemed to instantaneously lead to loathing and bitterness, but I couldn't get anywhere near either emotion, even though the repercussions of what David had done had been so mortifying. Perhaps if I hadn't felt so responsible for the mess our relationship had become I would have been able to conjure something stronger, but I did feel responsible and therefore I couldn't.

'If only I could at least really lose my temper with you,' I said out loud, while wondering if an angry outburst would purge me of some of the pain.

'Perhaps you can't lay into me because we aren't meant to go our separate ways,' David said hopefully. 'If you really can't hate me then perhaps that means we should try and patch things up. I could go to therapy, counselling or something.'

I knew that all the counselling in the world wouldn't be able to give me the outcome I had been craving.

'No, David,' I said firmly, 'absolutely not. The decision's been made and now we have to stick to it. I want to stick to it,' I reminded him, just in case he was still labouring under the illusion that there was a glimmer of hope for us.

'Where did you say you were moving to again?' he asked quickly, trying to catch me off guard as he stood back up.

'I didn't.'

It had been hard not telling him about my new home in Norwich. It was neatly nestled in a place called Nightingale Square and sat opposite a grand Victorian pile called Prosperous Place. The pile was just the sort of property we had been employed to furnish and I knew he would have been as intrigued by its fascinating history as I was.

'But it's not all that far,' I added. 'And you can get in touch via my solicitor, should you need to. Try not to get into too much mischief now you're young, free and single again, won't you?'

'I only want to be one of those,' he said sadly.

And that summed up part of the problem, which I had realised far too late; there was a piece of David which had always been the naughty boy who didn't want to grow up.

Chapter 2

Being a cash buyer, and buying from a vendor with no chain, meant that the purchase of the house was simplicity itself and as the survey didn't throw up anything untoward I was able to leave London and David's broken vows behind almost immediately. Thankfully I could afford to take a year out, which would give me time to adjust to life on my own and update my new home.

I was very happy to be moving to somewhere where no one knew me. My London friends had all been David's friends originally and the majority were nearer his age than mine. It was only natural that when the moment came they had rallied round, but then drifted back into his orbit. I didn't mind that my own was empty. In fact, the clean slate this move was offering had become the one welcoming beacon in the sea of sadness I had been treading water in.

'Thanks for everything,' I called from the gate as the

removals men set off back to London with a hefty tip, and heartfelt thanks, for lugging about and rearranging some of the furniture that had been left behind.

'You're welcome love. Good luck.'

'Thanks,' I said, heading back down the path, but not before I'd spotted some curtain-twitching antics in the house on my right. 'A little bit of luck wouldn't go amiss,' I muttered as I closed the door and surveyed my box-filled new abode.

I was annoyed that my mother had been right about everything, even if she had miscalculated the timing; however, it had been one of her perfectly crafted comments which had led me to Norwich rather than back to Wynbridge. 'You know it's the only sensible thing to do,' she had said while trying to convince me to return home, and she was right. Returning to my childhood home and the nurturing embrace of my family would have been the 'sensible' thing to do, and that was exactly what stopped me doing it.

As out of character as it was, I didn't much feel like being sensible any more and I certainly didn't feel up to facing the head-bobs and pitying glances that I knew would be waiting for me in the flat Fenlands of Wynbridge should I return home to nurse my broken heart.

It had been my brother, Tom, whom I had called on for support when I found what looked, online at least, like the perfect sanctuary for an emotionally drained, and soon-to-be divorced, thirty-year-old woman who was having to face the rigours of creating a whole new life for herself because her seemingly perfect happy ever after had fallen so spectacularly apart.

Smiling out from the screen the little house in Nightingale Square looked like the answer to my prayers. Somewhere unassuming I could hide away in and nurse my shattered soul in peace and privacy. Yes, I had fallen head over heels in love with it at first sight, and yes, that was admittedly an impulsive trait which hadn't served me well in the past, but I had everything crossed that it was going to be just the distraction I needed.

My sister-in-law, Jemma, however, hadn't been convinced.

'Are you sure Jemma can spare you?' I asked Tom as we made arrangements to view the house via Skype.

'Of course she can spare him,' she butted in. 'Although she's really hoping you'll hate it and decide to come home.'

It was interesting that practically everyone in the family still assumed I considered Wynbridge my 'home' even though I had left over a decade ago for university and hadn't properly lived there since.

'Norwich is hardly the other end of the earth,' I reminded her as her knitted brow popped into view and I cringed at the thought of moving back into my childhood bedroom.

'But it's hardly next door either, is it, Kate?' she pouted back.

'It's only two hours away, Jem. One hundred and twenty short minutes along the A47, that's all.'

'That feels like two days with this pair in the back,' she moaned on, jerking her head in the direction of where my feisty niece and nephew were tucking into their dinner. 'We just want to look after you. You've been through so much . . .'

'I'll be there,' Tom cut in, 'but I'm not telling Mum.'

The train journey from Liverpool Street to Norwich had given me ample opportunity to mull over the nightmarish events of the previous few months and strengthen my resolve that not moving back to Wynbridge was the right thing to do. I had stared out of the window as the world flashed by, the landscape becoming steadily cleaner and greener.

I just knew that the house was going to be the ideal bolt-hole for me; it was still in a city, albeit a far smaller one than London, but it would offer the same urban level of anonymity I craved and that was just as appealing as the original sash windows and stained-glass panelling in the front door.

I had initially been drawn to Norwich because of its history and unusual castle. The fact that it wasn't somewhere I was familiar with was an added bonus. The newness of it all certainly felt right. I didn't want to live somewhere where memories and ghosts lurked around every corner, threatening to leap out and remind me of all that had gone before. My life was facing an unexpected fresh start and Norwich was a blank page with a fascinating past that I was looking forward to learning more about. Besides which, it conveniently put enough miles between me and Wynbridge to stop the family popping in to re-stock the fridge every five minutes, yet was close enough for an organised day trip.

'You're too thin,' Tom had predictably said when he hugged me at the station, 'and you have bags the size of suitcases. I had rather hoped Skype was just showing you in a bad light, but . . .'

'I'm heartbroken,' I answered him simply, but truthfully. 'What did you expect?'

I dreaded to think what he would have said had he known the details of everything I'd had to cope with. Had it simply been a case of good old-fashioned infidelity which had pulled my marriage apart, as I had let everyone believe, I might have been able to gradually piece it back together, but there had ended up being so much more to it than that and not even my rose-tinted desire for a Disney-inspired happy ever after could make me forget it.

'But you still don't hate him?' Tom frowned.

'No, I still don't hate him.'

Had my brother been privy to the part I had played in the catastrophe, and the colossal guilt I lugged about as a result, he would have understood why I was incapable of hating David for what he had done. I knew that had I not tried to force my beloved into changing his mind about something I had been so readily prepared to sacrifice when we first met, then our marriage would have merrily skipped along much the same as it had for the last few years. I would have still been living my fairy-tale dream rather than sweeping up the leftovers of a Hammer House Horror.

You see, I was a firm believer in one true love, a fully paid up member of the club in fact and now I had been blackballed. I had single-handedly screwed up my one shot at eternal happiness, and David's too, so hate was an emotion I simply couldn't reach, unless of course you counted the self-loathing which crept in during the darkest hours of the night.

'Mum would have forty fits if she could see you,' Tom tutted as he slipped his arm through mine and studied my face.

I knew my blue eyes had lost their sparkle and my usually jaunty ponytail was a little on the limp side, but thankfully he forbore to comment further.

'Of course she would,' I agreed, refusing to give in to the tears his familiar and comforting bulk threatened to unleash. 'And that's exactly why I don't want you to show her how to Skype.'

I knew it wasn't fair, my selfish desire to keep her at arm's length, but the sticking plaster she would try to apply to cover the hurt would be accompanied at some point by the inevitable, 'I did try and warn you, Kate.' And I was nowhere near ready to admit that I hadn't heeded a single one of her warnings but had rushed, like a giddy schoolgirl, headlong into trust and consequently, heartbreak.

Not that the blow had struck within the rather mean six months she had given us on our wedding day, but it had come nonetheless, and I sometimes wondered if she was as furious for herself as she was for me. My mother, as David had predicted, hadn't been easy to win over, but his unremitting charm and flattery had worn her down in the end; I couldn't help thinking she felt as much of a fool as I did, albeit for very different reasons.

'I did warn you it was a bit of a hole,' the estate agent, who was leaning against a sleek black Audi, had called out before he had even introduced himself when Tom had pulled into Nightingale Square. 'I hope you aren't already thinking you've wasted your time. You are Mrs Harper?'

I had winced, jarred out of my stupor by the sound of my married name as it tripped off his lips.

'Yes,' I remember nodding, 'I'm Kate.'

The estate agent matched the clichéd image I had conjured up during our telephone conversations to a T. The second he had discovered where I was travelling from he had assumed I had London money to throw around and then spent most of his time trying to convince me to look at far bigger properties with far more impressive postcodes, but my heart was already set on Nightingale Square and keeping the rest of my money safely in the bank.

My eyes had swept beyond him to the slightly wonky wooden gate and overgrown front garden and I realised that the house, which was the smallest of seven situated around a lush, fenced-in green, was just like me. Clearly it had been loved once, but was now in need of a little TLC. The clever wide-lens photographs online had played down the shabby state of the place, but I didn't care about that at all. I was in love with it and its interesting story already.

My fascination with history had led to me spending hours on the internet and in the library researching all about the Square and the man with the philanthropic vision who had built it. Burying myself in the past was thankfully still the one thing that I found I could focus on doing for longer than five minutes.

Charles Wentworth had been the wealthy owner of one of the twenty-six shoe factories which, from around 1860, had overtaken weaving as the main industry in Norwich and, from what I could deduce, he was the perfect man, the archetypal romantic hero. Not that I was sure I still entirely believed in them any more, my faith having received a hefty knock, but as he was consigned to the history books, I reckoned he was about as close to perfection as I was likely to get.

An astute businessman, with a heart as large as his financial resources, he had chosen to live in the sprawling Victorian mansion house which stood directly opposite the factory, so he could keep an eye on his investment. Once satisfied with the set-up he had then overseen the building of seven homes on the land in between to accommodate the factory managers and their families.

Once upon a time there had also been houses for the general workers but they, along with practically everything else from that time, were gone now. The back to back terraces had been demolished decades ago, replaced with larger, more attractive, villa-style properties with gardens, and the former factory site now housed a row of little shops.

From what I could make out, the only things left of Mr Wentworth's legacy were Nightingale Square and his home Prosperous Place which, I had noticed when I turned around to admire it, also happened to be for sale and looked to be in a similar state to the house I had set my heart on.

From what I had read, Charles Wentworth had left his family well provided for, but in earning his fortune he hadn't stepped on anyone's toes or exploited any of his workers as so many others did at that time and I hoped his descendants were proud to be related to such a worthy forefather.

'Shall we get on?' I had said to the agent, my eyes moving back to the gate.

'Of course,' he had smiled, his misplaced confidence restored. 'I'm Toby Fransham by the way. Let's have a quick look here and I'll take you to view a couple of those hi-tech new-builds I was telling you about, next to the bypass. This place might be dead in the water, but those beauties on the other hand . . .'

'Are worth twice as much in commission,' Tom had cut in before I had a chance.

Toby Fransham did at least have the grace to blush.

'Why don't you show me the garden?' my clever brother had suggested, 'and we'll let Kate look around inside in peace.'

The golden glow of a late September afternoon showed the house in a halcyon light, but as I stepped over the threshold, stooping to pick up the pile of post that had become wedged behind the front door, I knew the place would have seduced me even in the depths of winter.

'It's been in the same family ever since it was built,' Toby Fransham had sniffed as Tom quickly steered him along the hall towards where the kitchen led to the garden. 'The last resident lived here all her life, but by the looks of it she never had much done by way of modernisation, hence the price.'

'You said the family were keen to secure a sale,' I had called after him. 'I do like the place, Mr Fransham, but I'm not about to make a fool of myself over money.'

He had carried on while I took my time exploring first the little sitting room with the bay window which overlooked the front garden, and then the dining room with the intensely swirling orange and brown carpet that led to the archaic kitchen. There was a large cupboard under the stairs and as I followed them up, I found a double bedroom at the front, and two singles, one of which you had to walk through to access the bathroom. Although the avocado suite and MFI kitchen had clearly been fitted a long time ago, everything appeared to be in working order, despite a thin layer of dust.

'What do you think?' Tom had asked when he caught up with me as I was looking out of the front bedroom window again.

There was an uninterrupted view across the green to Prosperous Place and I imagined Mr Wentworth and his wife doing the rounds, making sure everyone was happy and that the houses were all up to scratch. The vision was almost enough to stir my jaded romantic heart a little.

'I think I could be happy here,' I had sighed, bracing myself for the arguments against buying the place that my sensible brother was bound to come up with. 'In spite of the . . . interesting upholstery.'

I hoped he wasn't going to protest too strongly because I was amazed that I had even entertained the idea that I could ever be happy again, let alone suggested it out loud.

'I think you could too,' he had agreed, taking me completely by surprise. 'This place is right up your street, isn't it?'

'You don't think I should be moving back to Wynbridge then?'

'No,' he had said, taking my hand and giving it a squeeze. 'You don't need us lot fussing around you, and like you said to Jemma, it's only a couple of hours away in the car.'

'Thanks, Tom,' I had said, smiling up at him and feeling relieved.

'There's plenty to do here,' he acknowledged, looking around at the few bits of furniture that had been left behind and the thick gloss paint that covered the little fireplace and mouldings, 'but that's no bad thing. It'll keep your mind off—'

'Come on then,' I had interrupted before my mind was filled with what I was moving here to forget. 'Let's go and find Mr Toby Fransham and tell him he needs to keep looking for someone else to stick in those new-builds he's so fond of.'

Considering we were standing on the pavement in the middle of a city, there had been little to hear beyond a lone scolding blackbird and the distant rumble of the ring road. It was a far cry from the constant barrage I had grown accustomed to in my marital home in London.

'I daresay it livens up a bit in the evenings when everyone comes home from work,' Tom had said when I commented on the quiet. 'There'll probably be cars parked everywhere then.'

'You aren't trying to put me off buying it all of a sudden, are you?' I had responded as a movement behind an upstairs curtain in a house on my right caught my eye.

'Of course not,' he had grinned. 'I wouldn't dream of it. Just don't tell Jemma.'

'You're actually thinking of putting in an offer, are you?' asked an astounded Mr Fransham, who until that moment had been annoyingly engrossed in something on his phone.

'I most certainly am,' I had quickly replied. 'I'm going to suggest seven less than the asking price.'

He had drawn in a sharp breath and shook his head. It was the classic estate agent's reaction to hearing numbers they didn't like.

'I'm not sure they'll go for that,' he had frowned. 'And the office rang a minute ago to say there's been another enquiry about the place today.'

I had been pretty certain that he was bluffing. The girl I had spoken to had told me the place had been languishing on their books for well over a year.

'Well, they won't get a penny more out of whoever buys it, with that disaster of a bathroom still in situ, will they?' I had told him briskly. 'And I know it's been empty through one harsh winter already, so I'm fairly confident the vendor will snatch my hand off.'

Tom had winked and then began to laugh.

'I'll be in the city for the rest of the day,' I had shouted as I marched purposefully back to the car and Mr Fransham muttered something about number crunching. 'Let's just see if we can get the ball rolling before I'm back on the train, shall we?'

I had felt certain I wasn't going to need to worry about crunching anything.

'I thought you were down,' Tom had beamed as he helped me with my seatbelt because my hands were suddenly shaking so much.

'I am,' I had willingly confirmed, 'but when it comes to parting with money, I'm not completely out.'

Less than an hour later my offer had been accepted and I had started to brace myself to face a change of life that I didn't feel at all ready for; but at least lovely Nightingale Square was as good a place to be moving to as any.

I was interrupted from my musings by a sharp rap on the front door knocker. This was wholly unexpected and I froze, a mug in one hand and a jar of coffee in the other, staring at the door and the silhouette the other side of it. Another knock finally galvanised me into action.

'Sorry,' the woman was apologising before I'd even seen her warm smile and friendly hazel eyes. 'Sorry. I know you've literally only just arrived and I don't want to interrupt your unpacking, but I thought you might like these.'

She nudged a carrier bag at her feet and it was only then that I noticed she had a smallish child tucked under one arm and a pumpkin under the other.

'Well, not this, obviously,' she laughed, hoisting the boy a little higher up her hip, 'but the pumpkin and sweets are all yours if you want them.'

I was at a loss.

'It's Hallowe'en,' she explained, her smile faltering as she no doubt began to wonder whether I was going to say anything at all. 'The Square will be crawling with kids by teatime and I thought if you put these on your step you might get some peace.'

'Right,' I said, transferring the jar and mug to one hand before stooping to pick up the bag, 'sorry. Thanks. That's very kind of you.'

'When I spotted the lorry turn up I thought you probably wouldn't have had time to sort anything for yourself.'

The little boy under her arm began to wriggle so she set him down.

'Do you want to come in?' I asked. 'I've just found the coffee and some mugs.'

'Well, as long as you're sure.'

I wasn't really, but I hadn't expected a neighbour, assuming that's who she was, to descend so soon after my arrival and I wasn't familiar with Nightingale Square's visitor etiquette yet either. In London I didn't know a single one of my neighbours. I probably couldn't have picked them out in a line-up.

'Of course,' I said, holding the door further open as

the little lad toddled into the hall. 'Come in. I'm Kate by the way.'

'I'm pleased to meet you,' said the woman, following his lead. 'We were all so excited to see the sold sign go up. This little place has been empty since Doris moved on and we've all been hoping someone lovely would take it.'

I wasn't sure I was capable of living up to everyone's expectations of loveliness.

'Anyway, I'm Lisa,' she added. 'I live two doors along that way,' she pointed vaguely in the direction of her home, 'and this is my youngest, Archie.'

Not the curtain-twitcher then.

'Hello, Archie,' I smiled, and he grinned up at me, babbling something I couldn't make out.

'I also have Tamsin and Molly,' his mum happily continued, 'and a husband called John. He's the biggest baby of the lot, but that's men for you!'

I was amazed that she had three children, four if you counted the husband. She only looked about my age.

'We were childhood sweethearts,' she giggled when I didn't say anything. 'We started young. Have you got any of your own?'

'No,' I said, 'no kids.' I didn't add that I had no husband either. 'How do you take your coffee?'

A few minutes later, and much to my surprise, Lisa had made herself completely at home. She arranged Archie on the kitchen floor with a few pots and pans and a wooden spoon from the nearest packing box to bang on and then began to scoop out the belly of the pumpkin on the Formica-topped kitchen table, which she had thoughtfully covered with the free newspaper I had found on the doormat when I arrived.

'I'll leave you to carve it,' she said, when she spotted me watching. 'And I've put a couple of tea lights in with the bags of sweets and my spare gas lighter thingy.'

'Thank you,' I said, tipping out the bag and marvelling at the array of sugar-coated items. Archie began to make mewing noises when he spotted the brightly coloured bags.

'No chance,' Lisa told him sternly. 'If you're anything like your big sister you'll be hyper for days.'

Archie, clearly used to not getting his own way, went back to his drumming.

'You'll have to tell me how much I owe you,' I said.

'Don't worry about that,' Lisa laughed, 'it's all from the pound shop anyway, but I'll take this pumpkin flesh and the seeds, if that's all right?' she asked, pointing at the plastic container she had been decanting it into. 'I'm making soup for us all tonight and roasting the seeds for my other half to snack on. We're both trying to lose a few pounds,' she added confidingly.

I was impressed she could find the time to make soup from scratch with three children to look after, but I couldn't help thinking that it was a shame she was trying to lose weight as her curvy figure suited her. Although I didn't tell her that, obviously.

'I used to be really skinny before I had the kids,' she tutted, 'but never mind.'

We had another coffee and she explained that everyone who lived in the Square was getting together on 5 November to have a little bonfire and let off some fireworks.

'We do it every year,' she told me, which came as something of a shock given that I had been expecting the same level of remoteness from my neighbours here as I'd experienced in London. 'We're all a very friendly bunch. We also have a summer party and go first footing on New Year's Eve. There's a real sense of community here.' She sounded very proud.

'First footing?' I queried.

'Yes,' she grinned. 'Have you never heard of it? The first person over your threshold after midnight on New Year's Day brings gifts.'

'Gifts?'

'Coins, bread, coal, whisky, that sort of thing.'

They sounded like unusual 'gifts' to me.

'It's for good luck,' she elaborated, with a smile. 'And a year filled with warmth, food and flavour. You'll soon get the hang of it,' she laughed. 'And us.'

'Well, that all sounds lovely,' I swallowed, my tummy rolling at the thought of getting roped in when all I really wanted to do was draw the curtains and hide away from the world as well as my neighbours.

'I was hoping you'd say that,' Lisa beamed. 'You and your husband would be most welcome to join us for the fireworks. In fact, we're all hoping you will.'

I had no idea where she'd got the idea that I had a husband to bring to the party, but I felt obliged to accept her kind invitation and before I knew it I'd been talked into providing a tray of toffee apples for the children along with some extras for bobbing.

'I won't bombard you about who lives where,' she said, scooping Archie up into her arms and kissing the top of his head as he leaned keenly back towards his instruments. 'You'll meet everyone at the fireworks and you can tell us all about yourself then.'

'I'll look forward to it,' I swallowed, following her back through the house to the front door.

'I can tell you're going to fit right in here, Kate,' she said, turning her lovely smile on me again. 'You're really going to love living in Nightingale Square!'

I hoped she was right.

Chapter 3

I was very grateful for the Hallowe'en-themed moving-in gift Lisa had dropped off. The trick or treaters arrived at tea-time, just as she had predicted, and were still hanging around late into the evening. Thankfully no one had knocked on my door, but I had heard plenty of activity as I settled down for an early night and when I went out to retrieve the pumpkin the next morning the bowl of sweets was completely empty.

'Morning, Kate!' called a man's voice to my left, making me jump.

'Good morning,' I called back while surreptitiously looking around to see if anyone else was going to pop up unannounced and scare me half to death.

'Sorry, love,' he chuckled, leaving his van and wandering over. 'I didn't mean to make you jump. I'm John. I'm Lisa's other half.'

Looking at him, he couldn't possibly have been anyone

else. He had the same easy-going manner as his wife and the lines around his eyes suggested he spent just as much time smiling as she did.

'You didn't get any trouble last night, did you?' he asked with a nod towards the pumpkin and empty sweet bowl.

'No,' I said. 'No one even knocked, but the treats have all gone.'

I was pleased to see the rest of the Square and the little green weren't littered with wrappers and eggshells. Clearly the local trick or treaters were a considerate bunch.

'Lisa warned them all to leave you alone,' John said with a wink. 'No one would dare defy my Mrs.'

'Well, her warnings certainly worked and actually,' I said, feeling surprised, 'I had the best night's sleep I've had in a while.'

I had fully expected to toss and turn for a few nights under my new roof. I had got used to being home alone in the London house since David had moved out of course, but being somewhere new was always unsettling, what with the unfamiliar creaking floorboards and water pipe rumblings, but I had gone out like a light.

'That's good,' he said. 'You'll no doubt need your energy for unpacking today.'

'That's true,' I said.

I was looking forward to arranging my things just as I wanted them, even if I was going to have to pack them all away again when I made a start on the decorating and refurbishing.

'Fortunately, there's not too much to do.'

'What about your cooker and stuff?' John asked. 'Have you got your white goods sorted?'

'They're all new and coming later this morning,' I told him. 'The fridge-freezer I can turn on myself and I've paid for the retailer to sort the cooker installation, but I think I'll need to call someone to plumb in the washing machine. That's way beyond my DIY capabilities.'

'I can do that for you,' John laughed. 'You don't want to be paying someone.'

'No, really,' I said, embarrassed that he might have thought I was angling for a favour.

'It's no bother,' he shrugged, walking back to his van. 'I can do washing machines standing on my head. Our brood have got through enough of them in their time. Just give Lisa a knock when it arrives and I'll pop round after work. Unless your other half would rather have a crack at it himself?'

The thought of David knowing how to change a simple tap washer, let alone plumb in a washing machine was laughable, but rather than take the opportunity to set John straight on either my husband's domestic shortcomings or my marital status, I simply thanked him and rushed back inside.

*

I spent a contented couple of hours arranging books on shelves, hanging curtains and cleaning windows and, in spite of the outdated décor and the lawn that was badly in need of a cut, the little place felt very homely indeed. As foolish as it might sound I couldn't shake off the feeling that it was enjoying being lived in again. I might not have got away with shutting out the world so far, but I was certain that purchasing number four Nightingale Square had been the right thing to do.

The post brought various notices and bills along with a couple of 'welcome to your new home' cards from my parents and Jemma and Tom. I knew it wouldn't be long before they would be expecting to pay a call; in fact I was surprised Mum hadn't beaten the removals van, but so far, she was respecting my request for privacy, encouraged in no small part by my dad and Tom, I was sure.

I arranged the cards on the mantelpiece in the sitting room and made a mental note to call a chimney sweep sooner rather than later. The evenings were getting cool already and the room would be even more cosy and snug with a fire burning in the grate.

The house was a far cry from my upmarket home in London and I wondered what David would make of it, not that he was ever going to set foot in it. I had to accept that my life with him was over and there was no point in wondering what he would think of my choices and decisions, but it wasn't going to be easy to move on from that shared mindset. A van pulling up on the pavement stopped me brooding further and I rushed out to welcome in my shiny new kitchen appliances.

'I just wanted to bring this back,' I said to Lisa late that morning, when I had plucked up the courage to pop round and return her lighter.

I don't know why I felt so shy. When I was growing up Mum and our neighbours used to be in and out of each other's houses all the time, as did us kids. I guess it was a friendly habit I had become unaccustomed to.

'And I wanted to say thank you for coming over yesterday,' I added. 'It was a lovely welcome to the Square and much appreciated.'

'Well, you're more than welcome,' she said, ushering me inside. 'Come and have some lunch. I've got pumpkin soup coming out of my ears. The kids weren't overly impressed with it for some reason.'

'No, no,' I said, taking a step back, 'I didn't mean to intrude. You must be busy.'

'I am,' she said, 'busy having lunch. Come on. Then I'll ring John and tell him your washing machine has arrived. That was the delivery for you, wasn't it?'

Lisa and John's house was much larger than mine, not that you'd know it with all the kids' stuff strewn about. It was teetering on the right side of chaotic however and felt comfortable and very lived-in. The fridge was covered in a muddle of messy artwork, as was a large pinboard which filled the wall above the table.

'Excuse the mess,' said Lisa with a dismissive wave of her hand. 'Although,' she added, looking around her, 'by our standards this isn't too bad. I've always said there's more to life than hoovering. As long as the right bits are bleached that's all I'm bothered about. Here, Kate,' she said, indicating the stove, 'give that a stir, would you?'

I did as I was told while she strapped Archie into his high chair and he dazzled me with yet another of his cheeky smiles.

'Doesn't he look like his dad?' I laughed, now able to see the likeness for myself.

'Funnily enough,' chuckled Lisa, 'you aren't the first person to say that. I reckon it's the belly.'

'No,' I said, not realising she was joking, 'it's his eyes. They're definitely John's eyes.'

I looked up from the pan again and we both burst out laughing.

'What's all this about then?' called a voice from the hall. 'I'm not sure we allow laughing on an empty stomach.'

'Come on through, Harold!' Lisa called back. 'Come and meet your new neighbour.'

Harold, it turned out, was the octogenarian who owned the house between me and Lisa and John. Like Doris, the lady who had owned my house, he was a long-term resident and he came and had his lunch with Lisa most days. He was also a little hard of hearing.

'What did you say your name was again, love?' he asked as I was helping Lisa serve up her fragrant soup and home-made rolls.

'Kate!' I shouted in his ear as loud as I dared.

I glanced nervously at Archie who I was sure would dissolve into tears at any moment.

'Don't worry about him,' said Lisa. 'He's used to plenty of volume.'

'Kate,' said Harold, finally grasping it. 'That's a very pretty name. Are you married, my dear?'

'Yes,' I said, not untruthfully. 'Would you like one of these rolls?' I offered, holding up the plate.

'Oh, no thank you,' Harold smiled. 'Not with my teeth.'

'I'll have you know this batch is much better than the last one!' Lisa shouted at him good-naturedly.

When we had finished eating I loaded the dishwasher while Lisa put Archie down for his nap and then I walked with Harold back to his front gate.

'I hope you, or that husband of yours, are keen gardeners,' he commented with a nod towards my overgrown plot. 'Doris had some lovely plants in there, but they're getting choked out by all those weeds.'

I knew enough about gardening to be able to separate the

good from the bad and ugly and promised that I'd cut it back and tame it properly before the winter took hold.

'I can see you're going to fit into our little Square a treat,' said Harold, squeezing my hand. 'I only hope whoever buys Prosperous Place is as lovely as you.'

We both turned to look at the large house and the for sale board that one of the more prestigious local agents had hammered up just behind the metal gates.

'All overgrown like that,' said Harold with a little shudder, 'it reminds me of Satis House.'

'The house in *Great Expectations*, you mean?'

'That's the one.'

Looking at its abandoned state, he had a point.

'There are rumours about developers buying it and turning it into apartments, you know.'

He sounded outraged and I have to say I felt rather perturbed myself by the thought of Mr Wentworth's once beautiful home being carved up.

'You should have seen it in its heyday,' said Harold wistfully.

'I've seen photographs on my computer,' I told him. 'I researched the history of the place when I was making up my mind about—'

I quickly stopped before I really put my foot in it.

'Lots of my family worked in the factory, you know,' he went on, thankfully, rather than pushing for an explanation. 'I've got dozens of snaps if you'd like to see them one day.'

'Yes, please,' I said enthusiastically. 'That would be lovely.'

'I'm chuffed you know about the area,' he said, turning back to his house. 'It's good that folk know how this place started out. It'd be a real shame if it all disappeared and no one remembered anything about it at all.'

'I couldn't agree more,' I told him, thinking it would actually be more of a tragedy than a shame.

'And believe me,' he added mysteriously, 'there's more to know about that place than the number of bedrooms and acreage of the garden.'

I felt a little shiver as I looked back at the boarded-up windows. Clearly Harold's knowledge of Prosperous Place extended way beyond the 'happy times' I had been reading about.

Chapter 4

When I opened my bedroom curtains on 5 November, a sold banner had been plastered across the for sale board at Prosperous Place and, from what I heard during my first trip into the wider neighbourhood, it sounded as though Harold's worst fears for the house were going to come true.

Realising I was becoming a little too comfortable with pottering about at home and brooding over thoughts of David, I took myself off for an exploratory ramble to the lovely row of shops which were just a couple of minutes' walk from my door. There was a grocery store, an artisan bakery and café, a gift shop selling local arts and crafts, as well as a florist, butcher, post office, second-hand book store and a couple of well-stocked charity shops.

As far as I could tell the community spirit, in this part of the city at least, extended far beyond the reaches of Nightingale Square and everyone was very friendly. I might have kept my front door closed for a few days, but beyond it there was no sign of the urban anonymity I had been expecting.

Distractedly I rifled through my purse counting change as I steered myself towards the grocery store, which had old-fashioned crates of seasonal veg artistically arranged along its frontage. More intent on checking I had enough money to buy the apples I had promised to provide than watching where I was going, I didn't see a man also heading for the shop door and he, distracted by his phone screen, didn't see me either.

'Sorry,' he automatically blurted out as we collided with a heavy bump. 'Sorry.'

My handful of coins were knocked from my grasp and drunkenly rolled across the pavement in all directions.

'I wasn't looking where I was going.'

'No, I'm sorry,' I insisted. 'I wasn't watching either.'

It wasn't until the coins had been retrieved that we straightened up and faced one another.

'There you go,' said the man, carefully tipping the money from his palm into my open purse. 'I don't think any escaped.'

'Thank you,' I faltered as our eyes momentarily met.

His were a deep, intense chocolate brown, heavily lidded and his thick, dark lashes would have been the envy of any girl who was a martyr to Maybelline.

'No problem,' he smiled, pulling off his woolly hat to

reveal a head full of curls as dark as his stubble. 'Are you going in?' he asked with a nod to the door when I didn't move or say anything.

'Yes,' I said, 'yes, sorry.'

I made a grab for the handle, but he reached it before me and stood back to let me go in first.

'Thanks,' I smiled.

I felt my cheeks flush as I squeezed past, quickly forgiving him his preoccupation with his phone.

We worked in embarrassing synchronicity around the shop floor, each reaching for exactly what the other wanted on more than one occasion, but I managed to make it to the counter ahead of him.

'Do you have any avocados?' I asked the young woman who was operating the till.

'Just those two there,' she said, vaguely pointing, her eyes not surprisingly focused on the next customer in the queue.

I added the slightly over-ripe fruit to my basket and she turned her attention back to me as I dropped one of the shop's reusable jute bags on to the counter.

'Aha,' said a loud voice behind me, 'we meet at last. You're the lovely young lady who's moved into number four Nightingale Square, aren't you?'

'Oh,' I said, taken aback, as I turned to see a tall man daubed in flour step around the queue and stand right next to me. 'Yes, I am, but how did you know that?'

'Oh, he knows everything,' grinned the girl as she bagged up my bananas. 'You really have to watch this one.'

'Thank you, Poppy,' the customer in question smiled warmly, before offering me his hand. 'I'm Mark. I live at number seven with my husband, Neil.'

'Pleased to meet you, Mark,' I said, shaking his floury hand. 'Have you been spying on me, by any chance?'

'Of course,' he laughed. 'We all have.'

I thought again of the avid curtain-twitcher and realised he probably wasn't joking. Fortunately, I didn't think I'd been doing anything too embarrassing to make the scrutiny something I should be worrying about, but I was fairly certain the absence of a man about the house would have been noted by now.

'Are you coming to the party tonight?' he asked. 'I'm guessing Lisa has told you all about it.'

'She has,' I confirmed, 'and I am. I'm supplying the apples,' I added with a nod to the bag Poppy, the shop assistant, was now packing. 'Are you and Neil going to be there?'

'Well, I am,' he said, sounding suddenly less cheery, 'but I'm not sure if Neil will make it. He's work-obsessed these days, so he might not get back in time.'

'Oh dear,' I said.

'Yeah,' he shrugged. 'Don't even get me started. That man of mine needs to have a good look at his work-life balance and reassess his priorities.'

Clearly the mention of the party had hit a nerve.

'Anyway,' he said, shaking off his annoyance, 'I didn't come in here to have a moan about the state of my marriage.'

'What did you come in for then?' asked Poppy with another wide grin.

'Cranberries, if you have some. This chilly turn in the weather has got everyone asking for something with a slightly festive flavour.'

'I might have some dried ones,' she said, biting her lip. 'Bear with me and I'll have a rummage when I've finished serving.'

With my shopping paid for, Mark waited in line close to the man I had collided with on the street. Given the way he surreptitiously looked him up and down I guessed he had taken on board how handsome he was too.

'Did I hear you say there were no more avocados?' asked the liberator of my loose change.

'Afraid not,' Poppy sighed, looking for all the world as if she'd like to give him something far more exciting than an avocado. 'That lady had the last two.'

'Sorry,' I shrugged.

'That's twice you've beaten me to the punch then,' he said, pushing his thick curls away from his face.

'What do you mean?'

'Didn't I hear your friend here say that you've just moved into Nightingale Square?'

'That's right,' Mark quickly jumped in, keen to claim his spot in the conversation. 'I did.'

'I thought so,' he nodded, as he finished paying. 'I can't believe the house had been on the market all that time and I hadn't known about it. Apparently, your offer was accepted the day I enquired.'

I thought back to Toby Fransham, the estate agent, telling me there had been another interested party. Evidently, he hadn't been bluffing to get me to up my offer after all.

'Well, I'm sorry about that,' I said, reaching into my bag and pulling out one of the avocados. 'Let me give you this by way of compensation.'

Laughing, he took it and added it to his own purchases.

'You're sure you wouldn't rather part with the house?'

'Sorry,' I smiled. 'I'm staying put.'

'I don't blame you,' he smiled back, his dark eyes shining even brighter. 'I'm Luke, by the way.'

'Kate,' I responded, my voice catching in my throat.

We chatted until Mark had paid for his dried cranberries and then all walked back together in the direction of the bakery.

'I suppose you've spotted the sold sign?' Mark asked me. 'For Prosperous Place I mean.'

'Yes,' I said sadly, 'you can't really miss it, can you?'

'Such a shame,' he went on, shaking his head. 'Rumour has it that a developer has snatched it up with the intention of modernising and turning it into exclusive apartments. That's not you, is it?' he suspiciously asked Luke, who had stuck with us. 'You didn't set your sights on something bigger when you realised you'd missed out on Nightingale Square?'

'No,' Luke frowned. 'I had no idea that had been sold too. It's such a beautiful house.'

'But it won't be for much longer,' I said sadly. 'My neighbour, Harold was telling me about the potential plans, which would tie in with the rumour you heard, Mark. I've no doubt that if the new owners have their way, they'll rip the guts out of it. It'll be all about adding square footage rather than preserving the past.'

'Harold's really cut up about it,' Mark said, stopping outside the bakery door. 'But then, we all are. We'd been secretly hoping someone would step in and set about returning it to its former glory.'

'That would have been wonderful,' I agreed. 'I did some research about it before I moved and it looked amazing in its heyday, but I guess it's too late to turn the clock back now.'

'You're not wrong,' sighed Mark. 'Anyway love, I'd better get back to work. These cranberry buns won't bake themselves. Are you coming in?' he added, turning to where Luke had been standing. 'Oh,' he said, sounding disappointed. 'He's gone. Probably just as well though. If he'd hung around I'd never have got any work done!'

We both laughed.

'You didn't recognise him, did you?' He frowned.

I shook my head.

'No,' I said. 'I don't think so. Did you?'

'I thought I did,' he shrugged, 'but I can't quite place where from.'

'Well, never mind,' I said, swapping my heavy bag from one hand to the other. 'I'll see you tonight.'

'Yes,' he said. 'I'll catch you later. And don't be late,' he added with a wink. 'We're a friendly bunch but remember, we know where you live.'

I laughed again as he pushed open the door and called over his shoulder.

'And whatever you do, don't let Lisa talk you into sampling any of her bread. You could crack a tooth on her cottage loaf!'

I sat and ate my avocado salad that evening wondering if its twin was equally as delicious and then turned off the lights to peep in privacy around the upstairs curtains. I could see there was quite a crowd gathering on the green and the little bonfire was already lit, the flames casting dancing shadows up into the trees and bathing the scene in a golden glow.

I could pick out Lisa and John, along with their brood, and Harold, as well as Mark who looked to be very much on his own. My stomach squirmed at the thought of venturing out to meet the other half-dozen or so Nightingale Square residents I could see ambling about.

'I'd almost given up on you,' Lisa teased, taking the tray of apples and setting it down on an already packed trestle table. 'Come and say hello to everyone.'

First in the line-up were a couple in their sixties who lived in the house with the twitching curtains. It didn't take many seconds to work out who was responsible for them dancing about along their poles.

'I'm Carole,' said the woman briskly. She was immaculately turned out for a bonfire party, 'and this is my husband, Graham.'

Neither Graham nor I had time to exchange pleasantries before she launched off, filling me in on the nuts and bolts of living in Nightingale Square, which Lisa had neglected to mention.

'Bins go out on a Tuesday night, ready for collection on Wednesday,' she reeled off.

That much I had already worked out for myself but I didn't dare interrupt her. Carole was clearly the kind of woman who thrived on organisation and order.

'And the green here is cut by the council every month from April to October, so it's best not to leave anything lying about. There was very nearly a nasty incident last summer when your eldest left her bike out overnight, wasn't there Lisa?'

'Yes,' said Lisa, theatrically rolling her eyes. 'Very nearly Carole, but not quite.'

Graham took the tense moment as an opportunity to take a step away from his wife, but she quickly called him back to heel.

'Don't go disappearing,' she said, out of the corner of her mouth. 'I'm sure there's still plenty that needs doing.'

I felt Lisa bristle beside me and wanted to laugh. I didn't think Nightingale Square was big enough for two queen bees and wondered who would win the battle for overall supremacy. Lisa's approach to life was disarmingly laid-back while Carole's was the epitome of efficiency. It was too tough to call.

'Are those the apples you brought for bobbing, Kate?' asked Mark, stepping in with all the diplomacy of a skilled mediator.

'They are,' I nodded, handing over the bag. 'Maybe you and Graham could go and find a bowl to put them in.'

Graham was gone before Carole had time to object.

'That was a good idea,' she smiled, although her tone suggested otherwise. 'He's recently retired,' she confided, 'so I like to keep him busy. He'll just sit about reading the paper all day and nothing would ever get done.'

'I'm sure he'd quite enjoy that,' snapped Lisa. 'Isn't that what retirement is supposed to be all about?'

'What about your other half, Kate?' Carole asked, ignoring Lisa with aplomb and looking over my shoulder back towards my little house. 'Is he going to come out and say hello?'

Given that I had no idea of the current whereabouts of the man whom I could no longer claim as my other half, I didn't think it very likely that he would be putting in an appearance anytime soon, especially as he didn't know where I'd moved to.

'No,' I said, feeling my face turn ruby red and not because of the heat from the bonfire. 'I'm living here on my own. I'm separated.'

'Separated?'

'Soon to be divorced, actually.'

Without thinking I rubbed my gloved right hand over my left. My ring finger still felt odd without the band of gold, but the impression it had left on my skin was starting to fade a little.

'Well, it was very nice of him to come and look at the house with you,' said Carole, her beady eyes snapping back to me. 'And given the way you looked together I'm guessing it's been an amicable parting.'

The cheek of the woman!

'Is there any chance of reconciliation, do you think?' she asked, bulldozing on.

'Carole!' Lisa put in. 'You can't just go around asking folk things like that.'

The penny suddenly dropped and I realised that Carole had spotted Tom the day we came to view the house. It was a logical enough assumption to make, but her insensitive questioning ensured I was in no rush to set her straight.

'Who's that?' I asked, drawing both her and Lisa's attention away from the uncomfortable conversation. 'Is he another Nightingale Square resident?'

'Yes,' said Carole, waving in the man's direction, 'he is. Glen!' she called out in a sing-song voice while Lisa went off to check on John and the kids. 'Come and meet Kate.' I couldn't believe Lisa had abandoned me and hoped she wasn't feeling put out that I hadn't mentioned my marital status before.

Glen, his wife Heather and baby daughter Evie, as Carole explained by way of introduction, lived in the first house on the left as you entered the Square.

'We haven't been here all that long,' Glen told me while unsuccessfully trying to stifle a yawn, 'and to tell you the truth it's all taking some getting used to, for Heather anyway.'

I got the impression he was talking about more than just the house move.

'Where is your good lady wife this evening?' Carole asked, turning her attention to the direction Glen had come from.

There was a light on in the hall, but the curtains were drawn and the downstairs rooms were in darkness. Glen followed her gaze.

'She's having a nap.' He frowned. 'She's trying to get some rest before Evie sets her sights on keeping us up again all night.'

'You need strict routines with newborns,' Carole knowledgeably spouted off, 'and there's no harm in letting them self-soothe. No harm at all.'

Glen didn't say anything, but the set of his jaw told me he didn't agree with Carole's suggestion.

'I'd better go and check on Graham,' she said, the second she realised he'd managed to slip out of sight. 'It's been lovely to meet you, Kate. You must pop round for coffee so we can really get to know each other.'

She rushed off before I had time to answer. Personally, I was in no hurry to get to know her any better at all.

'Do you think she's right?' Glen asked, running his hands through his hair. 'About the self-soothing thing, I mean?'

'Sorry.' I shrugged. 'I have no idea. I haven't got kids so I don't think I'm qualified to have an opinion on that.'

'I don't feel like I have much of an idea at the moment,' Glen said with a nervous laugh. 'Most of my opinions on parenting have come from books and the majority of those seem to be contradictory.'

'It must be difficult,' I said, thinking back to when Tom and Jemma had their first baby, Ella.

Jemma had always been an absolutely brilliant mum, but she'd be the first to admit what a steep learning curve it had been. I'd heard her say many a time that she'd rather single-handedly ice a thousand cupcakes than go through the rigours of teething again.

'It is difficult,' Glen said seriously, 'and poor Heather's exhausted. She's missing her work and her friends and Evie hasn't been the easiest of babies so far. Heather had everything organised and catalogued before she gave birth, but Evie doesn't seem to want to follow the rules.'

I nodded, but didn't know what I could say to make him feel any better.

'Sorry,' he said, shaking his head. 'I don't know why I just told you all that. I'd best get back and make sure she's OK.'

'Maybe you could all come out for something to eat,' I suggested, not wanting him to leave feeling as fed up as he sounded. 'It's not too cold tonight.'

'Maybe,' he said and then he was gone.

'So, how's Miss High and Mighty finding motherhood then?' asked Lisa, who returned with a plastic cup containing what looked like a terrifying cocktail. 'It's only juice,' she said as I peered inside.

'And what are the bits bobbing about?'

'Fruit,' she said, before taking a closer look, 'I think. John's letting the kids drink it so it must be all right.'

'What do you mean "Miss High and Mighty"?' I asked, taking a tentative sip and feeling grateful that she hadn't taken the opportunity to ask for more details about my failed marriage.

'Glen's Mrs,' she elaborated. 'I popped round a couple of times when they first moved in thinking she might appreciate getting the low-down on the Square.'

'What happened?' I asked, risking a bigger sip and guessing the pair hadn't exactly hit it off.

'Snooty cow didn't even let me over the threshold,' she sniffed. 'I clearly wasn't polished enough to grace her impeccable abode.'

'Well, I get the impression she might need a friend now,' I said. 'I don't think motherhood is panning out quite how she planned.'

Lisa shrugged. 'Well, she knows where I live,' she said brusquely. 'Come on, let's get you something to eat and then it'll be time for the fireworks.'

I was rather taken aback by her response. Lisa struck me as someone who would go out of her way for everyone. Heather's snub must have really upset her.

Stuffed full of hot dogs and topped up with another glass of non-alcoholic Rocket Punch, I stood and watched the fireworks and listened to the excited squeals of the children, before drawing love hearts and my name in the air with a sparkler which still had the ability to scare me a little as it burnt down towards my fingers.

The last family I had to meet was single dad Robert and

his twin boys, Alfie and Jack, both of whom Lisa's eldest, Tamsin, had been batting her lashes at all evening.

'Come and say hello to Robert,' Carole said, steering me determinedly by the elbow when she realised our paths hadn't yet crossed. 'He's single just like you,' she added plenty loud enough for him to hear. 'And I've no idea how he manages all on his own with those two boys and no woman about the place. He's an absolute hero.'

Robert smiled awkwardly and Carole, thinking her *Blind Date* moment was sealed, rushed off to make sure Graham wasn't enjoying too much freedom.

'You must be Kate,' Robert said, his smile now marginally more relaxed.

'I am,' I smiled back. 'Pleased to meet you, Robert.'

'Please call me Rob,' he said, before hastily adding, 'and I'm not actually single.'

'It's all right,' I told him, 'I'm not going to try and collar you for a date.'

'No, no,' he said, stepping away and sounding embarrassed. 'I wasn't suggesting you were.'

I raised my eyebrows.

'I just didn't want you getting the wrong idea,' he stumbled on. 'Not that I had assumed you would, of course.'

I didn't say anything.

'God,' he groaned, 'sorry. Let me explain. What I meant was, I'm not single . . .'

'You've already told me that,' I cut in.

'I'm seeing someone,' he whispered, pulling off his hat. 'Sarah. We work together.'

'That's nice,' I nodded.

It really was of no interest to me, but the way he was carrying on you'd think it was a state secret.

'No one here knows,' he said, as he finally hit on the heart of the matter. 'You see, I'm trying to keep it from Carole.'

'Aha,' I laughed as the penny suddenly dropped. 'Now I see.'

'Sarah's a single parent like me,' he elaborated, encouraged by my reaction, 'so there's a lot at stake and if Carole finds out about us, she'll make me invite her along to things like this and we're simply not ready for such a public declaration.'

The words fell out in a jumbled rush and I decided I rather liked Rob and his urge to protect Sarah from Carole's scrutiny. Catching my understanding, he finally relaxed.

'I'm ever so sorry if you thought I was rude.'

'It's fine,' I said, nodding in Graham's direction as he ducked out of Carole's sight in what looked to be a well-practised manoeuvre. 'I'd pretty much already worked out she's a force to be reckoned with so I can understand the cloak and dagger.'

'She means well,' Rob laughed, 'but sometimes she makes it tricky to remember that.'

'So I gather.'

'Has she coerced you into helping with the greenspace community project yet?'

'The what?' I asked, as we wandered over to help pile up plates and cups.

'The greenspace project,' he repeated. 'This summer, we thought it would be a good idea to get a communal growing space up and running.'

'That sounds like a wonderful idea,' I said, imagining everyone pulling together to grow their own pumpkins and potatoes. Not that I wanted to be involved with it myself, of course.

'Yes, well, unfortunately,' Rob sighed, 'I'm sorry to say that's all it is because we still haven't found a suitable plot.'

'Aren't there any allotments available?'

I knew they had become highly sought after in recent years, but couldn't imagine that somewhere the size of Norwich wouldn't have at least one patch available to offer a group of keen growers.

'A couple of sites have empty plots,' Rob explained, 'but they're all on the other side of the city and nowhere near big enough really.'

'What we want is somewhere within walking distance,' added Harold, picking up the thread as he joined us. 'Somewhere nearby that will give everyone a chance to get involved.'

'Well, what about right here on part of the green?' I

suggested, thinking I'd struck gold on my first attempt. 'You won't get any closer to home than this and you could keep an eye on it from the comfort of your armchairs.'

'We've already tried that,' said Graham, who had abandoned the pint he had been trying to enjoy to help with the tidy up. I stood back as he deftly flipped over a trestle table and tucked in its legs. 'But the council said no.'

'What's it got to do with the council?' I frowned.

'Apparently, the responsibility for this little bit of grass was passed on to them when the Wentworths left Prosperous Place,' explained Harold. 'I'm not sure if that will alter now the house has changed hands again.'

'Perhaps we should ask,' suggested Rob. 'You never know, the sale might make a difference.'

'That sounds like a good idea,' I agreed. 'It certainly couldn't do any harm.'

'So, you like the sound of all this, do you, Kate?' asked Harold, his eyes shining with excitement. 'You'd be up for a bit of grow-your-own with us, would you?'

It hadn't been my intention to imply that, but as I looked around at the friendly faces of the people I could now boast as my neighbours, I felt far more settled than I had expected to when I posted the front door key of my London home back through the letterbox for David to find. I felt something shift inside me and surprised myself by changing my mind about wanting to maintain a completely solitary existence.

'Yes,' I smiled. 'I don't see why not. In for a penny, as my nan used to say.'

Perhaps, if I approached the project with enough gusto, it would become an excellent way to keep fit and a distraction from thinking about David all rolled into one.

'Great,' said Rob, clapping his hands together and making me jump. 'In that case I'm sure Graham won't mind getting the paperwork all in order and dropping it round to you. Perhaps you might be able to make more headway with the council than we have.'

Chapter 5

A few days later, and true to his word, or should that be Rob's word, Graham was standing on my doorstep bright and early, holding a manila folder full of paperwork.

'Everything's in there now,' he told me as he backed down the path having refused my offer of a coffee because Carole was waiting to start breakfast. 'The only people who haven't contributed anything are Glen and Heather because they moved in after everything was originally sent off. You might want to talk to them before you get the ball rolling again.'

'Assuming it's worth getting the ball rolling again,' I reminded him. 'Are you sure you don't want to carry on with it yourself, Graham? After all, it's you the council have been talking to up until now.'

I still wasn't sure how I'd ended up being elected as the resident most suited to take up the cause, especially as I'd only recently moved in. Sowing a few seeds I was happy to sign up for, but spearheading the whole campaign was something else entirely. Surely Graham was the better candidate to carry on; what with being recently retired he must have more time on his hands than he knew what to do with – assuming Carole let him sit still for two seconds together, of course.

'No,' he said, shaking his head. 'I've more than enough to do in the house, but please don't make it sound like a lost cause, Kate,' he added, looking crestfallen. 'I need something to get me out and about, even if it is just for a little while every day.'

He put forward a very strong case and confirmed my suspicions. I could see Carole loitering in her trademark spot behind the upstairs curtains, no doubt monitoring her husband's progress. Taking on the project would give me something else to think about other than why David hadn't at least tried to get in touch. Not that I wanted him to, but his good behaviour had come as a surprise and I had taken to spending far too long thinking about it.

'Glen was very keen when I mentioned it to him the day they moved in,' Graham carried on, pulling my thoughts yet again in the direction of my concerns about Heather. 'But I haven't got around to talking to him about it since.'

'I see.'

'If you could get him and Heather on board then it might make a difference to freeing up the green,' Graham added.

'Getting them involved would mean that *every* resident was looking to take part.'

'I'll see what I can do,' I promised, waving the file in Carole's direction so she knew I'd seen her. 'I'll make a start this week.'

'Great.'

'Just as soon as I've had a chance to read through this lot, that and drink a vat full of coffee.'

I hadn't been sleeping particularly well since the bonfire party and needed an extra caffeine hit to get me going in the mornings. My mind was buzzing and not only because my phone had been unnervingly quiet.

No matter what I tried to settle to doing, my thoughts kept straying to Heather and everything Glen had said about her. I had barely been in the Square five minutes before Lisa was in my kitchen, establishing herself as my new best friend and sharing her dodgy dough and yet just a couple of doors away, Heather had been living here considerably longer, but still wasn't part of the Nightingale Square community at all.

Lisa had left me in no doubt that Heather's isolation was of her own making, but now she was a struggling new mum and I didn't think it would do any harm to try and extend the hand of friendship and help her feel less like a fish out of water and more like part of the shoal, just as Lisa had done for me. If only I could find a way to make Lisa see it like that.

*

'So, you really think we'll have more of a chance of securing a plot closer to here if everyone signs up?' Lisa frowned from her station behind the ironing board in her homely kitchen later that week.

I had now skimmed through most of the contents of the folder, but had taken my time reading the letters everyone had submitted to the council to explain why they wanted a growing space they could collectively call their own. Lisa's was by far the most passionate. Manipulative it might have been, but I was using her desire to 'cut down on her family food bill' and 'teach her kids some essential life skills' as the way to convince her to try and make a friend of Heather again.

'Definitely,' I nodded, crossing my fingers. 'I'm certain it could make all the difference.'

'And you aren't just saying that to make me go around there?'

'Of course not,' I said, feigning shock that she would suggest such a thing.

'Well, all right then,' she caved, 'but if she keeps me on the doorstep today I won't be going back a third time.'

I couldn't ask more of her than that.

With Tamsin, who was off school because it was a teacher training day, listening out for Archie who was having a nap, Lisa and I walked around the green and up the path to Heather and Glen's front door. Everything looked remarkably smart and I thought again of my promise to Harold to sort out my own little front garden. I surprised myself by thinking that I didn't want to be the one letting the side down.

'You can knock,' Lisa sniffed, still not convinced that we were going to receive a warm welcome.

The seconds ticked slowly by and I became convinced that we weren't going to receive any kind of welcome at all. I raised a finger to press on the doorbell, but Lisa put her hand out to stop me.

'Believe me,' she said wisely, 'playing a tattoo on that thing when there's a baby on the scene is not going to be conducive to neighbourly relations.'

She was right of course. If Evie was asleep the last thing her mum would want was two strangers from the street noisily disturbing her peace.

'Oh, bugger it,' Lisa tutted. 'Come on. Let's go. I've still got a massive pile of ironing and it won't sort itself. You can come and try again later when Glen gets home from work.'

'No wait,' I said, nodding back to the door. 'Look.'

I could distinctly see a shadow moving in the hall and when I quietly knocked again it moved forward and the door opened.

'Hello,' I smiled. 'I'm Kate, your new neighbour. Are you Heather?'

I couldn't believe I was doing this. All the time back in London when I had been waiting to move I had been thinking about peace and quiet and privacy and yet here I was pushing myself into someone else's living room before I'd finished properly settling into my own.

'Yes,' said Heather. She sounded a little weary and looked dog tired. 'Hello. Glen said he'd met you at the bonfire party.'

'And I'm Lisa,' said Lisa, after I had nudged her. 'We met a few months ago,' she couldn't resist adding, 'on this very doorstep, actually.'

A slight blush crept across Heather's face and for a moment I thought she was going to cry.

'Could we possibly come in for a minute?' I quickly asked, hoping to stave off any tears. 'I promise we won't keep you long.'

'All right,' Heather nodded holding the door further open. 'But we'll have to be quiet because I've only just got Evie to sleep.'

'OK,' I whispered, feeling relieved.

'And would you mind taking your shoes off? We've just had new carpets laid.'

Lisa prodded me sharply in the back as I bent over to untie my laces. She and Heather really were nothing alike at all. Given the amount of Lego debris littering Lisa's floors it was far safer to keep your footwear firmly in place when you crossed the threshold into her and John's house.

'And please excuse the mess,' Heather added, showing us into the sitting room which was a cream and soft grey haven of peace, tranquillity and tidiness. 'I'm afraid I'm a little behind with my housework.'

Lisa and I sat perched on the very edge of what looked and felt like a very expensively upholstered sofa while Heather went to check on Evie.

'What mess?' Lisa hissed in my ear. 'Has she seen the state of my sitting room? Is she taking the piss? Do you think she has any idea that this décor won't last five minutes when Evie's old enough to wield a paintbrush?'

I put my fingers to my lips to 'shush' her lest Heather should hear her griping.

'And I'll tell you something else,' she went on, completely ignoring my silent warning and raising her voice a little, 'she wouldn't have let me in at all if I hadn't been with you.'

'Actually,' said Heather, suddenly appearing around the door, 'I would.'

'Heather.' I jumped, dropping the file and scattering the papers all over the recently vacuumed carpet. 'This room is beautiful. Have you modernised throughout? And as for being behind on your housework—'

The compliment was clearly too much. She plonked herself down in the armchair opposite and began to sob as if her heart would break.

'Well done,' Lisa mouthed to me as I scrabbled to pick up the strewn letters and vainly searched in my pockets for a tissue. 'There, there love,' she said to Heather in a tone of surprisingly sympathetic understanding as she passed her a handkerchief, 'let it all out. You'll feel much better for it.'

We spent the next half an hour listening to Heather unload. She told us how hard she was finding motherhood, what a job it was keeping on top of the hoovering and how her friends and work colleagues, none of whom had children yet and lived on the other side of the city, had gradually cut her out as she couldn't muster the energy to meet up with them or pick up the life she had pre-Evie.

Lisa nodded along, evidently empathising with every word and when Heather eventually ran out of tears and apologised for being so snooty when she had visited before, she wasted no time in giving her a hug.

'It's not as easy as you make it look, is it?' Heather sniffed. 'This motherhood lark, I mean.'

'I'm sure I don't make it look easy.' Lisa shrugged, but I could tell she was pleased.

'You do,' Heather cut in before she had a chance to say anything else. 'You lot look like the Von Trapp family compared to the mess I'm making of everything.'

'Oh dear,' said Lisa softly. 'It's a dangerous business, that.'

'What?'

'Comparing yourself to other people.'

'I agree,' I said, 'and that doesn't just apply to paralleling parenting styles either.'

I had spent far too long obsessing over the woman David

had broken my heart for and wondering if she was the complete opposite of me, or worse, if she was exactly the same.

'And what on earth,' said Lisa, raising her eyebrows and sounding borderline bolshie, 'are all these?'

'I thought they might help,' said Heather, turning as red as a beetroot as she bit her lip.

'And have they?' Lisa asked, flicking through the pile of hardback books featuring flawless mums and contented tots which were carefully displayed on the coffee table. 'I'm in no doubt they would have contributed beautifully to our bonfire, but what about your life, Heather? Have you gleaned anything really useful from the pages of any of these?'

'No,' Heather gulped as the sound of Evie beginning to snuffle came through the monitor which was sitting next to the books. 'The only thing they've helped with is toning my upper arms as I've lugged them about.'

We all began to giggle and Evie began to cry properly.

'I better go and see to her,' Heather sighed wearily. 'She just won't settle today and she's feeding all the time. My nipples are red raw. Sorry,' she smiled, 'too much information. Anyway, I'm thinking of putting her on the bottle.'

She was beginning to get tearful again.

'Tell you what,' Lisa kindly suggested, 'why don't we go together and I'll check her feeding position while Kate puts the kettle on. I managed to feed all mine, but getting going was tricky in the beginning. It can take a while.'

'All right,' Heather nodded, leading the way. 'Thank you, Lisa.'

The pair were upstairs for what felt like forever, but when they came back down Lisa was carrying Evie and Heather was grinning. I tried to avoid looking at the bundle of loveliness in her arms and wondered if I had made a mistake calling round after all, although I was pleased Lisa and Heather had finally hit it off.

'Growth spurt,' Lisa announced, settling herself on the sofa and beckoning me over to look at the softly snoring baby.

'Don't you go getting broody,' I told her after taking a very fleeting glimpse.

'Not much point,' she tutted, stroking Evie's tiny pink fingers, 'John's had the snip. He made me agree to it after I fell for Archie.'

She sounded rather sad and I got the impression that if it had been up to her she would have been popping babies out forever.

'Do you have any children, Kate?' Heather asked as she began pouring the tea I had made.

'No,' I said taking a shuddering breath and trying to sound blasé. 'And I'm on my own now so I can't imagine I'll ever have a family.'

'You'll meet someone,' said Lisa. 'A gorgeous girl like you won't be on your own for long.'

'I don't think so,' I told her. 'David was my chance

at happiness and I blew it. We blew it,' I added as an afterthought.

'I think you'll find there's more than one Mr Right in the world,' Lisa laughed. 'And anyway, Mark already told me that the day the pair of you met there was some gorgeous guy in the grocers who couldn't take his eyes off you.'

'I'm sorry I didn't tell you I was separated,' I said, ignoring her delusions about what Mark had said. 'I let you and John and everyone assume I was happily married when I'm anything but.'

'That doesn't matter.' She shrugged. 'It's no one else's business, but trust Carole to bring it up at an inopportune moment.'

'Mmm,' I agreed, happy to move the conversation on. 'She's the archetypal nosy neighbour, isn't she?'

'But she means well,' said Lisa, echoing Rob's words as she fondly looked down at Evie again. 'Her heart's in the right place, even if it pains me to say it.'

I could hardly believe my ears.

'Are you sticking up for her?' I frowned.

Lisa was the last person I would have expected to champion someone like Carole, but she refused to answer.

'Shush,' she said, looking at Heather, who had fallen fast asleep in the chair.

Talking quietly in the kitchen after Lisa had settled Evie back into her bassinet we decided not to leave before her mum woke up again. Heather was clearly in need of a friend or two and I surprised myself by thinking that Lisa and I could fit the bill, even if it did mean getting drawn into cooing over Evie.

The three of us might have had little in common beyond our addresses, but I got the impression that we all needed one another for some reason and I realised that having been married to David, I had missed out on forming friendships with women my own age. Not only because his friends were so much older than I was, but also because there had always been the unspoken suspicion that my dear husband might show a little too much interest in anyone under thirty I introduced him to.

It pained me to think it, but perhaps my marriage hadn't been the perfect fairy tale I thought it was, after all? The realisation came as a bolt out of the blue and I began to look forward to the possibility of a few nights in with a bottle of wine and my new friends.

'You're still here,' Heather yawned almost an hour later when the sound of Evie snuffling again pulled her out of her nap.

'We didn't want to just leave,' said Lisa.

'Especially as we still haven't told you why we turned up on your doorstep in the first place,' I added.

'It's nice to have some company,' Heather smiled as she stood up and stretched out her back. 'Some days here with

Evie I wonder if I'm capable of having a conversation with another adult who isn't Glen.'

'Haven't you been to the mother and baby group yet?' Lisa quizzed. 'It's only up the road.'

Heather shook her head.

'In that case, why don't you go and sort Evie out,' Lisa suggested, 'and then we'll go for a quick walk.'

'That's a great idea,' I jumped in as Heather began to shake her head again. 'It will be so much easier to explain why we called round outside and the fresh air will do us all good.'

'I don't know,' she said doubtfully.

Lisa aimed straight for the heart of the problem. She told Heather that when she had first had Tamsin she didn't leave the house for weeks and as a result fell into a deep depression that was hard to pull herself out of. Her frank admission clearly struck a chord with our new friend, who promptly bundled up her baby and followed us outside without another word.

Left to her own devices I was fairly certain she wouldn't have left the house all day, possibly all week, but it didn't take many minutes out in the crisp November air to put some colour back into her cheeks and a spring in her step.

'I know Glen really liked the idea of this vegetable-growing lark,' she said after I had explained the reason behind Lisa's and my impromptu visit. 'But neither of us would have a clue what to do.'

'We could all learn together,' I told her, 'although you know what you're doing already, don't you, Lisa?'

Lisa's letter to the council had explained how she used to go to the allotment with her granddad when she was a girl.

'I think so,' she said. 'It's been a while since I've handled a spade, but I'm sure it will all come back to me. I used to be at the family allotment every weekend and even after school sometimes. Thinking about it again has made me realise what my kids are missing out on and if we all chip in together it isn't such a big responsibility.'

'We could draw up a rota,' said Heather, who clearly liked to keep things organised. She was going to get along like a house on fire with Carole. 'So that way everything gets watered and weeded, but no one has to be accountable for everything.'

'That sounds great,' I agreed, 'and having everyone singing from the same hymn sheet is bound to go down well with the council. The green is lovely, but I reckon transforming it into an allotment will make it even more popular.'

'Mum!'

We all spun around to see Tamsin standing on the doorstep with a wriggling Archie in her arms.

'I'd better go,' said Lisa. 'I need to pop down to the shop for some milk before I do the school run and the rest of the ironing and that little terror looks like he needs the exercise.'

'And I want to make a start on perfecting this file,' I added. 'The sooner we can get cracking the better.'

73

'Will you be all right?' Lisa asked Heather. Clearly our new friend's welfare was fixed at the forefront of her mind.

'Yes,' Heather nodded, 'in fact, if you fancy the company, I wouldn't mind a walk to the shops myself.'

Lisa looked at me and winked.

'Some company would be great,' she smiled. 'I'll show you where the mum and tot group meet up if you like.'

I watched the pair of them walk away, thinking that we were all going to get a whole lot more out of a community garden than just carrots and coriander. A communal garden would fill our hearts and minds as well as our bellies and I was looking forward to enjoying the benefits which could be harvested from a lungful or two of fresh air.

Chapter 6

Having been privy to my brother's working pattern at the council in Wynbridge I knew it wouldn't be long before the thoughts of the Norwich team would be distracted by Christmas and so I headed to see them the day Glen dropped round his and Heather's letter. However, my attempt was nowhere near as successful as my efforts to bring Lisa, Heather and me together and, in spite of my determination to put our case forward with renewed vigour, our reorganised file fell on deaf ears.

'It's all down to the Wentworth legacy,' said the young man behind the protective glass as he squinted at his computer monitor. 'The residents know this.'

To my mind he only looked about twelve and doubtless had no authority to consider the matter further at all. The thought annoyed me because it was *exactly* the sort of thing my mother would have said, and it wasn't long ago that I would have been rolling my eyes at her attitude; yet here I was, adopting it as my own.

'But we don't want to rip down the railings or park on the grass,' I tried again. 'Our efforts would improve the space. The diverse planting would encourage more insects and we don't need storage or water because it's practically on our doorsteps.'

'Exactly,' he pounced, passing back the file of papers, 'if it's that close to home, then why don't you just turn over your gardens instead?'

'But you're missing the point,' I said, trying to push the file back again. 'We want somewhere where we can all grow together. We want to make it a community project and the green is accessible to everyone.'

I still baulked at the words coming out of my mouth – all this from the woman who had moved to the Square determined to hide from the world. The young man opened his mouth on the counterattack, but was stopped by a stern-looking colleague wearing tweed. She nudged him out of his seat and dumped her solid frame in his place. The swivel chair groaned in protest.

'Are you representing the residents of Nightingale Square?' she demanded over the top of her glasses.

'I am,' I said, drawing myself up and strengthening my resolve that I wouldn't be fobbed off a moment longer. 'I'm a resident myself there now and—'

She nodded, snatched back the file and slid off the chair.

'Come with me,' she said, pressing a buzzer to allow me access to the holy inner workings of the county council.

'Thank you for your help,' I said to the young man who was now bright red and had been no help at all.

'The thing is,' began the woman once she had shut us in a windowless office. 'And this is strictly between us.'

'Of course,' I agreed, trying not to think how claustrophobic the room was.

'It's all rather a mess.'

'Oh dear,' I said. 'Is it?'

'Yes,' she said, slapping the file down and offering me a chair. 'It is. And I'm not just talking about the green.'

'Oh dear,' I said again.

'When the Wentworth family left Prosperous Place,' she explained in a low voice, 'the council were asked to take responsibility for certain areas related to it.'

'Such as the green,' I interrupted.

I knew this already.

'Exactly,' she said, 'and that responsibility still holds. We really don't have the power to be able to grant a change of use. Our job is simply to maintain it as it is.'

'I suppose we all knew that, but we hoped—'

'The only way anything can change,' she cut in, 'is if a direct descendant of Mr Wentworth himself buys back

Prosperous Place. If that were to happen,' she added, 'then the responsibility of the green would revert back to the family and they could do whatever they liked with it.'

I sighed. 'Well, I can't imagine that's going to happen, unless of course, they're part of the company who has put in an offer to tear what's left of the place apart.'

'Afraid not,' she told me. 'From what I've heard, there's no rich relative on board, so the green will stay firmly in the council fold.'

'Shame,' I tutted, 'we might have been able to appeal to their sense of family values.'

'Huh,' she grunted. 'I don't think that sort of thing exists any more, certainly not in this instance anyway. You don't know the half of what's going on.'

'We know there are plans to turn the house into apartments,' I informed her, 'and I have to say we're pretty appalled.'

'Hmm,' she said, shaking her head. 'That's just the tip of the iceberg. There are plans afoot to build far beyond the house. If it all goes through then the grounds are going to be swallowed up as well. They want to extend, you see. Apparently, the juxtaposition of the old and very modern will appeal to those looking for executive living in the city.'

'You mean they're going to slap up some steel and glass construction and call it progress?'

'From what I've heard,' she seethed, 'that's exactly what they're hoping to do.'

I was dismayed and given her disapproving tone, so was she.

'But they can't just do that,' I protested. 'Surely the history associated with the place should warrant it some sort of protection.'

'You'd think so,' she went on. 'But there's no listing on the building and a lot of people are in favour of the changes. According to some, a development like this will put Norwich on the map.'

I thought back to my estate agent, Toby Fransham. This was just the sort of development he'd love to get on his books. It would knock his hi-tech new-builds into a cocked hat.

'A love affair with the past,' the woman sighed, 'doesn't fit in with the kind of future most people are looking to invest in I'm afraid, and you aren't the first person I've said that to today either.'

'Do you really think there's no hope at all?'

Her expression wasn't encouraging.

'Everyone is going to be so disappointed,' I said, thinking of more than the green.

'I know,' she nodded, pulling a scrap of paper from her pocket, 'and I shouldn't be doing this, but if you give me your number, I'll let you know if I hear anything else.'

'Thank you,' I said, feeling too deflated to appreciate the

risk she was taking. 'I won't say anything about this to my neighbours until I've spoken to you again.'

'So,' I said to the dejected group of faces looking back at me, 'to sum up, we aren't going to get our community growing space *and* to make matters worse, we're going to potentially lose our lovely view as well.'

'I can't believe it,' said Mark, shaking his head.

'But it hasn't gone through yet,' countered Rob hopefully. 'Has it? I mean, there's still a chance it won't happen.'

'I've had it made very clear to me,' I hated telling my neighbours, 'that it really is just a formality now. Unless there's a miracle between now and the New Year, Prosperous Place as we know it is doomed.'

I had gone out of my way to avoid making the announcement for as long as I could, but now that we were well into advent calendar season and Susan, the woman from the council, had offered nothing more helpful than the name of the architects in the time since my visit, I had to fill them in. Despite being gathered together to bask in the warmth of the first fire in my very own grate there was still a chill in the air, but it had little to do with the declining temperature.

'I'm surprised your place hasn't heard anything about this,' said Mark to his husband Neil, who had finally made it out of his office before the ten o'clock news.

I had been rather taken aback when Mark had landed on

the doormat with Neil on his arm. Still in his impeccable designer suit, but with his silk tie loosened, Neil was the complete opposite of his casual other half who favoured fatigues over formality, and I had been embarrassed when Mark had picked up on my surprise.

'You think I'm punching above my weight, don't you?' he had teased, gazing adoringly at his handsome beloved. 'You're thinking I'm his bit of rough.'

'Ignore him,' said Neil, passing me a very lovely bottle of already chilled champagne. 'Welcome to the Square, Kate. I'm sorry we haven't met before.'

Looking at his expression I got the impression that he was wishing we still hadn't met. Based on the little I had gleaned from Susan and a timely conversation with Mark when I popped to the bakers, I had made some enquiries about the team of architects who were working on the plans for Prosperous Place and discovered Neil's name on the list of employees. I had been wondering if he was going to say anything about it when we finally met, but apparently not.

'Yes,' said Lisa, catching what Mark had said. 'Perhaps you could put a few feelers out, Neil. Try and find out exactly who's behind this travesty.'

He was saved from having to say anything further as Evie began to cry and it was impossible for the conversation to continue with her in the room. She certainly had a decent set of lungs on her, but Heather was looking far happier now she had set foot back out in the real world and knew she had friendly faces close by on whom she could call.

'I think we had better head back home,' said Glen above the din as he jiggled his daughter up and down in his arms and moved to the hall. 'Sorry to break up the party, Kate.'

'Don't worry,' I told him, 'I only wish I had better news to share with you all.'

'You tried your best,' said Graham consolingly as Carole continued to scrutinise the books on the shelves while surreptitiously checking for dust.

'As did you,' I reminded him. 'Unfortunately, this is one green conversion that isn't meant to be.'

'We'll start looking for somewhere else in the New Year,' said Harold determinedly. 'Perhaps we should turn our front gardens over to growing carrots instead of clematis. It's what happened here in the war.'

Having spent hours tidying and rearranging my diminutive frontage I wasn't all that keen to pull it up and start again.

'Like you said, we'll wait until the New Year,' I said firmly. 'Who knows what the next few months will hold.'

'Never mind the next few months,' tutted Lisa. 'I'm more concerned about the next few weeks. Christmas is on the horizon and in case you hadn't worked it out, that means madness in our house.'

'More madness than usual?' Rob laughed as he pulled on his coat.

He had told me when he arrived that he couldn't stay long because he was meeting Sarah in the city. Carole had caught us whispering in the hall and looked well pleased but, in spite of my annoyance I hadn't said anything to blow his cover.

'Cheeky bugger,' Lisa laughed, before thoughtfully adding, 'yes actually, far more madness.'

'Are you up for that, Kate?' John asked. 'Do you fancy spending Christmas with our crazy brood?'

'If only you'd asked yesterday,' I told him with a sigh.

'What difference would that have made?' Lisa asked. 'You're only two doors away. You can't escape us that easily.'

'I'm going to be rather further away than that this Christmas I'm afraid,' I explained.

'What do you mean?'

'My mum phoned last night.' I swallowed. 'She's guilted me into going back to Wynbridge for a few days.'

I still wasn't entirely convinced it was going to be a good idea. I'd spent last Christmas at home because things with David had been decidedly rocky and it had been quite a tonic, distracting myself by helping out in the Cherry Tree Café and with my niece and nephew, but this year was different. Everything was signed, sealed and sorted. Perhaps I should have turned Mum down and set about creating some new traditions and Christmas routines for myself, but it was too late now. The deal was made.

'Can't you just say you've changed your mind?' John suggested.

The 'tut' which escaped Lisa's lips was loud enough for everyone to hear, even above Evie's wailing.

'Would *your* mother let you go back on Christmas arrangements?' she scolded.

'Um,' he said, looking sheepish. 'Yeah, point taken.'

'I won't be gone long,' I reassured them. 'I'll definitely be back in time to celebrate New Year.'

'Well, that's something,' said Lisa who had told me on more than one occasion that the party in our small part of Norfolk was one not to miss. 'I want to make sure your new year gets off on the best foot possible, if you know what I mean!'

I did know exactly what she meant, but wasn't all that convinced that a lump of coal and a dram of whisky was going to be enough to get my life completely back on track.

Chapter 7

I have to admit it felt comfortingly familiar crossing the bridge which spanned the River Wyn and parking up in the prettily frosted market square. Sitting in the car I had hired for the occasion, I could see Jemma and her business partner, Lizzie Dixon, clearing tables in the Cherry Tree Café.

That little café had been Jemma's dream for almost as long as I could remember, and with the support of her husband, my dear brother Tom, and with her best friend-turned-colleague working tirelessly by her side, it had soon become a reality and was now one of the most popular daytime eateries and craft workshops in the local area.

I had never been jealous of Jemma before, so I didn't much care for the pang I felt slyly slithering about in the base of my belly, but my dear sister-in-law really did have it all. A loyal and loving husband, two adorable children and a thriving business made her, in my eyes at least, the luckiest woman alive, and her outstanding successes showed up my own dismal failures in flawless HD.

The second I had acknowledged, and shut out, this caustic feeling I realised exactly why this Christmas was going to be so much tougher than the last. Last year I had been deluded, hanging on to the belief that I had willingly immersed myself in every festive thing my mother had thrown at me, but what I had actually been doing was acting on autopilot.

The way I was feeling now as I watched Jemma bustling about was a sharp contrast to last year, because then I had been numb. I had gone through the motions, ticking all the merry boxes and letting everyone think I had a handle on things when in fact I had buried myself in a mountain of mince pies so I didn't have to face up to the reality of what was waiting for me back in London. Perhaps my reawakened feelings were a positive sign, even if they were angling on the side of mean.

A sudden sharp tap on the passenger window pulled me out of my maudlin meandering.

'You going to sit there all night or are you going to come and say hello?'

'Jesus, Tom,' I scolded, my hand flying up to my chest as he opened the door and leant inside. 'Are you trying to finish me off completely or what?'

'Well, I don't know about that,' he grinned, 'but you look a damn sight brighter than when I saw you in September.'

That was hardly surprising, considering he had just given me the scare of my life and every drop of blood in my body had rushed to my face, but I was reassured to hear him say it nonetheless, and the relief in his tone suggested he felt the same. If he thought I looked more like my old self then Mum wouldn't have too much to fuss about and, as far as I was concerned, the less fuss I had to face during the next few days the better.

'Of course I do,' I told him. 'I've been moving on, haven't I? And, as we all know, time's a great healer.'

'Bullshit,' he replied, a smile playing around his lips.

'Yeah,' I agreed, even though it pained me to do so. It really was bullshit.

There hadn't been a single day when I hadn't missed David, when I hadn't ached to feel his strong arms around me, when I hadn't wondered what would have happened if I had packed away my guilt, seen beyond his bad behaviour, sacrificed my heart's desire and made a concerted effort to try and mend our marriage.

The passing of time had healed very little of the deep ache and emptiness nor purged me of the responsibility I lugged around because I believed I had been the one who pushed him to do what he did. It had taken two of us to make the marriage, but breaking it, turning the fairy tale into a horror story, that was down to me and consequently, I had paid the ultimate price.

I swallowed and took a deep breath, forcing myself to

think of my little home and the life I was carving out for myself with the help of my new friends. I knew I was lucky to be living in Nightingale Square. I was more settled than I could ever have imagined possible and surprisingly thankful for the neighbours I had initially planned to distance myself from, but now it was Christmas, and Christmas was capable of doing funny things to even the most sensible of folk when they found themselves all alone in a king-size bed and wondering what might have been.

'Look who I've found!' Tom called out as we crossed the café threshold, the bell above the door enthusiastically announcing our arrival.

'Kate!' squealed Jemma, rushing through from the kitchen and giving me a smile I wasn't sure she would have thought I deserved had she been privy to my earlier thoughts.

Her hands were covered in bubbles and she hastily dried them on her cupcake-patterned apron before pulling me into a tight hug.

'God, I've missed you,' she said, stepping back to scrutinise my complexion just as Tom had done.

This was something I knew I was going to get a lot and I was pleased I had had the foresight to pack my blusher and highlighter. An outwardly healthy, rosy glow was guaranteed courtesy of the contents of my make-up bag, even if I was feeling rather wrecked underneath.

'You look well,' Jemma nodded. There was the same edge

of relief in her tone that had crept into Tom's. 'Doesn't she look well, Tom?'

'She does,' he agreed.

'I feel well,' I told them both, doing my best to sound convincing as I breathed in a lungful of the spicy cinnamon-scented air.

Physically I was tip-top and they didn't need to know about the turmoil that still bounced about in my head as soon as I was quiet and still for more than a minute.

'And I'm looking forward to a fun-filled family Christmas.' Tom rolled his eyes.

'More bullshit,' he smiled, 'but as I'm sure you will have worked out, Mum has really pulled out the stops for this one.'

'That she has,' Jemma sighed, her eyes never leaving my face. 'Personally,' she added, sounding more than a little concerned, 'I can't help thinking she might have pulled out one stop too many.'

The second Lizzie appeared through the beaded curtain the atmosphere returned to what it had been before, but Jemma's words loitered uncomfortably in my head and I hoped Mum hadn't gone too overboard in her efforts to try and make me enjoy my few days at home. I wasn't sure I had the energy to keep a grin in place for that long without looking manic.

'Hello, Lizzie,' I smiled. 'Wow, you look amazing. Are you going somewhere special?'

'Ben and I are having a night out in Peterborough,' she explained as she smoothed down the skirt of her holly and mistletoe-patterned dress. 'It's been ages since we went out on a proper date.'

'Well, enjoy yourselves,' said Jemma, 'and don't worry about rushing down in the morning because Angela has promised to come in and cover the early rush.'

'Fantastic,' said her friend as she pulled on her coat, her red curls bouncing. 'I'm looking forward to this *so* much. It's important to give the old ball and chain some attention every now and again, isn't it?' she added, wrinkling her nose. 'Otherwise things can go a bit stale.'

The words had left her mouth before she remembered I was soon to be divorced and that my own 'ball and chain' had surpassed stale and was now completely redundant.

'Oh God, I'm so sorry, Kate,' she mumbled, her cheeks flushing as red as her vibrant hair.

Thankfully her awkward apology was cut short by her partner Ben's arrival.

'I'll walk with you to the car,' said Tom, hastily ushering the pair towards the door. 'I need to nip back to the office for something.'

'Well, don't be long,' Jemma called after him. 'We have to pick the kids up from your mum and dad's soon and I'm sure Kate can't wait to get settled into her old room.'

Once everyone had gone I followed her into the kitchen

so we could carry on chatting while she finished tidying away for the day.

'I'm so sorry about what Lizzie said.' She blushed, her eyes firmly fixed on the washing-up bowl.

'It's fine.'

'She just forgot—'

'Jemma,' I cut in, 'it's fine. Honestly.'

'OK,' she nodded.

'So, come on then,' I said, keen to move the conversation on, 'tell me what Mum's been up to. She hasn't got a string of eligible, local bachelors lined up for me to choose from, has she? Or signed me up for the next series of *First Dates*?'

Urbane relationship humour had apparently become my default setting. Just to prove that I really was beyond caring about what had happened, I joked about my almost single status, and I might have been pulling the wool over Jemma's eyes by carrying on so flippantly, but I wasn't really fooling myself.

'No,' said Jemma, sounding surprisingly more guarded than I would have expected, 'nothing quite like that.'

'Well, that's a relief,' I said brightly. 'I might be nearly single again, but I'm not ready to leap into the rigours of another relationship just yet.'

Why was I babbling on? Why was I contradicting my 'one true love' conviction? I knew I would never find love again, so why was I going overboard to suggest otherwise?

'I'm enjoying my "me-time" too much,' I added inanely for good measure, my shrill voice gradually trailing off along with my enthusiasm.

'But do you miss David?' Jemma blurted out, still staring at the sink. 'Even after what he did, do you still have feelings for him?'

Her line of questioning was completely unexpected and I felt my heart contract, the cruel band David's deception had wrapped around it tightening its grip once again. There had been moments when I had almost got used to existing with it in situ, but Jemma's inquisition was a painful reminder that it was still there, still waiting to make its presence felt when stretched even just a little too far.

'Of course I miss him,' I said, the words catching in my throat.

'But would you have him back? If he was truly sorry, would you try again?'

This was exactly the sort of moment when I wished I had shared the full details of everything that had gone on. If Jemma had known it all she would never have asked.

'He is truly sorry,' I told her, feeling nettled. 'He's told me that a million times, but his being sorry won't stop him making the same mistake again, will it? I mean, you have met David, haven't you, Jemma?' I went on, sticking to the ladykiller thread I had adopted when discussing the situation with anyone. 'We are talking about the same not-quite-tamed Lothario I married a few years ago, aren't we?'

'I'm sorry,' she said, shaking her head. 'I shouldn't have said anything.'

'It's all right,' I told her, even though it wasn't. 'You're just a romantic at heart, like I used to be. You want everyone to find their happy ever after, but unfortunately, I haven't been as lucky as you. My Prince Charming turned out to be just a slightly older frog after all.'

Christmas Eve, Christmas Day and even Boxing Day all thankfully passed without incident and I knew that my initial pang of jealousy towards Jemma really was nothing more than a sign that my emotions were waking back up. When my mother's well-meaning efforts to jolly me along and feed me up got too much I took myself off for bracing walks around the town and spent a lot of time thinking about Nightingale Square and what everyone there was doing. In truth, I was itching to get back.

I'd left strict instructions for Lisa to call me if I hadn't appeared by the twenty-ninth on the pretence of some trumped-up household emergency, a burst water pipe or the like, which would smooth the way for me to leave Wynbridge without a fuss. However, on the evening of the twenty-seventh, just as I was all set to tumble into a turkey-curry-induced stupor, I realised I should have told her to ring far sooner.

'You do know your mother means well, don't you, Kate?' my father panicked me by saying as we cleared away the dinner dishes together. 'And that she loves you very much.'

'Oh Dad,' I groaned. 'Are you going to tell me what she's done? I know there's something.'

Earlier that day she had cornered me in the kitchen and subjected me to a barrage of questions which weren't all that dissimilar to the ones Jemma had asked the evening I arrived. Dad opened his mouth to enlighten me, but the doorbell snatched his words away.

'I'll get it,' said Mum, drifting down the stairs in a heady cloud of Dior and wearing a dress I hadn't seen before.

'No,' I said, 'I will.'

The solid silhouette of my soon-to-be ex-husband was unmistakable and as I reached to open the door, I cursed my traitorous heart as it began banging away in my chest in much the same way as it had that very first day our paths had crossed.

'Kate,' David gasped, his blue eyes flying wide open and the colour draining from his face when he emerged from behind the gargantuan festive floral centrepiece he was holding out in front of him. 'I had no idea.'

He had never been able to lie, especially when caught off guard, and I had no reason to believe he had been given any inkling that I was going to be there. This was my mother's doing, although why he would have accepted her dubious invitation to visit was beyond me.

'David,' I sighed, opening the door a little further so he could step around me and inside, 'likewise.'

The familiar scent of his aftershave almost took my breath away as he brushed by and I momentarily closed my eyes, allowing myself to drink him in. For some inexplicable reason my mother had decided to roll the dice in my game of life and send my head and my heart straight back to where they had been in the summer.

I had no idea why she had done it, but I knew that both Jemma and Dad were privy to her meddling and felt just as furious with them, for not putting a stop to it, as I was with her. Yet again I found myself wishing that I had told them the whole story as to what had gone on between David and me.

'David,' said my mother, looking anxiously from him to me, 'how very lovely to see you.'

Suddenly she didn't look quite so sure of herself and I hoped she had registered the chaos she had caused, even if she did 'mean well', as Dad and everyone else kept suggesting.

'These are for you,' David stammered, holding out the flowers towards her with hands that didn't appear to be all that steady.

'Thank you,' she smiled. 'How beautiful. Aren't they beautiful, Kate?'

'What are you doing here, David?' I demanded.

I was quite happy to dispense with the niceties and move things along.

'I ...' he began, shoving his hands deep in his pockets, 'well. I was invited.'

'Why was he invited, Mum?'

'I thought it would be nice for us all to be together,' she said, biting her lip. 'It's Christmas, after all.'

I wondered how the infant Jesus would feel about the interfering that went on around the world on the excuse of it being his birthday.

'I had no idea you were going to be here, Kate,' David said quickly. 'I would never have agreed to come if I had known.'

'So why did you agree?'

'I wanted to apologise,' he swallowed. 'I wanted to explain to your parents in person ...'

'But why did you feel as though you had to?' I asked with a shrug. 'You aren't—' I stopped to correct myself. 'You *weren't* married to my parents. You were married to me and you've told me on more than one occasion how and why you couldn't keep your trousers zipped. Or are you here to tell them *everything* else?'

I didn't usually give my tongue an opportunity to run away with itself. Given the dangerous nature of what it could blurt out, I had kept it in check for months, but the sight of David standing in my parents' living room had a frighteningly detrimental impact on my ability to keep it buttoned.

'Kate!'

This was from my father and it stopped me in my tracks. I

closed my eyes and took a deep breath as the ground swayed a little beneath my feet. I didn't need a living and breathing reminder of what I had thrown away. A top-up of the guilt tank or an extra opportunity to think about what I had wasted really wasn't required. I was more than capable of conjuring both myself, but for some mad reason Mum had seen fit to supply me with them anyway.

'I'm going to the pub,' I snapped, snatching up my bag and forcing myself not to knock her over the head with it. 'Merry Christmas, David.'

Chapter 8

Far from being the peaceful sanctuary I had hoped for, The Mermaid was heaving with post-Christmas revellers all sporting new chunky knitwear, but I managed to slip in under the radar and bagged myself a table out of view of the door. I sat with my back to the jovial crowd, nursing a glass of wine and trying to collate my scattered thoughts.

Next year, I vowed as I took a long and nerve-settling sip, I would happily run the risk of upsetting my family and follow my gut as well as my heart. Next year I would be celebrating Christmas with Lisa and Heather and everyone else in Nightingale Square.

'Kate?'

The hairs on the back of my neck stood to attention.

'What?'

I refused to turn around.

'I'm so sorry.'

'You know, had I thought of it sooner, I would have had that printed on a T-shirt and sent to you via Santa.'

'Can I sit down?'

I shrugged.

'Your mum really hadn't told me that you were going to be there, you know.'

'But I daresay you worked it out anyway, David, didn't you?' I said, swallowing down a mouthful of wine.

He didn't say anything.

'But it makes no difference to me.' I shrugged. 'If you want to spend the holidays with my family then go ahead. I'm leaving in the morning, so you can have my room if you like.'

'Kate, please don't be like that.'

'Well, how do you expect me to be?'

'Not like this,' he said, sounding infuriatingly bewildered. 'When you left in October I thought we were OK. I thought we had at least parted on friendly terms.'

We had really. There had been no destroying of possessions or prawns in the curtain poles, so I could hardly dismiss his confusion. However, I had assumed that our courteous parting had been final, or failing that, our last for at least a good long while. But now, just weeks later, here he was, smelling delicious and looking as lovely as ever.

'Friendly or not,' I snapped, 'that's no justification for turning up to ruin my Christmas, is it?'

'It wasn't my intention to ruin anything,' he sighed.

'Of course,' I said, slapping my hand against my forehead. 'I was forgetting, you came back to spill the sordid beans, didn't you? Were you really planning on telling my parents everything?'

'I don't know.' He shrugged. 'Probably not.'

'So, you were lying, again,' I sniffed.

'No,' he said, finally sitting in the chair opposite mine. 'I was just so surprised to see you that I ended up saying the first thing that came into my head.'

'A lie.'

'It's been agony not seeing you,' he went on, ignoring my scathing monosyllabic response. 'Not being able to even talk to you on the phone has been torture.'

'Has it?' I asked, hating myself for letting the words escape. Hating the fact that I still cared.

'It has,' he said. 'It's been killing me, Kate.'

I was annoyingly pleased that he had found it so difficult to keep his distance. I had been thinking he hadn't struggled with my terms at all, so it was good to know I had actually left a mark on his heart that in some way matched the depth of the one he had carved into mine.

'I've been trying to break that solicitor of yours,' he admitted when I didn't say anything, 'but she won't crack. I still don't know where you've moved to.'

I drank another mouthful of wine, eager to banish all thoughts of the many seductive tactics in his arsenal that he could have called upon to break down her defences, and reminded myself that she was a professional woman, a woman of principle with firm morals.

'And there's absolutely no reason why you should,' I said, draining the glass and putting it back down on the table.

'I miss you, Kate.'

'Good.'

'Do you miss me?'

Why did everyone keep asking me that?

'Of course I miss you,' I bit back. 'You've been a part of my life for the last goodness knows how many years and now you're not there.'

David looked encouraged by my admission and I quickly backtracked lest he get the wrong idea.

'But then I also miss the espresso machine,' I told him, 'and those sugar-coated biscuits from Fortnum's.'

'You can order those things online,' he said, sliding his hand across the table until the tips of his fingers touched mine. 'You can replace both of those things easily enough, but you can't replace us.'

I sat back and put my hands in my lap.

'I have no desire to replace us,' I said starchily. 'Or even to pick up the pieces of what's left of us. You can't mend what's been broken, David.'

'But you can,' he said. His voice was eager as his eyes searched out mine. 'You can glue things back together and make them even stronger than they were before, if you really want to.'

The wine was turning my thoughts to mush and there was a tiny but determined voice in my head telling me I should at least give that suggestion a few minutes' consideration. I shouldn't dismiss the idea without turning it over first.

'We could create a new bond,' he said temptingly. 'A bond so strong, that this time it couldn't possibly be broken.'

'We're not talking about some piece of lustreware you're having restored for a client,' I sniffed, trying not to get carried away with the vision of us renewing our vows on some far-flung beach.

'I know that,' he said. 'And I know you don't want to risk your heart all over again, Kate, but please, at least think about it. This is the real reason why I drove all the way up here in the hope of seeing you.'

I shook my head.

'We could wipe the slate clean and start afresh. I would never hurt you again if you gave me a second chance. I would take proper care of you, this time. Perhaps ...' he added, 'perhaps we could even have that conversation about children after all.'

Had I not already been sitting I would have fallen down. The man who had always insisted that a baby wasn't part of the deal was now using one as a bargaining tool to try and win me back. I wasn't sure how I felt about that. Had he forgotten that it was his desire not to talk about starting a family that had driven him to reassert his independence in the arms of another woman? If all of that had slipped his mind, then I certainly needed to remember it.

'I need another drink,' I said, pushing back my chair.

'I'll get it,' he said, rummaging in his pockets before jumping up and reaching for my glass. 'You think about what I've said and if this is on your finger by the time I come back, then I'll be the happiest man on the planet.'

I looked down at my wedding band and then I watched him walk to the bar. I watched how quickly he caught the eye of the pretty young girl serving, even though there were at least half a dozen other customers already waiting. I watched the entire exchange. David was on his best behaviour. He didn't flirt, he didn't leave an outrageous tip, he didn't stand and chat, but none of that altered the fact that I had watched him like a hawk.

I hadn't been able to tear my eyes away and I knew that if I allowed myself to slip back into our marriage, baby or no baby, I was going to face a lifetime of watching. Watching to see if he fell back into his old ways and then waiting to see if those 'ways' developed into something more serious. I didn't think I could hold my breath for that long. I didn't think I wanted to, and I certainly didn't want to do it with a child in tow. I might have longed for the whole kit and caboodle that came with the perfect marriage, but I wasn't stupid enough to think that having a child was going to be a cure-all.

'Don't worry about that drink,' I said, quickly snatching up my things before the glasses were even on the table. 'I've changed my mind.'

'But I thought you'd be pleased,' David said, looking from the ring to me and back again, confusion pulling his face into a frown. 'I thought, this was what you had wanted all along—'

'I know what you thought,' I interrupted, 'and it was, but it isn't what I want now. I can't risk giving you a second chance, David, and if you think about everything from my point of view rather than your own for once you'll understand why.'

'But what about your happy ever after?' he pleaded. 'It's what you always said we were creating.'

'I'm beginning to think I'm a bit too old to believe in fairy tales.' I swallowed, determined not to cry in front of him, 'and besides, you may well have denied me mine.'

I packed my bags before I went to bed that night, knowing that I wasn't going to see out my time and wait for the phone call from Lisa before I made the journey back to Nightingale Square. Had it not been for the large glass of wine I'd drunk in the pub I wouldn't have even waited until first light, but I wasn't going to risk failing a breath test on top of everything else.

'You're not leaving?' said Mum when I appeared at the breakfast table with my suitcase in tow. 'You can't really be considering going already.'

We had had a terse exchange of words when I got back from the pub and I had warned her I would be leaving sooner than originally planned, but looking at the disappointment on her face I guessed she thought I'd sleep on it and change my mind.

'I really can,' I told her bluntly. 'In fact, I think it's best if I do.'

'Aren't you going to say anything?' she demanded of my father.

He didn't say a word until he was helping me carry my bags out to the car.

'I did try and warn her,' he said. 'I did tell her it was a bad idea, but she'd got it into her head that all you needed was a nudge in the right direction and everything would be back to how it was before. What with it being—'

'Christmas,' I finished for him.

'Exactly.'

'I do know that she did it with the best of intentions,' I sighed, 'but I'm too angry to tell her that right now. I don't want to let her off the hook just yet.'

'Of course,' he said, pulling me into a hug which threatened to unleash more tears than the rest of Christmas put together. 'I told her you wouldn't thank her for it, but she thought she knew best.'

I nodded, but couldn't get the words to jump over the lump in my throat.

'Perhaps if you told her everything, Kate,' he continued. 'Perhaps if she knew the whole of what happened she'd be more willing to leave it alone and let you move on?'

I pulled myself out of his embrace and blinked back my tears.

'What do you mean?'

'It doesn't take a genius to work out there was more to your decision to leave David than what you told us, love,' he said softly, shaking his head. 'Whatever else that husband of yours did, it must have been pretty bloody bad.'

'Dad!' He never swore, not even mildly.

'Because I know, we all know, that you loved him with each and every bit of your heart and it must have been something far worse than a drunken one-night stand to make you walk away forever.'

I stepped forward and kissed him on the cheek.

'Thanks, Dad,' I said huskily. 'I'll ring you when I get back.'

I pulled into a lay-by on the outskirts of town and fired off a quick text to Tom, explaining why I had left early and asking him to apologise to Jemma and the kids, and then I sent another to Lisa in the hope that she would have time to go around to the house and turn the heating thermostat up a notch.

There was a chill in my bones that couldn't be warmed, no matter how high I turned up the car heater and as I drove on, I couldn't help thinking that there was nothing left in the whole world that would be capable of thawing my cold heart now.

Chapter 9

When I pulled back into the car hire depot in Norwich I realised I couldn't actually remember any of the journey at all. I had driven for almost two hours on autopilot, mulling over every look, nuance and reaction I had given the one man I had ever been in love with and wishing with all of my heart that I hadn't gone back to Wynbridge for Christmas. Thanks to Mum's meddling, the year felt set to end on a depressing low rather than the high I had been aiming for and I wasn't sure I could forgive her for that.

Whether it had been Christmas or not, I knew the trip had happened far too soon and I thanked my lucky stars that I had had both the strength and the sense not to move back to my home town for good. The nurturing embrace of kith and kin might have been ideal for some, but for me it was the last thing I needed. What I needed was to surround myself with my new friends, and live peacefully for a while in my new home, neither of which were tainted by the life I was trying to leave behind or littered with loitering shadows all waiting to trip me up at every opportunity.

I was relieved that David still hadn't discovered where I had moved to and, given Mum's disastrous attempts at a not very subtle reconciliation, I was fairly certain she wouldn't dare hand out my address, and Tom knew it was more than his life was worth. As the taxi I had taken for the final leg of my journey swung into the top of Nightingale Square I caught the first glimpse of my lovely house and knew that I was going to be left in peace, for now at least.

Leaving my bags in the hall, I explored each and every room, much the same as I had the day I came to view it with Tom and Toby Fransham, only this time my possessions were all in situ and looked as though they had been there forever. Every room felt cosy, thanks to Lisa's thermostat tweaking; the fire was laid ready to light and the fridge was fully stocked. She had also left a 'welcome home' note on the table along with some brightly coloured artwork from the children which I happily propped up above the sink as I filled the kettle. I would have to follow her and John's lead soon and buy some magnets for the fridge so the pictures and scribbles could be properly displayed.

With a large mug of restorative tea and a slice of the Christmas cake Mum had insisted I come away with, I curled up in the armchair and flicked through the TV channels in the hope of finding a cheesy film to fall asleep in front of. The tranquil moment lasted for less than half an hour.

'Come on!' I heard a voice shout from the green. 'We can do this. It's just what we need to blow away the cobwebs.'

'You do know some people are trying to sleep off the excesses of Christmas, don't you?' I bawled through the bedroom window after rushing upstairs to get a better view of who I thought was disturbing the peace.

'Kate!' beamed Heather, her face pinched from the cold and her nose aglow.

'Get your butt out here!' Lisa demanded, jumping up from the bench she had looked firmly glued to. 'Come and talk some sense into this crazy woman, will you?'

Wrapped in the thickest coat, scarf and gloves combo I could throw together and carrying a fresh mug of tea, I trotted over to the green, keen to see my friends and find out what all the fuss was about.

'I've missed you so much,' said Lisa, rushing over the second she caught sight of me and giving me a hug.

'So have I,' said Heather, joining in so the three of us were tightly squashed together, my tea in danger of being worn rather than drunk.

'And I've missed you,' I managed to blurt out before the last gasp of air was squeezed out of my lungs.

'And not just because I love you to bits of course,' said

Lisa, loosening her grip, 'but because I've had to take sole responsibility for this crazy lady.'

I stepped back and took in Heather's beaming face. She didn't look crazy to me, just very happy.

'Don't let the soppy expression fool you,' warned Lisa before I had a chance to say a word. 'Now she's finally been getting some sleep her true personality has come to the fore and to be honest I'm already thinking I should never have let you talk me into darkening her front door.'

'That's a bit mean,' said Heather, stamping her feet to stave off the cold. 'If it wasn't for you two ...' her words trailed off. 'Well,' she eventually said, 'let's just say I wouldn't be in the happy place I am now.'

'Exactly,' said Lisa, patting the empty space next to her on the bench for me to sit on. 'And you wouldn't be trying to talk me into this blasted, get off your butt and run 5K thing, you've got your heart set on.'

I let out an ill-timed snigger and Lisa turned her attention to me.

'And I don't know what you're bloody laughing at, she's roping you in as well!'

'What?'

'We need to start the New Year with a sense of purpose,' said Heather, still bouncing about, although I was sure the circulation to her toes must have been sorted by now. 'I'm going to start running again and I want you two to join me.

I'm going to have Evie in her buggy and we can take turns to push her as we run. What do you think?'

'I think you've had one glass of mulled wine too many and completely lost the plot,' Lisa groaned, turning to me for support.

'You know I haven't had a drop because I'm still feeding Evie,' Heather shot back.

'Well, I think it's a great idea,' I interrupted.

I didn't really. My armchair was comfortable enough to hunker down in until the blossom was in full bloom at least, but it was fun to wind Lisa up, and actually Heather was right; in just a few days we'd be hanging up new calendars and opening fresh diaries so starting a new healthy regime really couldn't be better, or more predictably, timed.

'Think of the summer in shorts and skinny jeans,' I said, giving Lisa a nudge for good measure.

'Think of years living here as an outcast,' she shot back.

We all burst out laughing and I made a mental note to spend my Christmas money on a new pair of trainers as well as the fridge magnets.

'So,' said Heather once we had all got our breath back, 'how was Christmas in the sticks? I thought you were planning to stay a bit longer?'

'I had been,' I told her, taking a sip of the rapidly cooling tea, 'but my mother put a rather large spanner in the works.'

'Do you want to talk about it?' Lisa asked, turning to face me.

Gosh it was good to be back. For the last twenty-four hours I had felt as though I was carrying the weight of the world on my shoulders, but just five minutes in the company of this pair and the gloom had lifted and I was feeling like a new woman. Well, almost.

'You know, I think I would,' I said, 'but not out here. It's too cold.'

I had begun to shiver as the slate-grey day started to bite and the wind picked up a little, worming its way into any nook and cranny that wasn't swaddled in at least three layers.

'How about you both come around to mine tonight?' I suggested. 'We could have a non-turkey-themed takeaway or something and—'

'Wine,' Lisa butted in before I had time to suggest *Bridget Jones's Diary*. 'That's allowed, isn't it, Heather? We don't have to give up the booze just yet, do we?'

'Hang on,' I said, 'no one mentioned giving up wine.'

'And takeaways,' said Lisa, standing up and stretching out her chilled limbs. 'No wine and no takeaways after the New Year.'

'But I didn't realise . . .' I began.

'You should have backed me up then, shouldn't you?' she said, her hands now firmly planted on her hips. 'That'll teach you for trying to be a clever-clogs and picking the wrong side. I'll see you at seven. Can you be out of the house by then?' she asked the woman who was all set to deny us each and every one of life's simple pleasures.

'Better make it half past,' answered Heather. 'Glen and I like to bath Evie together, but I'll be over as soon as she's settled, and I've got some expressed milk in the fridge so Daddy can be in charge of the late evening feed.'

'Perfect,' said Lisa as she walked back towards her house, 'see you both tonight.'

'You can have a glass of wine at the weekends,' giggled Heather with a wink as we watched our friend sashay away. 'I just haven't told Lisa that yet.'

By half seven the curtains were drawn, the fire was roaring, the cushions were plumped and the candles were lit. The house was cosy, warm and relaxing – *hygge*, I think the Danes call it – and I felt the tension in my shoulders ebb away for the first time since I had told Mum I was going home for Christmas.

'As it's our first ever girls' night in,' said Lisa, as she let herself in through the unlocked front door, 'I thought we should go all out and make the most of it.'

'Sounds good to me,' said Heather approvingly as she ducked through the door just before it closed. 'What are you suggesting?'

'Three bottles of Prosecco for me and Kate,' said Lisa,

pulling two out of a carrier bag with a flourish, 'and the last tub of Celebrations that I'd hidden at the back of the boot cupboard.'

Heather didn't look particularly impressed, but Lisa was determined.

'Lighten up, love,' she grinned. 'By this time next week you'll be forcing alfalfa sprouts down our necks and making us join in with yoga DVDs, so we're allowed at least one last night of heady indulgence.'

'Actually,' said Heather, biting her lip as she peeled off her coat, 'I have been wondering whether we should sign up for a Pilates class or something as well. It would be good to balance the running with something more calming.'

Lisa rolled her eyes and pushed Heather down the hall towards me.

'Right,' she said, taking charge. 'No more talk of fitness or faddy diets tonight. I want to hear all about what Kate got up to on her big trip home.'

With a glass of fizz apiece, lemonade with a slice for Heather, and the tub of chocolates fast disappearing, my two friends sat together on the sofa while I claimed the armchair and told them everything that had happened.

'But what on earth was she thinking?' Lisa gasped when I finally got to the part about the doorbell ringing and David being the one who had pressed it, courtesy of my mother's invitation. 'What on earth made her think you'd want to be faced with your ex before you'd had a chance to get over him?'

It was a relief that she understood how I had felt and why.

'Beats me,' I said, shaking my head and helping myself to another mini Mars and a Bounty.

'I'm sure she meant well,' said Heather, echoing the words of practically everyone in Wynbridge.

Trust her to try and see the good in what Mum had done.

'I know,' I concurred, 'and David and I did part on civil terms in October so—'

'How is it possible to be civil when you're pulling apart a life that's wrapped around someone else's?' Lisa asked. 'Not that we know *why* you were pulling that life apart and not that I'm asking,' she quickly added. 'I'm just surprised to hear the word civil being used to describe a divorce, that's all.'

'He was unfaithful to me,' I said before I thought about it too much. 'He had a one-night stand with another woman, at least he always maintained it was just one night, and I decided to end our marriage as a result.'

Heather shook her head and leant forward to top up my glass.

'No, love,' said Lisa softly, 'he decided to end it when he dropped his pants. I'm sure his wandering eye wasn't your doing.'

I still couldn't bring myself to admit out loud that actually it had been, but I did explain the sort of man that David was;

how he had always had an eye for a pretty girl and that I had known what I was getting myself into when I accepted his proposal. I didn't elaborate too much however, because from what Lisa had intimated already I guessed she was more of the 'cut off his balls and fry them' brigade when it came to dealing with infidelity, whoever felt responsible for it.

'So perhaps,' said Heather, 'because your mum knew that you had parted on a reasonably amicable footing she could have thought there was a chance of getting you back together. Does she know the reason why you're divorcing him?'

'Yes,' I said, a tell-tale blush blossoming, 'she knows. Everyone knows, but you're probably right. Her soppy old heart no doubt thought there was a chance we could patch things up, especially as we'd been so polite during the break-up.'

'Didn't you *ever* want to shred his suits?' Lisa asked incredulously.

Clearly, she was having a hard time getting her head round the idea of a gracious parting.

'No,' I said truthfully, 'I'd seen enough of that kind of thing courtesy of some of our friends, and worse. To tell you the truth I was just really, really sad about it all. I didn't have the energy to turn what was happening into a vengeful free-for-all.'

I felt my face go even redder as I thought about the real reason behind why I didn't have the energy to turn our parting into Armageddon and Lisa looked at me and narrowed her eyes.

'What?' I frowned.

'Nothing,' she said with a shrug.

'So, I take it David was rather shocked that you were less than pleased to see him when you answered the door at your parents' house?'

'You could say that,' I sighed. 'He insisted Mum hadn't told him I'd be there, but it didn't take a genius to work out I'd be home for the holidays. When I stormed out he followed me to the pub and within minutes started going on about putting everything back together, renewing our vows and making a fresh start.'

I didn't mention the baby he had dangled as if I were a donkey chasing a carrot.

'But you weren't tempted?'

'Oh, I was tempted all right,' I reluctantly admitted, avoiding Lisa's outraged expression, 'right up until the moment I watched him ordering drinks at the bar.'

'What happened then?'

'Nothing,' I shrugged, 'absolutely nothing.'

'I don't understand.'

'Well, I couldn't take my eyes off him, could I?' I sniffed. 'I was watching his every move, taking in how comfortably he was talking to the barmaid and watching her flutter her lashes in response and that was when I realised.'

'What?' asked the pair together.

'That was the moment I knew that if we got back together then I was heading straight back to waiting for him to do it to me again. If I put myself back in that relationship I would be watching him forever and just papering over the cracks that have run too deep to be filled.'

'So, you finally figured out that what you really need to do is scrape it all back, sand and smooth those cracks away and paint yourself a brand new colour,' Lisa said astutely.

'Exactly,' I agreed, looking at the dated décor around me. 'Just like this place.' I sighed as I swallowed a mouthful of fizz. 'It's not David's fault,' I tried to say, but heavy tears were suddenly threatening to fall and I shook my head to stop them. 'It's just the way he is. The way he's always been.'

I felt such a fool for believing that I had changed him.

'Do not,' said Lisa sternly, as Heather abandoned her glass and rushed to my side when I began to sob, 'let that man's personality explain away what he did to you, Kate. Do you hear me?'

I nodded, but couldn't speak.

'And don't look at me like that, Heather,' she said crossly, 'because there's more to this story than we know. But it'll keep for another night.'

'Is there?' Heather asked me. 'Is there something else, Kate?'

'Yes,' I said, 'there is, but as Lisa said, it'll keep.'

As far as I was concerned it could keep locked away forever.

I took myself off to the bathroom to compose my thoughts and when I came back the fire had been stoked and the DVD was cued up ready to go.

'All right?' Lisa asked, without looking at me.

'Yes,' I said, 'thanks. Much better.'

'That's two out of three now, isn't it?' she tutted. 'I suppose it'll be my turn next.'

'What do you mean?'

'Well, Heather here blubbed the first time we met her and tonight it's been all about you, so I reckon I'm due a sobbing session of my own sometime soon.'

'You wait until I take you for your first run around Whitlingham Lake,' Heather laughed, digging her sharply in the ribs. 'Crying will be the only thing you'll be capable of after that!'

More tears followed her comment, but they weren't sad ones.

Chapter 10

Thankfully, with the Nightingale Square New Year celebrations to organise, there was little time to dwell on my reacquaintance with David and, having shared the details of pretty much everything that had happened with my girls, it didn't take me long to work out that my mother's well-meaning meddling hadn't turned me back into the wreck I had been in the summer after all.

Had I really been back there I would have been wearing my dressing gown, sleeping in until the afternoon and then mooching aimlessly about the house until it was time to fall back into bed, but I hadn't even considered sinking to those depths again and not only because I had Lisa hammering on the door at all hours, but also because I discovered I didn't want to.

'I can't help thinking your mum actually did you a favour by inviting Mr Wrong round to stuff up your Christmas,' the lady herself pronounced as we set about blowing up yet more balloons and counting out party poppers.

My house had been designated as Party Central and was consequently filling up with all manner of celebratory accoutrements. Glen had offered his and Heather's place, but Heather was worried about sodden shoes spoiling her carpets and there was no way Lisa's house could be deemed suitable. The place was already stuffed with over-excited children so it certainly didn't need piles of balloons and mini-combustibles cranking up the atmosphere. I had wondered if Carole might step into the breach, but her excuses had echoed those Heather had come up with and the role of warehouse stockist had been left to me.

'Oh, really?' I gasped between puffs. 'How do you work that one out?'

I already knew what she was going to say, having felt my way to the same conclusion, but I had no intention of stealing her thunder.

'Well, look at you,' she said, nodding at my freshly polished nails and recently re-coloured hair. 'For a start you've been sale shopping in the city, you're wearing make-up and your sweet breath is minty fresh.'

'So?'

'So,' she continued, precariously balancing another balloon on the steadily growing pile, 'that goes to prove that you aren't wallowing, doesn't it? You're getting on with things in spite of the setback. If you were as broken by seeing him again as you initially thought you had been, you'd still be sitting around in your sweats with the curtains closed.'

'Not that there would be much chance of actually doing that,' I tutted. 'Not with you hanging on the bell every two minutes.'

'Rubbish,' she said firmly. 'If you really weren't ready to move on you wouldn't let me in. You would have opened a window and told me to f—'

'Not that you would,' I interrupted.

'No, of course I wouldn't,' she laughed, 'but I'm just saying, you should be proud of yourself, Kate. I'm not sure I'd be where you are right now if John had done something to me like David did to you.'

I was surprised to hear her say that. I hadn't thought there was anything in the world capable of stopping Lisa in her stride or knocking the wind out of her bubbly and exuberant sails.

'Right, that's it,' she groaned, slumping back against the sofa for support. 'I'm going light-headed here. If anyone wants more balloons they can blow the bloody things up themselves. Now, let's check we've got enough of everything we need for everyone to join in with the first footing.'

New Year's Eve was bright and dry and I was grateful that the weather was kind because the party turned out to be far larger than I had expected. Lots of people had turned up from neighbouring streets, including Poppy, the pretty girl from the grocers, and they were all happy to congregate on the green where John, Rob and Graham had set up a collection of gazebos and braziers to warm hands at a safe distance.

The dozens of balloons Lisa and I had lent our puff to were strewn in the trees, along with strings of brightly coloured lights, and Carole was standing guard by the punch bowl to stop the enthusiastic revellers adding even more alcohol to the occasion. Thanks to the amiable weather it was all a far more welcome set-up than having the hordes traipsing through my little house, even if I did have well-worn out-of-date psychedelic carpets rather than new cream pile.

'Are you all right sitting there?' I questioned Harold, who had asked John to fetch the garden chair he kept by his front door to watch the world go by.

'I'm grand, thank you, Kate,' he smiled, tucking a tartan blanket tighter around his knees. 'How did you enjoy your Christmas?'

'Let's just say it's nice to be home,' I shouted down at him as Graham wandered up with some plastic half-pint glasses of punch on a tray.

'Can I tempt you?' he asked. 'I'd have a couple now before it's too lethal, if I were you,' he advised.

'But I thought Carole was keeping watch,' I said, looking back in her direction. 'She's in charge of drinks, isn't she?'

I was amused to see Poppy was engaging her in conversation, while a chap with thick blonde dreadlocks, whom I didn't recognise, was emptying what looked like a hipflask into the fruity concoction on the table behind her.

'Ah,' I said, quickly taking one glass from the tray for myself and another for Harold. 'I see. Thanks, Graham.'

'We'll all be half-cut by midnight,' Harold chuckled, taking the drink from me and downing half of it in one big swallow. 'Just as well it's a bank holiday tomorrow and a Sunday, so no one has to go to work.'

Graham and I nodded in agreement.

'That's actually something I've been meaning to ask you about, Kate,' said Lisa, who had joined our little group with a slightly squiffy-looking John draped around her shoulders.

'What?'

'Work,' she said. 'What is it that you do for a living?'

'Oh,' I said, trying to find the words to explain succinctly what it was that I did, or used to do. 'My field is history. I'm enthralled by the past. I work with antiques mostly.'

'Restoring them?' Graham asked.

'No,' I said, dismissing the image of David sitting in The Mermaid and offering me the chance to stick us back together, 'not restoration. I used to run a business sourcing specific antiques that people wanted to buy. I had a list of clients who paid me to find particular pieces they were looking to fill their homes with.'

'Nice,' slurred John, attempting to give me a thumbs up, but not quite making it.

'That sounds exciting,' said Lisa more soberly, her eyes shining.

'It was,' I said. 'My searches often took me all over the world. It was great fun tracking down certain pieces.'

'Some folk have more money than sense,' Harold tutted in thinly disguised disgust.

I couldn't disagree with him there. Some of the figures involved made my stomach roll. I wondered if David had convinced Francesca Lucca to give him a chance to furnish her latest Italian abode yet. The loss of her account alone would be quite a blow to the business I had left behind, and it wouldn't take many deserting clients for the little empire we had worked so hard to create to crumble. Not that that was my problem.

'I'm not sure you'll find much call for that sort of thing around here,' Harold added.

On that point I could correct him, but I didn't. In my experience the world was full of wealthy people happy to pay the price for what they thought they couldn't live without but they, and their demands, didn't much interest me any more.

'That's all right,' I said, taking an exploratory sip of the punch and quickly discovering that the smell alone was enough to make my head spin. 'I'm not going to do that now. I'm going to take some time out to work on the house and I want to explore the history of the city, get to know the Castle a little better and perhaps even offer my services there as a volunteer at some point in the future.'

'And help us find somewhere to grow our greens,' John reminded me. 'You did say you were still going to help with that.'

'Of course,' I said, 'don't worry. I haven't forgotten.'

'It's a shame you won't get the chance to go and have a nose around Prosperous Place before it's had the guts ripped out of it,' Harold sniffed. 'The house and grounds over there are packed with enough history to keep you entertained for years.'

'It's an absolute disgrace that it's all going to be lost,' sighed Poppy, catching the conversation as she wandered over to join us.

The house was in darkness, but its silhouette stood tall and strong. Its solid presence was a comforting full stop to the Square, but for how much longer? How long before it would be bedecked in tactless spotlighting and was housing ill-informed residents who harboured the illusion that their hi-tech abodes were preserving a part of Norfolk history, when in fact their very construction had ripped the heart out of an important piece of it.

'Have you heard anything else from that woman at the council?' Lisa asked.

Neil and Mark had joined us now and as one we all looked towards the house.

'No,' I confirmed, 'not a word. I really think the place is done for.'

A little later, as I was taking a moment to check the bags of coal, bread and miniatures of whisky for first footing at midnight, Neil came and found me.

'You know, don't you?' he said, his handsome face twisted with worry and his eyebrows knitted together.

'That you work for the firm who are responsible for drawing up the plans to decimate Prosperous Place, you mean?'

He nodded and looked over his shoulder to where Mark was standing with Heather and Glen. Mark was looking adoringly at Evie who was strapped to her father's chest in some sort of snug-fitting sling. Clearly the late hour suited her as she was giggling and kicking her little legs with abandon.

'Yes,' I said. 'I know.'

'So why haven't you said anything to any of the others?'

'What would be the point?' I shrugged. 'It will all come out sooner or later and anyway, it's not really any of my business, is it?'

'You're a Nightingale Square resident now,' he reminded me. 'Of course it's your business, and between you and me, Kate . . .' he went on, lowering his voice to little more than a whisper.

'Yes?'

'. . . The whole development is balanced on a knife edge now.'

'What do you mean?'

'I reckon,' he swallowed, 'if there's enough objection to the plans to hold them up for any length of time then the whole project will fold. It wouldn't take much. The finances are already far tighter than they should be, not that I should be telling you that, but I can't say I'm as enamoured with the project as my boss thinks I am, and not just because it's happening right outside my front door.'

This was interesting news indeed, a definite beacon of hope, but only a temporary one of course.

'But if this project goes to pot then the place would be back on the open market,' I hissed, my voice as quiet as his. 'And we'd be back where we started.'

'Well, there is that possibility I suppose,' he shrugged, 'but I thought you'd like to know. In truth I don't want to see the heart ripped out of the place any more than anyone else, but I wouldn't want to see it razed to the ground either.'

'What?' I squawked.

'It's prime building land,' he said darkly, 'if it isn't developed, the only other option would be demolition.'

'Surely you're not serious?' I demanded.

'I'm afraid I am,' he told me. 'And, if it is flattened to make way for more bog-standard flats, then the entire area will be changed forever.'

I felt my stomach drop to the floor. That sounded even worse than the current development plans. At least the proposition on the table at the moment meant that, in one guise or another, some part of the original structure of Prosperous Place would remain in situ.

'What are you two whispering about?' demanded Mark, who had sneaked up unnoticed.

'We were just trying to work out the alcohol content of the punch,' I said creatively, my mind reeling as I imagined Prosperous Place reduced to a pile of rubble, my body trembling at the thought.

'Oh, it must be millions of units by now,' Mark laughed with a hiccup. 'Squillions.'

'Are you drunk?' Neil tutted in amusement.

'A bit,' Mark sniggered.

'I'll leave you to it,' I said, ducking away. 'Happy New Year.'

'And to you my lovely,' Mark slurred as Neil steered him away from the punchbowl.

'If I come round to your house,' I asked Harold, who was still holding court with quite a crowd around his chair, 'will you tell me a bit more about Prosperous Place and your family who worked there? Will you show me those photographs you said you had?'

I was determined to build a picture of the place and its past in my head before it was changed beyond all recognition.

'Absolutely, dear girl,' he said, sounding delighted. 'I would be honoured. I'm surprised you haven't been before now.'

I did feel guilty about that. He had invited me to look on my very first day living in the Square.

'It's a shame you never met Doris.'

'Doris?'

'The lady who lived in your house before you.'

'Ah, yes.'

'Her family had a far closer connection to the Wentworth family than mine,' he said meaningfully.

There was a definite twinkle in his eye and I guessed that Harold had been privy to far more than his own share of secrets and memories over the years.

'Did they?'

'Mmm,' he said mysteriously. 'You pop round and I'll fill you in.'

The rest of the evening whizzed by and as we all congregated together on the green to listen to the countdown to midnight on the sound system John had rigged up and we linked arms to sing 'Auld Lang Syne', I didn't feel any pang of regret that I was standing in Nightingale Square rather than in my parents' house or the pub in Wynbridge, and thinking about what David was up to was even further down my list of thoughts.

'Three, two, one . . .'

As Big Ben began to chime I looked around at the faces of my neighbours and friends and thought how lucky I was to have made my way to Nightingale Square and the warm and welcoming embrace of such a close-knit community. Not that that was what I had been looking for when I spotted my little house online, but as Lisa handed round the first footing goodie bags and everyone exchanged kisses and hugs, I realised that I felt truly at home.

I knew I had a very real part to play in this vibrant slice of the city, and although I wasn't entirely sure what my role was yet, one look back at the outline of Prosperous Place, now dramatically backlit by an explosion of city centre fireworks, I knew it wouldn't be too much longer before I had worked it out.

Chapter 11

By mid-January winter had tightened its icy grip. The New Year hangovers had barely been forgotten before Lisa's brood were enjoying snow days and Heather, her tone loaded with disappointment, had declared conditions were too treacherous for us to run in. A brisk walk down to the shops and into the city for healthy lunches and sale shopping was about all we could manage, but Lisa didn't seem to mind and to be honest, neither did I, even though our other friend was keen to remind us that we needed to make a concerted effort to get in shape sooner rather than later because 'a summer body was made in the winter'.

Rather than worrying about whether or not I was going to be beach-body ready, I spent my days gathering together paint charts, fabric samples and the details of various local kitchen and bathroom fitters in preparation for the refurbishment I planned to begin in the spring. I was content to while away the chilly afternoons flicking through pages and swatches in Lisa's kitchen with Radio 2 providing a cheery backdrop whenever the chatter was low enough for us to hear it, which admittedly wasn't all that often.

On the days when she wasn't meeting up with other local mums we would go to Heather's instead, but with Evie becoming more beautiful and more alert by the day it was hard spending time with her, not that I had told either of my friends that. I didn't want them to feel sorry for me any more than I wanted them to feel annoyed that I hadn't told them the whole story about David and me right from the start.

Inevitably, as I watched Evie being jiggled about on someone else's knee my mind tracked back to the child David had offered me as compensation for his infidelity and I wondered if a little bundle of my own, should I have been so lucky, would have made up for the pain and heartache he had caused. Would my life have been any better if I had attempted to fulfil my broody biological needs and settled for that half-arsed and slightly wonky fairy tale ending after all?

January turned increasingly bleak and it began to drag by at a snail's pace. What I needed was a decent distraction before the novelty of the names Farrow and Ball had creatively come up with for their paints no longer beguiled me and I fell to more frequent and gloomier brooding. Fortunately, Harold was on hand to provide an adequate diversion.

'You *still* haven't been and had a look at these photographs of mine,' he scolded one particularly cold afternoon when I called round to collect him en route to Lisa's for lunch. 'I've got them all ready. There are boxes of them along with a fair few newspaper and magazine clippings.'

This was just what I needed to take my mind off memories which were as murky as the weather.

'I'm sorry, Harold. I can't believe I've left it this long. How about tomorrow afternoon,' I suggested, knowing the change of scene would do me good. 'How does that suit?'

'Well, I go to the library in the afternoon,' he reminded me as he slipped his arm through mine, 'and then there's the Friday club on Friday,' he reeled off. 'I wouldn't like to miss that.'

At least I didn't have to feel guilty that my absent-mindedness had meant Harold was home alone every day. He had more weekly activities planned than Lisa, Heather and I put together.

'Monday then,' I said, carefully closing his garden gate behind us. 'How about I come on Monday afternoon?'

'Perfect,' he agreed. 'I'm always at a loss on a Monday after a busy weekend.'

I shook my head and laughed. I would never have believed the day would come when I was envious of an eighty-year-old's social life, but my neighbour was clearly out more often than he was at home by his fireside.

The pre-arranged Monday turned out to be the gloomiest of the year so far. The daylight hours were dark, the sort that required the house lights to be blazing from dawn till dusk and if it wasn't for checking, you'd never be able to hazard a guess as to what the actual time was.

As promised, Harold had sought out his photograph albums of Prosperous Place, along with a variety of fragile, yellowed newspaper and magazine clippings which chronicled its fortunes over many decades. I was looking forward to adding another layer to the information I had already discovered about the business and the goodhearted man who had created it. It would be a comfort on such a dreary day to feel the warmth of human kindness and hear a tale or two which hopefully culminated in a happy ending.

'I thought I had more than this,' Harold tutted, when we were finally settled at the dining table with a cup of tea apiece and a slice of Victoria sponge which Neil had dropped round from the bakery.

'I shouldn't worry, Harold,' I told him, reaching for an album. 'I think there's more than enough here to be going on with.'

There were dozens of small black and white images along with a few larger ones in dazzlingly bright colour and they recorded the gardens and grounds, as well as the house, in all their glory.

'Would you look at these,' I gasped, as I flicked through the pages of an album dedicated to the grounds in high summer. 'I had no idea the gardens were so extensive. These herbaceous borders must have run the entire length of the perimeter walls, and who on earth are all these people milling about?'

'Just a minute,' said Harold, reaching across the table. 'There should be a newspaper article to go with those. They were taken when the gardens were opened up for charity. My great-grandfather wrote in his diaries that hundreds of people would come and visit, whatever the weather. Judging by what he recorded, everyone wanted to peek over the wall and catch a glimpse of how the other half lived.'

I skimmed over the clippings, amazed by the amounts of money that had been raised.

'That was typical of the sort of thing old Mr Wentworth set up,' said Harold with a nod, 'and not many people know this, but whatever was raised on the day, he would match it out of his own pocket. Generous to a fault, he was.'

'That was the impression I got from the things I found out about him online,' I smiled.

The photographs of the interior of the house were every bit as beautiful as the gardens. It looked exquisitely kept and was packed full of furniture and paintings that David and I, along with our clients, would have drooled over.

'Do you know who this is?' I frowned, pointing at a close-up of one of the paintings, a portrait, which was hanging next to a large and elaborately decorated fireplace.

Harold readjusted his glasses.

'Oh now,' he said with a heavy sigh. 'There's a tale for you. That's Mr Wentworth's eldest son. He was a rather special friend of Doris's great, or should that be great-great-aunt, Abigail.'

'What exactly do you mean by *special* friend?' I asked, moving the photograph further into the light and noticing just how much he took after his father.

'No one ever talked openly about it of course,' Harold continued. 'Because it was such a scandal at the time.'

'Go on.'

He sat back in his chair again and took his time over another mouthful of cake.

'Well, I don't know all that much,' he eventually said, 'and much of what I do know I've had to patch together from snippets of overheard conversations from when I was younger.'

'Yes?'

'Let's just say it was often whispered that Doris's family were rather more connected to the Wentworths than perhaps they should have been, if you take my meaning.'

'You mean there was an affair?' I asked, feeling intrigued and shocked in equal measure.

'Well, I'm not sure I would put it quite like that,' Harold smiled, his eyes twinkling, 'but that's the gist of it. The chap in the painting, Edward Wentworth, was very taken with Doris's great-great-aunt Abigail, even though she had only just turned sixteen when they met and he was twenty-four.'

It all sounded very romantic to me, in spite of the age gap.

'Apparently,' Harold continued in a low voice, 'she used to wait for him at the end of the road and then they would go off together for the day. By nightfall, when they'd had their fun, she'd trot home as if butter wouldn't melt. It went on for months and her parents were beside themselves.'

The secrecy and clandestine nature of the suspected relationship tugged a little at my bruised heartstrings. Edward and Abigail must have been very much in love to go to such lengths and take such risks.

'How long did they try to keep their relationship secret for?' I quizzed. 'I thought the Wentworth clan would have been more open-minded than to judge a girl by her social standing.'

I had a sudden sinking feeling that what Harold was going to tell me wasn't going to end well. I had created an illusion of perfection around Mr Wentworth and his philanthropic credentials and had everything crossed that it wasn't about to be shattered. I had to hang on to the belief that sometimes life really did turn out to be as idyllic as I hoped.

'It wasn't actually the Wentworth family who turned

out to be the problem,' Harold explained and I let out a premature sigh of relief. 'It was Doris's family. When they discovered what was happening they said they wouldn't have the girl getting ideas above her station.'

I shook my head in disappointment.

'You have to remember,' Harold was quick to remind me, 'that Doris's family, like mine, had all worked hard in the factory and were very lucky to be living in Nightingale Square. My guess is that Abigail's father thought that if the relationship ended badly then they would all have ended up without a home *and* a job.'

'But Charles Wentworth wouldn't have been that vindictive,' I insisted. 'That would have gone against everything he claimed to believe in.'

Harold shrugged.

'We know that, but Abigail's parents weren't prepared to take the risk,' he told me, 'and after one liaison too many she was forbidden from ever seeing Edward again.'

It all sounded tragic, very Romeo and Juliet. I hoped the love story was going to end with a joyful reunion, but the expression on Harold's face wasn't suggesting wedding bells and a blissful ever after.

'Do you know what happened to them after that?' I ventured.

Harold nodded. Considering he'd told me he didn't actually know all that much, he had managed to piece together rather a lot.

'Abigail refused to do as she was told and was sent away in the end,' said Harold, shaking his head, 'to a relative who lived somewhere along the south coast, and Edward,' he added with a shudder, 'met an unfortunate end beneath the copper beech.'

'You mean,' I could barely get the words out. 'You mean, he killed himself?'

Harold nodded.

'In the gardens at Prosperous Place?'

Harold nodded again.

'That's dreadful,' I shuddered. 'I don't remember reading anything about any of this,' I said, thinking back over everything I had discovered about the place before my move. 'I would have remembered something this terrible. There was no mention of the tragedy anywhere,' I continued as Harold went to boil the kettle again.

'I can't imagine it's the sort of family history Mr Wentworth or his wife would have wanted to have made public, is it?'

'Well, no,' I conceded, 'but even so. That wouldn't usually stop the press from having a field day or events being recorded elsewhere, would it?'

I thought back over my internet research and wondered if subconsciously I'd stopped delving into the past once I'd created the perfect picture of it.

'Did Abigail ever come back?' I swallowed.

'No,' said Harold. 'She never returned. There were rumours that she'd had a child, but there was never any proof.'

'How sad,' I said, my eyes filling with tears as they returned to the photograph of the portrait hanging next to the fireplace.

'Yes, well,' said Harold, 'as my old mum used to say, the path of true love never did run smooth.'

She was certainly right about that.

We spent the remainder of the afternoon looking through the rest of the photographs while Harold filled me in on more details about the factory, along with talk about the many members of his and Doris's families who had worked there.

'I would say my lot and Doris's were the lucky ones,' he smiled, as he explained about the supervisory roles they had worked their way up to in the factory, 'but they had all worked hard to move themselves off the shop floor and into the Square. However,' he insisted, 'Mr Wentworth looked after everyone, irrespective of their position. He made sure a fair wage was paid for a hard day's work and even the terraced houses around here were palaces compared to some.'

'So, when did it all start to go wrong for the business?' I asked. 'When was the turning point for the factory?'

'Understandably, things went off the rails for a while after Edward died,' Harold explained, 'and by the time Mr Wentworth rallied, his other son Lawrence had developed gambling debts beyond comprehension. The only way his father could help him was to sell off certain assets and by the time he died, the empire he had created was dwindling.'

It was devastating to think that all his hard work hadn't secured a future for those who came after him; all his efforts had actually amounted to nothing. It was heartbreaking.

'Eventually Prosperous Place was the only thing left,' Harold continued, 'and that was sold out of the family after having been in the care of a distant branch of the clan for some time. Luckily for Doris's lot and mine, old Mr Wentworth left our families the houses we lived in and his wife made sure that we got them when the time came.'

I couldn't begin to imagine how he and his wife must have felt, watching it all fall apart after the death of their son. It was a testament to them both that they hadn't banished Abigail's family from the Square, and indeed the county; I wondered if the girl had ever been told the fate that had befallen her beloved.

'I'd like to see more pictures of the factory,' I said, my eyes flicking back over the muddled plethora of photos.

'You and me both,' Harold tutted. 'I have no idea where they've all got to, but I hope this has given you some idea of what the place was like in its heyday.'

'It certainly has,' I confirmed as I started to gather everything together. 'Thank you for showing it all to me, Harold. I appreciate it, even if you did have things to say that didn't match my rose-tinted view of the place.'

Far from feeling comforted, I felt as though I'd been pole-axed with a cruel hard dose of reality and wished I hadn't honed in on the portrait of Edward or made certain assumptions about the Wentworth legacy.

'Like I said earlier,' Harold shrugged. 'I don't really know all that much about the finer details, but I can't help wishing that this didn't feel like the end.'

'I agree,' I said sadly. 'I can't believe that all this history and knowledge is going to be lost. You should write everything down you know, Harold. The human stories at least. The things you've told me this afternoon are the things that keep history interesting and alive for people, even if their outcomes are tragic. If you don't pass them on, they'll be lost forever.'

'Well,' he chuckled, 'I've told you now, haven't I? Perhaps you could write them down.'

'Yes,' I said, 'perhaps I could.'

We were interrupted by an urgent knocking at the front door.

'Now who could that be?' frowned Harold.

'I'll go,' I said.

It was Carole and she was looking more than a little agitated.

'Have you seen?' she demanded, pointing towards the end of the Square.

'Seen what?'

'The sign,' she urged, 'it looks like it's been ripped down and there's been a car parked at the gates all afternoon.'

I looked to where she was pointing and she was right, the developers' sign had indeed been pulled apart rather than dismantled, but there was no sign of a car.

'It's happening, isn't it?' she sniffed. 'By this time tomorrow you won't be able to move down here for bulldozers and builders' vans.'

I had no desire to join in with her melodramatic wailing, but I had a horrid feeling she was right. If that was how the new owners treated the sold sign then I dreaded to think what was going to happen inside the house.

'I think you're right, Carole,' said Harold, as he joined us on the step. 'Things are finally afoot.'

'I wish I could have seen it as it was,' I sighed. 'I wish I could have at least seen the gardens as they were in the photographs you've got, Harold.'

'I daresay it's all still there,' he said. 'Overgrown and uncared for I grant you, but I bet it's all there. The place has been through a fair few hands since the Wentworth family departed, but I can't imagine all that much has changed really, especially outside.'

'But it will now,' Carole sniffed, pulling a crumpled tissue out of her cardigan pocket.

'So, why don't you go and have a look before it's gone?' said Harold, the mischief back in his eyes. 'There'll be no one there now, will there?'

'What do you mean?'

145

'There's a wooden gate around the far side,' he said, pointing towards the end of the Square with his stick. 'You could try that. You could probably climb over it if it's locked. It's not even as high as the wall.'

'Harold!' said Carole snootily. 'That's trespassing.'

She was right.

'Go and have a look before it's gone,' Harold temptingly urged in my ear. 'There won't be much to see by way of flowers I grant you, but go and have a look before what's left is lost forever.'

Chapter 12

'I can't believe we're doing this,' Carole hissed as we casually walked around the perimeter wall of Prosperous Place looking for the gate.

'I can't believe you're coming with me,' I hissed back.

Once I had decided I was going to follow Harold's crazy instructions there had been no shaking Carole. It didn't seem to matter what was going on, she had to be a part of it, even if it did potentially mean trouble, or in this case, possible arrest.

'It's here,' I said, taking a step back. 'This is it.'

The wooden gate was there, just as Harold had said; only now it was hidden beneath a thick tangle of clinging ivy.

'Is it locked?'

I grabbed the handle and twisted but it wouldn't budge, even with all my weight behind it.

'I think so,' I puffed, looking back over my shoulder to where Carole was making a right show of trying to look as if she wasn't up to anything out of the ordinary. 'Come and give me a leg up, will you?'

'What?'

'Come and give me a leg up,' I said exasperatedly. 'Help me reach the top and I'll pull myself over.'

Pulling on her gloves so my boots wouldn't muddy her hands, Carole hoisted me up and over the gate with a force that rather took me by surprise. I landed on the other side with a thump and took a moment to catch my breath and look about me, hoping the developers hadn't left a guard dog or two roaming about to keep an eye on the place.

'What can you see?' Carole's voice came through the gate.

'Not much from here,' I said. 'It's all too overgrown.'

I turned my attention back to the gate. It was bolted at the top and bottom and after I'd pulled away the ivy and given it a hefty tug or two it finally, reluctantly, yielded. Carole quickly slipped through the gap and between us we wedged it shut again as best we could.

In silence, and with our breath streaming ahead of us, we set off to explore. It was difficult trying to equate the colourful photographs back on Harold's dining table with the neglected frosted jungle, but once I'd spotted the top of the ornate fountain over the thick yew hedges I began to get my bearings.

'It's just like Narnia, isn't it?' Carole whispered. 'I had no idea anything as magnificent as this was lurking behind the walls.'

She was right. We had been exploring the icy landscape for what, thanks to the cold, felt like hours, but in reality was nowhere near as long. We had walked around what I knew had once been sweeping striped lawns; then along the furthest lengths of the walls, which had showcased the borders packed with stunning herbaceous displays, and finally through a series of smaller garden rooms which held tucked-away summerhouses, gazebos and secret corners.

'How about this for a vegetable garden then, Carole?' I said, as we worked our way around the back of the house and found a walled garden, half a dozen greenhouses and what would have once been a beautiful orangery.

'Wow,' she said, shaking her head.

It was the first time I had ever known her at a loss for words.

'Shall we go and see if we can get inside the house?'

I don't know what had come over me, but I was suddenly desperate to see it all, even if the venture was risky. I knew without a doubt that if the gardens were any indicator, then the house was going to be spectacular and was therefore more than happy to manipulate my neighbour's subdued state if it meant I could use her as an accomplice to get inside.

'I don't think so,' she sniffed, her vocabulary and voice returning at the most inopportune moment. Her nose was glowing and her eyes were watering. 'Even if the windows weren't all boarded up, I think that really would be pushing our—'

The words had barely left her lips when our attention was caught by the light shining off an upstairs window which had just been pushed open.

'Oh no,' I swallowed, my heart thumping hard and fast in my chest. 'That one's not boarded up. That one's wide open.'

'Hey!' shouted a man's voice. 'Can I help you?' He didn't sound at all happy.

'Shit,' I squeaked, tugging at the sleeve of Carole's fleece. 'I think we'd better go.'

'I think you're right,' she squeaked back, pulling herself free and setting off like Usain Bolt springing out of the blocks.

For a second I stood with my mouth open and then set off to try and catch her up.

More haste, less speed, had always been one of my mother's favoured proverbs, but I'd never really understood the wisdom behind it. That is until I came hurtling around the corner and found Carole spreadeagled across the path.

'Carole!' I shouted.

'I'm all right,' she said, pulling herself into a sitting position and brushing herself down. 'I'm all right. I just slipped.'

I quickly helped her to her feet, keeping one ear open for the sound of approaching footsteps behind us while encouraging her to get moving again, but it was no good. She couldn't bear to put any weight on her right foot and, given the slippery conditions, hopping was definitely not an option.

'Just leave me,' she said, waving me away. 'You can make it to the gate if you leave me.'

She sounded like a wounded soldier in one of the war films my father always fell asleep watching on Sunday afternoons and I had to force myself to resist the temptation to laugh. She plonked herself back down on the gravel with a groan and, knowing I couldn't really abandon her, I joined her to await our fate. I wasn't going to let Harold forget about this in a hurry. In fact, if our names ended up appearing in the local press I was going to cite him as the brains behind the whole escapade.

We didn't have to wait many seconds before the inevitable footsteps drew closer and I was just thinking about struggling back to my feet when a man with a headful of dark curls and a shocking vocabulary shot around the corner, slipped on the same patch of ice that had been my companion's downfall and landed in a heap at my feet.

'Fuck me!' he shouted as he hit the deck.

The scene was so comical that we all began to laugh, even Carole.

After the worst of the giggles had died down, I held out my hand and between us, my pursuer and I pulled ourselves awkwardly to our feet.

'Are you all right?' I asked.

'No,' said Carole exasperatedly. 'I'm cold and I'm hurt and I'm beginning to think it's all your fault.'

I bit my lip and looked back down at my narky neighbour.

'Sorry Carole,' I said lightly, 'I wasn't asking you and besides, you said you were fine a minute ago.'

'Well, I'm not fine now,' she snapped back.

'And neither am I,' said the man, brushing the ice and frost from his jeans. 'My ego's taken one hell of a wallop and the bruise on my backside is going to make it impossible to sit down for at least a week.'

He looked at me, a shadow of a smile playing around his lips, but I thought it best not to laugh again.

'We could probably sue you,' moaned Carole, as I carefully helped her stand upright and offered her my arm to lean on.

'Carole!'

'Well, we could,' she winced.

'Now that would be interesting,' said the guy who I was now certain was the man I'd shared my avocado haul with before Christmas, 'considering you're both trespassing on private property.'

'He does have a point,' I reminded Carole via a sharp nudge. 'I daresay he could probably sue us if he wanted to, and worse.'

'I daresay I could,' he agreed.

'It's Luke, isn't it?' I asked, just to make doubly sure.

'That's right,' he grinned, 'and you're Kate, avocado sharer and the newest arrival in Nightingale Square.'

I was both surprised and, if the somersault my stomach performed was any sort of indicator, flattered that he had remembered. Carole simply looked astounded.

'Now you really do have the upper hand,' I shivered, 'because you know a whole lot more about me than I know about you.'

I allowed myself just one second of contact with those mesmerising eyes, but it was long enough to send the heat flooding to my cheeks. I hastily turned my attention back to keeping Carole on her feet, or should that be foot, before I made a complete fool of myself.

'So, what are you doing here?' both Luke and I asked at exactly the same moment before succumbing to laughter again.

'Look,' groaned Carole, leaning heavily on my arm and making my shoulder throb, 'as lovely as this getting to know you moment is, my ankle isn't feeling any less painful. I need to go home and strap on an ice pack.'

'Shouldn't that be a hot water bottle?' Luke asked, his eyes briefly meeting mine again.

I quickly looked away, unsure if he was teasing Carole or offering her bona fide first-aid advice. He certainly seemed to be brimming with confidence, but given that he was potentially in the right and we were very definitely in the wrong, I supposed he had every right to say and do as he liked.

'Right now,' Carole barked back, 'either would be welcome.'

'Then in that case,' said Luke, stepping forward and smoothly sweeping her into his arms, 'I suppose I'd better drive you home, hadn't I? And on the way Kate can tell me why I've caught you both prowling around the grounds of Prosperous Place in the near dark and without permission.'

'You'd better drive slowly then,' said Carole coquettishly to her Colonel Brandon-esque hero.

'Oh and why's that?'

'Because the journey will be over as soon as it's started,' she sighed. 'I'm a Nightingale Square resident too.'

'Here,' said Luke, after we had taken what I guessed was a short cut around to the side of the house, 'reach inside my coat pocket would you, Kate, and grab my car keys?'

'What?'

'My car keys,' he said. 'Unlock the car then I can slide Carole straight on to the back seat.'

She didn't even look embarrassed that we had heard the little sigh that had escaped her lips. She just appeared thoroughly smitten, as well she might. Mark had been right about Luke, not that I was in the market or really looking, but facts were facts.

'Tell me, Luke,' Carole smiled, the pain in her ankle

obviously obliterated as she gazed up at his chin and I rummaged through his pockets from behind, trying not to let my fingers linger where he felt warmest. 'Have we met before?'

'I don't think so,' he said doubtfully.

'Only you look very familiar,' she frowned.

'I get that a lot,' he said. 'I think I just have one of those faces. Have you found the keys yet, Kate?'

'Yes!' I said, triumphantly pulling out the fob and quickly pressing the button to unlock the car.

'You might have to clear the back seat a little,' he told me, his voice beginning to sound ever so slightly strained. 'Just shove everything in there to one side.'

I did as instructed and my heart sank when my eyes fell upon a bundle of papers and a pack bearing the logo of the developers who I knew had secured the purchase of Prosperous Place. I thought back to the conversation Luke, Mark and I had had outside the bakers before the Bonfire Party and tried to rack my brains as to what he had said when we were talking about the sale.

It had been a while ago, but from what I could remember he had told Mark he definitely *hadn't* set his sights on Prosperous Place when he'd discovered he'd missed out on my little house; but then he'd disappeared within the next ten seconds, and why else would he have one of the development packs in his car if he wasn't a part of it?

'All sorted?'

'Yes,' I said, covering the paperwork with a jacket so Carole wouldn't catch sight of it. 'Here you go.'

Once she was carefully deposited in the back I climbed into the passenger seat and waited while Luke ran back to the house, presumably to lock it.

'I think he must be one of them,' came Carole's voice from between the seats.

'One of who?'

'The developers of course,' she said, her voice adopting a tone which suggested she thought I was an idiot for not working it out for myself. 'Why else would he have access to the house?'

I swallowed but didn't say anything. I had no desire to blot Luke's copybook until I had all the evidence. But what more evidence did I need? His credentials had been spread across the plush interior of his posh car.

'I'm going to ask him,' said Carole.

'No,' I quickly countered. 'Don't do that.'

'Why not?'

'Well, it's none of our business for a start and . . .'

'And what?'

'And we might end up wanting to keep him onside if he is part of the development. Don't forget he might be one of the people who has the final say when it comes to deciding whether or not we can start growing on the green.'

'Oh, I hadn't thought of that,' she said, patting my shoulder. 'You ask him then.'

'Why should I ask him?'

'Because you're young and pretty and you've met him before, so it won't sound as intrusive coming from you.'

'Honestly, Carole,' I groaned.

'And you were the one who agreed to take on running the greenspace project. Finding us a site is down to you now, isn't it? You need to go out of your way to make a friend of him, Kate.'

'Look out,' I said, catching sight of Luke in the wing mirror. 'He's coming back.'

There was barely time for any sort of conversation let alone an explanation of what we had been up to before we were back in the Square and Luke was helping Carole hobble to her front door.

'I would ask you in,' she said as Graham came rushing along the hall to see what all the fuss was about, 'but I really need to get this ankle elevated.'

'What's gone on here then?' Graham demanded.

He sounded far from impressed to find his wife in the arms of another man on his own doorstep.

'Be quiet, Graham,' Carole said warningly. 'I'll explain in a minute.'

'It's fine,' said Luke, backing away. 'I understand, Carole, and I'm sure Kate here will be happy to explain to me why I caught the pair of you breaking and entering.'

'You caught the pair of them doing what?' shouted Graham, turning puce.

'That's a wonderful idea,' said Carole, nodding meaningfully over Luke's shoulder at me. 'Kate will explain everything, won't you, my dear?'

Chapter 13

'So, how are you settling in?' Luke called through from the sitting room to the kitchen where I was taking some time out to collect my thoughts, on the pretence of making us tea.

'I think I've been here long enough to consider myself completely settled,' I called back.

It had been almost three months since my moving date and I was well used to the rattles from the plumbing and the kindness of my neighbours now.

'You like it here then,' he said, his voice suddenly closer.

I looked up from where I was fiddling about with mugs and spoons to find him leaning comfortably against the doorframe.

'Yes,' I said, clearing my throat. 'Yes, I do, very much.'

'Do you live alone?'

'Yes,' I said, feeling warmer. 'Do you always ask so many questions?'

He shrugged and began to unravel his scarf and I reminded myself that until I had worked out if he was friend or foe I needed to keep him onside; otherwise Carole would be wearing my guts for garters before I knew it.

'I'm on my own too,' he said sadly. 'I don't much like it though.'

'Why not?' I asked as I poured the water and stirred.

'Do you always ask so many questions?' he mimicked.

I passed him a mug and began rifling through cupboards for the packet of dark chocolate digestives I knew I had stashed away in case of a low moment.

'Would you like me to put a match to your fire?'

'Sorry?'

It was a simple enough question, but somehow he managed to make it ooze innuendo and I couldn't help thinking about Carole and her obviously burning loins further along the Square.

'I noticed the fire in the front room is laid,' he said innocently. 'Do you want me to get it going for you?'

'Yes, all right,' I swallowed, thinking it was an odd request for a guest to make in a stranger's house. 'I'll be through in a minute.'

'You can't beat a real fire,' he said enthusiastically, disappearing back along the hall.

By the time I had found the biscuits, he had the fire roaring up the chimney and had settled himself in my armchair next to it. I sat on the sofa with my legs curled under me and watched him staring intently at the licking flames. He looked distracted, a frown knitting his brow as he concentrated on something I couldn't see.

'Are you all right?' I asked, when the silence became too loud to ignore.

'Yes,' he said, tearing his eyes away from the crackling blaze. 'Sorry. I was miles away.'

He took two digestives from the packet I offered and then sat back, munching away and looking around the room.

'You haven't decorated yet,' he observed. 'The décor still matches the details the estate agents had online.'

He obviously had a good memory.

'No, I haven't done anything yet.' I swallowed. 'I'm waiting until the spring.'

'That sounds like a good idea.'

'I thought it would be better to take a few months to get a feel for the place in case I ended up doing something rash and regretted it.'

He nodded in agreement and I carried on.

'The lady who lived here before me had been here all her life and I know it probably sounds strange, but I feel I kind of owe it to her not to rush into changing anything. Once you start ripping things apart, you can't put them back together, not in quite the same way anyway.'

I hoped he had the sense to interpret the deeper meaning

of what I was insinuating. It was my feeble attempt to say a whole heap of things without spelling out the finer details.

'So, tell me,' he said, picking up his mug. 'What were you doing wandering around the gardens of Prosperous Place this afternoon? I didn't have you down as the trespassing type.'

'I'm not,' I said quickly.

He raised his eyebrows.

'All right,' I accepted. 'I'm not as a rule.'

'So, what tempted you today?'

'It was Carole,' I said, passing the buck. 'Well, a combination of her and my neighbour Harold. He and I had spent the afternoon looking at old photographs of the house and gardens and when Carole called round and pointed out that the for sale board had been pulled down, he suggested we should go and have a look at the place before the bulldozers moved in.'

'I see,' Luke said thoughtfully. 'And what makes Harold think that the bulldozers will be moving in?'

'We all think it,' I said bluntly before I could check myself. 'We aren't stupid. We know what this so-called group of developers have got in mind for the place.'

'But why do you all care so much?'

'Well, obviously I can't speak for everyone,' I carried on, 'but I know Harold and I have a definite fondness for the house's history, a respect for what it once was, for what the whole area once was to Norwich really.'

'Are you talking about the Wentworth legacy?'

'You've heard of it, then?'

I knew I needed to rein in the sarcasm, but the fact that he, and I daresay the rest of the development consortium, knew all about what Mr Wentworth had given and sacrificed only made their determination to obliterate it even more distasteful.

'Yes,' he said, 'I've heard of it.'

'We residents have a vested interest in the little of what's left of it, actually,' I added, thinking it was now or never as far as the green was concerned.

'What do you mean?'

'The green here,' I said, getting up and moving to the window. 'We want to turn it into a community growing space, one big allotment where we can all come together and grow our own.'

Luke joined me at the window.

'I think it looks good as it is,' he said, staring out into the gathering dark. 'From what I saw of it earlier. And isn't this all a part of the Wentworth legacy as well? This little Square and the green is still exactly how Mr Wentworth wanted it to be, isn't it?'

He had a point.

'Surely if you lot dig it up, even for such a worthy cause, then you yourselves will be chipping away at another tiny bit of all that's left of his creation, and what you say you're so keen on preserving.'

I hadn't looked at it like that and I wasn't too sure I liked the taste of my own medicine.

'Can't you go and grow somewhere else?' he suggested.

'We would if there was somewhere close enough for everyone to be able to access it,' I said, feeling suddenly less convinced about our plans. 'The key to the whole idea was maintaining the sense of community,' I explained, trying to justify what we were proposing and make it sound very much like something Charles himself might have put into action, had he thought of it. 'We all want to work together.'

'I see,' said Luke, moving across the room to peruse the bookcase.

I decided not to say anything else.

'You have some lovely books,' he said, bending his head to read the spines.

'Thank you.'

'I take it you're a bit of a history expert?' He smiled, running his finger along the shelf.

'Something like that.'

'Hence your interest in the Wentworth legacy?'

'Exactly.' I nodded. 'Sometimes I can't help thinking that looking back into the past is preferable to living in the present.'

I instantly regretted the admission, but thankfully he didn't start questioning me about what I meant.

'That thought has crossed my mind recently,' he said

simply, before dazzling me with an almost too perfect smile. 'Tell me about this neighbour of yours.'

'Which one?'

'Harold,' he said, reclaiming the armchair and looking instantly at home. 'The chap with the photographs.'

I was happy to fill him in about Harold and how his family, like Doris's, had lived in the Square ever since it was built. I even suggested he should call round and ask to look at the photographs for himself. It might make all the difference to what happened next and I felt determined to make him fall in love with Prosperous Place, just like I had. I was beginning to feel as though I would go to any lengths to stop him and his cutthroat crew ripping the heart out of the place.

'But won't he think it's a bit funny if I just turn up on his doorstep?'

'Not if you tell him your connection to Prosperous Place.'

I waited for him to explain his connection to me, but he didn't say a word.

'You obviously have one because why else would you have been in the house this afternoon?'

Still nothing.

'I could go with you if you like,' I suggested, when it became obvious that he wasn't in the mood to share. 'Because you really should take a look at all the stuff he's got. It might make a difference to your plans. Assuming you have some of course?'

You couldn't blame a girl for trying.

'I might take you up on that,' he said thoughtfully. 'Have you thought about getting a cat?'

'A cat?' I frowned. How on earth had the conversation gone from Prosperous Place to cats in two seconds flat? 'What are you talking about?'

'If you don't like living on your own,' he said seriously, pinning me with his dark eyes as he pushed an errant curl away from his face.

'I never said I didn't like living on my own,' I reminded him. 'You were the one who said that.'

'Was I?'

'Yes.'

'Then perhaps I should consider getting a cat.'

'You don't strike me as the cat type.'

'What type do I strike you as then?'

'I couldn't possibly say,' I said, busying myself with the biscuit packet and gathering the mugs together on the expectation that he would take the hint and leave.

Not only had he cleverly steered the conversation away from his connection to Prosperous Place, he had also made me blush. He really could be a most infuriating guy.

'I don't suppose there's a chance of another tea, is there?' he asked, making himself more comfortable in my armchair again.

*

'If I were you,' said Luke, looking out at the back garden as we washed up the mugs after our third cup of tea, 'I'd be inclined to replace this entire back kitchen wall with a concertina-style glass window.'

'Would you?' I yawned.

I was feeling tired and rather shell-shocked. Somehow Luke had ensconced himself in my little house, next to my fireside, in my armchair and we had spent almost two hours discussing life, but not love, the past, but not our own and the joys of a real fire versus the electric alternative. I was still none the wiser as to what his role, interest or financial invest-ment in Prosperous Place was, but I didn't think there was any harm in getting to know him. He might still turn out to be very handy if we needed a direct link with the developers, as Carole had pointed out, and I was sure she would be over-joyed that I was going to such lengths to secure us an ally.

'Yes,' he said. 'Your patch of garden out there, it's slightly terraced, isn't it?'

'It is,' I confirmed.

'Don't you think it would be lovely if this whole end of the house looked out over it?' he said, conjuring the image in my mind's eye.

'It would,' I agreed. It would certainly be glossy magazine stylish. 'But I also think it would be far too modern for this place. You have to remember I'm trying to preserve what's already here.'

'Rather than enhance it?' he questioned. 'Preserve it in aspic; keep the antimacassars firmly in place, that sort of thing. Is that what you had in mind?'

'I'm not creating a museum,' I tutted, 'and besides, I thought you said you preferred the past.'

'I do,' he admitted, 'in some ways, but that doesn't mean you can't meld it with the new and modern to create something even better. Architecturally speaking, I'm all for it.'

I narrowed my eyes, wondering if this was a glimpse of the modern versus old architectural juxtaposition that Susan from the council had hinted would be happening when the developers got their paws on Prosperous Place.

'So that's the sort of thing you'd go for, is it?' I asked lightly. 'If this was your place, you'd be all for ripping out that back wall and opening up the view?'

'Definitely,' he said.

I couldn't help but feel disappointed.

'But only if it could be done sympathetically of course.'

Was that a glimmer of hope?

'Of course,' I agreed, trying to reel him further in, 'and I suppose it would be nice to bring the outdoors in a little,' I conceded.

'And it would lighten this end of the house no end,' he went on.

'Well, I'll think about it,' I said, knowing I wouldn't and that even if I had wanted to, the cost would have been prohibitive.

'Let me know what you decide,' he said. 'I might be able to put you in touch with someone who can help.'

Oh dear.

'And you'll introduce me to Harold and his many photographs, won't you, Kate?'

'Happily.' I was pleased he hadn't forgotten about that at least. 'I'll even help you choose a cat,' I generously added. 'If you do decide to get one.'

'I'll hold you to that,' he laughed, walking back to the sitting room and finally pulling on his jacket and scarf.

The front door was barely open an inch before I saw the curtains twitching in Carole's front bedroom. I was amazed she had managed to negotiate the stairs and wondered how long she had been perched in the window waiting for Luke to leave. I wanted to ask him if he was heading back to Prosperous Place, but I didn't.

I had enjoyed his company, and his sense of humour, even if for a while he had felt like the house guest who was never going to leave, and didn't want to end his visit knowing for certain that he was going to be one of the team responsible for destroying the last piece of the Wentworth legacy.

His views on architectural improvements were almost enough to take the shine off his appeal and I didn't want to tarnish his personality further.

'Thank you for your hospitality, Kate,' he said, turning

back to me after he had opened his car and in the process lit up half the street.

'And thank you for not reporting Carole and me to the police,' I smiled, wondering how many more upstairs windows were now privy to his departure.

'I really will hold you to your promise to help on the pet selection front you know,' he grinned, taking a step towards me as I instinctively took one back. 'Well,' he said, looking a little confused, 'bye then.'

'Bye.'

I had shut the door before he had even closed the gate, my heart hammering in my chest. I was certain he had been going to kiss me; granted it would have only been a peck on the cheek, but it was a very long time since any man, other than David, had kissed me and I wasn't sure I wanted to be kissed, innocently or otherwise.

And, I reminded myself, Luke could still turn out to be the enemy for all I knew and more intimate fraternising with the enemy, however handsome they were, was definitely not a depth I was prepared to sink to.

Chapter 14

I couldn't resist taking a walk back to Prosperous Place early the next morning. I didn't go through the gate again for obvious reasons, but I could see what I thought was the window that Luke had yelled through. It was firmly closed and the place looked as deserted as ever. If he was still loitering behind the walls he was certainly keeping a low profile.

It was eerily quiet, almost too quiet, and there were no tell-tale wisps of smoke coming from any of the chimneys to suggest that he had lit his own fire. He had seemed mesmerised by mine. In fact, he seemed to relish the cosiness of both hearth and home and I wondered if he really was lonely, with no such simple comforts in his own life.

After all, he had readily admitted he didn't like living alone but then, I reminded myself as I turned my back on the empty house and strode back to the Square, if he was a ruthless property developer looking to make a quick million then he deserved to be on his own, and unhappily so.

'Where have you been?' Lisa's voice called out the second she spotted me crossing the road back into the Square. 'Did you not get any of my messages?'

Heather's car was parked in front of my house and she was sitting inside it with Evie strapped into her car seat in the back.

'No,' I said, shaking my head. 'What's going on? Is everything all right?'

'Everything's fine,' Heather called from the car, clearly keen to temper Lisa's impatience. 'She's just in a bad mood, that's all. Get in and I'll explain where we're going on the way.'

'And turn your phone on for goodness sake,' Lisa moaned, taking her place next to Evie while I quickly climbed in the front. 'Anyone would think you didn't want to be disturbed while you were entertaining handsome strangers late into the night.'

'Oh, I see.' I laughed as a dozen or so messages lit up my phone screen. 'Is this an ambush?'

'Got it in one,' Heather winked as she pulled smoothly away from the kerb.

'So where are we going?'

'You'll have to wait and see,' said Lisa before Heather had a chance to tell me.

Evie was happily gurgling away next to her, completely oblivious of Lisa's sullen mood.

'But you can tell us all about your cosy evening in when we get there,' she added.

'And don't even think about leaving out any details,' Heather chipped in as she joined the rush hour traffic. 'Or worry about old misery guts in the back there. Apparently, she'd rather be at home this morning than out in the fresh air.'

'Are you talking about Lisa,' I teased, twisting round in my seat to look at her, 'or Evie?'

Thankfully it didn't take too long to wend our way around the city and less than twenty minutes later we pulled into the car park at Whitlingham Lake.

'We aren't running, are we?' I asked Heather as she man-handled Evie's buggy out of the boot and set it up with all the speed of a seasoned pro. 'I haven't got my trainers on.'

'Of course we're not running,' said Lisa. 'If you'd read the messages you'd know that.'

Clearly the journey had done little to lighten her mood.

'I can't read in the car,' I told her. 'It makes me feel sick.'

She rolled her eyes and zipped up her coat.

'It's still too slippery for running,' said Heather as she buckled her baby in and snuggled her under an extra blanket. 'I thought we'd ease ourselves in to some exercise with a nice walk instead.'

'And I thought we'd end the torture with some coffee and a slice of cake,' Lisa added, pointing to the café at the opposite end of the car park.

Thankfully her voice sounded warmer with the mention of cake and I guessed if the birdsong and gently lapping water didn't cheer her up, the promise of a toasted teacake probably would.

This time it was Heather who rolled her eyes as she pulled on her gloves.

'Well, we don't want to go mad and push ourselves too hard,' insisted Lisa. 'You don't want us going into shock, do you?'

The lake looked beautiful, even if the breeze cutting across it was enough to take our breath away; we hadn't got far though before we were pulling off our hats, look-ing rosy-cheeked and feeling slightly out of puff. Perhaps Heather was right and our fireside hibernation had gone on for a little too long.

'So how did you know?' I panted, thinking I might as well get the inevitable interrogation off and running. 'Was it the bells and whistles of the central locking that gave my visitor away last night?'

'No,' said Heather.

'It was Carole,' puffed Lisa beside me. 'She was on the phone the second that allegedly gorgeous fella had dropped her off on her doorstep.'

I might have known. I could hardly believe she hadn't already limped to my door and demanded an update.

'So . . .' said Heather.

'So?' I said, shrugging my shoulders and stepping ahead.

'So, what happened?' said Lisa, hanging on to my arm to make me slow back down. 'Did you snog the face off him? Carole was fairly certain you'd go to any lengths to find out who he really was and given the description she gave me of him, I can't say I'd blame you if you did!'

'Lisa,' said Heather, with a frown.

'Sorry,' she said, clapping her hands together and not sounding sorry at all. 'I'm just too excited. I've been hoping to conjure you up a new Prince Charming, Kate,' she beamed, turning back to me again, her bad mood conveniently forgotten. 'And poof! Here he is.'

'He's no Prince Charming,' I said, trying to shake her off. 'Well, not mine anyway.'

'Of course he is,' she persisted. 'And I'm your personal Fairy Godmother.'

The idea was laughable. For a start she wouldn't suit pink tulle and she didn't look to have a star-tipped wand secreted anywhere about her person.

'And given that, according to Mark, this is the same guy you met in the grocers. The very one who fancied the pants off you,' she went doggedly on, '*and* that you know your onions when it comes to antiques and stuff, we're rather hoping you'll be able to steer him in the right direction when he and the other developers start work on Prosperous Place.'

Now it was my turn to roll my eyes. What she was suggesting was absurd and I wondered if there was anyone in the Square she hadn't talked to about the situation. Heather, sensing that I wasn't happy, pulled her back and tried to shut her up.

'I really don't think Kate's on the lookout for a new Prince Charming,' she said sagely to our over-exuberant friend. 'And I don't think she's looking for a wild fling that may or may not help save Prosperous Place either,' she quickly added before Lisa had a chance. 'Are you, Kate?'

'No,' I said firmly. 'Of course I'm not. No torrid romance required here, thank you very much.' I was trying my best to sound less nettled than I felt, but I wasn't sure I was succeeding. 'I certainly don't need a Prince Charming. Besides, I've already had mine and he's long gone.'

I swallowed and dropped my eyes to the path and Lisa took the opportunity to start up again.

'You do know there's more than one Prince for each of us, don't you?' she nudged. 'You do realise that you get to have another crack at the relationship game. One failed marriage doesn't condemn you to a life sentence of spinsterhood.'

'I don't think you can be a spinster if you've been married,' said Heather thoughtfully.

'Well, whatever. A sentence to singledom then,' Lisa

impatiently added. 'You know what I mean. You need to get back on the horse, Kate before you completely forget how to ride.'

Heather looked as though she wanted to laugh, but I didn't find our friend funny at all.

'Says the woman who's happily married to the man of her dreams,' I bitterly cut in. 'A man who is so loving and loyal, he's no doubt looking after your three beautiful children on his day off, so you can have a break.'

Lisa shook her head, but I didn't give her a chance to interrupt.

'Believe me Lisa,' I told her, 'you'd soon feel the same way if you found yourself in my position. If John broke your heart, you'd soon understand that when it comes to true love, there are no second chances.'

Heather gave Lisa a look which both suggested that she needed to stop pushing and that she deserved the telling off I had just given her, but it still didn't stop her.

'Are you actually telling me that you *really* believe there's only one person in the world for everyone?'

'Yes.'

'And that if the relationship with that person, that once in a lifetime so-called soulmate ends, then that's it? Bye bye romance and love and sex and everything else?'

'Yes.' I shrugged. 'The chance to have a truly meaningful relationship has gone.'

There, I'd admitted it. I'd finally said that if the fairy-tale idyll turned out to be anything but, then that was it, game over. The flame was extinguished, never to be as brightly relit.

'But what if the person you were madly in love with broke your heart,' asked Heather quietly, 'just like David did, and then, somewhere down the line, you fall for someone else.'

'You couldn't possibly fall for someone else in the same way or love that deeply again,' I told her. 'If you had already given your whole heart to someone there wouldn't be any of it left for anyone else. You might think you were having a second time around romance, but it wouldn't really be a patch on what had gone before.'

'So, what you're saying,' said Lisa, stopping in the middle of the path, 'is that it's the happy ever after for you or nothing?'

'Exactly.'

'Even if the first fairy tale ended through no fault of your own and there was an opportunity to write another, you wouldn't?'

'No,' I said firmly. 'I wouldn't. If you'd already had the best, then why would you bother with the rest?'

I was rather pleased with my 'I'm a poet' moment, but Lisa just scowled.

'That's ridiculous,' she snapped, her chin thrust stubbornly in my direction.

'Let's just agree to disagree on this, shall we?'

'Well, perhaps we should, because if you're thinking that this soon to be ex-husband of yours was the best,' she said, her hands firmly planted on her hips, 'then I feel pretty damn sorry for you, Kate.'

'Lisa!' gasped Heather.

'What?' She frowned. 'It's true. He treated her like shit and now she thinks she's doomed to spend the rest of her days on her own. Well, I'll tell you lady,' she said in a voice she usually reserved for when her kids had been up to no good. 'Some day some lovely bloke will fight his way through to your heart and he'll want to whisk you away and I really hope you will have seen sense by then.'

'I wouldn't bank on it,' I said, walking away. 'And if you're really thinking that I would be interested then you don't know me very well at all and besides, I'm actually the reason my marriage failed, not David so I'm entitled to think I'm getting my just deserts, thank you very much.'

'I can't believe you're still blaming yourself for what happened,' she began to mutter, but Heather stopped her.

We continued to walk in silence around the lake and back to the car park. Heather had made a few vague attempts to point out the wildfowl and the change in the weather which was looming on the horizon, but she soon gave up when neither Lisa nor I responded.

'Shall we just go home, then?' she asked wearily when we were halfway between her car and the café in the car park.

'I don't bloody think so,' said Lisa, linking arms with me as if our argument had never happened. 'I only came for the cake.'

'Not the scintillating conversation?' I asked, shoving my hat back on.

It felt cold now we weren't striding along.

'No,' she said, pulling me in the direction of the café. 'Not really. I have this infuriating mate who has some very weird ideas you see, and she insisted on coming along this morning.'

I couldn't believe she thought I was the infuriating one.

'You mean a mate who won't agree with your way of thinking?'

'Exactly,' she said.

'Shocking,' I gasped.

'It is,' she said, 'she's a total nut job, but I'll grind her down in the end.'

She wouldn't, but I had no intention of telling her that and starting the whole argument up again.

'And before you start cross-examining me about last night,' I said, eyeing the pair of them as Evie began to fidget, 'I have absolutely no idea what this guy Luke has to do with Prosperous Place, or what he and his developer pals have lined up for it.'

Lisa tutted.

'In that case you definitely should have snogged the face off him,' she said.

I opened my mouth to protest.

'Not for any romantic reasons,' she quickly cut in, 'just so you could pump him for information.'

'That's a terrible thing to suggest,' Heather said disapprovingly as she pushed Evie's buggy through the café door. 'I'm sure Kate would never use her feminine wiles in that way.'

'Given what she told us on our walk around the lake, I'm a little concerned that she'll never use them for anything ever again.'

I ignored the remark.

'I did, however,' I said instead, 'tell him about our desire to turn the green into an allotment, so if he or any of his cronies have the power to make a decision about that, then I'm sure we'll hear about it soon enough.'

I pushed away the thought that if we did get the go-ahead we would be changing one of the last remaining pieces of the Wentworth legacy, as Luke had been quick to point out, to suit our own ends.

'Well, that's something I suppose,' Lisa said graciously. 'The evening wasn't a total waste, then?'

I didn't tell her that the evening hadn't been wasted at all. Rather it had actually turned out to be one of the nicest I'd had since arriving in Nightingale Square, but I knew that if I admitted that, then there'd be no stopping her.

*

'Can you hold Evie while I nip to the loo?' Heather asked, while Lisa was queuing up to pay for our snacks and drinks. 'I'm absolutely bursting.'

'Can't you just hang on until Lisa comes back?'

I had no desire to be left, literally, holding the baby. In fact, given the tumultuous thoughts our walk around the lake had stirred up, that was the very last thing I wanted.

'Nope,' she said, dumping the snuggly wrapped-up bundle into my arms. 'Sorry. I'll be quick.'

I took a deep breath and carefully readjusted my position at the table so I could get a more comfortable hold on her.

'So,' I sighed, looking at Evie's pretty, plump face. 'What are we supposed to talk about then, Miss Evie?'

She rewarded me with one of her beautiful smiles and then reached out a pudgy hand and started pulling at my scarf. Her little softly padded body felt heavy in my arms and I realised she was feeling far more relaxed than I was. I fathomed, as I began to gently jiggle her up and down and watched her giggle in response, that I'd been a constant in her life for as long as she could remember. She beamed up at me and stretched her arms out to reach my face and I kissed her fingers, making her properly squeal.

'Now look at you,' said Lisa, resting the packed tray on the table. 'Are you seriously telling me that you'd take a pass on a second time around romance and miss out on making one of these for yourself?'

Tears had sprung to my eyes even before I'd had time to think up either a witty or scathing retort and as I bent my head, trying to blink them away, one escaped and rolled down my cheek. It was quickly accompanied by another.

'Now, do you want chocolate or strawberry?' Lisa asked, holding aloft two cupcakes, completely unaware of the growing torrent her timely comment had unleashed. 'I got Heather the nuts and seeds tray-bake thing she asked for, but I bet she'll be begging for a bite of these when she sees them.'

'Kate?'

Heather was back from the loo.

'Can you take her?' I sniffed, standing awkwardly and passing Evie back to her before she'd even had time to unzip her jacket.

'What have you said now?' she asked Lisa accusingly.

'What?' Lisa responded. 'I only asked her which cake she wanted.'

'I'm just going to the loo,' I said, keeping my head bent as I made my escape.

When I came back to the table the tea had been poured, the cakes distributed and Heather was discreetly feeding Evie under a muslin square.

'Are you all right?' Lisa asked. 'I didn't mean to upset you. I was just trying to make you see sense.'

Heather tutted loudly.

'Sorry,' Lisa corrected. 'I was only trying to make you see what *I* think is common sense.'

'It's all right,' I told her, pulling off my jacket. 'It's not your fault. You weren't to know.'

'Know what?'

'It doesn't matter,' I shrugged. 'Can we talk about something else?'

Heather deftly burped her baby and swapped her to the other side.

'She's still as voracious as ever then?' Lisa said with a nod to the bump under Heather's muslin.

'Oh God, yes,' she smiled, 'I can't keep up with her. I'm going to have to start weaning her soon. I know it's a little early but—'

'Mother knows best,' Lisa interjected. 'Better than those bloody books weighing down your coffee table, anyway.'

'Oh, they've gone,' said Heather.

'Charity shop?' I asked, taking a first delicious bite of the strawberry cupcake and forcing myself to join in with the conversation.

'Box in the garage,' she replied. 'Glen and I didn't think it was fair to pass on all that paranoia about how things should be done to someone else.'

Lisa laughed.

'It'll be November the fifth again before we know it and we can have a sacrificial burning.'

'It's only January,' Lisa tutted. 'I'm still not over last Christmas yet, I don't need to be thinking about the next one. How are plans coming along for the christening?'

'Slowly,' Heather groaned. 'But there's one thing Glen and I have decided on.'

'Yes?'

'We'd love it if you and Kate would agree to be Evie's godmothers.'

The second bout of tears her kind words set flowing ensured that I really did have no option other than to explain what could have been construed as an aversion to babies and everything that came with them.

'You can't blame me this time,' Lisa was quick to protest. 'I hadn't even opened my mouth. You were definitely the one who set her off,' she said, taking hold of Evie while Heather rearranged her clothes.

'It's no one's fault,' I sniffed, blowing my nose on a paper napkin and screwing it into a tight ball. 'It's just baby talk in general.'

'Go on,' said Heather, passing me another napkin.

'It was my incessant baby talk that broke up my marriage,' I said, the words leaving my mouth for the first time ever.

'I thought you said David had been unfaithful.'

'He was,' I said, still sniffing, 'he was, but only because I drove him to it.'

Heather reached out and put a hand over Lisa's before she launched off on her '*you can't blame yourself*' speech again.

'When David asked me to marry him, before then even,' I began in a rush, 'he had always been adamant that he didn't want children. He said he was too old to start a family. He was always very up-front about his feelings and I, being so in love with him, was happy to sacrifice becoming a mother if it meant I could keep him.'

'So what changed?'

'It wasn't even something I thought about until a couple we knew, who were only a little bit younger than David, had their first baby. It was a boy and David seemed besotted by him. He coddled him and cooed over him and even became his godfather and I, seeing the change in him, began to think that perhaps he would consider us having a baby of our own.'

'But he wouldn't?'

'No,' I said, shaking my head. 'He was adamant that he wouldn't be up to the job full-time, that he didn't want to be. He said he enjoyed the freedom associated with the life and business we had created too much, and that a baby was all well and good providing it went home at the end of the day.'

'How did that make you feel?'

'Wretched. Once the idea had begun to grow in my head I couldn't stop it. I did try but before I knew it, it was cropping up in practically every conversation we had. In the end David's patience with me wore out and he decided that he was going to go to an auction in France, which we always attended together, on his own. He said he needed a break.'

'And that was where . . .?' Lisa asked, her eyebrows raised.

'Yes,' I nodded, 'that was where it happened, and so you see, it was all my fault.'

Lisa shook her head.

'It certainly was not,' Heather jumped in, taking up the tone she was always berating Lisa for using. 'He should have been more understanding. It was cruel to act like that around someone else's child and then punish you for the feelings the sight aroused.'

'Did he tell you he'd been unfaithful?' Lisa asked. 'When he came back, did he tell you?'

'No,' I said, knowing I needed to get off the subject. 'He carried on as if nothing was amiss. He was attentive and apologetic and I just put his change in attitude down to the fact that he'd had time to think things through and was trying to see the situation from my point of view.'

'What a bastard,' said Lisa, handing a very drowsy Evie back to Heather.

I shook my head. I was about to shoulder the blame once again, but the look on both their faces made the words die in my throat. 'Shall we have another pot of tea?' I said instead. 'My treat.'

*

Neither of my friends really seemed to have grasped the gravity of my guilt. Had I not got it into my head to try and change David's mind about having a baby, then I'd still be happily married, contentedly living in London and working alongside the man I loved, and who had been my one chance at a happy ever after.

Or would I?

The fact that David had chosen not to mention his 'foolish indiscretion' (his words, not mine) until circumstances forced his hand, had set my thoughts off and running to every unsavoury and distasteful place imaginable. Had he succumbed to temptation before? Had the night he eventually described to me in mortifying detail actually been a one-off or more like one of many?

'It's not too late, you know,' said Lisa, twisting between the front seats while Heather strapped Evie back into her little seat next to me.

'It's not too late for what?' I asked.

I hadn't really been tuned in to what she had been saying as we left the cosy warmth of the café and walked back over to the car.

'For you, you numpty,' she laughed. 'I know what you said earlier, but there's still time for another shot at love and romance and even a baby of your own.'

I shook my head, but she didn't give me a chance to voice my objection again. Heather looked at me and smiled sympathetically. She and I both knew it was pointless trying to stop Lisa when she was in her stride. I would just have to wait it out until she'd said her bit and nod along when necessary. It was easier that way.

'I know you've got this squiffy take on love and that it's a once in a lifetime thing, but I'm telling you right now, you're wrong, completely off your rocker.'

I wasn't, but I bit my lip. Some people could handle an existence where things happened out of sync, but that wasn't for me. I liked my life events to be neat and tidy, organised and all happening in the correct order. Diversions from the path were all right for some, but I had always preferred the traditional route.

I would never in a million years have imagined that divorce would be a major feature of that route, but it had happened and now I was steering my own safe and sedate course. I was navigating a passage which limited hurt, upset and disappointment and I daresay, had Lisa been aware of it she would have added passion and unpredictability too, but that was fine. I was more than happy to live without both if it meant not risking my heart again.

'Didn't I hear you only yesterday, Lisa,' said Heather, unable to resist challenging our friend's determination to bend my thoughts to match hers, 'lecturing your Tamsin about the importance of respecting other people's opinions, even if they aren't necessarily the same as yours?'

'You did,' said Lisa, yanking on her seatbelt. 'But that doesn't count in this case.'

'Why not?' Heather and I chorused.

'Because Kate's wrong and she needs telling.'

'Simple as that,' I said.

'Simple as that,' she agreed. 'And I'm going to prove it.'

Chapter 15

A week later I was back in Harold's house, sitting at his dining table and drinking tea, only this time I was surrounded by pieces of paper and notebooks, rather than photographs and magazine clippings.

'I'm still not sure this is worth the bother, Kate,' the old man grumbled, 'or your time for that matter. You must have something better you could be doing.'

'Not really,' I shrugged, sharpening my pencil again, before I set about recording more of what he could remember, 'not until the weather improves anyway. And like I've told you a hundred times, it's now or never because once the sun starts to shine and spring puts in an appearance, then I will have better things to do. Plenty of better things, like stripping wallpaper for a start; you won't see me for dust then.'

'Literally,' chuckled Harold.

'Exactly.'

I was looking forward to making a start on the refurbishment of my cosy little abode, but I wasn't so enamoured with the fact that I couldn't rid myself of the thought of the kitchen wall being replaced by a retractable sheet of glass. I had even taken to drinking my first caffeine hit of the day standing in front of the space with my eyes closed, imagining the view beyond the bricks and thinking how lovely it would be to invite the outside in in such a dramatic way.

'But really, Kate,' came Harold's voice again. He sounded more like a sulky teenager than a man in his eighties. 'What's the point? Not even that young man of yours has bothered to come and look at the snaps, so I can't possibly imagine that anyone else will be interested in these tall tales. It's all in the past and should probably stay there.'

I was as annoyed with Luke's continued no-show as I was with myself for not being able to shake off his interior design suggestions. When he had been warming his toes at my fireside, I'd had absolutely no reason to doubt his sincerity when he said he was keen to meet Harold and look through his old photographs. He had sounded genuinely eager to discover more about the history of Prosperous Place and yet I hadn't caught so much as a glimpse of him, or anyone else for that matter, hanging around either the house or the Square.

'He's certainly not my young man,' I corrected Harold

perhaps a little too sharply, 'and we aren't just doing this for his benefit anyway.'

'Who are we doing it for, then?' he demanded.

I didn't have an answer for him right at that moment, but was thankfully saved from admitting it by the sound of the letterbox being rattled.

'I'll go,' I said, jumping up.

There was just the one letter, a rather smart envelope with Harold's name written in beautifully curvaceous handwriting on the front.

'Who is it?' he called.

'No one,' I said, rejoining him at the table. 'It was just the post.'

'The post came hours ago,' he frowned.

'Well, this was sitting on the doormat,' I told him. 'It's been hand delivered; look, there's no stamp or address.'

'Who delivered it?'

'I don't know,' I said, handing the letter over. 'I didn't see.'

Harold took the envelope and turned it over in his hands, taking in the weight of the expensive stationery.

'Feels like money,' he sniffed suspiciously.

I couldn't help but smile at his canny observation.

'I thought the same thing,' I agreed. 'It's beautiful thick paper, excellent quality and not many people write with a fountain pen these days. Aren't you going to open it?'

Still frowning, Harold pointed towards the little table which occupied the space next to his armchair by the fire.

'Oh my,' I said, passing him the slender bone-handled letter opener he had indicated. 'This is rather beautiful.'

He stared at it intently, as if he hadn't really looked at it properly for a very long time.

'It was my grandmother's,' he told me. 'Possibly her mother's, now I come to think of it.'

He slid the end of the blade into the paper and slit the envelope neatly open with one deft twitch of his hand.

'Could you please pass my reading glasses as well, my dear?'

I watched as he slowly read what looked like a prettily decorated card and shook his head.

'It's money all right,' he said. 'Have a read of this.'

The card was actually an invitation, but it had been made to look like a Victorian valentine. It was decorated with a violet border and although very beautiful I wouldn't allow myself to be seduced by such pretty packaging, especially as I read on.

'Dear Harold Brighton,' I read out loud. 'You are cordially invited to Valentine's Day dinner at Prosperous Place on Friday February the fourteenth. Drinks at seven thirty, dinner at eight, carriages at ten thirty.'

'Carriages,' Harold sniffed again. 'That's a bit fancy, isn't it? Considering it's only at the end of the road, and what's with the hearts and flowers?'

'It doesn't say who it's from, does it?' I observed, turning it over to look for clues just as the doorbell rang. 'There's just a mobile number to RSVP to.'

The long line of numbers didn't quite match the prettiness of the card, but whoever had sent it had certainly gone to a lot of trouble to make it look appealing.

'Well, I'm not going.' Harold's stubborn voice carried along the hall as I went to answer the door. 'I'm not turning out after dark. It's probably one of those scams you hear about on the news. Whoever sent it no doubt wants to empty the house and by the time I've worked out there is no fancy dinner I'll have been robbed blind.'

I shook my head and tutted. It was an awful lot of trouble for a potential housebreaker to go to. What an imagination he had.

'Oh goodie, you've got one as well!'

I discovered Lisa on the doorstep and she was brandishing a similar invitation to the one I still held in my hand. Carole, Graham and Heather were close behind her and they all held theirs up in a show of unity. From what I could see, each one was decorated slightly differently, but carried the same wording.

'This is Harold's, actually,' I pointed out to my friend who was looking most excited about the prospect of a Valentine celebration inside the walls of Prosperous Place. 'I've been here all afternoon, so I don't know if I've got one.'

'Well, go and see,' ordered Carole. Her flushed cheeks suggested she was enjoying the excitement every bit as much as Lisa. 'And then we'll decide what we're going to do.'

They all bundled into Harold's front room and I went home to retrieve my own envelope which, sure enough, was waiting on the doormat.

'I take it we've all got one?' asked Rob, who had heard the kerfuffle and come out to join in with the speculation.

'Looks like it.'

'Bit odd, isn't it?' he said. 'Not saying who it's from, I mean.'

'Yes,' I agreed. 'It is a bit.'

Not surprisingly, Carole's voice was the first I heard when I crossed the threshold into Harold's again.

'They're obviously from the developer,' she said sagaciously. 'No doubt they think they can win us over with a fancy card and a classy dinner. It will be champagne all round to soften the blow of whatever it is they're planning to do, you mark my words.'

At least one of my neighbours had worked out the justification for the elaborate invitations, even if she hadn't mentioned the role her handsome hero may have played in distributing them.

I stared down at my own card which was decorated with all sorts of beautiful spring flowers and a smattering of pale pink hearts. I had to hand it to whoever had come up with the designs because they had certainly done their homework.

The motifs they had picked out were perfect and I remembered what I had once read about the Victorian postal system being almost overwhelmed when the popularity of the cards really took off.

'So, who cares?'

This came from Lisa and it made my heart sink.

'I'm going to make the most of it,' she rushed on, 'and besides, if they've gone to all this bother for us, they can't really be that bad, can they?'

'That's exactly what they want you to think,' Carole pressed on, before I had a chance to say exactly the same thing. 'This will be some clever exercise in the art of seducing potential problem neighbours.'

'Well, you've changed your tune,' Lisa snapped. 'When your knight in shining armour carried you home in his executive carriage you were all smiles. You sounded more than a little seduced yourself then, Carole.'

I let out a long, slow breath, convinced that this in-house sniping was exactly what the team at the end of the road was hoping for. If we carried on talking to each other like this and starting to fall out, we were going to be playing right into their hands.

'Look,' I said, risking Lisa's wrath. 'Let's not get caught up arguing about the whys and wherefores, let's just have a show of hands as to who thinks it's a good idea to go.'

Lisa's hand shot up straightaway and Heather's was only a

nanosecond slower. I raised mine in a show of solidarity and Lisa looked smugly at Carole.

'I'm not siding with you because I want a fancy night out, Lisa,' I quickly told her. 'I want to find out all I can about the development, and this will be a great opportunity to do that, and don't forget, at the end of the day, the new owners might have some influence over the green. We don't want to jeopardise our chances of securing that, do we?'

'She has a point,' Rob shrugged at Carole before raising his hand. 'I think we should all go. After all there's safety in numbers, right?'

'Exactly,' I agreed, thinking that I was going to have to keep a close eye on Lisa and wondering if Rob was sacrificing a romantic evening out with Sarah to come along. 'And hopefully, what one of us forgets to ask, someone else will think of.'

'Fine,' Carole finally caved. 'If that's what you all want, then we'll go.'

'Do you think I've got time to slim into that dress I found in the New Year sales?' Lisa asked Heather as we discussed the evening. 'Such a posh invitation warrants a posh frock, doesn't it?'

I knew we needed to be amenable, but I couldn't help feeling my friend was rather missing the point.

There were no trinkets or bouquets for me on Valentine's

morning which wasn't unexpected, but it was the first time in a long time that I hadn't received an elaborate floral arrangement, complete with hidden jewellery and I hastily switched off the television when the so-called early morning *news* programme resorted to showing surprise live on-air wedding proposals complete with Princess-cut diamonds and horse-drawn carriages. If I couldn't have my own fairy tale I certainly wasn't going to get all doe eyed watching someone else's.

'You all set then?' asked Lisa when she landed on the doorstep wearing the self-satisfied expression of a woman who had been treated to the love of a good man before she left the house.

'Not really,' I said, slamming my front door behind me. 'I still can't believe you've managed to talk me into this.'

'We have to have our armour polished and intact before we go into battle, as you and Carole keep saying,' she reminded me, waving to Heather. 'We need to be strong and show them we mean business,' she mimicked.

'And I still hold to that,' I said, climbing into the back seat of Heather's car and hoping that Lisa hadn't caught Carole's matchmaking virus and was harbouring a motive that involved pushing me in Luke's direction should he happen to be there that evening. Not that I'd given it much thought, hardly any in fact. 'But we were thinking more along the lines of metaphorical armour really. I personally don't think that an appointment with the hairdresser and then a manicurist is necessary at all.'

'Well I do,' she said firmly. 'In order to play the part, you have to look the part. And besides, this is the first time in forever that John and I will be anywhere other than the sofa on Valentine's night, so I'm going to make the most of it; anyway, you want to look your best for lovely Luke, don't you?'

'Believe me,' I told her as she unwittingly confirmed my fears. 'He's the last person on my mind.'

Heather looked at me in the rear-view mirror and grinned.

'He is,' I said, slumping back in the seat.

I knew neither of them believed me, but it was true. Luke was the last person I was hoping to see sitting at the head of the dining table or dishing out cocktails at Prosperous Place because if he was there, that would mean he was definitely involved in what was going to happen to it and I wasn't sure I could stomach that on top of everything else.

His no-show at Harold's front door and his proprietorial handling of my fireside might have annoyed the hell out of me, but there was still something about him that had me hoping he would turn out to be one of the good guys. Obviously, I wasn't going to try and explain that to my friends though, so I turned my attention to the view as they exchanged knowing looks in the front.

*

As one, with Harold steering the mobility scooter he loathed, but for the purpose of that evening relented was a necessary evil, we braved the freezing February air and set off from the Square at exactly twenty minutes past seven.

'Kate, you look stunning,' Mark whistled, as he took in my simple black gown and diamanté embellishments before I buttoned up my coat. 'Is that a vintage ensemble by any chance?'

'It is,' I told him. 'Thank you, Mark.'

In the end I had followed Lisa's lead and taken my time choosing what to wear. I'd finally opted for the only outfit that didn't hold memories of evenings gone by. I had tracked down this particular dress for a specific occasion, but circumstances had cheated me out of wearing it, a fact that I was suddenly surprised to note I was rather grateful about.

'It's Dior,' said Neil, cocking his head to one side. 'Isn't it?'

'Yes,' I laughed. 'How did you know that?'

He shrugged and looked a little embarrassed.

'It's all in the details,' he smiled.

'She's gone for the classic Hepburn,' said Lisa, quoting what had been said in the hair salon as the stylist sprayed my elegant up-do. 'She's pure class, this one.'

'Pure class indeed,' said Neil and Mark slipping either side of me and linking arms.

As far as I was concerned we all looked pure class. John couldn't take his eyes off Lisa's elaborate lashes and Heather was revelling in wearing a dress that Evie wouldn't have the chance to spit up on. The look Glen was giving her left me in no doubt that they would be ducking out of the evening and dismissing the babysitter as soon as they could.

We crossed the road and found that the wooden gate which I had previously vaulted over during my 'visit' with Carole had been pulled open. It was flanked with heart-shaped helium balloons and the winding path beyond was lit with glowing torches and tea lights in jars which illuminated our way around the side of the house and up to the open front door. There still wasn't a soul to be seen and, having carefully stowed Harold's scooter out of sight, Neil hammered on the doorframe and we all tentatively stepped inside.

The cavernous oak-panelled hall was softly lit with dozens more candles of all shapes and sizes and I could make out the gentle strains of classical music coming from the room to our right. It looked very elegant and impressive; however, I soon realised it was as cold inside as it was out and we all looked blankly at one another wondering what on earth was going on. Something was definitely amiss.

'Anyone at home?' John called out, his voice echoing off the walls and making us all jump.

'Jesus,' gasped Mark, theatrically clutching his chest with one hand and clinging to Neil with the other. 'We're here for cocktails and dinner John, not to play Cluedo.'

'What do you mean?'

'You nearly gave me a heart attack!' he laughed, before adding in a deep voice that didn't sound like it belonged to him at all, 'It was John who did for Mark, in the hall, with his booming baritone.'

We all giggled and then fell silent as we heard heavy foot-falls thundering down the stairs.

'You're here,' said a voice I instantly recognised before any of us had eyes on its owner.

I felt my heart sink in my chest and my shoulders slumped a little. How lovely it would be, just every now and again, not to be disappointed.

'You're *all* here,' said Luke, looking straight at me as he pushed his unruly curls away from his face.

His gaze lingered longer than was entirely necessary and my knees, no doubt as a combined result of the frustration that he was there at all and the cold which was penetrating my very marrow, felt a little wobbly in response.

'Kate,' he swallowed, 'how very lovely to see you again.'

'Luke,' I nodded, unable to raise a smile. 'Hello.'

'Oh my god,' Lisa started. She was tugging at my coat sleeve and whispering urgently in my ear the very second he moved on to ask Carole if her ankle was feeling any better. 'You never said it was *him*.'

She pinched my arm so hard I almost cried out.

'Who?' I hissed under my breath while discreetly trying to shake her off. 'What on earth are you talking about?'

'I knew I recognised him,' said Mark's voice on my other side. He sounded every bit as excited and out of puff as Lisa. 'Didn't I say that day we met him in the grocers, Kate, that I thought I recognised him, but what on earth is he doing here?'

'So,' said Luke looking at me again before Mark had a chance to hazard a guess. 'Here you are then.'

Now that we were there he didn't seem at all sure what to do with us. I looked around the hall and up the stairs, but there was no one else around to help him out.

'The invitation did say seven thirty,' Rob reminded him as the seconds ticked awkwardly by.

He sounded a little tetchy, but that was hardly surprising. He had confirmed earlier in hushed tones that he was indeed missing a romantic evening with Sarah in order to bolster our united front.

'Of course.'

'Sorry mate, but I've got to ask,' said John, pointing at the frilly pink number Luke was wearing and that we were all aware of, but had been too polite to mention. 'What's with the apron?'

Luke looked down at it in dismay and opened his mouth to answer, but was interrupted by the sound of a loud buzzer.

'Oh, crikey, that'll be dinner,' he said, looking slightly panicked. 'Come on everyone. Follow me.'

He rushed off into the room on our right with the apron

still in place and, having exchanged what can only be described as looks of incredulity, we followed on behind him.

The dining room was another wood-panelled beauty, but there were no polished candelabras or sparkling cutlery. In place of a shining mahogany table there were three mismatched pine ones which had been pushed together end to end and were all slightly different heights. Not one of the motley collection of chairs was a pair and there was a strong whiff of something on the wrong side of cooked coming from what I guessed was the kitchen area. Heather caught my eye and pointed to where the classical music was emanating from what looked like a wind-up radio.

A frustrated roar met our ears and we all huddled a little closer to the thankfully blazing fire to work out what on earth was going on and how best we could plan our immediate escape.

'Does anyone happen to know the number for the takeaway pizza place down the road?' Luke asked sheepishly as he reappeared in the doorway, still wearing the apron which was now singed around the edges and holding a large pan with something very burned welded to the bottom of it. 'I'm afraid it's looking like that dinner I invited you to is off.'

Chapter 16

Thanks to Lisa's ability to feed the five thousand on a tight budget with few ingredients, combined with Mark's professional skills at keeping calm in a kitchen crisis, everything was soon back under control and we all formed an orderly line, helped ourselves to ladles of fragrant vegetable curry and chunks of the fresh bread Mark fortunately had at home, before taking our places around the rather unconventional dining tables.

The rest of the development crew were still conspicuous by their absence, but the whole evening already felt so surreal that no one thought to ask if and when they would be joining us, or noticed that there were no extra places set at the tables. So much for Carole's carefully planned-out strategy and list of questions.

'I'm sorry about the lack of cocktails,' Luke apologised, before taking his seat, 'and the lack of ambience, heat and illumination. It wasn't my intention for us to eat solely by candlelight, but the electricity still hasn't been reconnected, in spite of the promises from the power company, and the furniture which was due for delivery this morning hasn't turned up yet either.'

We all looked at him and smiled sympathetically.

'This was the best I could muster at such short notice I'm afraid. The acrid smell of burnt risotto is all my own doing of course. I hadn't realised just how tricky it would be to cater for so many guests on a two-ring gas camping stove.'

He stopped to take a breath and Neil jumped in to console him.

'It's all fine, honestly,' he said kindly, looking straight down the table to beam at our host and in the process making his husband huff. Evidently it was acceptable for Mark to gush over Luke's handsome good looks, but not for Neil to try and make him feel better about his disastrous culinary efforts. 'Don't worry about it.'

'I should have cancelled,' Luke continued. He was sounding more disconsolate by the second. 'But at such short notice it just didn't feel like the right thing to do.'

I looked first at Luke and then around the table. This was not what any of us had been expecting, but given the way Lisa was batting her lengthy lash extensions at our fine host, I knew the evening had already surpassed her hopes even if not in quite the way she had imagined. She was clearly taken with Luke, and Heather, fanning her flushed face, was also looking a little smitten.

'Perhaps you should have opted to wine and dine us elsewhere?' Rob suggested.

'On Valentine's Day?' Luke laughed. 'I don't think so and anyway, it had to be here.'

'Did it?' Mark muttered, clearly nettled as he dunked his bread in his curry.

'Yes,' said Luke. 'It did. Now please, I promised you all dinner, so let's just finish eating and then I'll explain everything.'

I don't think any of us had ever eaten so fast in our lives and no sooner had the last mouthful been swallowed than Luke was back on his feet.

When he excused himself to check on a fire in one of the other rooms, Lisa began automatically piling everyone's plates together as if she was at home rather than a guest at a dinner party. If that indeed was what the evening could still be categorised as.

'Well, this is a turn-up for the books,' she began. 'Carole gets carried home by one of the world's top male models, Kate has him warming his toes at her fireside and the pair of them don't even have the sense between them to recognise him!'

I wasn't sure I'd heard her right.

'Perhaps they don't spend as long perusing the aftershave

ads as you do, my love,' said John, giving his wife a squeeze and making her giggle.

Clearly, he was happy to allow his wife a mild flirtation, but with whom exactly?

'Hang on a minute.' I frowned. 'Lisa, what on earth are you talking about?'

'And what about you?' demanded Mark of Neil. 'I can't remember the last time you smiled at me like that. Am I going to have to jump to my own conclusions about how you feel about him?'

'No one's going to have to jump to any conclusions about anything,' said Luke, walking back in, only now without the apron. 'Let's leave this mess and go and sit in the staff quarters. It's warmer in there.'

'Warm enough to perhaps take off our coats?' Carole asked.

'Hopefully,' Luke smiled.

It was a squeeze for us all to fit into the little sitting room at the back of the house, but it was definitely warmer and with mugs of steaming coffee and packets of biscuits tipped out on to plates in lieu of dessert, we were all ready to thaw out and listen to whatever it was that Luke had gone to so much trouble to gather us all together to say.

'I have a feeling,' Lisa said to him before he had a chance to finish his first chocolate digestive, 'that I might know who you are.'

'Not that it matters,' he sighed, 'but if you're thinking I'm the chap who was trying to sell you the champagne lifestyle last Christmas courtesy of a spritz from the right bottle of aftershave then yes, I am who you think I am.'

He didn't look particularly pleased about the admission, but Lisa was agog.

'See,' she said to me, her eyes sparkling. 'I told you he was a model. His photos from the Man! Christmas campaign last year were to die for. If you're into that toned torso sort of look of course,' she hastily added with a nonchalant shrug to save what little was left of her dignity.

Luke looked from her to me and I added a shrug of my own. I didn't know if he expected me to be impressed, but I wasn't. If anything, I felt let down. A man I had thought was nice had made money out of his looks and was now ruthlessly developing his property portfolio. As far as I was concerned, he was turning into the ultimate cliché before my very eyes.

'Sorry,' I said. 'I'm not much interested in aftershave ads so I'm still none the wiser.'

Lisa rolled her eyes in annoyance and I wondered whether Luke, if he was as famous as she and Mark suggested, was frustrated to discover that his face was as unfamiliar to me as the next man's in the street, even if it was rather more impressively chiselled.

'Well, that's good,' he shocked me by saying.

His reaction was the polar opposite of the one I had

anticipated. I had assumed that models were shallow, self-centred creatures that lived frivolous, pointless lives, or perhaps that was just my own limited experience of them.

'I'm pleased you don't know,' he continued, 'because my days of posing in front of a camera in my undies are well and truly behind me now.'

'But you managed to stick it out long enough to make lots of money and enjoy the benefits of living the so-called champagne lifestyle?'

The words were out before I could check them, but that didn't stop Lisa giving me her best death-glare. I knew it was nothing to do with me, but I couldn't help feeling upset that he had used his looks, rather than his brains, to boost his bank balance. Suddenly he had completely lost his appeal.

'Yes,' he said, biting his lip and frowning. 'I suppose I did for a while.'

'Well,' cut in Carole, steering the conversation back to where it was supposed to be, 'as fascinating as this all is, none of it explains what you're doing here, Luke, or for that matter, how you know so much about us. Those pretty invitations we received were all personally addressed. I'm guessing they were from you?'

There was a general murmur of agreement among the group.

'Yes,' he said, 'they were from me. So, why do you think I'm here?'

He was still addressing me. Still staring and in the process making me feel scrutinised and more awkward than when he'd caught me trespassing. Perhaps given my scathing comment and assumptions about his former career I deserved to feel like that.

'Kate?'

'All right,' I said bluntly, ready to dish out the truth, even if he wasn't going to like it. 'I think you've made a fortune from flashing your perfect pecs and now you've come here to make yourself some more money. You're following the trend and establishing your property portfolio, along with the rest of the developers who were listed on that board, and in the process the lot of you are going to rip the heart out of Prosperous Place.'

I had no idea where the ferocity had sprung from. I would never normally express myself so aggressively, even if I had felt singled out, and the look of hurt which flashed across Luke's face produced a stab of guilt which twisted itself into a knot in my gut. I took a deep breath to steady my heart rate and looked everywhere but back at him and the sea of shocked faces swimming before me.

'Is that what you all think?' he asked quietly, looking now around the group.

'I think it's a logical enough assumption to make when we don't know any different,' spoke up Glen. 'I mean, you are one of the developers, aren't you?'

Luke dropped his gaze to the floor and shook his head.

'I thought we were supposed to be keeping the evening on an even keel,' Carole reminded me in a low whisper as she tried to pass me a bourbon biscuit I didn't want. 'You haven't forgotten about our plans to grow on the green, have you?'

My out of character loss of temper had ensured that I had completely forgotten about it. I had been so looking forward to finally getting to see inside Prosperous Place, the pinnacle of Charles Wentworth's philanthropic empire, but now I was so disappointed about Luke and the sad state of the house and the inevitability of what was going to happen to it next, that our carefully choreographed plan had fallen by the wayside. The whole evening just felt like another nail in the fairy-tale coffin to me.

'Luke knows a little about you all because he knows me,' said Neil.

I watched Mark's mouth fall open as Neil crossed the room to stand next to Luke and another piece of the jigsaw puzzle slowly slid into place. Neil worked for the firm of architects who had been responsible for the dreadful set of futuristic plans and Luke had the keys to the castle. It didn't take a genius to add the two sides of the equation together.

They must have been in cahoots all along. I had obviously been wrong about Neil. He had just been spinning me a line at the New Year's Eve party. He had told me that he hated the project and that it was poised to fail, but that wasn't right at all. He just wanted me to think that seeing Prosperous Place demolished would be worse than seeing it modernised.

'I gave Luke your names,' said Neil. 'He wanted to personally invite you here this evening because he was keen to get off on the right foot.'

'I'll bet he was,' said Mark.

He sounded bolshie and bitter and I was pleased there hadn't been any sign of the cocktails that the invitations had promised. Tipsy guests would have made for an uglier scene than the one I imagined was going to play out now.

'For goodness sake, Mark,' said Neil crossly. 'Stop being such a diva—'

'No,' said Mark, putting up his hand. 'I'm sorry, but this has gone on long enough. Everyone deserves to know the truth.'

'I can't argue with that,' said Luke, shoving his hands in his trouser pockets.

'My husband here,' said Mark, ignoring Luke, 'is a part of the team who has drawn up the plans to destroy this place. I've been sworn to secrecy about this, but I think you all have a right to know. He works for the firm which has formed an alliance with the developers.'

There was a collective intake of breath and Neil put his head in his hands.

'Well I never,' said John.

'A traitor in our midst,' tutted Graham.

This was going even worse than I had imagined and judging by the look of disbelief on Luke's face, this wasn't what he had envisaged when he had delivered his fancy cards. He had doubtless intended an elegant evening culminating with us all loving the plans, thanks to the soothing gin slings he would pour down our throats.

'Is that true?' asked Heather. 'Did you really have a hand in the plans, Neil?'

'Yes,' he shrugged. 'I did.'

Luke began to laugh and everyone's attention swung back to him. Confusion was being edged out by annoyance and the fact that he found the situation amusing was endearing him to no one. If this was supposed to be an elaborate evening to smooth the way for when the diggers descended then it had turned into an unmitigated disaster.

Perhaps Luke should stick to what he knew best – posing on a deserted beach in his pants – because life as a property developer was not going well for him so far. But then, perhaps he was far cleverer than any of us gave him credit for. Perhaps showing the house in the worst possible light was how he was hoping to convince us that in its current state, it really was a lost cause.

'Is that all you're going to say?' he asked, elbowing Neil who was still glued to his side. 'Aren't you going to tell them the rest?'

'You're the host,' said Neil. 'I think I'll leave the party tricks up to you.'

'Oh, I've had enough of this,' said Harold, struggling to his feet. 'Will you get my scooter and take me home please, Kate? I'm too old for all this silly game-playing.'

'Certainly,' I said, offering him my arm.

'No, please,' said Luke, fixing me with those heavily lashed eyes again. 'Just wait. Let me explain. This evening has obviously been a complete catastrophe, but let me at least try and salvage it by putting you all properly in the picture.'

'Are you and your associates going to instruct the council to let us turn the green into a growing space or not?' Carole piped up.

Clearly, she was as keen to leave as the rest of us and no longer willing to play along to get the result we had all gone there to secure.

'No,' said Luke, 'I'm afraid not and who exactly are my associates, Carole?'

'The rest of the development crew,' said Lisa, stepping up. 'I take it they wheel you out as the front man when the girls and the gays need something pretty to look at, do they?'

Luke burst out laughing again, but no one else joined in.

'I only helped you in the kitchen,' Lisa pressed on, turning redder by the second, 'because I thought you'd be able to get us the green.'

I thought she was going to cry and it dawned on me that I wasn't the only one to have had my fairy tale crushed in the last couple of hours.

'Me too!' piped up Mark.

'And there was me thinking you were being helpful and kind,' Luke sighed.

'Yeah, right,' sneered Mark. 'Come on Neil, we're leaving.'

'No,' bellowed Neil, shutting us all up, 'we're not going anywhere. What a bloody cock–up. Just sit down the lot of you and listen.'

I sat Harold back in the chair he had struggled to pull himself out of, and since we were clearly not leaving any-time soon, I took off my coat and sat back down in front of the fire.

'Kate,' Luke swallowed.

'What?'

He didn't say anything else and I looked up at him.

'What?' I demanded rather than asked.

Neil gave him a nudge.

'Nothing,' he stuttered. 'Sorry. It's just that dress . . . you look so . . .'

His voice trailed off.

'It's Dior,' smiled Neil. 'Vintage.'

Luke nodded but continued to hold my gaze.

'I was paying more attention to the way it was being worn rather than who designed it,' he said eventually.

'Apparently, our girl's a classic Hepburn,' Lisa smiled, her annoyance with him momentarily forgotten.

'And then some,' Luke smiled back. 'Kate, you look utterly exquisite.'

It might have been a line, one he'd even used before, but that didn't stop my cheeks reddening and my hands starting to sweat. For a second it felt like there were only the two of us in the room. I was grateful when Harold jumped in and broke the spell.

'So,' he demanded. 'Come on then, out with it, my lad. Some of us have homes to go to.'

'All right,' said Luke, taking a breath before leaning across me to throw another log on the fire. 'The truth of it is that I'm actually here because of you two.'

Now he was looking at both me and Mark, who was perched on the arm of the chair opposite.

'Us?' questioned Mark.

'Yes,' said Luke. 'You. Do you remember the day we met in the grocers?'

'Avocado-gate,' Mark nodded. 'Yes, I remember.'

'We talked about how I had beaten you to the punch and secured my house before you'd managed a viewing,' I added.

I was surprised my voice sounded so normal.

'That's right,' Luke agreed, 'and between you, you also told me that Prosperous Place had been sold and what you thought the plans were for it.'

'And you denied you were anything to do with it,' Mark quickly reminded him.

'Because I wasn't anything to do with it,' he went on, 'at the time.'

'So how come we're sitting here and you're the one with the keys?' asked Carole. 'You look pretty at home to me.'

'I am at home,' Luke smiled dreamily, his expression momentarily transformed.

'Just tell them the rest, for pity's sake,' encouraged Neil.

'All right,' he said again, taking another breath. 'When I discovered that Prosperous Place had already been sold, and to developers to boot, I decided to do some digging. A very nice lady at the council put me in touch with the then current owner and gave me the name of the development consortium and their architectural team.'

I thought back to my meeting at the council. Susan had mentioned that she had spoken to someone else about the situation. She must have meant Luke.

'From there it was a short leap to our mutual friend Neil here, who wasted no time in telling me that he wasn't happy with what was in the offing for the place and when I approached the vendor and enlightened him as to what was *really* going to happen, as opposed to what the development crew had told him was going to happen, he was of the same opinion.'

Perhaps I should have believed that Neil wasn't happy about the plans after all.

'But why would the vendor care?' I asked. 'Surely he just wanted to get the place off his hands?'

'He didn't actually want to part with it at all,' Luke explained. 'He just couldn't afford the upkeep any more. A place like this can become a complete money pit if the little niggles aren't sorted soon enough and, well, you can see for yourself we are on the cusp here.'

I didn't know what everyone else thought, but I'd been inside long enough to know that it wouldn't take many more winters before things were in need of serious repair. I was no structural engineer, but I had eyes in my head and they could pick out the peeling paint, the underlying smell of damp and the bone-chilling cold, none of which would do a property like this any favours at all.

'So,' Luke carried on, 'I told him that I would match the price the developers were going to pay, but that I would restore Prosperous Place to its former glory.'

As one our eyes swivelled back to him and there was a sharp intake of breath from all corners. Had he really just uttered the words that we had all been longing to hear?

'So, you don't want to tear it down or slap some glass monument to the side of it?' Lisa gasped. 'And you aren't a part of the group of developers?'

'No,' said Luke. 'I have no intention of doing anything like that. I want to do the complete opposite in fact and I'm absolutely not part of the group of developers. There are no developers now. It's just me.'

'And did the vendor believe your intentions were honour-able?' Carole butted in.

Clearly she wasn't ready to pop the champagne cork before she was in receipt of all the facts.

'They weren't sure to begin with,' he said, fiddling with the fire again, 'but I convinced them in the end.'

'And how exactly did you manage to do that?' Lisa demanded.

'It was easy,' he shrugged. 'I'm the pretty front man, remember? I just wheeled myself out, whipped off my shirt and they fell at my feet.'

Lisa shook her head, mortified.

'Sorry,' she mouthed.

'It's all right,' he laughed.

'So, what *did* you say to make him believe that your intentions towards the place were so different to the devel-opers'?' I asked.

'I told him the truth,' he said, turning his attention back to me.

'Which is?'

'That I've recently discovered I'm a descendant of the Wentworth family and that I have every intention of reclaiming and restoring my family home.'

Chapter 17

The ensuing silence lasted long enough to confirm that everyone, aside from Neil who it turned out had been the ultimate double agent, was deep in shock.

'Shall I go and make some more coffee?' Luke offered. 'Give you all time to take my announcement in.'

'I'll give you a hand,' said Neil, gathering mugs.

I looked at Luke, trying to gauge his reaction to ours. If I were in his position I wasn't sure how I'd be feeling. It wasn't as if he owed us an explanation, but I appreciated the effort he was making to put us in the picture.

Prosperous Place was now legally his, thankfully back in the Wentworth family fold – assuming he was telling us the truth – and whatever he decided to do with it was up to him. I had wondered before if any of Charles Wentworth's descendants had inherited his generous and benevolent spirit and it turned out the affirmative answer was standing right in front of me, offering to make coffee while planning how to restore his family home to its former glory.

Was it possible that we had a real-life hero in our midst? The question popped unbidden into my head and I quickly batted it away and reminded myself that, thanks to my husband's deception, I didn't believe in those any more.

'Well, what about that then?' Lisa exploded before Luke was out of earshot. 'That's a turn-up for the books, isn't it? You should see your faces!'

'You,' said John, giving her another of his trademark squeezes, 'are a total minx. How do you think I feel knowing that you're standing there drooling all over Mr Gorgeous?'

'I can't imagine you care two hoots because you know I love you and I know you drool all over that calendar I gave you of Kylie last Christmas.'

'Fair enough,' John laughed, 'and well played.'

'Thank you,' Lisa bowed.

'Will you two stop, for goodness sake,' Carole scolded. 'This is—'

'What is it, Carole?' snapped Harold, shutting her up.

I could tell from her tone that she was going to try and twist the situation and turn it into a drama and Harold had obviously picked up on that too.

'Well . . .' she faltered.

'It's our dream come true, isn't it?' he said, quickly cooling the words that were poised to pour out of her mouth. 'The most unexpected, but the very best outcome any of us could have hoped for.'

'It really is, isn't it?' joined in Graham, unaware that his wife had been going to try and put a quarrelsome kink in the plot. 'Prosperous Place isn't doomed after all. There'll be no pillaging or pulling apart.'

'There certainly will not,' said Luke, who, with Neil's assistance, had made coffee in record time. 'Not on my watch.'

'So, tell us then lad,' said Harold, taking the mug Luke offered. 'How exactly are you related to Mr Charles Wentworth and how come it's taken you so long to find your way home?'

Luke looked from one of us to the other and it was then I realised that his eyes did look familiar, but not because I'd seen them in an aftershave advert. I had gazed upon them when I had researched Prosperous Place before my move to Nightingale Square and again since, seated at Harold's dining table admiring a certain portrait.

'It's Abigail, isn't it?' I couldn't resist butting in as I stirred a heaped spoon of sugar into my drink. 'You're related to Doris's family. That's why you were so interested in my house.'

'I thought you didn't take sugar,' Heather quietly reminded me.

'I do when I've had a shock.'

'Yes,' said Luke. 'You're almost right, Kate. It turns out I'm a descendant of the boy no one was supposed to know existed, but how did you know that?'

'It's your eyes, lad,' said Harold, thankfully saving me from having to become lost in them again. 'There's a definite family resemblance about the eyes.'

'I told you, you needed to talk to Harold,' I reminded Luke. 'And it's even more important that you should now.'

'And I will,' he said. 'I've been meaning to, but moving in here hasn't gone quite as smoothly as I'd hoped, as you've all no doubt worked out from this disastrous attempt at a dinner party.'

'It hasn't been that bad,' said Mark, moving to stand next to Neil. 'Even if it did turn into a bit of a muddle before the big reveal.'

'Is that your idea of an apology?' Neil frowned.

'It's the best I can come up with,' said Mark sincerely. 'You know I'm not very good at admitting when I'm wrong.'

'Crikey,' said Neil, fanning himself and feigning shock. 'That's a revelation in itself.'

Everyone laughed and Luke smiled at me again.

'I still hadn't quite made the connection between Doris and Abigail before you moved into the Square, Kate,' he explained. 'I was certain Prosperous Place had been my family's home but I didn't think I'd be lucky enough to buy it. When I looked into buying your place, that was simply as close as I thought I'd get. I didn't realise the true significance of number four until quite recently.'

'So, who is this Abigail you keep talking about?' asked John. 'I don't think I've ever heard of her before.'

'Oh, I think that's a story for another day,' Luke sighed. 'Suffice to say, I'm the new owner of Prosperous Place, I'm a descendant of Charles Wentworth, and I'm sure Harold can explain to you about Abigail and my link to her far more succinctly than I can.'

I wondered if he was reluctant to go through the details because of the sad circumstances surrounding his branch's connection to the Wentworth family tree or if he still wasn't actually in possession of all the facts. From the little he'd intimated, it sounded to me as if he had only recently become acquainted with certain details.

'I just want to reassure you that I have no intention of dragging the house into the new millennium when it sits so comfortably in the one that went before,' he concluded, 'but I do intend to make it wonderful again and that folks, as they say, is that.'

'Aside from the fact that you won't let us use the green to grow our greens,' Carole reminded him.

'Yes,' he nodded, 'I'm sorry about that but as I said to Kate, that green, in its current guise, is what Charles Wentworth envisaged when he built the Square. He provided a space where his workers could come together at the end of the day and relax and I'm not going to begin my time as custodian here by altering that. However,' he hastily continued before he was bombarded with objections and counter-arguments, 'if you come back here at ten o'clock tomorrow morning, and by that, I mean all of you, kids, cats and babies included, I'll explain the alternative that I have in mind.'

'Why not tell us now?' asked Glen.

'Because,' said Luke quietly, pointing to where Harold was dozing, 'I think we've heard enough from me for one evening. Come back tomorrow and all will be revealed.'

'Promises, promises,' Lisa sighed dreamily.

We all laughed and Harold woke up, flustered that the joke had been on him.

'I don't think anyone in the Square actually has a cat,' I said to Luke, as we helped Harold into the back of his car so he could drive him home and see him safely indoors.

'I'm surprised about that,' Luke said quietly. 'I was convinced there would be one cat person among you, but of course I already knew it wasn't you, Kate.'

He looked at me and smiled, and remembering the cosy evening we had spent together at my fireside I found myself smiling back.

'I think you and I should go on a date,' he whispered in my ear.

'Go on a date?' I spluttered.

His warm breath on my neck was the softest caress and I jerked my head away.

'That sounds like a fine idea to me,' came Harold's voice from the dark interior of the car.

'I thought you were asleep.'

'With you two yapping on,' he tutted. 'How could I possibly be asleep?'

'Well, I'm delighted you seem so taken with the idea, Kate,' Luke huffed. 'I don't think I've ever been subjected to a reaction like that when I've asked a woman out before.'

I wasn't sure if he was teasing or not, but given the circles he moved in, and the plethora of beautiful models he no doubt had clamouring to grace his arm, I could well imagine my response was far from the usual.

'It's just that I'm not really in a position to go on dates,' I said, trying to avoid his gaze again.

As lovely as Luke seemed to be, he certainly wasn't the man for me because, thanks to David, there was no man for me now.

'I wasn't suggesting a wine, dine and gentle seduction kind of date,' Luke hastily countered. 'Unless . . .'

'Sounds fine to me,' came Harold's voice again and Luke grinned and broke off from whatever it was he was going to say.

I couldn't help noticing how the lines around his dark eyes crinkled when he smiled so mischievously.

'What sort of date were you suggesting, then?' I asked primly.

'A trip to the local cat rescue place,' he said. 'See if we can't find ourselves feline companions to sit by our respective firesides.'

I wasn't sure how I felt about being a lone female living with a cat. There was a certain stereotype attached to it that, even though I was single, I didn't particularly want to conform to.

'I'll think about it,' I told him. I wouldn't, but I would have said anything to stop him looking at me like that and talking about dates. 'But right now I just want to go to bed.'

He waggled his eyebrows suggestively and I felt myself turning red. I half expected Harold to pipe up again, but he didn't.

'Well, we'd best get you home then,' Luke whispered. 'Hadn't we, Kate?'

Chapter 18

I couldn't vouch for anyone else in the Square, but I didn't get an awful lot of sleep that night. I lay awake, my mind playing over the evening in minute detail. I was shocked that we now had a Wentworth descendant living in Prosperous Place, but I was determined that my agitated state was more to do with the fact that the house had been saved, rather than the fact that there was a handsome prince at the helm.

The thrilling turn of events really were fairy-tale-tastic but I had enough common sense, and still harboured enough heartache, to know that there was a possibility that the ending might not turn out quite as happily as we all hoped it would.

'So,' said Heather, the next morning as we all set back off to Prosperous Place to retrieve Harold's scooter and discover what Luke had in mind for me and my neighbours, 'this is all a bit of a turn up for the books, isn't it?'

'Just a bit,' laughed Lisa, scooping little Molly up into her arms and falling into step, while John pushed Archie along in his buggy. 'And it's all down to you, Kate,' she beamed.

'And me,' butted in Mark, who was obviously eavesdropping with abandon.

'Yes,' Lisa conceded, 'and you, Mark. I'm sure it was your rugged good looks and wild ways with the sourdough that really convinced Luke that this was the place he needed to be.'

'Are you being sarcastic by any chance?' he asked.

'As if,' laughed Heather. 'Lisa's not the sarcastic kind and I'm sure you had just as much to do with capturing Luke's imagination as Kate did, Mark.'

'What are you all wittering on about?' I frowned. 'This is nothing to do with me. Luke is here to reclaim what's left of the Wentworth legacy.'

'His ancestors have called him home,' added Neil.

'Exactly,' I earnestly agreed, before I realised he was in on the act and teasing me as well. 'His being here has nothing to do with me,' I hastily reiterated.

'But we reckon he could be the one,' said Heather, plucking at my sleeve just as Lisa had done the night before.

'The one?'

'The one to reawaken your heart, Kate,' she said dreamily. 'He might not be here *because* of you, but he's here *for* you.'

'He's the one who can chop his way through to the tower

231

you've imprisoned yourself in,' added Lisa, 'and, after much kissing and canoodling, free you from it.'

'You're mad,' I told them both, striding ahead. 'You've both lost the plot.'

'No, we haven't,' Lisa called after me. 'We're just trying to get on board and see things from your perspective.'

'No,' I said, stopping dead so the pair of them almost fell into the back of me. 'You're not. If you were doing that you'd realise there is no tower, there are no *self-imposed* restrictions on my heart because it is irrevocably broken. Its only purpose is to measure time.'

'And you're still sticking to that crazy idea, are you?' said Lisa, lowering Molly to the ground and encouraging her to use her own legs for the final few steps.

'Yes,' I said, 'I am and it's not crazy thank you very much.'

'Luke might think it is,' said Heather.

'But Luke doesn't know about it, does he?' added Lisa.

'No,' I said, 'he doesn't and there's absolutely no reason why he should.'

'But that means he'll keep trying and his efforts will be in vain,' Heather burst out. 'Perhaps we should warn him that you really are untouchable before he makes a complete fool of himself.'

'What?' I scowled. 'What do you mean he'll keep trying? He'll keep trying to do what?'

'Make you fall in love with him,' Heather said lightly while bending to kiss the top of Evie's head as she wriggled in the carrier strapped to her chest.

I couldn't believe Lisa had managed to brainwash her and bend her ideas to match her own off-kilter ones in such a short amount of time.

'After last night, it's obvious to everyone that he's already smitten,' Lisa continued, her tone softer. 'You only have to think about how he kept looking at you, how his eyes kept seeking you out, to know that.'

I stood open-mouthed, unable to find the words. All this time I had thought I was the deluded romantic, but it turned out I'd made friends with two of the biggest dreamers this side of the Milky Way. What utter rubbish they had come up with. The only reason Luke had 'sought me out' was because I knew him slightly better than the rest of them. And he kept coming back to Neil as well; it wasn't all about me.

'They're right, you know,' John startled me by saying. 'It's as plain as the nose on your face.'

'Exactly,' said Lisa, high-fiving her husband as they disappeared through the gate and Glen nodded along in agreement.

'Only I don't think the poor lad realises it yet,' John called over his shoulder. 'So, let him down gently when you're explaining why you're destined to spend the rest of your life alone, won't you?'

*

I made sure I stood at the back of the group as Carole took the lead along the path and up to the back door, but it didn't make any difference because Luke strode out of the door and around us and everyone had to turn round to face him, which put me right at the front. I ignored the weight of Lisa's stare that I could feel burning into the back of my neck. At least she was going to keep me warm.

'Morning, everyone,' Luke beamed, wrapping his scarf a little tighter around his neck. 'Thank you all for turning out so early on a Saturday morning, especially as it's so chilly.'

The sun was shining, but there was a sharp frost clinging to everything. I wrinkled my nose and rubbed my hands together, grateful for the chunky gloves Lizzie from the Cherry Tree back in Wynbridge, had knitted me for Christmas.

'Some of us didn't have any choice,' grumbled Tamsin from somewhere behind me.

Lisa had promised her that Rob's boys would be putting in an appearance so the fact that their father hadn't even attempted to prise them from their beds had not gone down well at all. I wouldn't have been surprised to see her stomping back to the Square sooner rather than later.

'Well, in that case,' said Luke, 'let's get on and we can talk about the details back in the house in front of the fire.'

'Sounds good to me,' said Lisa. 'What do you think, Kate?'

I ignored her and tried to blend into the group as Luke led us along a path to the right which ran between the house and what had probably once been another of the beautiful borders Harold had photographic evidence of.

'Oh, my goodness,' came Carole's voice from a few paces ahead. 'Would you look at that?'

We stood in awe and gazed at the beautiful sight. Almost as far as the eye could see the ground ahead was covered with a thick carpet of nodding snowdrops. They were growing unchecked across the paths, beneath the trees and through the lawns and even Tamsin stopped grumbling when she looked up from her phone screen and took in the view.

'They're quite something, aren't they?' smiled Luke, as we admired the fresh green stems and pristine flower-heads. 'But they're not what I've asked you all here to look at. Let's keep moving before our feet freeze completely.'

We sidled around the snowdrops, trying not to crush them underfoot and then followed Luke through a gate and into the large walled area Carole and I had briefly glimpsed before. There were no plants, beyond a few bedraggled weeds which had braved the winter, but I could see now that the space was divided up into a series of brick-edged beds and along the wall on the far side there was what appeared to be a large and elaborate glass-fronted bothy.

'This is it,' Luke beamed, spreading his arms wide. 'The

old kitchen garden. Now very much neglected of course, but poised for renovation.'

Ten blank faces stared back at him.

'I thought this place would be far better than the green,' he went on, 'you could each have your own area you see, or not if you want to grow together. You can divide it up however you see fit really.'

'What exactly are you suggesting, Luke?'

I didn't want to have to be the one to ask, but everyone else was standing about like one o'clock half-struck and getting colder by the second. I thought I knew what he was offering but I wanted to hear him spell it out before I got too carried away.

'That this could be the Nightingale Square growing space,' he said, as if it was obvious.

Everyone looked back at the garden and the lone scolding robin who had swooped down from the top of the gate and was watching our every move with its beady eyes and then they began to talk together and laugh and cheer. Luke's offer, apparently, was a good one, a very good one indeed.

'But won't you want to do something with it yourself?' asked Graham above the din.

The colour had flooded his face and I could tell he was itching to start measuring and digging, even if his tone was cautious.

to human contact. 'There's no way someone could have got in here. I daresay their mother is a stray. Was there no sign of her?'

'No,' Tamsin sniffed. 'Nothing but these little guys wobbling about.'

'You really shouldn't handle them,' Carole warned, taking a step back, 'they're probably infested.'

They didn't look infested, but she was right; they could have had every parasite going. Her warning didn't stop Graham from trying to cuddle the black and white one with the quietest meow imaginable though.

'Gosh, they're sweet,' said Heather, watching from afar.

'What are you going to do with them?' I asked Luke, before the gushing got out of hand.

'Keep them,' pleaded Tamsin as she watched her little sister carefully stroking the one she had first spotted. 'There's seven altogether. That's enough for one for each house in the Square.'

You couldn't fault the speed of her mental maths skills when she could use them to her advantage.

'We can't have one,' said Neil quickly, 'Mark's allergic.'

I'd wondered why he was keeping his distance.

'And besides, with seven new cats prowling about we'd have no bird life left,' said Harold sensibly.

He had a point, but that didn't stop Tamsin looking mortified.

'We could have one, couldn't we, Mum?'

'Absolutely not,' Lisa said straightaway. 'I've enough of a menagerie with you lot to look after and the guinea pigs. I don't need a cat as well.'

'What do you think, love?' Graham asked Carole.

Luke didn't give her time to answer.

'I suppose I could keep a couple,' he said. 'Not all seven of course, but I'll take two on and they can have the run of the place. That way,' he added, looking meaningfully at Tamsin and Molly, 'no one would miss out.'

It was the perfect compromise. Yet again Luke had donned his cape and saved the day.

'See,' said Lisa in an aside to me, as she prised the diminutive puss from her youngest daughter's hands, 'he could scale that tower of yours, no problem.'

Heather giggled and Luke looked over at us, but didn't ask what the tittering was about. Thank goodness.

'I'll ring the rescue centre I was telling you about, Kate,' he said instead. 'See what we need to do with them. They'll probably need to see a vet at least and the centre may want to put a trap out for their mum.'

'I'm sure Kate wouldn't mind giving you a hand,' said Heather.

Apparently, she was as keen to volunteer my time as Lisa was to unlock my heart.

'Great,' beamed Luke. 'Thanks, Kate.'

'No problem,' I said, biting my lip and ignoring the dynamic duo.

'And the rest of you can start planning what you want to do with this place. We shouldn't be too long, but if you want to head off before we get back, don't forget the scooter and just shut the back gate when you leave, could you?'

'Will do,' came a chorus of voices. 'Thank you, Luke.'

What an accommodating fellow he was turning out to be.

Chapter 19

With their mother rescued and the kittens weaned it had been tough, trying to pick out just two who were destined to become the Nightingale Square community garden mascots, but in the end the little grey fluff ball and one of the black ones were deemed the most suitable. The grey, named Violet, stood out simply because she was so sweet and adorable, and her brother, Dash, because he was a bit of a menace and as Graham was keen to point out, if he couldn't keep the mice away from the pea seedlings then nothing could.

The Disney names had been picked out by Lisa and John's brood and, thanks to the thriving rescue centre social media accounts, the other five in the litter had already found happy homes. Our two were currently confined to barracks with Luke inside Prosperous Place, but would be back out in the garden as soon as they were old enough.

I wouldn't have been at all surprised if they decided to take up residence in the refurbished bothy, for the warmer months of the year at least. The pair were now real people-pleasers and when Lisa's three got tired of helping out in the garden they headed back to the house to play with the kittens until it was time to go back to the Square.

'Tea!' bellowed Carole from her station in the transformed shed. 'Come and get it.'

The entire area had gone through quite a transformation in the month since Luke had said we could use it and everyone had enjoyed playing a part, even me. I still hadn't made a start on stripping wallpaper at home, but I had helped dig over the beds and add the trailer-loads of well-rotted muck that had been delivered from a nearby riding school.

Lisa had taken me firmly under her green wing and taught me how to sow a variety of vegetable seeds. Some had gone directly into the soil of the beds which had been deemed ready to plant in, but the rest, which were fast becoming strong seedlings, were growing in regimented seed trays and would be transplanted once all risk of frost had passed.

I was surprisingly proud to have played a part in turning a humble seed into a healthy, albeit tiny, plant and my involvement with the project had provided a welcome distraction from the brooding I was still prone to when shut inside for too long. Don't get me wrong, I loved my little house with a passion, but the fresh air was a real tonic and I wasn't the only resident who was benefiting from it.

In response to Carole's shouts about a brew we all downed tools and wandered over to the bothy which now had decent lighting, a kettle, fridge, microwave, washing-up area and a little stove. It hadn't been a cheap conversion but everyone had contributed, the idea being that later in the year, when the garden was yielding a decent crop, we would be able to cook on site and enjoy impromptu parties as the sun set. Luke had even suggested a barbecue and pizza oven and Lisa was kept busy in the evenings stitching reams of bunting for hanging from Easter onwards.

'How's it going?' I asked John who, with the help of Glen, was stringing up some lights along the front of the building to add to the party atmosphere.

'Almost done,' he said, taking a mug and stepping back to admire his handiwork. 'This place is going to be self-sufficiency central by high summer.'

'Excellent,' I smiled, looking about me at the faces of the enthusiastic party who had turned up most days and every weekend, come rain, snow or sunshine, to do something.

Even Tamsin was benefiting from spending time outside, when she wasn't in the house playing with her brother and sister and the kittens of course, and it had been her idea to suggest we could keep a few chickens, but I wasn't sure anything was going to come of that.

'How are the workers?' called Luke as he appeared through the gate, carrying a massive pile of post and grinning from ear to ear.

'I think we're nearly done for today,' said Graham, scraping his boots on the back of his spade. 'Practically all the beds are ready for planting in now and if the weather stays with us, we should be able to get some of the seedlings in the ground soon.'

Between us Nightingale Square residents and Luke, we had decided to run the garden communally, rather than each taking our own spot. We were planning to grow some fruit as well as lots of vegetables and herbs and Heather and Carole had been keen to establish a cut flower bed, along with a space among what would be the bean bed, for some wigwams of fragrant sweet peas.

'What have you got there?' Lisa asked Luke.

'I think it must be the catalogues you ordered,' Luke explained. 'They arrived this morning and I thought, if you aren't all in a rush to get off, we could have lunch back at the house so I can tell you about something else that's going to be delivered soon.'

'I wonder if it's the key to your heart, Kate,' murmured Lisa, but thankfully quiet enough that only I could hear.

'I doubt it,' I told her in an equally quiet voice. 'David tossed that on the wayside months ago.'

*

We all sat in the Prosperous Place kitchen around what Luke had been ecstatic to discover was the original Victorian table. It had been moved to one of the outbuildings for some reason and was in a right state when he found it. Graham and John had helped him carry it inside and some paperwork discovered in one of the end drawers, along with some crudely carved numbers underneath, confirmed its age and authenticity. Luke was over the moon and had set about restoring it with gusto.

Tracking down original pieces for the house was proving hard, so the discovery of any little gem, even if it was just a kitchen table, was treated with reverence and care. I was every bit as enthusiastic as Luke to see things returned, but I was careful not to let my excitement run away with me. Lisa and Heather's teasing about how Luke felt about me might not have been in any way true, but I didn't want to take the risk of inadvertently giving him the wrong idea and therefore had made a point of keeping my excitement to myself.

The pair of us did have one thing in common that I couldn't shy away from though: his efforts with the table aside, we had both been spending far more time setting up the garden than getting on with repairing and refurbishing our respective homes. But with the feel of spring in the warm breeze and the sunshine and increasing birdsong, it was impossible not to turn up.

'Have you told them?' asked Tamsin, as she scooped up

a protesting Dash and kissed him on the end of his little black nose.

'Not yet,' said Luke, handing out the post before stirring the large pan of soup which was warming on the stove.

Mark and Neil weren't with us as they had set off early for a weekend away, but Mark had dropped round a batch of crusty rolls, fresh from the bakery, before they left and I passed them around.

He had insisted they should get away as Neil was now chained to his job for even longer hours than before, courtesy of the guilt he felt for losing his company the Prosperous Place account. I could tell, by the expression on Luke's face that when he heard that, he felt every bit as responsible, but surely it was all for the best? Between them, they had saved Prosperous Place and I hoped that, in time, Neil would see he had done the right thing and perhaps even think about looking for a position with another, more sympathetic firm.

'Told us what?' asked Harold as he took a sneaky bite of his roll before Luke had ladled out the soup.

I looked at him and shook my head.

'What?' He shrugged. 'All this digging makes me hungry.'

I raised my eyebrows.

'All right,' he acquiesced, 'sitting in that deckchair telling you lot how to dig makes me hungry.'

We all laughed and I began distributing the bowls Luke was filling.

'So, you were saying?' Rob asked Luke.

'You mentioned a delivery,' Graham added importantly.

I was sure, even though we had agreed there was no hierarchy among the group, that Graham saw himself as the chief of our little tribe. I guessed that, whatever he had done for a living before he retired, a fair bit of responsibility had gone with it, and he had missed that, being stuck indoors with Carole all day.

'That's right,' said Luke, taking his seat at the table. 'Tamsin here,' he said, making her blush, 'as you all know, mentioned the possibility of keeping some chickens a couple of weeks ago.'

'She did,' said John, 'and she's not shut up about it at home ever since.'

'Well, that's just as well really,' beamed Luke, 'because we're taking on some rescue hens in a couple of weeks' time and I was hoping she would be in charge of looking after them.'

'Really?' Tamsin gasped, restoring Dash to his basket, which he promptly jumped out of.

'Really,' nodded Luke. 'I've found an old henhouse in the trees at the bottom of the fern garden. Goodness knows why it's there, but it just looks like it needs a good clean and a repair to the roof and it'll be good to go.'

'And we'll need some sort of enclosure,' Graham mused.

'Definitely,' agreed Heather. 'I was feeding Evie early

this morning and that fox was back, rootling around in our garden. We'll have to find a way to keep that out.'

'But you're all happy with the idea?' Luke checked. 'Fresh eggs every day is something you like the sound of. I've been warned the hens will take a little while to grow all their feathers and look the part, but I'm sure they'll be content enough to see out their time here.'

Everyone nodded and voiced their approval and Tamsin, her moody teenage persona forgotten, looked thrilled.

'And are you making progress in here?' I asked Luke, looking around. 'I know you've been with us in the garden a lot, but you haven't said much about the house recently. Any joy on the furniture hunt?'

'No,' he said, 'afraid not. I'm giving up on that for a bit now and turning my attention to more specific family pieces.'

'Such as?'

'Some jewellery, but paintings mostly,' he explained, 'and there's one portrait in particular I want, although of course if I can track down more things than that, it would be wonderful.'

I swallowed a mouthful of soup and tore at my roll, but said nothing. On more than one occasion during the last few weeks I had been going to offer to try and help him source some of the things that should never have left Prosperous Place, but I had always changed my mind at the last minute.

I had left that part of my life behind, but it didn't stop me feeling bad about not stepping in when I almost certainly could have helped.

'What's this?' Lisa asked.

'I'm trying to find some of the original things that Charles Wentworth and his wife would have had in the house,' he told her. 'Portraits and paintings, that sort of thing.'

'Well,' she said, looking pointedly at me as I felt my heart begin to race, 'you're talking to the right person then, aren't you?'

'Am I?' he frowned, looking back to me because I was the only person he had been talking to.

'Are you going to help him, Kate?'

I could have throttled her.

'How could Kate help?'

'That's what she used to do when she lived in London,' said Harold, unwittingly putting his foot in it even further than Lisa. 'When rich folk wanted something fancy for their homes, Kate here helped them track it down, didn't you love? I'm surprised you haven't told him that already.'

Lisa refused to meet my eye and became preoccupied with dipping her roll in her soup. She knew full well that I hadn't said anything, and why.

'I already knew you were a history buff,' Luke said quietly. 'But is that really what you used to do?'

'Yes,' I said. 'Sort of.'

'Then you must have loads of contacts in the trade,' he said.

I couldn't bring myself to look at him.

'Yes,' I said, trying not to think of David and our many friends. 'I suppose I must.'

Luke didn't say anything else and I knew he was hurt. Hurt that I had the knowledge and the wherewithal to help him in his quest and that, in spite of all the kindness that he had shown to me and my neighbours, I hadn't seen fit to return the favour. He had already mentioned, during his bouts of digging, what a struggle it was going to be to fill the house and not once had I offered to help or even suggested that I would know how to go about it.

I began to tear my bread into even tinier pieces, thinking that I was going to have to offer him an explanation now, whether I wanted to give one or not.

'If you pop round to mine later today, Kate,' Harold sealed my fate by saying, 'then I could give you the photos Luke hasn't seen yet. Between the pair of you I bet you can find some snaps of what Luke here is after. I think we both know which portrait he's talking about, don't we?' he added with a wink.

'No, it's fine,' said Luke, shaking his head. 'I can manage. I'm sure Kate has far better things to do with her time than help me.'

There was that hurt tone again.

'No, she hasn't,' interrupted Lisa. 'We were supposed to be

having a girls night in, but Heather has had to cancel and I really should make a dent in the ironing pile so she's on her lonesome tonight, aren't you, love?'

'Yes,' I said, through gritted teeth. 'Yes, I am.'

'Well, if you really do have the time,' said Luke. 'Any ideas about how to go about re-stocking and researching would be much appreciated. Shall we say here, at seven?'

He didn't sound keen for us to get together at all. He was obviously only going along with the suggestion because he knew Lisa wouldn't shut up until he caved.

'No,' I said, thinking I would be able to explain everything better on my own turf. 'Why don't you come to mine?'

'All right,' he shrugged. 'I'll come around seven and I'll bring a takeaway. What do you fancy?'

'You,' said Lisa under her breath while I glared at her and wondered why we were friends at all.

It was the first time I had felt really awkward in Luke's company and I knew he felt the same way.

'It's nice to be back,' he had said as he crossed the threshold and nodded at the fire burning merrily in the grate. 'Although I have to say, my first visit here feels like forever ago now.'

'I suppose it does,' I agreed. 'But then, an awful lot has happened since you caught Carole and me trespassing.'

'I thought you said you weren't trespassing.'

I didn't contradict him, but couldn't suppress the smile which was tugging at the corners of my mouth.

'Anyway,' he said, handing me a bag which was giving off yummy smells courtesy of the Chinese takeaway up the road. 'You're right. A lot has happened since then. I'm the cat person you said you couldn't see me as for a start.'

'So you are,' I agreed.

We ate the takeaway on trays on our laps and the silence became so stifling that I had to resort to flicking through the television channels until I found some brash reality show to drown it out. Once we had finished I turned it off again, cleared away the plates and lifted the box of photos from Harold's up on to the coffee table.

'You know, Kate,' said Luke as I carefully prised off the lid, 'I'm well aware that Lisa dropped you in it earlier and I'm sure you have a perfectly good reason for not telling me about your former job, so please don't think I've come here tonight expecting an explanation. You don't owe me anything, OK?'

'I know,' I said quietly.

'We all know what a nuisance Lisa can be,' he smiled, confirming that the only reason we were having this conversation at all was because of her, 'but she means well.'

It wasn't all that long ago that everyone was saying that about my mother and look what she had done. Our phone calls were still frosty and far between and I had already told her that I wouldn't be going back to Wynbridge for Easter. I had also reiterated that I didn't want her and Dad to see the house until it was refurbished.

'I mean,' Luke continued when I didn't say anything else, 'I knew you were passionate about the past because we talked about it before, but—'

'Look,' I said, cutting him off. 'I am going to tell you because, well, because it feels impossible not to now.'

'Not impossible—'

He might have been saying that, he might even have meant it, but I couldn't forget the earlier look of hurt on his face and I didn't want him to feel like that because of something I had or hadn't said. I wanted to clear the air between us and lay my cards on the table so he knew why I had kept schtum for all these weeks, even though he had gone out of his way to help me and everyone else in the Square.

'My work, as Harold suggested earlier, used to revolve around finding antiques and things for wealthy clients to fill their houses with,' I said quickly. 'I was good at it,' I told him. 'I had a knack for finding the right thing for the right person, and my husband and I built up a solid and successful business doing exactly that together.'

'I see.'

'But when our marriage broke down last year, I left him and the business behind and it's not what I do any more. In fact, I don't think I'll ever want to do it again.'

'And that's why you've never said anything,' Luke quickly cottoned on, 'because if you offered to help me it would potentially mean getting back in touch with people who knew you when you were married.'

'Exactly.'

'It might even put you back in touch with your husband.'

'Quite,' I swallowed. 'And I have no intention of ever getting back in touch with him, for any reason.'

'Of course not,' said Luke, coming to sit beside me and resting a hand on my shoulder. 'I'm so sorry you've felt obliged to tell me this, Kate. It was nobody else's business. Bloody Lisa,' he tutted.

'Oh, never mind her,' I said, quickly laying my hand over his and absorbing its warmth. 'She meant well.'

We both laughed and broke apart before the hand touching led to eye contact and then on to the possibility of goodness knows where. Not that I wanted to look into Luke's eyes again or even contemplate the destination of goodness knows where.

'So,' he said, 'let's forget all about it and have a look at what Harold has put in here instead.'

I was more than happy to do that and Luke was soon as mesmerised by the photographs as I had been.

'This is all amazing,' he said, as the time ticked by and the fire sank lower in the grate; it was now little more than glowing embers. 'These are going to help me no end.'

We had sorted the images into piles – one each for the different rooms in the house and another for the gardens.

'I know I'm not going to be able to make it look exactly the same, and I don't want to really, but at least having access to these will keep me on the right track.'

'And this,' I said, with a flourish, 'is the one that I think you'll be most pleased to see.'

It was the portrait of Edward. No one could deny Luke's connection to the Wentworth family when they looked at Edward's handsome face, dark curls and even darker eyes.

'It's as if someone dressed you in period costume and painted you,' I laughed, shaking my head.

'Do you really think so?' Luke smiled, staring intently at the photo. 'Do you really think I look like him?'

'You could be him,' I insisted. 'It's uncanny.'

'I can sort of see it,' he said, squinting and turning his head.

'Although it's a bit different to the kind of images of your-self you're no doubt used to looking at.'

'Yes,' he agreed. 'Just a bit.'

Was it my imagination or had he turned a little flushed at the mention of his modelling days?

'So,' I swallowed, 'how did a nice guy like you end up posing for a living?'

I'd wanted to ask him for weeks, almost ever since Lisa had revealed his supermodel status.

'I'd just been about to graduate from university,' he told

me, 'and was visiting a friend in Brighton to celebrate hand-ing in my thesis when I got "spotted".'

'Spotted?'

'Yeah,' he shrugged, 'you know, by an agency scout. He was there on a shoot with some other models. It was actually one of the girls who first noticed me, then the guy gave me his card and told me to give him a call if I fancied having some test shots taken.'

'And your ego got the better of you?'

'Hardly,' he laughed. 'It was my bank balance that got the better of me.'

'You were in it for the money?'

'Absolutely,' he unashamedly confessed. 'I had thousands of pounds worth of student loans to pay off and standing in front of a camera turned out to be a pretty simple way to clear them.'

'I see.'

'I settled my debts,' he went on, 'and then carried on. I got to travel the world, visit some spectacular places and then, before I started to get bored with it all, decided to call it a day. That was just before Dad died.'

'I'm sorry,' I said. I hadn't realised he'd had a parental bereavement to cope with.

'He'd been ill for a while,' he sighed, 'but was obsessed with tracing our family tree. There was only me and him so I promised that I'd carry on with it if . . .'

He stopped and took a breath.

'If he didn't get a chance to,' he finished quickly.

'And that's what led you to Prosperous Place?' I asked quietly, 'his quest for finding family?'

'Yes,' he nodded. 'Dad had almost got as far as the Wentworth connection, but not quite; I put the final pieces together,' he said, turning his attention back to the photograph of Edward's portrait and studying his ancestor's features intently. 'Dad would have been stoked about all this and I want to carry the legacy on, but I'm not quite sure how to. And how on earth am I going to find this blessed painting? I don't even know where to start.'

I knew exactly what he should do and where he should start, but didn't think I had it in me to tell him for fear that it would take me straight back to where I didn't want to go.

Chapter 20

It took me a few days of intense soul searching to make up my mind as to whether or not I was going to help Luke track down the portrait which he believed would be the crowning glory in the Prosperous Place collection.

Discovering that he had made copies of Harold's original photograph, and carried one around with him in his wallet like some sort of talisman, did nothing to strengthen my resolve not to get involved.

'This is the one thing,' he said when I found him sitting in a chair outside the bothy one sunny afternoon and staring at the picture: 'This is the pinnacle, Kate.'

'Is it?' I asked, as I busily filled the watering can, averting my gaze as he pulled off his jumper to soak up the early spring sunshine in a clingy and well-worn T-shirt.

The walled garden was now totally transformed and I was pleased that Rob (who still hadn't plucked up the courage to even introduce Sarah into a conversation, let alone invite her to the garden) had had the wherewithal to photograph every stage of our progress. Each of the beds now had green shoots peeking out in regimented rows, or an array of canes and markers, complete with handwritten labels, all offering a hint of the harvest to come. Mark and Rob had gone to great lengths restoring the henhouse and even Neil, who was the least keen to get his hands dirty, had lent a hand in making sure the run was as fox-proof as possible.

It was good to see him in the garden and I noticed he was popping back more and more often, especially at the weekends. It didn't take a genius to work out that our green gym was giving a mental boost to everyone, as well as becoming the ideal way to burn off the lingering winter pounds.

'If I don't manage to find another single thing,' Luke sighed wistfully as he tucked the paper carefully away again, 'I won't care.'

I was sure he would.

'As long as I have this,' he said, patting his wallet with its treasured piece of paper stowed back inside, 'I'll feel as though I've made amends to the generations of my side of the family who had no idea of their connection to this place.'

He stood up and stretched, his T-shirt parting company with the waistband of his jeans.

'What?' he said, when he caught me staring.

'Nothing,' I mumbled, feeling a sudden heat coursing through my veins which had nothing to do with the spring sunshine.

I was finding it increasingly difficult to tear my gaze away when he ran his fingers through his curls and licked his lips. I'd noticed recently that his hands often strayed to his hair when he was caught off guard, but he didn't appear to be aware of the habit at all. It was endearing.

'What?' he said again, pinning me with his most seductive stare.

'You really love it here, don't you?' I asked, holding back what I was thinking.

'I really do,' he sighed, staring back at the house. 'It's hard to explain, but living here feels so right and it's a comfort to know that I've finally managed to do something that would make Dad proud. I'd let him down in so many other ways.'

'How?'

He turned his attention from the house back to me again.

'Sorry,' I blurted out, 'it's none of my business.'

'No,' he said, 'it's OK, but I'm not going to shock you with the worst of the details. Let's just say that my father was a pretty cut and dried conventional kind of a guy. He and Mum had met early. They were almost childhood sweethearts. Theirs was the fairy-tale love story. The kind you usually find in the cinema or in a book.'

That kind of love story sounded fine to me. To be honest, it was a relief to know it existed beyond the big screen and a book.

'He never understood my serial dating days.'

'Oh,' I said lightly, 'I see.'

'Playing the field was frowned upon.' Luke laughed. 'He was forever lecturing me to stop messing around and wait for "the one".'

'But you enjoyed playing the field so much you thought all that could wait, yes?'

Having recently been a victim of the laissez-faire attitude towards relationships myself, I could understand how his father, the archetypal one-woman man, felt. But how Luke chose to conduct his sex life was nothing to do with me.

'Sort of,' he said, 'plus the fact I never believed in this whole fantasy about finding "the one". I didn't think it was possible that there was just one person in the world who could capture your heart so completely that you would never want to be with anyone else ever again.'

I dreaded to think how he would tease me if he ever learned of my take on one true love.

'You should talk to Lisa about that,' I told him, waving at her as she appeared through the gate with Archie in tow. 'She thinks it's all a load of rubbish as well.'

'But that's the thing,' said Luke, his dark eyes return-ing to rest on my face. 'I'm not sure that's what I do think now at all.'

'Hi, Charlie, it's Kate.'

'Kate! Oh my god! How are you? You're the last person I expected it to be.'

As I had reluctantly punched his number into my phone I'd had a feeling he was going to say something like that.

'But you don't mind that I've called?'

'Of course I don't mind that you've called,' he boomed. 'Hold on.'

I could hear a clicking sound in the background and knew he was lighting one of the fat, fragrant cigars everyone asso-ciated him with.

'So, how are you?' he asked after the first big puff.

I could almost smell the Cuban from my kitchen.

'And more importantly, where are you? Are you coming back? I miss you. Our dinner parties have been so dull since you left.'

I knew he was massaging my ego. I'd heard him do it to other people a thousand times before, but I didn't mind. It was nice to be on the receiving end of his New York drawl again. Charlie was one of the more flamboyant members of the group David and I had worked with. I was certain the pair would still be in touch, but as Charlie was also the go-to guy for paintings, pictures and portraits, I considered it worth the risk.

'No,' I said, ignoring that Charlie had asked *where* I was, 'of course I'm not coming back. I think I've provided enough after-dinner gossip for you guys, don't you? It's time you moved on to someone else.'

Charlie was quiet for a second.

'You know,' he said, 'it was never like that.'

'I know,' I sighed. 'I was only teasing.'

'We all told him he was a fool,' he said seriously. 'We all said he was an idiot. In fact, we're still telling him.'

'Well,' I said, swallowing away the lump in my throat.

This was not how I had planned the conversation would go. It was supposed to be all business. David, and what his friends did or didn't say to him, wasn't supposed to figure in any of it. I soon realised how naive I had been to believe that was going to happen.

'Well, it's all water under the bridge now, so—'

'But it isn't, is it?' Charlie interrupted. 'David's still as dull as dirty dishwater. He's no fun at all these days.'

'Isn't he?'

I had assumed that after I had spurned his advances at Christmas he would go off on his merry way, lick his wounds for a day or two and then set about finding someone else to make him feel better.

'No,' said Charlie. 'He's not. I have no idea what happened

at Christmas, Kate, beyond the fact that his attempt to woo you back didn't go according to plan, but he's practically been a recluse ever since. He doesn't come out, he works all hours and I know for a fact that he hasn't so much as looked at another woman.'

That didn't sound right at all. I thought he would have been stretching his wings and enjoying his freedom to return to the wandering ways I assumed he had missed during the years we were married.

'Are you sure we're talking about the same David?' I couldn't resist asking.

'I'm sorry to say we are.'

'Well, I'm sure he'll snap out of it soon,' I said stoically. 'He just needs a bit more time.'

'He says that if he can't have you, Kate, his one true love, then he doesn't want anyone.'

That was not what I wanted to hear. I couldn't believe he had said those actual words. Surely if I really was his 'one true love' he would have taken better care of me, wouldn't he? Was all this, I wondered uncharitably, what David had primed Charlie to say, should I happen to get in touch?

'Well, it's a shame he didn't realise that before he did what he did then, isn't it?' I retaliated.

These days I felt less inclined to listen to the voice in my head reminding me that I was the one who pushed him to do 'what he did'. As Lisa had pointed out on more than one occasion, David was a grown man, responsible for his own conscience and his own trouser zip. I had to stay strong. What he was, or wasn't, up to these days was of no interest to me. I was managing to move on, even if he wasn't.

'Of course it is,' Charlie agreed as he took another massive puff, 'but isn't everyone entitled to make one little mistake?'

Had the repercussions not been so dreadful, this could have been the point in the conversation when I broke down and agreed that yes, everyone was entitled to make one little mistake and that I would take David back and try to forgive him even if I couldn't forget. However, the repercussions *had* been dreadful and I was still feeling far from forgiving.

'Look,' I said, 'I haven't called to talk about David.'

'Sorry,' said Charlie. 'I know it's none of my business, but you can't blame a chap for trying. He'd never forgive me if he knew you'd called and I hadn't tried on his behalf.'

Was that a hint of what I already suspected?

'Charlie,' I said forcefully, bringing the call back to heel. 'I don't want you to breathe a word about this call to David.'

'All right, all right.'

'I have a job for you.'

'What kind of job?'

'I want you to track down a portrait for me.'

'Oh really?' he said, taking yet another long drag.

This was the line I should have started with. Getting Charlie to talk about work was as easy as distracting a cat with a cardboard box.

'Do tell.'

'I will tell,' I said sternly, 'but only if you absolutely promise that you will not mention either this phone call or the painting I'm looking for to David.'

'I promise,' he said hungrily. 'Scout's honour, whatever you say.'

'I mean it Charlie, if this gets back to David I'll know you've broken your promise and I think I've been let down enough recently, don't you?'

'Yes,' he said, sounding chastened. 'I think you have. I promise.'

'Good. I'm pleased we agree about that.'

'Now tell me,' he said, the old familiar excitement back in his tone. 'Tell me, what exactly is it that you want me to find?'

'Who's Charlie?'

I had no idea Lisa had slipped into the house and I dropped the phone in shock at the sound of her voice.

'Sorry,' she said. 'Did I make you jump? The door was open.'

'It's fine,' I said, retrieving the phone and returning it to its base. 'Are you ready to go now? I thought we said half past?'

'Change of plan. Heather's back already. Who did you say Charlie was?'

'I didn't,' I told her. 'And anyway, what's it got to do with you?'

I knew I sounded annoyed, but that was fine because I was. Lisa always liked to have her nose in everyone's business, but recently she'd been pushing things a bit too far.

'I'm sorry,' she said, for once sounding like she actually meant it. 'I know you think I'm a nosy old bag, but I'm only interested because I have no life.'

'What?' I frowned, grabbing my coat.

'It's true,' she sniffed. 'Beyond the confines of this square and the garden I have nothing.'

'Neither do I,' I reminded her, 'and neither does Heather at the moment.'

'But you both used to,' she said, her shoulders sagging, 'you both used to have jobs, and Heather's getting ready to go back to hers. All I've done is raise babies. Sorry,' she quickly added, knowing that was the one thing I had wanted, but hadn't been allowed to have.

'It's all right,' I told her, my annoyance evaporating. 'I'm finally beginning to accept that we don't all get what we want in life, irrespective of whether we sign up to the fairy-tale formula or not.'

'Do you really mean that?' She sounded aghast.

'Yeah,' I said, wrestling on my coat. 'I really do.'

For a second I thought she was going to cry but a knock on the door broke the spell and she blinked a few times before answering it. I dismissed her unusually emotional state, blaming it on her monthly hormone imbalance.

'We're coming,' she said when she found Heather on the doorstep, 'and I'm going to try and make it at least halfway round today. I promise.'

The whole get fit plan from the New Year hadn't been going all that well. When we should have been pounding the pavements, we'd been checking out the cafés and coffee houses in the city instead, but now the weather had improved we were starting over and even Lisa had vowed to take it more seriously.

'Why is Evie in her pushchair?' she asked Heather. 'I thought we were driving to the lake. You said as soon as you got back from your meeting with HR we'd be going.'

'Change of plan,' said Heather, biting her lip. 'Sorry girls, but I don't feel much like going for a run now.'

I grabbed my house keys and we walked over to sit on the bench on the green. Evie was content to watch the birds and shake her cloth book while we waited for her mum to tell us what had happened, because something clearly had.

'Has something happened at work?' Lisa asked when she couldn't bear the suspense a second longer. 'Was there a problem about your return date?'

Heather had been telling us how she was planning to go

back to work part-time. She didn't particularly want to, but knew that if she didn't do it soon she never would. I got the feeling that her desire to be a stay-at-home mum after the pressure and intensity of her career, which had been her sole focus for so long, had come as something of a shock. It hadn't been until Lisa had offered to look after Evie, so she wouldn't have to send her to a nursery further afield, that she began to come around to the idea of going back at all.

'I don't have a return date now,' she said eventually. 'I've decided I'm not going back.'

Lisa and I exchanged glances.

'Well, that's good isn't it?' I said cheerfully, trying to rally her. 'That's kind of what you wanted, isn't it?'

'I guess,' she shrugged. 'But I'm sorry I won't be able to offer you the work now, Lisa. I know you were looking forward to taking care of Evie.'

'It's fine,' said Lisa. 'I can still see old gorgeous whenever I want and perhaps this is just the push I need.'

'What do you mean?' Heather asked.

'Oh, I don't know,' Lisa shrugged. 'I was just saying to Kate that I have no life beyond this place. Perhaps now's the time to get my act together and find a job of my own.'

'But what about Archie?' Heather asked. 'You wouldn't want to send him to day care, would you?'

'No,' said Lisa, chewing her lip. 'I suppose not. I probably wouldn't even earn enough to cover the cost.'

'Perhaps you could look after him, Heather?' I suggested. 'He could be a playmate for Evie.'

Heather shook her head and slowly breathed out.

'She'll have one of her own soon enough.'

I shared another look with Lisa.

'What are you talking about?'

'That's why I'm not going back to work,' she said in a rush. 'I'm pregnant again.'

'Oh my god,' gasped Lisa.

'I know!'

'Did you plan to be?' I asked.

'No.'

'Do you want to be?' Lisa said next.

'Yes . . . no . . . maybe.' Heather laughed. 'I don't know. It hasn't really sunk in yet. It wasn't meant to happen like this.'

'Crikey, Heather,' I said. 'You're really going to have your hands full.'

'I know,' she said, 'but at least I have friends nearby to help out.'

'That's true,' I smiled.

'You don't mind, do you?' she said, reaching for my hand. 'About the baby, I mean.'

'No, of course not,' I told her. 'I'm thrilled for you. Please don't think that I'm not happy for you, my darling, because I am. I really am.'

'Thanks,' she said shyly. 'That means a lot.'

271

'How's Glen taken the news?' Lisa asked.

'I don't know,' Heather giggled. 'He's like me, still in shock. It's very early days so we're not telling anyone yet.'

'Apart from us two,' I laughed. 'And possibly Carole.'

We all waved over to where we could see our nosiest neighbour loitering behind her curtain pole and I stole a glance back at my pregnant friend. Like me, her life plan had been scattered to the four winds, in fact it was all a right old muddle and yet here she was, still smiling brightly and embracing the changes. I admired her adaptability.

'I guess this is yet another scenario which disproves the fairy-tale theory, isn't it?' Heather smiled at Lisa.

It was as if she could read my thoughts.

'No, it doesn't,' I was quick to respond as I rejigged the new twist in her story to make it fit what I had hoped would have been my own. 'Fall in love, get married, have baby, then second baby, happy family, happy ever after. It's textbook. If anything, it goes to prove that happy endings do exist.'

'That's not what you said back at the house,' Lisa pounced.

'Back at the house,' I corrected her, 'I said that we don't *all* get the fairy tale, I never said that no one does.' My mind tracked back to what Luke had said about his parents.

'So, you think that my life conforms to the fairy tale, do you?' Heather frowned. 'Even now?'

'Pretty much,' I shrugged. 'I mean, your life fits the mould a darn sight more tidily than mine. I've completely given up trying to squeeze mine into shape, you know that.'

'I'll remind you of that in a few months,' she said with a smile on her lips, 'when I'm sleep deprived and up to my armpits in even more nappies; then we'll decide who's living the charmed life.'

'I'll hold you to that,' I said, leaning across to shake her hand.

Chapter 21

I hadn't grasped just how early in the year Easter was going to fall until I turned the month over on my kitchen calendar. Spring had very definitely sprung and I still hadn't put into practice any of the home improvements I had been planning when I first moved to Nightingale Square.

I could of course squarely and conveniently lay the blame at Luke's door for that because had he not seduced me, and everyone else, with our perfect community garden, and the brace of fluffy kittens, then I felt certain that my little home would have been totally transformed long before the supermarkets were filled with chocolate eggs.

As wonderful as it was to spend so much time outside watching green things growing and the rescue hens sprouting feathers in places they had never before realised were supposed to be covered, I knew I needed to make a start;

otherwise the year would be over and I wouldn't have achieved anything I had set out to do.

With my mind half on the impending Easter egg hunt and subsequent party I had been roped into helping with, and knowing that my friends were going to be otherwise occupied for the next few days, I decided that right then was as good a time as any to get going on my own plans.

Lisa had thrown herself with gusto into finding a new job, Heather was suffering what she described as 'morning nausea' rather than actual sickness, Luke had taken himself off on an impromptu holiday 'to think some stuff through', or so he had told John and Glen, and Charlie, despite exhaustive efforts, had so far drawn a blank in his search for the lost portrait.

'Are you absolutely sure that it's been sold?' he had asked for what must have been the hundredth time. 'It isn't tucked away in the house somewhere, under a dustsheet or something?'

I had even resorted to helping Luke look for it myself, getting into all sorts of uncomfortably tight spots and dusty cupboards with my newest neighbour, but the only things we had found were gargantuan spiders. At the end of the search we were both adamant the portrait wasn't at the property, but Luke couldn't lay his hands on a bill of sale or trace any paperwork suggesting where it might have disappeared to either.

Luke was finding it all very frustrating, but I still hadn't told him I was on the case. Beyond a couple of dates and the artist's name we had very little to go on, so what would have been the point? In fact, we had so little to work with that even Charlie, who could find the tiniest gem in a dragon haul, was poised to admit defeat, so it would have been heartless to get Luke's hopes up only to disappoint him.

'It's definitely not there, Charlie,' I confirmed yet again.

'Then I think you need to tell this chap I'm helping out and ask if he'll let you have a proper sort through the property paperwork,' he wisely suggested. 'I daresay he must have missed something. Penny to a pound if you have a look the mystery will be solved in a heartbeat. You have a nose for these things, Kate, you know you do.'

I had been thinking along the same lines myself, but my reluctance to get involved wasn't only due to my concerns about getting Luke's hopes up. The crux of it was that I didn't want him to know that I had asked Charlie to get involved in case he got the wrong idea about my intentions.

Luke had said himself that he could appreciate how difficult it would be for me to get back in touch with any of David's and my former friends and I didn't want him thinking that I had gone and done it anyway because I had feelings for him. Romantic or otherwise. Because I didn't.

Yes, he was one of the kindest and most generous men I

had ever met and yes, my stomach did flip when he brushed the cobwebs out of my hair, and yes, my heart did pound when he turned up day in, day out to help in the garden, but it didn't mean anything. My desire to track down the portrait and see it returned to its rightful place was purely professional. End of.

'Let's just give it a few more days, Charlie,' I said determinedly, 'and if there's still no joy, I'll tell him then.'

'All right, dear girl,' he said resignedly. 'I'll keep trying.'

I finally settled on redecorating my bedroom, which was at the front of the house, first. I knew that ideally the really laborious jobs which were going to involve the most dust and upheaval should have taken priority, and they were at the very top of my lengthy to-do list. However, I had failed to take into consideration how long I would have to wait for tradesmen, not to mention the fact that I still hadn't settled on a kitchen design because my head was filled with the blasted glass wall that Luke had suggested.

'Right,' I said to myself, rolling up my sleeves as I began to re-pack boxes and move the furniture so I could rip up the carpet. 'Let's get this show on the road.'

I hadn't been at it long when I heard someone let themselves in through the front door.

'Need a hand?' called a voice up the stairs. 'Lisa sent me over.'

'Come on up, John,' I called back. I had already worked up

quite a sweat and the added manpower was most welcome. 'I could do with a bit of extra muscle.'

I knew I would have to empty the room completely when I had the new carpet laid, but for now we were able to man-handle the bed and the wardrobe between us, pushing them from pillar to post as necessary. The old carpet came up with good grace and we shared a pot of tea and a teacake apiece while sitting on the bedroom floor poring over the yellowed newspapers that we had discovered covering the floorboards.

'How's Lisa's job hunting going?' I asked as we recovered our strength. 'Any joy yet?'

'That's actually why I'm here,' he explained. 'She wanted me out from under her feet.'

'Form filling and CV writing can be a tricky business,' I agreed. 'No doubt she wants the peace and quiet.'

'She's not form filling,' John explained as he handed over his empty mug and crumb-covered plate. 'And I don't think she's ever had a CV.'

'What is she doing then?'

'Following her heart,' he said mysteriously, 'like she should have done years ago. Like I've been telling her since goodness knows when.'

'What's that supposed to mean?' I frowned. 'What's her heart been telling her she should be doing?'

He looked at me and chewed his lip for a second.

'You'll need to hammer down those few nails,' he said,

pointing to the edges of the floor where we'd caught our hands on the sharp heads which stood proud. 'It'll be quicker and easier than trying to pull them out.'

Once he had shown me how to set up the wallpaper stripper he had lent me he then went home to collect the children and take them to the community garden.

'We're on egg duty today,' he said, 'and I'm going to have a measure up for this pizza oven Luke keeps on about. It'll give my good lady a few extra minutes' peace.'

He still refused to elaborate as to what it was she was doing and why she needed peace in which to do whatever it was.

'I don't suppose Luke told you what he had gone on holiday to think about, did he?' I asked, hoping he might feel some way inclined to enlighten me about something.

My curiosity was piqued, and I didn't like looking across the Square to the empty house. I hadn't expected to miss its new owner, but I did. Not that I would have told John that.

'Well, if you can't work that out for yourself,' he said with disdain, 'then you haven't the brains I'd credited you with.'

He'd disappeared downstairs before I had the opportunity to think of a response.

The wallpaper stripper made light work of the multiple layers, but I made a point of keeping a few of the patterned pieces which were salvageable. They were a part of the house's history after all and an interesting reminder of how tastes had changed since the last time anyone had stripped the walls back to bare plaster.

By late afternoon there was just the one wall left. My arms were aching and the steamy air had turned my hair from smooth and tidy into a mass of kinks and curls. I pinned it up into a messy bun, made myself the biggest mug of coffee I could find and traipsed back up the stairs for one last push. All I really wanted to do was sink into a lavender- or rose-scented bubble-filled bath, but I was too close to the finishing line to put off crossing it now.

Thankfully the last wall had the least paper to strip. It was the wall furthest from the door and the addition of the original little ornate cast-iron fireplace meant it wasn't too big, which was why I had left working on it until last. I knew when I started that I was going to need something simple to finish on at the end of the day when my impetus was flagging. But as it turned out, the wall wasn't simple to deal with at all.

The recess to the left of the chimney breast, the bottom half of it at least, seemed to have far more layers than the rest of the room put together and I wondered how I hadn't noticed the bulge at the bottom of the wall before. However, the mahogany chest of drawers which had been left behind by Doris had been positioned there until this morning and I knew that the sprigged floral wallpaper was capable of playing tricks on the eyes if you stared at it for too long.

'Migraine inducing', my mother would have called it, just like the swirly carpet in the dining room, but I thought it had a certain old-world charm. The paper, not the carpet.

I was pulled up short as I realised the wallpaper stripper in my hand was hitting something hard, certainly not wallpaper, and I turned off the steamer and ran my hands over the area which was now damp. I could definitely feel the solid outline of something.

'Have you still got my husband up there?'

I almost jumped out of my skin as Lisa's head appeared around the door.

'No,' I told her, all plans to winkle out of her what she had been up to quickly forgotten, 'and I haven't got your kids either. They're all over at Prosperous Place.'

'What on earth are you doing?' she asked when she spotted me tapping away with my ear pressed to the wall.

'There's something under this paper,' I told her. 'Listen, it's hollow.'

Carefully we scraped around the edges and I noticed that the skirting board had been cut in line to match the shape on the wall above.

'I bet it's a cupboard,' said Lisa, her eyes wide. 'A cupboard full of forgotten treasure, that's been papered over.'

I rolled my eyes and shook my head, but she was probably right, about the cupboard part anyway.

'Told you,' she said smugly a few minutes later as we sat

back on our haunches and stared at the edges of what definitely looked like a door.

'I wonder what's really behind it.' I swallowed.

I wasn't sure I liked the idea of having a secret cupboard in the room where I slept. I still hadn't mustered the courage to brave venturing far into the dark cupboard under the stairs yet. There looked to be far too many cobwebs for my liking and I could all too easily imagine this recess would be similarly adorned.

'Only one way to find out,' said Lisa, reaching for the metal scraper. 'Use this to work around the sides,' she ordered, while reaching across to grab a screwdriver. 'We need to chip off the paint to free the edges so we can lever it open.'

'I think I'll leave it for today,' I said, jumping up and brushing down my jeans. 'I've been at it for hours and shouldn't you be home cooking dinner, or ironing, or something?'

'No,' she said, sounding disappointed. 'All that can wait. Come on,' she encouraged. 'I want to see. You aren't scared, are you?'

'Of course not,' I said, shaking my head. 'Just knackered and anyway,' I added artfully, 'I'm more interested in hearing about what you've been up to today. John mentioned something about following your heart.'

'Did he now?' she said, holding out her hand so I could pull her to her feet.

'He did,' I nodded, 'and I'm more interested in the

workings of your heart than what's inside some spider-infested cupboard.'

'Well, you'll just have to stay interested, won't you?' she said, swaggering across the room. 'Because it's supposed to be a secret.'

Oops, it sounded like I'd really dropped John in it, but at least she was almost out of the room and away from the cupboard.

'And you know you'll never get a wink of sleep in here tonight, don't you?' she added with a smile and a look back towards the little cupboard door.

I didn't want her to be right, but she was of course. I had my dinner, my longed-for bubble bath and my evening watching rubbish on the TV and by the end of it I was still dead on my feet, but no sooner had my head hit the pillow than my eyes, which had been so determined to close when I was curled up in my armchair, sprang open and I began imagining all manner of things that could be hidden in the cupboard next to me.

It had to be something pretty important, didn't it? Something someone had decided they didn't want anyone knowing about because why else would they go to all the trouble of making it look like the cupboard didn't exist? Or was I making too much of it? Was it just the lateness of the hour and Lisa's taunting making my mind play tricks?

As the lady herself said, there was only one way to find out.

It seemed to take forever to chip away enough paint to get the leverage I needed to force the door open. I did it as carefully as I could, taking every precaution not to damage the door. I might have been wary about what may have been stashed behind it, but extra storage was always a bonus and some simple furniture rejigging could mean this space became a shoe cupboard, or somewhere to stow the Christmas decorations, assuming of course there wasn't a body bundled in there and the whole house was going to end up being ripped apart by the police.

I shuddered, as with an ear-splitting creak the door finally began to move and I wondered which planet I had been on when I had decided that tackling this on my own in the dead of night had been a good idea. Before I pulled any harder I checked the torch on my phone was fully functioning.

'Shit,' I swore as it sprang into life, the annoying jingle alerting me that there was unusually both a text message and a voicemail awaiting my attention.

Both would have to wait because I currently had far more pressing matters to attend to. I took a deep breath, and with the phone in one hand, I used the other to open the cupboard door wide enough to see inside. I snatched up the screwdriver to defend myself from whatever beastie lurked within and braced myself to explore.

*

'Nothing?' said John. 'Not a thing?'

It was early the next morning, after what had eventually turned into a reasonable night's sleep, and John had popped over to see how I was faring with the wallpaper stripper. Lisa hadn't taken much notice of the walls apparently, but was all agog as far as the cupboard was concerned.

'No,' I shrugged, looking over at the space which I had spent a good long while de-cobwebbing.

It wasn't as if I had wanted to find anything sinister of course, but the fact that it was completely and utterly empty was a bit of a let-down. I had, in one mad moment, just before I pulled it open, imagined that I was going to find Luke's elusive portrait inside. I had imagined myself presenting it to him at the Easter party and him being so grateful that he ...

'Kate?'

'Sorry,' I faltered. 'What?'

'I said,' John repeated, 'do you mind if I take a quick look?'

'No,' I said, 'not at all. Do you want to borrow my phone? The torch is pretty decent.'

He whipped a torch from his back pocket and proceeded to dazzle me with it.

'Lisa's always telling me that you're prepared for every eventuality,' I smiled.

'Is she now?' he laughed.

'I'll go and put the kettle on,' I told him. 'Have you got time for tea?'

I was barely halfway down the stairs before he started hollering. I shot back up to the bedroom.

'I haven't got public liability insurance you know,' I warned him. 'You'd better not have done yourself a mischief.'

I was pulled up short by the fact that rather than crawl into the cupboard – not that he could have got all that far because he was a big bloke – he had gone in on his back and was reaching up in the direction of the chimney breast.

'How did you miss this little lot?' he choked, as his fiddling dislodged as much dust and as many spiders as I had already hoovered up. 'How did you not see all this?'

Two minutes later and I found myself gazing in shock at the astonishing loot with Lisa's words about 'forgotten treasure' ringing in my ears. It wasn't the lost portrait from Prosperous Place, but it might well offer up some clue as to where it had disappeared to.

I made John promise that he wouldn't mention what he had discovered to anyone, not even his good lady wife. The most I could get out of him was that he would do his best, but if she used her feminine wiles then he couldn't guarantee his discretion. It was about as good a commitment to keeping the secret as I could have hoped for and in turn I promised him that when I had had a chance to show everything to Luke, then I would free him of his obligation and tell Lisa all about it myself.

Chapter 22

'We were beginning to think you weren't going to come back,' Carole scolded Luke the day before Easter Sunday as we all gathered together in the bothy to finish the preparations for the party. 'We were beginning to think you'd gone for good!'

Lisa rolled her eyes at Heather who returned the gesture. Our friend was looking a little peaky, but had rallied enough to help with the arrangements and stop everyone trying to second-guess why she hadn't been putting in an appearance in the garden recently.

I looked at Luke and his topped-up tan and shook my head. No one had *really* thought that at all.

'Oh, Carole,' said Lisa, determined not to let her get away with her over-the-top comment. 'You do love a drama, don't you? Even if it is of your own making. I hardly think Luke would have gone to all the trouble of buying Prosperous Place just to abandon it again, do you?'

Carole didn't say anything, but her lips became a very thin line and she went back to ticking things off on her clipboard when the man himself refused to elaborate.

'So, how's everything going then?' Luke asked.

He rubbed his hands together as he cast an appreciative eye over the garden and the area John had measured up and cordoned off for the pizza oven and potential fire pit which had also been added to the list now. Clearly, he didn't want to become embroiled in the women's spat any more than he wanted to enlighten us as to where he had been.

'It all looks good to me,' he smiled, 'but then I'm no expert.'

'It's doing wonderfully well,' said Graham proudly. 'It's all thriving.'

'And there's even enough of the cut-and-come-again salad to feed us all tomorrow,' joined in Glen. His increase in hours recently, working with Evie looking on in her buggy, had more than made up for his wife's absence from the garden. 'It will be our first little harvest. These cloches have been a godsend. Thanks for putting them together, John.'

Lisa reached up and kissed her husband's cheek.

'He can turn his hand to anything,' she sighed. 'What would we do without him?'

'Oh, for god's sake, get a room,' Tamsin muttered, disgusted. 'I'm going to take Archie and Molly to check on Violet and Dash.'

'And I'll go and collect the meat from the butchers,' said Rob.

I had suggested to Rob that he might bring Sarah along to the party tomorrow, but he declined. He was as keen as I was to stop Carole dropping hints and pushing the pair of us together, but not willing to subject the woman in his life to our neighbour's scrutiny and interrogation.

'I'll give you a hand,' said Neil, 'and we can pick up the rolls that Mark has set aside from the bakery on the way back. Are you still happy to keep all the food and drink at yours tonight, Carole?'

'Yes,' she said, double-checking her list again, just to make sure everything was in order, even though she knew it was. 'There's plenty of room in our fridge in the garage.'

The two men went off and after Carole had coerced Heather and Lisa into helping her, Luke and I were left alone.

'I think I'll go and see if there are any eggs,' I said, turning back to the bothy for the basket.

I wasn't sure why I felt so awkward alone in his presence but the sudden thundering in my chest left me in no doubt that I had missed him rather more than I considered appropriate.

'I'll give you a hand if you like,' he said, fumbling a little as he took the basket and our fingers touched. 'I haven't had a chance to see how the girls are getting on since I've been back.'

'Did you enjoy your holiday?' I asked.

I didn't feel it was right to ignore that he'd been away but didn't want to end up sounding like Carole either.

'You look like you've been somewhere hotter than Norfolk.'

'It was more of a retreat than a holiday,' he cut in the second I had finished. 'I had stuff to think about.'

That was what the guys had said he had told them before he left, but clearly what that 'stuff' was wasn't up for discussion.

'Here they are then,' I said when we reached the run. 'What do you think?'

Luke couldn't believe his eyes and refused to accept they were the same scrawny-necked pitiful little specimens that we had taken delivery of just a few weeks before. I couldn't help but laugh at his reaction and felt myself beginning to relax again.

'You've swapped them,' he said forthrightly. 'You must have done. They can't possibly be the same birds.'

'They are,' I told him, laughing at the sight of his stunned expression. 'Of course they are. This just shows what a few weeks of clean living can achieve, doesn't it?'

'I suppose it does,' he laughed back. 'Although I never would have believed it if I hadn't seen it with my own eyes.'

'And actually, it's not just the hens,' I said, as I added the perfectly smooth eggs to the basket. 'Everyone who comes here is looking and feeling better, thanks to you.'

'Except for Heather,' he frowned.

How frighteningly observant he was. I hoped he hadn't spotted the silly happy dance I had indulged in when I had discovered his car back on the drive.

'She's looking a little off colour to me. Is she all right?'

'Blooming,' I said, then quickly rushed on in case he put two and two together and came up with quads. 'I was wondering if you might have time for a chat tomorrow,' I asked before I was quite ready to. 'After the party perhaps?'

'I can talk now if you like,' he said, looking down at me with his beautiful brown eyes. 'Or perhaps tonight? We could have another takeaway. I haven't tried the pizza place yet.'

'It would be better tomorrow.' I swallowed.

I flushed at the thought of us spending another evening together, but I wanted a bit more time to think carefully about how it would go. I needed to talk to Charlie, then decide whether I was going to tell Luke what I had been up to before revealing what John had pulled out of my clandestine cupboard.

'All right,' he nodded. 'But I'm going to apologise in advance if I'm not the best company.'

I was about to ask why he thought he wouldn't be, when Tamsin bellowed from the garden gate that he had a phone call at the house.

Easter Sunday was sunny and warm, almost unseasonably warm for the end of March, not that any of us were complaining. The party would have been a total flop if the weather was a washout but, as it was, the early spring sunshine ensured the bunting could be hung in perfect safety and cotton frocks were favoured over sweatshirts and jeans, for the girls among us anyway.

Lisa, Heather and I were the earliest to arrive at the garden and set about hiding eggs of all shapes, colours and sizes for the children to find. My initial concerns that Tamsin and Rob's twin boys were too old to enjoy that sort of thing were soon forgotten as Carole handed out the lamb-patterned buckets Lisa had stocked up on from the pound store and the competition to find the most eggs began.

'Well, now,' boomed a large and jolly lady who arrived late in the morning weighed down with bags bursting with yet more chocolate treats and an equally jolly gent following on behind. 'How lovely is all this?'

'Grandma!' squealed Lisa and John's eldest two as they rushed over, Archie being carried by Tamsin, to greet John's parents.

They weren't the only guests to pay the party a visit that day. Both Glen's and Heather's parents put in an appearance as did Poppy and some friends of Mark and Neil along with a pal of Harold's from his luncheon club. The elderly pair commandeered a table and enjoyed a lively game of cards, gambling away their fortunes of pennies which they had stored in old coffee jars.

I had more than enough on my mind, as I played out my evening with Luke in my head, and felt relieved rather than guilt-ridden that I had asked my Wynbridge family not to descend on me. Easter was always a busy time for Jemma and Tom and, according to phone calls with Dad, letting Mum stew on her actions at Christmas for such a long time was doing her no harm at all.

'Having fun?' Luke asked, when he finally put in an appearance just before we were getting ready to set the tables for lunch.

'I'd almost given up on you,' I smiled. 'We were going to send the kids to come and drag you out.'

'I've been watching you all from the house,' he explained. 'I didn't realise the morning had almost gone until I looked at the clock.'

'Why were you watching from inside?' I quizzed. 'The party can't properly start until it's been officially opened by our host.'

'Oh, I don't know about that,' he said, looking wary, 'and besides I might not be the bubbliest company today.'

'Is everything OK?' I asked, remembering that he had suggested as much the day before.

He didn't have a chance to answer before Lisa was dragging him off to meet her mother-in-law, Beryl, who came over all peculiar when he gave her one of his stunning smiles and thanked her for coming. It took a glass and a half of

John's spring cocktail and a sit down to settle her complexion back to something less alarming.

'I'm going to fire up the barbecue in a minute,' John's voice boomed above everyone else's, 'but before we all get stuck into this fabulous feast, I think it's only fitting that Luke says a few words and we all raise a glass to thank him for giving us residents of Nightingale Square a part of this fabulous garden to grow in.'

'Hear, hear!' everyone agreed amid a flurry of cheers and whistles.

'This time last year,' John continued, eloquently expressing how everyone felt, 'our ambitions were limited to what we could achieve if we ever got permission to dig up the patch of grass outside our own front doors, but thanks to the generosity of this man here, we have a real community garden to be proud of now and I hope the next six months prove to be as successful and bountiful as the first couple. To Luke,' he finished, raising a glass and smiling broadly.

'To Luke,' everyone else chorused, joining in the toast.

Luke shook his head and looked disarmingly embarrassed. He shuffled from one foot to the other and cleared his throat before looking at the group of neighbours he was for the most part responsible for turning into a group of firm friends.

'I don't really know what to say,' he began, then stopped and took a deep breath.

I still struggled to believe that the bloke who smouldered

from the pages of the multiple magazine adverts Lisa had since thrust under my nose could be so reserved and unassuming. His current stance and stammering was a far cry from the passionate poses he assumed when selling aftershave and designer labels. I felt my heart go out to him as he struggled to find the words to fit the occasion.

'When I lost my dad . . .'

The unexpected beginning pulled me out of my trance.

'Two years ago today as it happens . . .'

Everyone gasped and listened even more intently. That was no doubt why he said he might not be good company and had lingered in the house this morning. I wish he'd have said something sooner. We could have arranged to have the party another day. Sitting out in the sunshine with us lot was probably the last thing he felt like doing.

'When I lost Dad,' he continued, 'and decided that I would take up his obsession to retrace our family tree, I had no idea that it would lead me here or give me the opportunity to transform anyone else's lives. I selfishly assumed that the exercise would be about me finally managing to do something that would make him proud.'

'And he would be proud of you, lad,' Harold interrupted. 'And don't forget, we're your family now, and we couldn't be more honoured to have you in the fold.'

'Thank you, Harold,' Luke nodded.

I wondered if he was alluding to how he felt about the life

he had once led and that his dad disapproved of. Was that perhaps what he had been thinking about on his 'retreat'?

'But what I'm trying to say,' he continued, 'incoherently I know, is that I never for one second imagined all of this.' He looked around him at the beautiful space we had managed to create in practically no time at all. 'It just goes to prove that what Charles Wentworth had in mind for this area of the city is still as relevant today as it was when he was building his philanthropic empire. Things really are better when they're done together,' he smiled, 'and I hope that we will continue to work together for as long as we're all destined to be here.'

'I'll drink a toast to that,' responded Glen, quickly handing Luke a glass when he realised he was the only person present without one.

'Thank you all so much,' Luke nodded, holding his glass aloft, 'for welcoming me home and helping me fall in love.'

'Cheers,' we chorused again.

I felt my heart drum in my chest as Luke's eyes met mine and I allowed myself to briefly wonder whether he was talking about more than the bricks and mortar.

'Now please,' he summed up, 'enjoy the rest of this very special day, and if anyone who hasn't seen it yet would like to join me for a tour of the house after we've devoured this delicious meal, I would be more than happy to show you around.'

'Thank you for helping me fall in love,' Lisa hissed in my ear as we smoothed out the polka-dot patterned paper cloths and laid out the mismatched crockery and cutlery, along with the Easter-themed crackers and glasses. 'What do you think he meant by that?'

'Look around you, Lisa,' I said firmly, refusing to show any sign of weakness under her scrutiny. 'You can't look at this and tell me you haven't fallen at least a little bit in love with it yourself.'

The scene was idyllic. Carole was dotting the pots of bright spring bulbs she had prepared along the length of the table and the heady sweet scent of the hyacinths combined with the herbs from the barbecue rubber-stamped the day as one of halcyon proportions. If this was a taste of the summer to come, then we were all in for a treat.

'Who would fail to be seduced by a setting, right in the heart of the city, like this?'

'You know full well that's not what he was getting at, Kate.'

This was from Heather, and I could hardly believe my ears. Ordinarily when Lisa was off on one of her 'dog with a bone' rants she and I would stick together. Say whatever the other needed us to say when faced with such a barrage, but on this occasion, I was out of luck. I looked at her and frowned.

'Well, I'm sorry,' she said, 'but it's obvious, isn't it? Luke's falling for you, Kate.'

I opened my mouth to contradict her, but she didn't give me a chance.

'He might not have told you as much yet,' she said resolutely, 'he might not even know it yet, but he is. That's why he took himself off "to think things through"!'

She sounded as smug as if she'd worked out the final clue in a murder mystery.

'And you can forget all about that bloody one true love crap,' cut in Lisa, adding her own subtle and unique layer to the conversation. 'Life is messy and muddled and sometimes what might have looked like the perfect relationship at first can turn out to be nothing more than an elaborate dress rehearsal.'

'She's right, you know,' said Heather. 'Gobby, but right.'

'Hey,' pouted Lisa. 'I know what I mean.'

'I know what you mean,' I told her, 'I just don't believe it.'

By the time we had eaten our fill and the tables had been cleared, the sun was setting and the warmth afforded by the mellow old walls was beginning to wane. Harold and his card-shark companion had already headed back to the Square, as had Heather and Glen with Evie and their parents.

'I think we're going to head home,' said Rob, pulling on his jumper. 'The boys are going to stay with their mum for a few days next week and I don't want them too tired out when she comes to pick them up in the morning. I don't see why I should be the only parent subjected to their endless energy and Tiggerish behaviour.'

He had told me earlier, out of earshot of Carole of course, that he was planning to spend some quality time with Sarah and had finishing touches to plan.

'And we're going to make a move too,' said John. His parents had gone and he had Molly in his arms, her thumb was plugged in and her eyelids were heavy.

'You're all welcome to come back to ours, folks,' Lisa yawned as she scooped Archie up. 'That is if you fancy joining us for a non-competitive family game of Monopoly.'

'Hey,' said John, 'no one said anything to me about it being non-competitive.'

'We'd be up for that, wouldn't we, Mark?' said Neil.

I was delighted to see Neil entering into the spirit of things. Mark had told me earlier that his beloved was now seriously thinking about a change of career or even setting up a firm of his own. The Prosperous Place plans had sealed the deal when it came to deciding that he no longer wanted to be involved with preposterous projects which ultimately bene-fited nothing other than the project managers' purse strings.

'Definitely,' Mark agreed. 'I'll nip home and grab some beers and we'll be round.'

Graham and Carole took responsibility for locking the bothy and shutting up the hens and that just left me and Luke to arrange the rest of our evening.

'Come back with me,' he insisted, 'and we'll have that chat and a proper tour of the whole house.'

I had been thinking about putting him off, what with it being his dad's anniversary, but changed my mind now that he had suggested it again.

'She'd love that,' Lisa butted in. 'She's desperate to explore all your nooks and crannies.'

'All right,' I swallowed, turning my back on her and putting my sudden nerves down to revealing the contents of the cupboard rather than anything else. 'As long as you're sure you want company.'

'He wants you,' whispered Lisa, elbowing me sharply in the ribs.

Chapter 23

'I know Lisa was being silly,' said Luke, once we were alone.

I felt my face go hot as I thought he'd caught the gist of her childish innuendo, but fortunately he didn't seem to have cottoned on.

'But as you've already seen the less than impressive nooks and crannies, as she put it, in our search for the portrait,' he went innocently on, 'I really would appreciate the benefit of your expert eye over a couple of the other areas and rooms.'

'All right,' I nodded, 'I have to admit I've been hoping to have a proper look around, but I wasn't going to say as much in front of our friend, obviously. Thank you, Luke.'

I was relieved to discover that, in terms of architectural features and flourishes at least, not all that much had changed since Charles Wentworth oversaw the building of the house. The original décor and the majority of the furnishings were long gone, but that was only to be expected. However the elaborate ceiling roses and cornicing were still all in place, along with the grand fireplaces and panelling.

'What do you think?' Luke asked as we finished exploring the ground floor and headed up the stairs to check out the bedrooms.

I stole a quick glance at him and found a deep frown was spoiling his usually smooth brow. He was worried, I realised, genuinely concerned. I knew that the house meant a lot to him, but until that moment I don't think I had taken to heart just how much. His speech earlier had given me some indication, along with some of the things he had said to me in private, but the look on his face really nailed home the fact that Prosperous Place was everything to him.

'I think you should lose that frown,' I told him with what I hoped was a reassuring smile. 'The things that really matter have been perfectly preserved. You're not going to have too much trouble returning it to its original glory at all. Not with a canvas as beautifully, and originally, embellished as this.'

'Do you really mean that?' he said, stopping on the step below me.

'I really do,' I told him as I looked down into his face.

The creases which had been carved into his brow quickly vanished and his shoulders dropped back to more or less where they should have been.

'Thank you, Kate,' he smiled. 'I can't tell you what a relief it is to hear you say that. I can't help thinking that I've fallen on my feet having someone with your eye and knowledge living practically on the doorstep.'

'Well, like I've told you a thousand times before, you can call on me whenever you need to,' I said and I really meant it.

I know I had moved to Nightingale Square with the objective of taking a year out, but I had no intention of letting a project of such magnificent proportions as this slip through my fingers.

'I'll hold you to that,' said Luke, holding out his hand for me to shake.

'Good,' I swallowed, slipping my hot hand into his much cooler one. 'I'd be disappointed if you didn't.'

'Come on,' he said, squeezing hard and sending an electrical pulse from the tips of my fingers to somewhere deep in my belly, but not letting go. 'I probably should have shown you this before, but come and see where I think the portrait of Edward would have hung.'

'I'm pleased you've mentioned him,' I said, falling into step and trying to relax my fingers which were still in his grip, 'because that's who I wanted to talk to you about tonight.'

'And there was me hoping you were just here for my scintillating conversation,' Luke grinned, but using a tone which suggested he wasn't joking at all.

Looking at the fireplace in what had originally been the master bedroom, and thinking back to Harold's photographs, I was sure Luke was right. This definitely looked to be the place where the smaller family portraits had been displayed. I guessed they must have formed part of a more intimate collection that Charles and his wife kept aside from the bigger paintings which had dominated the rooms downstairs.

We had only been in the room for a matter of seconds before Luke inhaled deeply and thankfully moved the conversation away from my motives for joining him.

'Can you smell that?' he asked, sniffing the air.

'Yes,' I said. 'Well, I think so. I definitely just got a whiff of something, but whatever is it?'

'Pipe smoke I reckon,' he said, smiling broadly.

'Pipe smoke?'

'Yes,' he nodded. 'Whenever I come in here and look at this spot I get a whiff of it. It's happened ever since the day I arrived.'

'But where's it coming from?' I asked, looking around for the potential source. 'You don't think the place is haunted, do you?'

'I think it might be,' Luke told me. I was a little perturbed that he sounded so serious. 'I get the feeling there's some sort of presence in this room at least.'

I wasn't sure I believed in ghosts, but the smell was real and getting stronger by the second.

'Charles Wentworth smoked a pipe,' Luke elaborated.

'Did he?' I said, crossing to the window and trying not to show that I was spooked.

I might have been intrigued by the man who had built my house, but I didn't need the appearance of a ghostly apparition to seal my interest.

It was already dark outside, but I knew this window overlooked the garden and the main lawns. My body emitted a little shudder when I realised there would more than likely be a clear view of the tree under which Edward's brief life came to an abrupt and violent end. I closed my eyes and turned my back on the spectacle as a chill ran down my spine. I didn't want to see that tree or even imagine the scene which had happened under it. That was more frightening to me than the thought of Mr Wentworth's ghost suddenly springing up.

'Shall we carry on?' suggested Luke. 'I'm rather keen to hear what it is that you want to tell me now.'

I was relieved to find the rest of the house much as I expected and a little while later we found ourselves back in the old staff quarters where Luke was currently living. The conditions, thanks to the reconnection of the electricity supply, were a little more luxurious than those we Nightingale Square residents had endured on 14 February.

'I'm just going to go and check on Violet and Dash,' said Luke. 'Can I get you a drink; tea, coffee, something cold?'

'Something cold would be nice,' I said. 'I seem to have developed quite a thirst since the barbecue this afternoon.'

'Something cold coming up,' he beamed, heading for

the kitchen. 'I blame that spicy marinade John used on the ribs.'

'I think you could be right,' I agreed. 'Shall I put a match to your fire while you're gone?'

Luke turned back to me and laughed.

'You already have,' he told me.

Our eyes met briefly and again I recalled what he had said at the end of his speech, along with what both Lisa and Heather had intimated afterwards. More than intimated in fact.

'The matches are on the mantelpiece,' he said, finally letting me go. 'I won't be long.'

The fire was comfortingly crackling away by the time he returned carrying a chilled bottle of champagne and two flutes on a tray along with some leftovers from lunch.

'What are we celebrating?' I asked as he wrapped a napkin around the neck of the bottle and expertly eased out the cork.

'I'm not sure yet,' he said, 'that depends on what it is you have to tell me.'

As I watched him fill the glasses and pop an olive in his mouth I wished I had more exciting news to share than 'Charlie has drawn a blank'. I hoped he wasn't going to be too downcast that my efforts so far hadn't got us any closer to tracking down the portrait.

Perhaps the things John had discovered in the secret cupboard might lead us further along the trail. It had been difficult, once I realised what they were, not to sit and go through them on my own, but fingers crossed they were going to prove they were worth the wait.

'Well,' I said, once we had raised our glasses and I had taken a long and stomach-settling bubble-filled swallow. 'As I mentioned upstairs, it's about the missing portrait of Edward.'

'OK,' Luke nodded, his frown quickly falling back into place.

He was staring at me so intently I had to look away. I took another swig of champagne, a much bigger one this time.

'As you know,' I reminded him as the bubbles tickled my nose, 'I have contacts in the antiques field which might prove useful when it comes to tracking it down.'

'Contacts which you quite understandably said you didn't want anything to do with because they were connected to your ex-husband.'

'They're the ones,' I said, trying to make light of what I had said the evening I explained why I hadn't offered to help him out before. 'Contacts that could lead my path back to David, but fortunately, so far at least, haven't.'

'I don't understand,' said Luke, shaking his head. 'What exactly is it that you're trying to tell me, Kate?'

'Well, it's the mystery of the missing portrait,' I said quickly, drinking yet more champagne, 'the lure of it proved too much in the end and so I called my old friend, Charlie.'

Luke shook his head again, more vehemently this time.

'You didn't have to do that, Kate.'

'I know I didn't have to,' I said, 'but after you'd explained how much it meant to you, and to this place,' I hastily added to ensure he knew I had the interests of Prosperous Place fixed at the forefront of my mind, not his interests, 'it was all I could think about and so I did the only thing I thought I could do to help. Charlie's the best in the business,' I went on, 'and I've sworn him to secrecy. He promised not to mention any of this to David and he's been putting out feelers in the hope of turning up the portrait, or at least sniffing out an idea or two as to where it might be.'

Luke turned it all over in his mind for a moment.

'I can't believe you would do that for me,' he said. 'Not after you told me that you had absolutely no desire to ever have any contact with your ex, or anyone associated with him, again.'

'Well,' I said, finally draining my glass. 'I haven't had contact with *him* and I did it for the house really and like I said, Charlie has promised that word won't get back to David. He still has no idea where I'm living and I have every intention of keeping it that way.'

I was rather touched that Luke had taken my feelings, and the risk I had taken to jeopardise them, into account rather than asking straight out if Charlie had managed to track down the portrait, but that was testament to the kind of bloke he was.

'I only wish,' I told him as he refilled both our glasses, 'that I had something more positive to tell you, but I'm afraid Charlie has drawn a blank. He's searched high and low, sent emails to practically everyone in the business, along with the finest auction houses both here and abroad, but there's been nothing enlightening come back to him at all. There's not been so much as a single hint of where the portrait has disappeared to.'

'I see,' Luke nodded, twisting the delicate stem of his glass around in his hands. 'So, what do you think that means?'

'Well,' I carried on, 'as far as Charlie's concerned he's certain the painting must still be here, actually on site some-where. He's convinced it can't have been sold, not through any official channels, or via any of the larger houses that you would ordinarily expect to be involved, anyway.'

Luke shook his head.

'But between us we've had the place apart,' he sighed. 'I'm sure it isn't here.'

'I know,' I said, putting down my glass and reaching for the bag I had been lugging about all day. 'Which is why I'm hoping there might be something among this lot which will lead us in the right direction.'

'What have you got there?'

'Mostly letters,' I said, popping the lid off one tin and then the other. 'They were hidden in a secret cupboard next to the chimney breast in my bedroom. They're all pretty old by the looks of it and the paper is fragile so we need to be careful, but I'm sure they'll have some bearing on the situation.'

'Wow,' gasped Luke, as he peered into the tins and reached for a pair of dark-framed reading glasses which I hadn't noticed on the table behind him.

He shoved them on and I couldn't take my eyes off him. In less time than it took my heart to beat, he had gone from male model to model student. He looked for all the world as if he deserved the coveted cover shot on the 'hot dudes reading' calendar. I was grateful that the kittens were consigned to the kitchen because had one of those jumped on his lap I don't think I could have controlled myself when faced with such a sexy tableau. What the heck was wrong with me?

'What?' he blinked, when he caught me looking at him.

'Nothing,' I stammered, my face flushing scarlet as I forced myself to turn away.

'Is it the glasses?' he asked. 'They're pretty old. I keep meaning to get new frames.'

'No,' I croaked, 'don't change them. They suit you.'

'I didn't realise you went for geeky types,' he teased, looking at me over the rims.

'I don't actually go for any type,' I told him, trying to sound prim, but failing.

It was on the tip of my tongue to ask what he had been studying when he accrued his student debts before his modelling days, but I bit the question back and returned my attention to the letters.

They turned out to be even older than I had initially supposed and chronicled, among other things, the doomed love affair between Abigail and Edward and the relationship between her family and the Wentworths right up until around the time Doris must have been a young girl.

A number of the envelopes which had been sent to Charles had been returned unopened and I guessed that the shock of losing his son had led to him completely cutting all private communication with everyone in Abigail's family. There was no mention from either side of the child, Luke's ancestor, to whom Abigail had given birth.

'I suppose this goes to show what a great man Charles Wentworth was, doesn't it?' said Luke huskily as we trawled through it all. 'I bet anyone else in his position would have taken the house away and banished the entire family in a heartbeat, wouldn't they?'

'Yes,' I said, slipping one of the letters back inside its envelope, 'you're probably right. The fact that he didn't act out of spite, or otherwise, really shows us the mark of the man.'

It can't have been easy for him knowing that the family of the girl who had cost him his son was living practically on his doorstep, but then they, in a way, had lost a child too. If only Abigail and Edward had been born a century or so later, then their story would have stood a much better chance of having a happy ending.

'This letter from Charles's wife, Rose,' I said, picking it up again.

'What about it?'

It was the only one we had found written in her softly slanting handwriting.

'Well, as far as I can tell, it's the only one that helps us at all in our quest to find the lost portrait.'

'But does it?' Luke queried. 'I can't see how.'

'She mentions briefly a few things being sent to Abigail's mother,' I mused, running my fingers lightly over the paper, 'which makes me wonder if there's a possibility that Rose knew there was a baby, even if Charles didn't. Perhaps she sent things that had belonged to Edward to Abigail's family in the hope that the child would one day come to know who his father was.'

'You might be right about that,' said Luke thoughtfully. 'From the notes Dad left behind and the things he told me he'd discovered from our side, I'm certain that before she died, Abigail had told her son who his father was, even though she hadn't the evidence to prove it. In fact, it was that connection to Abigail's family further south which put Dad on the Norfolk trail.'

It was such a shame that he never had the chance to reach its conclusion, but I didn't think it necessary to point it out. Luke was no doubt thinking that for himself.

'There you go then,' I said instead. 'Maybe Rose wanted Abigail's family to have physical proof that the child was a Wentworth because she realised that the only way her husband's heritage would live on would be to leave behind something incontrovertible that would ensure the legacy continued. Her other son had proved himself less than capable of following in his father's footsteps, so maybe she felt this was the only way to give the Wentworth empire any chance of surviving.'

'But it didn't work, did it?' said Luke. 'The proof that Rose may have attempted to pass on didn't make it to either Abigail or her boy. The factory and houses disappeared and this place was eventually sold off without so much as a hint of another heir. Edward's son never stepped up to claim the title because he never had the proof to make the claim, even though he knew from his mother's own mouth the source of the blood running through his veins.'

'You're right,' I frowned. 'And it wasn't as if you could just pop along somewhere and ask for a DNA test in those days, was it?'

Edward's son had never been furnished with the evidence to confirm he was a Wentworth descendant and that was why the connection hadn't been made until Luke's dad had taken advantage of modern technology and genealogical records and found it. We sat in silence for a few seconds listening to the logs crackling in the grate.

'But you know, I can't imagine Rose would have given that portrait away.' Luke sighed, quashing my theory completely. 'And we know it was still in the house when Harold's photographs were taken.'

'Oh yes,' I tutted. I had forgotten about that. 'Of course.'

I drank another mouthful of champagne and began to feel thoroughly deflated in spite of the valiant efforts of the fizz. I had hoped the secret stash of letters would have provided Luke with some decent, solid answers, but all it had actually done was create more questions.

'I'm so sorry,' I said, sinking back into the cushions.

'For what?'

'All this,' I said, pointing at the piles of papers. 'I wanted to be able to help, but all I've done is produce more of a muddle.'

'Of course you haven't,' Luke disagreed. 'If anything, you've given us a new lead. Maybe the portrait went to Doris herself or one of her more recent ancestors. It must have been taken from Prosperous Place after those photos were taken. We just have to keep looking for the next link, one that doesn't veer so far back.'

'I suppose,' I said, wrinkling my nose.

'After all,' Luke went on, nudging my knee, 'Doris's family, who were my family, lived in your house right up until you arrived, so for all we know things could have been heading that way far more recently than we realise.

Who's to say the connection with the house ended when the Wentworths left here?'

'Maybe,' I said, scratching my head.

I knew he was trying to make me feel better, but it wasn't working. I was certain there was nothing left to discover in number four and it was all beginning to look like yet another happy ever after that was destined to remain unsolved.

'And anyway,' he said, reaching for my hand and stroking the back of it, 'as far as I'm concerned what we've discovered this evening goes to prove something far more important than where this blessed portrait has disappeared to.'

'Does it?' I swallowed.

Goose bumps had broken out along the arm attached to the hand he was still caressing and I sat up straight again as I caught the change in his expression.

'Yes,' he said, leaning closer, his eyes never leaving mine and his soft breath mingling with my own. 'It does.'

'And what's that then?' I whispered, my head spinning as a result of more than the bubbles.

'It goes to prove that the men of Prosperous Place have absolutely no power to stop themselves falling in love with the beautiful women who live in number four Nightingale Square.'

'I don't know what you mean,' I said, forcing myself to pull away a little.

I hadn't expected him to say anything as monumental as that.

'What I mean,' Luke breathed, as he took off his glasses and laid them back on the table, 'is that I've fallen for you, Kate. That I can finally understand what it was that my father meant by this whole one true love business.'

I shook my head, but neither of us moved. I had already been someone's alleged heart's desire and I didn't have any love left to share with anyone else. Surely Luke had made a mistake but the look in his eyes suggested he thought otherwise.

I had spent so long grieving for my own once in a life-time love that I hadn't seen the signs my friends had teased me about, or factored into the equation the possibility that I might just turn out to be someone else's.

'I don't think . . .' I stammered.

'Good,' Luke interrupted, shifting his body closer. 'Because recently I've been doing enough of that for the both of us and tonight I want you to forget all about thinking and logic and asking questions.'

He put our champagne flutes on the floor, then lifted my chin and softly brushed his lips with mine. My head was telling me I shouldn't want to 'feel' anything other than the desire to get the hell out of there, but my heart and some-where much further south were forcing me on. Imploring me to embrace the very real physical feelings which were determinedly pushing their way to the surface and battering the defensive dam I had built up during the last few months.

Whether he realised it or not Luke was bringing my body back to life, even if it was going to be at the expense of his heart.

'I want you, Kate,' he murmured, running his hands down my arms, along my thighs and under the hem of my dress, 'I want you in a way I've never wanted any other woman in my whole life. And not just for now and for this, but for always.'

It felt exhilarating to be wanted and my head was swimming, snippets of conversations I'd had with Lisa and Heather about love and second chances were swirling through my brain. I gasped with pleasure as Luke purposefully and thoroughly began to explore every inch of my quivering body.

'I want you too,' I whispered back, arching towards him.

My breath caught in my throat as in one swift movement he knelt in front of me and I wrapped my legs around his waist. His fingers fumbled with the buttons on my dress and for the briefest moment our eyes met and then my hands were in his hair and he was lowering his head, showering me with tender kisses in places I had almost forgotten existed.

I have no recollection of how long we spent wrapped around each other but afterwards my emotions felt as tumbled as my hair. Luke's words about falling for me, and how through me he was finally beginning to understand his father's take on love, should have stopped me but instead they had urged me on. I had been flattered and seduced and it wasn't all down to a pair of sexy glasses.

Perhaps it was the champagne, or the setting and the romance of the open fire, who knows, but I had never in my wildest dreams imagined I would give myself to another man, especially so wholeheartedly, ever again. My first boyfriend back in college and David made up the brief list of men I had slept with, but neither of them had offered me even half of the pleasure I had experienced with Luke.

I shifted a little in his embrace as I wondered uncomfortably if I had taken advantage of him and the intense feelings he believed he harboured for me.

'Are you all right?' he asked, kissing the top of my head as we lay still entwined.

'Yes,' I whispered. 'Are you?'

'Of course,' he said, nuzzling closer, 'although I didn't mean for things to go quite as far as that.'

I stiffened a little in his embrace, hoping he wasn't regretting it already. Even though I was feeling guilty about my inability to give him my heart, that didn't alter the fact that I had just experienced the most thrilling sex I had ever had.

'Didn't you?' I asked.

'No,' he said. 'I had this whole thing planned out in my head, you see.'

'Planned out?' I breathed.

'Yes,' he told me. 'I was going to woo you.'

'Woo me,' I laughed.

'Don't tease,' he said seriously. 'I went away before Easter to think this all through. I've never felt like this before, Kate and the plan I came up with was to woo you, then seduce you.'

'Perhaps you'll have to do it the other way around now,' I said, looking at him and wondering if there was a way I could kick the fairy tale into touch. Was I capable of change or was I too set in my ways, or as Lisa put it, brainwashed? 'Unless, now you've seduced me you're thinking there's no point in bothering with the wooing.'

Maybe it would be easier to pretend this hadn't happened.

'This isn't the sort of person I am, you know,' I said quietly.

'I'm well aware of that,' Luke smiled.

'I've never done anything as spontaneous as this in my entire life.'

I was just about to try and backtrack to what he had said about falling for me and work out how I could let him down gently when he started tickling me and making me squirm.

'Good,' he said, eradicating all sensible and serious thought. 'I wouldn't like to think this—'

'What?' I gasped, 'you wouldn't like to think this is what?'

'Did you hear that?' he said, his seductive tone lost as he looked towards the window. 'I think there's someone outside.'

'Oh no,' I yelped. 'Are you sure? It'd better not be Lisa.'

'You head upstairs,' he commanded, jumping up and gathering together my scattered clothes before thrusting them into my arms, 'and I'll see who it is.'

For a second I was transfixed by the sight of his tanned and toned back and biceps, not to mention his . . . but hammering on the back door brought me back to my senses.

'Hurry up,' he urged. 'Just go!'

It was too late. Apparently, whoever was hammering had discovered the kitchen door was unlocked and had taken it upon themselves to just walk in. Without another word Luke and I hastily pulled on our clothes and straightened the cushions before turning on the table lamp and ridding the room of its seductive ambience in one deft flick of a switch.

'Anyone home?'

It was a man's voice. Luke looked at me and shrugged and then crossed the room in two strides, before wrenching open the door to face the unwelcome intruder. I noticed he hadn't had time to pull his socks on and wondered if whoever had turned up unannounced would notice.

'David!' I gasped.

'Hello, Kate,' he smiled.

I felt the ground sway beneath my feet as a woman stepped out from the shadows behind him. She was holding the hand of a little girl who must have been no more than three or four.

'Candice,' said Luke, looking over his shoulder at me and sounding every bit as shocked.

'Hello Luke,' she said, ushering the child forward. 'I thought you might like to spend some of the Easter holidays with your daughter this year.'

Chapter 24

The curly-haired little girl surged forward and Luke lifted her into his arms as she buried her head in his neck. Silence descended as we all looked at each other and I could see from the stricken expression on Luke's face that the shock I was feeling about coming face to face with David in Prosperous Place, of all places, was not all that far removed from the utter bewilderment he was feeling.

I stole another look at the girl he had called Candice. She was very pretty, very young and a complete contrast to my ex, who was looking what could only be described as smug. She was apparently more than a little put out to find the father of her child enjoying what must have looked like a very cosy night in with another woman. I felt a surge of fiery heat flood through my body as I imagined what they would have witnessed had they turned up just ten minutes earlier.

Surreal didn't even come close to describing the scene and my spirits had switched from soaring to sunk in less than a breath. This was the first time I had opened myself up and allowed myself to really feel anything, either mentally or physically, since David's deception had ripped a ragged hole through my life, and it was definitely going to be the last. Suddenly I found myself wishing that the trio of intruders had arrived sooner, before I had taken that first drink of clothes-loosening champagne, and consequently stopped me making such a mortifying mistake.

Of course, Luke had told me that he had lived a life his father disapproved of, but I had never for one second entertained the idea that life might have resulted in a child. What a start for the poor little mite, and tethered to a mother who obviously thought nothing of keeping her out of bed and away from home at all hours of the night. But where on earth had they come from?

'We would have been here hours ago,' Candice huffed, answering my question as she dumped her holdall on the sofa and took another larger bag which David had carried in, 'but there were engineering works from just outside London so Jas and I were stuck on the replacement bus service for most of the way.'

'As was I,' David joined in. He made it sound as if it was the most natural thing in the world for him to be travelling to Norfolk late on a bank holiday Sunday. 'You can imagine what a surprise it was when we started chatting and realised that not only were we headed in the same direction, but also to the same destination!'

Candice looked at David and smiled. Trust him to seek out the prettiest passenger to strike up a conversation with.

'But at least it meant we could split the taxi fare,' said Candice, flicking her smooth curtain of dark hair over her shoulder as she unzipped the bag on the sofa.

She may have been young, but she was very groomed and glamorous. I wondered if she was perhaps one of the models Luke used to work with. She must have been practically a teen-mum when she had her daughter.

'You must let me pay my half, David,' she insisted.

'Not at all,' David chivalrously cut in, as he puffed out his chest which, I noticed, was looking a little more paunch than pecs these days. 'I wouldn't dream of it. It was my pleasure to be able to help you keep little Jasmine amused.'

I looked at the girl, Jasmine, still in Luke's arms. She looked exhausted and try as I might I couldn't shake off the image of David happily playing I Spy with the youngest passenger on the bus. In the past, before the arrival of his much-loved godson, he had always moaned if there were children travelling on any form of transport he was using, even if they were impeccably behaved. The irony that he was now determined to demonstrate what a model parent he could be after he had tried to lure me back to marital bliss with the promise of a baby of our own was not lost on me.

'But what are you doing here, David?' I demanded.

I was surprised that my voice was completely unaffected by events even though my stomach was churning and I was hoping I would wake up in the morning to discover this uncomfortable end to the day had actually been nothing more than a bad dream. Hopefully my real day would have ended after the party when I had gone home to Lisa and John's to play Monopoly along with everyone else.

'Do you mean this is David, as in your husband?' Luke asked incredulously.

Finally he had found his voice, but he sounded nothing like the man who had been whispering sweet and seductive nothings in my ear. His eyes snapped back to my former beau and he looked him over, mentally appraising every inch.

'Ex-husband,' I quickly corrected.

'Almost ex-husband,' said David, sounding hurt.

He stepped forward and held out his hand for Luke to shake. Which, to my annoyance and amazement, he did.

'I'm here because of the missing portrait,' David said smoothly.

'Charlie told you,' I seethed. 'I don't believe it.'

'I don't know why you didn't come straight to me, Kate,' he said shaking his head.

The deluded fool still didn't get it.

'Or at least pass on my details to Luke here, so he could get in touch with me himself. You know I'm the best in the business, next to Charlie of course.'

Oh, the arrogance of him; but actually, that wouldn't have been the worst idea. If Luke had been the one to get in touch, on the pretence of a random recommendation, the connection to me wouldn't have come up at all.

'I'm more than happy to be working with Charlie,' I told David peevishly. 'Or I was.'

I couldn't believe my cigar-smoking friend had gone back on his promise. There was no way I was sending him the thank-you box of Cubans I had been poised to seek out now. Was there no one left from my former life that I could trust? I threw another glance at Luke and little Jasmine and wondered if the folk populating the new life I was trying to build for myself were any better.

'Well, there's no harm done,' David smiled, 'and I've come because I have news.'

'Do you?' asked Luke.

I bit my lip, furious that he was interested in anything David had to say, but then I reminded myself he knew none of the darker details as to why our marriage had disintegrated, only that it had. Perhaps his reaction to my estranged other half showing up unannounced would have been very different if he knew the whole sordid story behind our separation. At least I hoped his reaction would have been different.

'So why didn't you just call?' I snapped. 'This is hardly the done thing, is it? Turning up unannounced on the doorstep of someone you don't know.'

'I did leave a voicemail message on your phone,' David quickly replied, 'and I sent a text. Did you not get them?'

Yes, of course I had got them, but they were both sitting unread and unheard on my mobile. If only I'd checked them I could have avoided this whole farce.

'And besides, I like to offer a personal service,' he enraged me by adding.

'Oh, now that is true,' I said, raising my voice, and unfortunately making Jasmine flinch. 'I'm going home.'

Luke looked at me for a second and I hoped he was able to interpret at least some of the meaning behind my loaded remark. I bent to pick up the bag which held the tins of letters, but then changed my mind and stacked them on the table. I didn't actually want them any more. I didn't want anything to do with Prosperous Place now David had turned up and tainted it and I didn't think I wanted anything else to do with Luke for that matter.

We may have just shared bodily fluids, but that was as far as the relationship was going to go. Yes, he had told me he had fallen for me and yes, for one mad minute I had been flattered, but that was before I knew he was lugging around a whole heap of baggage and a child he had never seen fit to mention. Cutting all ties, ripping off the sticking plaster was the only way to go. He barely knew me really, so I cruelly assumed he wouldn't be heartbroken for long.

'Do you live nearby, Kate?' David asked.

The cheek of him, what business was it of his?

'I was wondering if I could beg a bed for the night. Or even a sofa.'

'I'm miles away,' I said, pulling on my jacket and slipping my feet into my shoes. 'Not that that makes any difference. I wouldn't spend another night under the same roof as you if you paid me.'

'Don't be like that,' he pouted. 'I'm trying to make amends. Keep things on friendly terms, like you originally said you wanted when we were acting like grown-ups, remember?'

'I do remember,' I snapped, 'but I've changed my mind.'

'Kate,' Luke began but I cut him off.

'I don't want you to be my friend, David, or make amends!' I shouted, making for the door. 'I don't want you to even try. I just want you to disappear out of my life and never come back!'

I couldn't believe I'd lost my temper. Yet again David had managed to bring out the worst in me, and this time in front of Luke, someone I had for a moment thought I could perhaps care about in ways I thought would never be possible again. Not that any of that mattered now.

'I thought you said she'd be pleased to see you,' I heard Candice mutter as I rushed out.

'Kate!' Luke shouted, as Jasmine began to cry. 'Come back!'

I didn't go back, I didn't even look back. I rushed out into the crisp spring night air and ran all the way home.

There were myriad messages and texts waiting for me on my mobile when I finally got around to switching it on the next morning. Some were from Luke, but the majority were from David telling me that he had spent the night at Prosperous Place and that he had no intention of going anywhere until he'd seen me again and told me what he'd managed to turn up about the painting. I cursed myself for not having the sense to have changed my mobile number.

I didn't for one second believe that he had turned up anything. Charlie had been adamant that he had explored all avenues, unless of course he had been lying to give David a chance to wheedle his way back in to my affections. Knowing what I knew now I wouldn't have put it past him.

'Are you going out?' Lisa asked, as we collided on the doorstep. 'I was hoping for a coffee and a catch-up. I want to hear all about your evening's entertainment.'

I was in no mood for her saucy innuendos, even though I knew that she was just being her usual bubbly self.

'Kate, are you all right?'

'No,' I said, reaching for my umbrella as I realised just how hard it was raining. 'Not really.'

'Where are you going?'

'Into the city,' I told her. 'I have an appointment.'

'On a bank holiday Monday?' She frowned.

'Yes,' I said, biting back my tears as I bent to ostensibly check the zip on my boots. 'I won't be long. I'll come over to yours when I get back.'

'Let John run you,' she said. 'It's pouring. You'll get soaked.'

I stepped around her, slamming the door and jamming the key in the lock.

'I'll be fine,' I smiled as brightly as I could manage. 'It's only a shower. I'll see you later.'

I hadn't got far out of the Square before John drew up alongside me in his works van. He flicked on his hazards and the bank holiday traffic immediately began honking in response.

'You'd better get in,' he called through the passenger window. 'Otherwise I'm going to get lynched.'

'I'm not going to tell you,' I began to say as I shook out the brolly and climbed in.

'And I don't want to know,' he interrupted as he rejoined the traffic and the horn tooting subsided. 'Because if you tell me then I'll be forced to tell her indoors.'

I sniffed and nodded.

'I just didn't like to think of you catching cold, that's all.'

'Thanks,' I croaked. 'I appreciate it.'

'Especially when there's so much work still to do in the

garden,' he went on. 'We can't afford to have anyone taking time off.'

'So, you've only come to my rescue on this rain-soaked morning to make sure the garden won't end up being a man down?' I couldn't help but smile.

'Of course,' he laughed. 'Now, come on, where to?'

I had spoken to David briefly, very briefly, and agreed to meet at the Castle Museum. I made John drop me off on the dead-end road which accessed the shopping mall car park so, as far as he could work out, I could have been heading anywhere. Not that the destination itself was a secret. I was more concerned that he and Lisa didn't find out *who* I was meeting rather than *where* I was meeting them.

'Do you want me to pick you up?' John asked. 'It's no bother.'

'No, but thanks for the offer,' I said, thinking the walk home would help me clear my head if nothing else. 'According to the forecast it's supposed to clear up later, but I promise I'll ring if it doesn't.'

'Make sure you do,' John said sternly as if he was talking to Tamsin the terror rather than Kate the level-headed. 'And look after yourself, OK?'

'OK,' I promised.

David was all smiles when we met in the Castle foyer, but he looked dog tired. He was keen to tell me why he was so wrung out the second we were settled with tea and he had buttered himself a crumbly cheese scone.

'Excuse my manners,' he said, taking a mouthful and making short work of it. 'But I didn't get a bite of breakfast or a wink of sleep for that matter.'

I took a sip of the still scalding tea and hoped he wasn't about to tell me he had spent the night listening to the noisy bedroom gymnastics of Luke and the mother of his child.

'They were at it all night,' he said confidingly.

I thought my tea was going to make a return trip, but I managed to keep it down.

'I've never heard anything like it,' David went relentlessly on. 'How the child managed to sleep through it I have no idea.'

'What?'

'The shouting,' he said. 'And the language from Candice was shocking. I know her name doesn't suggest it, but I reckon she has some fiery Italian ancestry in her somewhere.'

'It didn't cross your mind that Candice might not be her real name, then?' I asked.

'No,' he said, turning bright red. 'It didn't.'

I could have capitalised on the moment. I could have quite easily milked the situation for all it was worth and reminded him that the pretty young model he had bedded had used a false name, which was why she turned out to be so difficult to track down, but I didn't. Judging by the puce shade David was currently displaying I didn't need to and really, what would have been the point?

'From what I could make out,' he carried on, 'there's some sort of ongoing paternity case between the pair of them.'

'Right.'

I didn't need to know. I didn't want to know.

'On the bus here last night,' David continued, 'she told me that Luke has been shirking his responsibilities for that little girl from the day she was born. Shocking, isn't it? He really doesn't strike you as the type, does he? But then I daresay you know him better than I do; what do you think?'

'You said you had some news about the portrait?'

'But she's very forgiving.' David smiled indulgently. 'She said that if he's prepared to do the right thing then she'll move in with him and give the relationship another go. She's quite a spark.'

And she'd also turned up just when Luke had secured himself his ancestral home. It was an uncharitable thought, but one I struggled to squash down now David had told me why she had turned up unannounced with her curly-haired daughter in tow.

'The portrait,' I said again, this time with more emphasis. 'My only interest in the place is to see it restored. I don't know Luke that well at all.'

'You're working for him, are you?' David asked, eyeing me over the rim of his cup. 'I didn't realise.'

I didn't contradict his assumption. It was far easier all round if he jumped to that conclusion rather than the other one. When he and Candice had burst in on us the night before it would have been perfectly logical to assume something very different, so I suppose I was getting off lightly if he naively thought we had been discussing antiques and restoration schedules late on a Sunday night.

'I just want to see Prosperous Place returned to its former glory,' I said, looking him straight in the eye.

It wasn't a lie. I had decided before I left last night that I had no further interest in Luke and his secrets, even though I had now experienced for myself his sizzling sensual technique. Or should I say techniques?

'Kate?'

'Sorry, what?'

'I said, have you thought any more about us?'

I could hardly believe my ears. I was so desperate not to hear what David was saying that I was almost tempted to track back to the memory of last night, which had haunted my dreams and was poised to play through in my head all over again.

'Have you thought any more about what I suggested when we met again at Christmas?'

He made it sound as if our get-together was something we had planned, rather than something my mother had sneakily orchestrated behind my back.

'No,' I said bluntly. 'I haven't, David. I really, really haven't.'

'But the baby . . .'

'There is no baby,' I spat, my temper thrusting its way up again. 'Thanks to you there will never be a baby.'

There, I'd said it. We'd skirted around the issue forever, but now it was out there, on the table, out in the open and I couldn't wait to see what he would do with it.

'All right,' he said, looking everywhere but at me.

Surprise, surprise, he was going to ignore it.

'Let me tell you what I've found out about this painting.'

Chapter 25

I was in no way convinced by what David told me he had discovered about the missing portrait of Edward, but he insisted that Luke was thrilled and happy to go along with what he had said to him without question. I was desperate to step in and potentially save Luke a whole heap of time, money and heartache, but really it was nothing to do with me now and of course there was the ghost of a chance that I might be wrong. I might have still wanted to see the house restored, but the price of achieving it was far higher than I was prepared to pay.

The photos David had shown me on his phone of the portrait he had tracked down in the US certainly looked like the painting in Harold's photographs, which I had copied and sent to Charlie to use as a reference, so all I was going on was a hunch. However, my gut had served me well in the past. Nonetheless, having mulled the situation over I decided that, on this occasion the best option, the only option in fact, was to butt out.

The downturn in the weather meant that the community garden required minimal watering and attention and so I made my excuses, telling Lisa I had a stinking head cold which I had no desire to share, and Luke to focus on his family and not think I had any expectations, even after what had happened between us. He looked tired and pale, but I didn't give him a chance to say a word before returning my attention back to decorating.

'Now,' I said to the cupboard next to the fireplace when I had finished sanding and priming the woodwork and painting the ceiling. 'What am I going to do with you?'

To be honest I didn't want any reminder of the connection number four Nightingale Square had forged with Prosperous Place and which I myself had reignited, but on the other hand, it was very useful storage in a house that didn't have all that many cubbyholes and closets.

'I'll give you a bit longer,' I told the door. 'Let's just wait and see what happens, shall we?'

Obviously, I didn't get an answer, but there was a tiny part of me that still couldn't bring myself to banish the cupboard, from either my mind or my sight, just yet.

I kept my door closed and my head down for almost three weeks, even though Lisa was insistent that no cold, common or otherwise, could last that long. I knew she was desperate to hear all about what had happened at Easter but I managed to keep her at arm's length until one afternoon when she sent a most unwelcome text about Heather.

'Are you sure she'll want us to go?' I asked as I climbed into the car and pulled on my belt. 'Did Glen say it would be OK to visit?'

'She's been given the all-clear,' Lisa reassured me. 'And she'll be home by the end of tomorrow, so it's fine. I just thought it would pass the time for her today and cheer her up to see us.'

'So, what exactly has happened?' I quizzed. 'And is the baby all right?'

'There's been some light bleeding,' Lisa sighed, 'which isn't all that uncommon in early pregnancy, but she's had some cramping as well so the hospital decided to admit her, just to be on the safe side.'

'Poor Heather,' I gasped, feeling guilty that I had lied to my friends about having a cold to ensure I was left alone. 'She must have been terrified. Is there anything practical we can do to help?'

'I asked Glen that and he said the family have gone into overdrive. I think she just needs us to be around, you know, be what we've always been since you moved here and interfered in our rocky start. Just be her friends.'

There was a smile on her lips as she said it, and certainly

no barb, but I felt the sting anyway. Ever since David and Candice had arrived on the scene I'd hidden myself away and avoided everyone. I knew I had good cause, but perhaps my behaviour had been a little over-indulgent given what I had discovered my poor friend had been going through.

'And how are things in the garden?' I asked, as Lisa pulled on to the busy ring road. 'Are the hens still thriving?'

'Everything's wonderful,' she said, 'it's all grown so much and the girls are grand. I can't imagine life without the place and I know things have changed a bit now that Candice and Jasmine are there, but Luke says—'

'It's fine,' I shrugged, cutting her off.

'I know it can't be easy,' she tried again.

'I've only not been going because I've been so busy,' I insisted, but which we both knew was a lie. 'And I've not been well of course,' I quickly added.

'It's been nothing to do with that ex-husband of yours showing up then,' she said, as she smoothly switched lanes, 'or anything that may or may not have happened after we left you and Luke alone at the end of the Easter party?'

'Did you say you had no change for the car park?' I said, reaching in the footwell for my bag and trying not to think about how she knew David had put in an appearance. 'Because I have plenty.'

*

Heather looked almost as pale as the pillow she was propped up against, but she was in good spirits and it took her and Lisa all of two minutes to track back to the conversation I had tried, and failed, to draw a line under during the journey in.

'So,' said Heather, after Lisa had offloaded a pile of magazines, two packets of biscuits and a bottle of Lucozade into the little locker next to her bed, 'any news from the Square?'

'Not much,' Lisa shrugged, 'but it looks like Candice and Jasmine are installed for the duration.'

'Really?' Heather asked, glancing apprehensively in my direction.

Lisa stopped talking and Heather cleared her throat.

'I don't know why you're so worried about what I might think,' I told them both. The only way to deal with the situation was to brazen it out. 'We've all of us admitted since he arrived that our horticultural benefactor is one hot bod, even Carole, but why you would think there's even the potential for anything to be going on between the pair of us is still beyond me.'

'Because for a start,' Lisa tiresomely began, 'at the Easter party he said he'd fallen in love with a whole lot more than just Prosperous Place.'

'He didn't exactly say that,' I tutted.

'And that night, after we'd purposely left the pair of you alone,' Heather carried on, 'you didn't get back to the Square until really, really, late.'

I had no idea that my movements had been so closely watched. Perhaps Carole wasn't the only curtain-twitcher in Nightingale Square.

'That was because my ex-husband and Luke's former partner and his daughter turned up!' I reiterated. 'I could hardly walk out as Luke let them in, could I?'

Not that he had actually let them in.

'Well, no,' said Heather, manoeuvring her pillow to get more comfortable, 'I suppose not.'

'There were introductions to be made and explanations to be heard,' I told them. 'It all took time. Believe me, it was the weirdest evening I've spent in a long time.'

I didn't mention that prior to the disturbance it had also been the most orgasmic.

'I suppose,' said Heather, chewing her lip.

'There's no suppose about it,' I said, 'it's a fact, so please don't be thinking you've got to be skirting around the issue of Luke's family when I'm in earshot. You both know my views on love and second chances by now—'

'Your crazy views,' Lisa cut in.

'I'm happily single,' I carried on in spite of her interruption. 'I've had my shot at love and I'm hardly likely to throw myself at the first man who might have dropped the tiniest hint that he was interested in me, or any man for that matter. Not that Luke has shown any interest in me in that way,' I clarified for good measure, 'so come on, Lisa, catch us up with the gossip and then I'll see if I can rustle up some coffee.'

I knew my little speech had fallen out in a rush and that my head was swimming with images of Luke and I wrapped around one another, but I'd said enough to convince Lisa that it was OK to carry on, even though it pained me to hear what she had to say.

'Nothing's officially been said,' she finally started, 'but anyone with eyes in their head can see that Jasmine is Luke's daughter and Candice has told me she's looking at local schools for September so she is obviously staying put.'

'Crikey,' said Heather. 'She's actually moving in for good then.'

'Yep.'

'And what about David?' Heather asked.

My head snapped back up.

'He's not still hanging around, is he?' I choked. 'It's been weeks!'

I couldn't believe he hadn't tracked me down if he'd been around all this time. Thank goodness I'd been keeping my head down and my door locked.

'No,' said Lisa, 'but Luke told me he's coming back this week. Apparently, he's been helping search for some painting that he wants for the house. It's being shipped from America and David has promised to come back to check its authenticity or something.'

'He's quite a smooth talker, that ex of yours,' Heather shocked me by adding.

'When did you meet him?' I asked.

'Easter bank holiday Monday,' she explained. 'We went back to the garden once the rain had stopped and he was there.'

I couldn't imagine David even sitting in the garden. He had always been an indoor type of guy, but then, until his godson came along and I saw them together I hadn't had him down as the paternal type either.

'Luke introduced him and when he realised we were your friends he started asking if you lived locally as well.'

'You didn't tell him, did you?'

'No,' said Heather, 'of course not.'

I could tell from the shifty looks they were exchanging that the pair of them had been subjected to David's charm offensive.

'What?' I snapped. 'What else did he say?'

'Well,' said Heather, 'not that it's anything to do with us . . .'

She'd got that right, but I got the impression that hadn't stopped them listening to whatever line he had tried to spin.

'Nor did we ask him to tell us anything,' added Lisa, 'but knowing how you feel about love . . .'

'Go on.'

'We know what he did to you was dreadful,' said Heather

quietly, 'and that you said you couldn't forgive him, but he told us he would do anything to win you back.'

'He said he wanted to start a family with you.'

I shook my head, but didn't comment. How dare he talk to anyone about any of that?

'He seemed nice—'

'My god, you've changed your tune,' I barked at Lisa, unable to stop myself. 'I seem to remember it wasn't all that long ago that you were the one who was ready to fry his balls!'

The people visiting the patient in the bed next to Heather cut off their conversation to tune in to ours, which was obviously far more interesting.

'Don't feel responsible for his behaviour, you've both said to me,' I went on. 'I told you my marriage ended because I wanted a child and he didn't and that it was my fault for pushing him into someone else's bed. It was my nagging that drove him to mess up, but that doesn't mean I'd take him back.'

Was it me, or had someone just turned the hospital thermostat up a notch?

'It wasn't your fault,' said Heather.

'You can't blame yourself for how he reacted to the situation,' Lisa went on, 'of course you can't, but if you keep insisting that he was your one shot at love and now he wants to have a baby with you, well . . .'

'Are the pair of you really suggesting that I should just get over what he did because now he's prepared to give me what I wanted all along?'

'Well, when you put it like that . . .' Heather murmured, sounding doubtful.

'I know it doesn't sound ideal,' Lisa carried on, still unbelievably championing the idea, 'but you don't strike me as the type who can be happily single, Kate, and if you refuse to give up this notion that you'll never love another man as much as you loved David, and he's desperate to have you back and start a family, then I thought you'd jump at the chance!'

I couldn't believe what she was saying. Something wasn't right here. I couldn't believe that Lisa, of all people, would have fallen for this. Heather maybe; she was more like me, softer round the edges and a romantic at heart, but Lisa, my ballsy best friend? No way.

'Do you really, really mean that?' I demanded.

'No.'

'Because personally, I think you're totally off your rocker. I thought you of all people . . . hang on. What?'

'No,' she said, reaching for my hand and giving it a squeeze. 'Of course I don't believe that.'

'What?' gulped Heather. 'I can't keep track here.'

'I just wanted you to acknowledge how ridiculous the idea was, Kate,' Lisa smiled at me.

The cunning wench.

'I thought that if I offered you the jaded idyll, with the not so perfect Prince, then you would finally be able to see how absurd it was and admit that it's not what you wanted at all. You'd see that what would have once been your happy ever after was actually more like a big bite from the poison apple.'

I shook my head in disbelief.

'And it worked, didn't it? You aren't going to go back to David because he's supposedly offering you a family?'

'Of course I'm not,' I frowned, 'but surely you realised that I wouldn't do that after I came back from Wynbridge after Christmas. I told you both that I'd sent him packing then, didn't I?'

'You did,' Lisa agreed, 'but you hadn't told us that he'd offered you a baby as a bargaining tool.'

'What difference does that make?'

'All the difference in the world,' she insisted. 'You can't quell the call of motherhood once it's taken root, even though you might try, and as Heather here was so taken with your ex, I just wanted to make sure that you weren't.'

'Oh dear,' said Heather, blushing profusely. 'Have I failed the ex test?'

'Spectacularly,' said Lisa. 'But we'll let you off.'

'Your hormones are all over the place,' I told her. 'We'll blame the presence of the baby you have on board just this once.'

It suddenly became obvious that the rest of the ward was holding its breath, waiting to see where the conversation headed next and Lisa, Heather and I looked at each other and laughed.

'We'd better get going,' said Lisa, standing up.

'But what about that coffee?' I reminded her.

'No time,' she said. 'I need to get back.'

We kissed Heather goodbye, made her promise to behave herself and told her we'd call in on her the next day, when she came home, to make sure all was OK.

'Glen's mum is going to stay for a few days to help out with Evie,' she told us. 'In fact, I can't help wishing I hadn't turned her down when she offered to help when Evie was born.'

She was clearly looking forward to the imminent arrival of her mother-in-law and some extra in-house support.

'But a visit would be good,' she said. 'You can keep me abreast of all the goss.'

As we headed back through the labyrinth of corridors I linked arms with Lisa and she planted a kiss on my cheek.

'That was a tricky game you played back there,' I told her. 'I was all set to walk out when I thought you were suggesting I should get back together with David.'

'I know,' she said. 'But it was worth it. You wouldn't be tempted to try again with him, would you? I mean, I know he's a charmer and everything and now he's on about wanting a baby.'

I pulled her to the side of the corridor and plonked her on a plastic chair.

'There's something else you need to know,' I said, as I dumped myself down next to her.

'What?'

I looked ahead for a moment and closed my eyes. There was no one in the world who knew about this final twist in the fling David had had. No one other than him and a few folk in the medical profession, that is.

'When David had his one-night stand,' I began, 'I didn't find out about it from him.'

'How did you find out then?'

'I—' I stopped, then swallowed and took a deep breath. 'I became unwell a little while after it had happened.'

I didn't elaborate on the details.

'Right.'

'So, I went to see my doctor and he ran a few tests.'

Lisa looked at me and shook her head, unable to join the dots.

'I had chlamydia,' I whispered, feeling thoroughly ashamed and realising that after what had happened with Luke I should book myself in for a check-up. 'David had caught it from this young woman, this so-called model he'd been with, and without realising, had passed it on to me.'

'Oh, Kate,' Lisa gasped.

'He was OK,' I said, 'but . . .'

'But, what?'

'But I wasn't. I was quite poorly and it took a while for me to recover.'

'But you're OK now?'

'In some respects,' I wept, 'but this baby he keeps promising, apparently there's a very good chance that I wouldn't be able to have one now anyway.'

I couldn't be sure from Lisa's expression exactly what she was thinking, but had David walked in at that moment, I was fairly certain she would have been able to conjure a frying pan and a fire from somewhere.

Chapter 26

As awkward as I felt about returning after my self-imposed exile, it was a pleasure to gaze upon the garden. The fruit, vegetables and cut flowers were looking healthy and lush thanks to the recent rains and the hens looked in fine fettle with their glossy feathers and fire-engine-red combs. Even Violet and Dash were out and about now they had both been neutered and were turning into beautiful sleek cats and, much to Graham's delight, proficient mousers.

'We would have lost the entire lot of peas if it wasn't for this pair,' he told me as he scooped them up, 'but there's been barely a nibble since Luke started to let them out and I haven't heard even the briefest of scrabbles in the bothy.'

I hoped they weren't as capable when it came to catching birds. We were all rather fond of the rotund robin and his bolshie ways.

'Well, that's good,' I said. 'I'm pleased it's all going so well.'

'And how are you?' Carole asked, handing me a mug of tea.

'Sorry?'

'Your cold,' she said. 'Has it finally gone?'

'Oh, yes,' I said, adding an obligatory sniff. 'I'm much better now, thanks, Carole.'

'Nothing worse than a head cold in warm weather,' she sympathised.

I nodded in agreement and tried not to notice that Luke had just wandered in to the garden carrying Jasmine and wearing a T-shirt that did nothing to disguise his physique, and low-slung cargo shorts that barely concealed the taut and defined abs I remembered sliding my fingers over, across and down.

'Are you sure you're all right, Kate?' quizzed Carole. 'You still look a bit flushed to me.'

'I'm fine,' I smiled, turning my back on Luke who had now put Jasmine down. I hoped he wouldn't notice me. 'My tea's a bit hot, that's all. I should have let it cool.'

'But you haven't had any yet,' Graham unhelpfully butted in.

Thankfully Violet chose that moment to dig her claws in and I was saved further embarrassment as he attempted to disentangle himself from her clutches.

'You're Kate, aren't you?' asked Jasmine as she came skipping up.

'That's right.' I swallowed, wishing she didn't look quite so adorable in her flowery little sundress.

'Mummy said you weren't coming back to the garden.'

'Did she?'

I wondered what else mummy had been saying.

'She said she wished no one would come back to the garden,' she added in a low whisper.

I felt rather sorry for Jasmine. I could well imagine she had been privy to far too many grown-up conversations in her short lifetime and I wasn't at all surprised that Candice wasn't as in love with the community garden as the rest of us.

'Daddy said I can have a little garden of my own,' the girl went on, looking longingly at the flowers, 'but he hasn't sorted it out yet.'

She sounded very mature and matter of fact. Another indicator that she spent too much time in adult company.

'How about in the meantime you start with this then?' I suggested, filling a seed tray with compost from the bag in the bothy doorway and handing her the tiny plastic fork and spade Lisa had bought for Archie.

'Oh, yes,' Jasmine squealed. 'Thank you, Kate.'

She arranged it all on the floor and began digging and poking and I slipped inside the bothy to busy myself tidying the trays and alphabetically organising the seed packets for absolutely no reason at all.

'Kate . . .'

I sucked in a lungful of air, determined to make the best of an awkward situation or at least not a complete fool of myself.

'Hello, Luke,' I said lightly, while staring intently at the instructions and reading all about how best to sow and thin rows of carrots to avoid the dreaded fly.

'Long time no see.'

I could hear he'd moved closer and purposefully took another step away.

'Mark said you hadn't been well.'

'Just a bit of a cold,' I shrugged dismissively.

'Well, anyway,' he said. 'I haven't come in here to check you were stocked up on tissues.'

'OK.'

I still hadn't looked at him, even though I knew he was looking at me . . . especially as I knew he was looking at me.

'I came in because I wanted to explain,' he started.

'About what?'

'Us, Candice, David and the painting, of course.' He was beginning to sound frustrated, as well he might with such an unwilling conversationalist to spar with.

'There's no need,' I said lightly.

'Well, I think there is.'

'But what's there to say?' I laughed, risking one fleeting glance from him to Jasmine before plunging my hands back into the organised assortment of packets.

'Plenty.'

'Look,' I interrupted, 'we've barely known each other long enough for there to even be an us, David is helping you find the portrait and your ex and your daughter have moved in with you. It couldn't be clearer.'

'What do you mean about that bit about us?' he demanded.

I didn't need to look at him to know he was scowling.

'Luke,' I sighed, 'I know you said you've fallen for me but you haven't, not really. You love the fact that I love this place and you've twisted those feelings into something else.'

I carried ruthlessly on, ignoring his poleaxed expression.

'It was just a bit of fun.'

'Not for me,' he began to say, but I cut him off again.

'Consenting adults,' I told him quietly, hoping his daughter couldn't hear, 'enjoying each other's company for a couple of uncomplicated, no-strings hours of fun.'

'You can't mean that.'

He sounded absolutely floored and I wasn't sure if that made me feel any better or not.

'I can,' I swallowed, 'I do.'

'*Really*?'

'Really,' I smiled, forcing myself to finally look at him properly, 'and even if I didn't, what would be the point in saying anything else?'

'What do you mean?'

I glanced out of the window at Candice who was striding in our direction.

'This whole situation,' I said, brushing by and trying not to breathe in the warm, heady scent of him, 'is what I mean.'

'Luke!' Candice shouted, from the bothy doorway. 'What's all this?'

She pointed to where Jasmine was happily playing.

'It's my garden, Mummy,' Jasmine beamed.

'She's filthy and her new dress is ruined!' Candice bellowed, ignoring the obvious delight in her daughter's voice.

Both Jasmine and her dress looked perfectly clean to me.

'It's my fault, Candice,' I piped up. 'Jasmine just wanted a little garden of her own, so I thought . . .'

Candice looked me in the eye and walked right over to where I was standing.

'You stay away from my daughter,' she hissed into my face. 'You stay away from all of us.'

'Candice!' Luke shouted. 'Don't talk to Kate like that.'

Candice turned her attention back to Luke and I managed to slip out of the bothy before their argument really kicked off.

'I'm sorry,' I said to Jasmine as I walked away.

'It's OK,' shrugged the little girl, distressingly sounding nowhere as upset as I expected she should.

It took a few more days for the portrait to arrive, along with my unwanted ex, and in that time a sickness bug swept through the Square knocking a fair few of us off our feet, but fortunately it passed in time for us to head back to Prosperous Place to watch the hanging. Of the portrait I mean, not my ex, although that perhaps would have been a preferable spectacle.

I was still reeling from Candice's behaviour, and, thanks to the bug, still feeling below par and dog-tired. I didn't think it would do me any harm to get away for a few days and so set about arranging a timely trip back to Wynbridge.

'Mum will be so chuffed you're coming back,' said Tom, when I called and asked if I could borrow his and Jemma's spare room for the duration of my stay.

I still felt guilty that I had put Mum and Dad off at Easter, but not so guilty that I was heading back to my childhood bedroom to keep my mum sweet.

'And I know she'd go nuts if she knew I wasn't encouraging you to go and stay with her and Dad, but with the kids already acting as if they're in summer holiday mode, I know Jemma would appreciate an extra pair of hands, especially in the mornings before she has to head to the café.'

I hadn't factored my feisty niece and truculent nephew into the equation any more than I'd planned on getting out of bed in the mornings. I hoped my getaway wasn't going to see me working as an unpaid au pair. If that was what my brother had in mind then I might as well move in with Lisa and John and save myself the journey to Wynbridge.

'I'll see you in a day or so, then,' I told him.

'Excellent,' he said.

'I'll text through the train times when I've booked my

ticket,' I added and quickly hung up, denying him the opportunity to apologise for assuming that I'd be happy to help out.

Planning the trip before heading to Prosperous Place for the portrait unveiling was supposed to have worked as a pick-me-up, something to look forward to after I had endured the sight of Luke and Candice playing happy families, not that the behaviour I had witnessed had suggested they were all that happy of course.

'What's all this?' I asked Lisa when I forced myself across the road to join everyone else and found the drive blocked by a couple of vans.

'Press,' she said, her unusually kohl-rimmed eyes shining with excitement and all traces of her post-bug pallor banished.

'And that one's local TV,' added Heather, who hadn't had the bug but had been allowed out of bed especially for the occasion, and was also sporting full make-up.

Clearly, they had both been made aware that this was going to be more of an occasion than I had.

'But what are they doing here?' I frowned.

Surely the arrival of one painting, no matter how much the family had missed it and paid for its eventual return, didn't warrant this amount of media attention. If it did turn out to be a fake, as I feared, then it wouldn't justify any at all.

'Didn't you get the note from Candice?' asked Glen.

'No,' I said. 'What note?'

He handed me a photocopied piece of paper which explained that now the media had been informed *who* owned Prosperous Place, and what the plans for it were, there was much interest in potentially filming the restoration and, although we were still welcome to watch the portrait hanging, we would only be allowed in if we were wearing something smarter than our ratty old gardening gear.

'What a cheek,' I tutted, shaking my head.

Given our last interaction I wasn't at all surprised that she hadn't made me aware of the situation.

'But forewarned is forearmed,' said Lisa, spritzing herself with perfume. 'I wouldn't have wanted to be on the telly or in the papers in my tracksuit bottoms and holey sweatshirt, even if it is only going to make the local news.'

She had more or less described what I was wearing to a T.

'And you never know,' beamed Heather. 'The story might get picked up by the nationals. I don't think you've ever really grasped just how famous Luke is, Kate.'

I was saved from having to answer by a familiar voice at my side.

'How thrilling is all this?' it said. 'This is going to be great for business.'

Lisa turned her back and walked away.

'Oh dear,' David continued, sounding crestfallen. He wasn't used to women turning their backs on him. 'Was it something I said?'

'I think it was more something you did,' I told him, as if he needed reminding. 'I'm guessing you were in on this charade then, were you?'

'Candice set it all up actually,' he said fondly. 'She's a very clever young woman,' he droned on, but was cut off from extolling her virtues when he caught sight of my face. 'Good grief. Are you all right, Kate? You look positively peaky and we won't want you in shot wearing that, will we? Why don't you ask Candice if she has a pretty dress and some heels you can borrow?'

It was on the tip of my tongue to tell him that I had a whole wardrobe full of pretty dresses just across the road, but then I remembered he still hadn't managed to work out where I lived and bit it back.

'It'll be fine,' I said instead. 'You needn't worry, I have absolutely no intention of being anywhere near a camera or a journalist. In fact, I think I might just slip off . . .'

I took a step away from David who was already engrossed in straightening his tie and turned straight into Luke's firm chest.

'Kate,' he said, putting his hands on my upper arms to steady me, 'you aren't thinking of going, are you?'

He looked every bit as sick as I felt, and thoroughly fed up to boot.

'I thought I might leave you all to it and pop back later,' I told him. 'I think that might be easier. After all, I'm still not feeling my best and I'm hardly dressed for the press, local or otherwise, am I?'

'Look, please don't go,' he said, catching me by the elbow and steering us away from David, who was running a comb through his hair. 'I need you here.'

'What on earth for?' I said, pulling gently free and wondering if my ex had always been so vain or whether I was only noticing it now because of the distance there was between us.

'Moral support,' shrugged Luke, 'a friendly face in the crowd.'

'You have Candice for all of that now,' I reminded him, 'I understand she's the one responsible for this media circus?'

'Yes,' he said bitterly, his expression darkening. 'And she knew perfectly well that I didn't want it but went ahead anyway. I didn't want any media hacks finding out that I had bought this place, let alone turn up to film it. All I really want is a quiet life, Kate, away from all of this kind of thing, but she still craves this ridiculous attention and publicity. She's always been the same.'

It sounded very much to me like they had got their wires crossed and I hoped they soon straightened everything out, for Jasmine's sake if no one else's. She was a lovely little girl, but it was more than obvious that she needed some stability in her life. However, I couldn't help thinking that the last thing Luke would be in for was a quiet life if he ended up spending the rest of his days with a media-obsessed other half.

As much as I disliked Candice, her manipulative manner and the hold she had over Luke, I had no choice but to hope that everything was going to work out for their daughter's sake. Even if her mother wasn't the best role model in the world, her father would be someone she could look up to and rely on, if he was given the chance to do things his own way, out of the limelight, of course.

I thanked my lucky stars that I hadn't had the chance to start relying on him myself. What had happened between us was bad enough, but any further emotional investment and I could have been in line for getting hurt all over again. I had got off lightly, hadn't I? Lisa and Heather might have believed in there being more than one true love for everyone in the world, but thankfully I had stuck to my beliefs and in the process saved myself a whole heap of delusion and unnecessary heartache.

The defensive route through the situation was the best, I decided.

'Well,' I began by asking, 'if Candice really does love all this attention so much, shall I expect to see you plastered across the pages of *Hello* magazine sometime soon?'

'Absolutely not,' said Luke, sounding furious.

'Or perhaps reclining on a chaise longue in one of the high-end interior magazines,' I teased.

'Whatever has got into you, Kate?' he demanded. 'I have

no idea what you're getting at, but I don't appreciate you making fun of the situation, especially as you know how I feel about it all.'

I didn't know really, but I couldn't seem to stop myself and I only had his word for it that he hated it as much as she obviously loved it. Laughing at Luke, and what Candice clearly wanted to turn him into, and them as a couple, wasn't funny at all; but I kidded myself into thinking that it was making me feel better.

'I think you're mistaking what I used to do for work for the real me,' he said sadly. I ignored the disappointment in his tone as he carried on. 'I never had you down as the sort of person who would do that, Kate.'

'You know, this place would make a great wedding venue,' I rushed on, looking around. 'Don't you think?'

An image of Candice wearing an excess of white and sweeping down the main staircase forced its way into my head. I was starting to feel sick again, but it was my own fault. If I had just focused on breathing in and out and being civil instead of coming out with such twaddle I would have been fine. Why wasn't I listening to what Luke was saying, what he was *really* saying?

'You aren't being serious?' he frowned as Jasmine skipped over with Candice in hot pursuit. 'Why are you talking like this? I can't believe you would think I'm in any way enjoying this, especially now you know me so well.'

But how well did I know him? I had been seduced by the Wentworth story and the house and the Square long before he arrived on the scene. Perhaps I had let my romantic inclinations slip out of the box I had sworn to keep them locked away in after David had broken my heart, but I knew it was time to pack them away again now and this time for good.

I'd never entertained the idea before, not even since Candice had arrived and upset the applecart, but for the very first time I wondered if buying number four Nightingale Square had been a mistake. Perhaps I should have listened to my mother and moved back to Wynbridge after all.

'You know that's not the sort of guy I am,' Luke whispered urgently in my ear.

'But that's the sort of guy Candice wants you to be,' I whispered back, 'and you need to think about what's best for your daughter,' I added as I tried to slip away.

'Kate,' nodded Candice, before I had moved barely an inch. 'I didn't think you would come.'

'Why wouldn't she?' Luke frowned. 'If it wasn't for Kate—'

'Well, as you can see,' I cut in, 'I'm hardly dressed for the occasion, so—'

'But as she didn't get your note, Candice,' said Lisa, who had realised what was going on and rushed to my rescue, 'that's hardly surprising.'

'Obviously I had no idea it was going to be such a big deal,' I added, bending to look at the little bunch of daisies

Jasmine had clasped in her hand and was trying to show me. 'Otherwise I would have unpacked my Prada pumps. These are pretty, Jasmine. Did you find them in the garden?'

Candice began to mutter to Luke and before I realised what she was going to do, she stepped between Jasmine and me and snatched the flowers from the little girl's grasp and threw them on the floor.

'Now we have to wash your hands again,' she said, pulling her away. 'You want to look your best for the cameras, don't you? You want to be a pretty girl like mummy.'

'Tell me,' said Lisa to Luke as we watched them march away, 'how did you end up hitching your wagon to a girl like that?'

Luke didn't say anything.

'Come on!' called David, ushering everyone together. 'Inside everyone, it's time.'

Even from my spot at the back of the gathered group I could tell within seconds that the painting Luke and David were carefully unwrapping was not the original portrait of Edward. Luke didn't know it of course, but the tell-tale throbbing vein in David's neck and the nervous glance he threw in my direction confirmed my fears.

'Oh, David, what have you done?' I asked him a few minutes later when everyone had surged forward to get a closer look.

The air was filled with the sound of cameras clicking and Luke and Candice had disappeared amid a flurry of clamouring journalists.

'Why on earth didn't you check it earlier?'

'Because I had no reason to doubt its authenticity,' he hissed.

I looked at him and raised my eyebrows.

'What?' he said, trying to sound innocent but failing miserably.

'Even after the exhaustive search Charlie had made,' I reminded him. 'Even after it turned out that there was absolutely no proof that the portrait had ever left Prosperous Place or the family, you still believed that a contact in the US could just happen to chance upon it and that everything we had uncovered here was wrong?'

David shrugged.

'You're out of your mind,' I told him. 'They'll rip you to shreds.'

He looked nervously over at the group who were still gathered around the painting, snapping away and studying it in minute detail.

'How could you have been so naive?' I scolded. 'You were excited the press were here an hour ago, you must have realised they were going to be the ruin of you.'

I couldn't believe he had been such a fool. I was going to get the hell out of there and fast. I didn't want my name associated with that painting. I was having nothing to do with it. I might have been taking a year out, but eventually I would want to work in the field again and I certainly didn't need a silly scandal like this dogging my reputation.

'I wanted to believe it,' he said, taking a step towards me and closing the gap between us. 'I desperately wanted it to be genuine because it was the only way I thought I could find my way back to you.'

Not this again.

'I thought that if I found this portrait for you, you would—'

'I would what?' I seethed. 'Fall back in love with you? Tell you I had made a mistake and that I didn't want a divorce after all?'

'Well, you made it clear enough at Christmas that you didn't want a baby,' he said, sounding hurt. 'So, I thought that if perhaps I could just show myself in a good enough light that *I* would become enough for you, like I used to be.'

How dare he sound hurt? And how dare he presume that I didn't want a baby.

'And I know that your passion for your work has always been your greatest love, Kate . . .'

'You ridiculous man!' I said, raising my voice. 'I don't suppose it ever even entered your self-obsessed head that I might still want a baby, but that I just didn't want to have it with you?'

He opened and closed his mouth, but no sound came out.

'And you seem to have forgotten that my having a child with anyone is a bit of a longshot now and as for this whole *you* being enough for *me* idiocy, what on earth makes you think that I would *ever* feel that way about you again, after everything you did?'

He didn't have time to answer, which was probably just as well, as I might have been tempted, for the first time in my life, to resort to physical violence; and that would have been far from ideal given the number of media men and women within a twenty-foot radius.

'So,' said Luke, bounding across the room in three strides and looking happier than I had ever seen him. 'What do you think?'

'I think it's a fake,' I floored him by saying.

I could have bitten my tongue off and shot David a look. It was his fault that I was in such a temper and now Luke was going to get the brunt of it.

'What?'

'It's a forgery,' I said firmly, 'a spurious imitation of the very lovely, but still lost, original.'

The next thing I knew Candice was at Luke's side, reaching for his hand and scowling at me.

'How dare you,' she spat.

I shrugged, but didn't take the allegation back.

'She's lying,' she said, keeping her voice low to avoid catching any unwanted attention. 'She's sulking because

David found it and now she has no reason to come over here for cosy nights in front of the fire with you.'

I looked at Luke and shook my head, wondering just how much he had told her.

'He told me all about your little tryst,' she laughed. 'And it doesn't matter to me in the slightest.'

'It doesn't matter to me either,' I laughed back.

'What are you talking about, Candice?' David demanded, sounding furious.

Clearly it was acceptable for him to have an assignation when we were married, but not for me to have one when we were very nearly divorced.

'Well, that's good then,' Candice continued in a spiteful sing-song tone, ignoring David. 'I'm pleased you realised that he was prepared to do whatever it would take to keep you onside and looking for his precious portrait.'

'Of course,' I said, crossing the room to the door and pointing back to the wall. 'The only problem he has now is that this isn't the precious portrait he's been looking for at all.'

Chapter 27

'Where did you disappear to?' Lisa demanded through the letter-box the next morning when I refused to answer the door.

'Here,' I shouted back along the hall. 'I wasn't feeling well again, so I just came home.'

That wasn't a lie. I'd been sick twice when I got home and then slept for hours, waking just before dawn and feeling no better for it. I was seriously thinking about cancelling my trip to Wynbridge.

'Are you going to let me in?' she continued to bawl. 'Or am I going to have this conversation on my knees with the rest of the Square listening in? Carole and Graham's curtains have gone into overdrive.'

'I don't think you should come in,' I shouted back. 'I don't want to pass this damn bug back to you again.'

'I don't think I can catch what you've got,' she said, her voice a little quieter, 'and besides, you know there's always some bug or another doing the rounds in our house. You don't have as many kids as I have traipsing through your house without developing a pretty cast-iron immune system.'

'So, what is it that you reckon I've got then?' I asked, as I finally gave in and opened the door.

'Well,' she said, looking me up and down and shaking her head as if she wasn't sure whether or not she should say it. 'I know this might sound completely insensitive in view of our recent conversation, but if I didn't know any better, I'd say you were pregnant.'

'Pregnant?'

'Mmm,' she said, cocking her head to one side before she pushed by and walked into the kitchen where she quickly filled the kettle and arranged two mugs. 'Sorry,' she went on, 'but given the way you look that's my humble opinion.'

I remembered how she had marched in, with little Archie on her hip, and taken over the very first day I arrived in the Square. She'd been doing it ever since and I couldn't imagine what my life would be like without her and Heather as my friends. That initial visit felt like such a long time ago, but actually it hadn't been all that long. Just a few months at the most.

'But,' she continued, 'given what you did tell me last week, combined with the fact that it's been allegedly well over a year since you had intimate contact with something that doesn't require double A's, I can't be completely sure.'

'You cheeky mare,' I told her, flushing scarlet and having a crafty look at the calendar while her back was turned.

'What?' she laughed, clearly feeling relieved that I hadn't been hurt by what she had said, about being pregnant at least. 'There's nothing wrong with—'

'I have absolutely no desire to hear what you're going to tell me there's nothing wrong with, thank you very much,' I said firmly, abandoning the search for the last star I would have marked in red pen and which would ordinarily be the first thing I would see. 'But can we just change the subject, please? I'm certain I've just got the same bug as the rest of you.'

'Fair enough,' she conceded, for once allowing diplomacy to intervene.

I was both surprised and relieved she was so willing to let the idea drop, but I knew that had she been aware of my Easter celebration she wouldn't have let it go.

'Have you seen the headline this morning?'

She quickly flattened the local newspaper out on the kitchen table.

'Front page,' I tutted. 'Must have been a slow news day when they set this up.'

'Slow news day my eye,' she said, looking over my shoulder. 'Look at the three of them. This editor knows what he's about. If that doesn't sell column inches I don't know what will!'

She was right of course. The sight of Luke, Candice and Jasmine beaming out at the camera was perfection itself, even if I thought the smile on Luke's lips didn't quite reach his eyes. I wondered if he was holding back because he was still annoyed about being unmasked as the owner of Prosperous Place or if he was thinking about what I'd said about the portrait.

'Did you stay long after I'd gone?' I asked Lisa as she stirred the two cups of steaming coffee.

I wasn't sure I was going to be able to drink mine. It smelled OK, but I wouldn't be responsible for how my stomach reacted to the taste.

'Not really,' she shrugged. 'As soon as the press disappeared Candice made it very clear that she wanted us lot gone.'

That didn't surprise me at all. She had all the makings of a stereotypical trophy wife, keen to keep the gates of her domain closed and guarded, not that I could imagine that was what Luke wanted. Yes, he was happy to keep the media at bay but he had welcomed the rest of us with open arms.

'I hope she doesn't make Luke shut the garden down,' I muttered, knowing that the last thing Candice would want would be us lot traipsing all over her private realm.

'She wouldn't do that, would she?' Lisa gasped. 'Not after all our hard work.'

'I wouldn't put it past her,' I shrugged.

I knew I sounded bitter, but I also knew there was more to this girl than met the eye. I hoped Luke had been very careful about ensuring he would hang on to his legacy should anyone ever try to prise it from his grasp.

'You really don't like her, do you?' Lisa asked.

Had she been privy to the dressing down Candice had given me in the bothy, and the way she talked to Jasmine, she wouldn't have had to ask.

'Not really,' I said, playing down my true feelings under her eagle-eyed attention. I didn't want Lisa to think that it was just jealousy that had turned me off Candice. 'But if she's here for her daughter's sake, then that's fair enough and I wouldn't have minded her half as much if she hadn't gone against everything Luke wanted yesterday to be about.'

'What do you mean?'

'All this nonsense,' I said, with a nod to the paper. 'He told me that all he wanted was a quiet life, with none of this press and media fuss. He's been trying to keep his family history and this place a secret from the world of celebrity, or whatever you call it, but at this rate he won't even be able to go down to the shops for a pint of milk without getting papped.'

'Oh,' said Lisa, looking back at the newsprint.

'He told me that when he left his career behind he thought – he hoped – it would be the end of seeing his face in print, but if Candice gets her way, it will be in there even more than before.'

'You might be more right about that than you realise,' Lisa agreed. 'I heard her chatting to the TV guy just before we left and from what I could make out she was hoping to set up a meeting.'

'What sort of meeting?'

'Apparently she's very taken with that *Normal for Norfolk* documentary. And if what she put on the note about yesterday is anything to go by, I reckon she fancies having some sort of docu-soap made about Prosperous Place and its restoration.'

'I can't see Luke agreeing to that,' I said. 'But if she does go ahead then that'll be the garden gone for sure.'

'How do you work that out?'

'Well, she's hardly going to want to share the limelight with you lot, is she?'

I didn't include myself in the scenario. If the cameras moved in then I would definitely be moving out, from the garden at least. I couldn't believe for one second that Candice's interest in televising the restoration of the house would lead to her sharing the details of the Wentworth legacy or any local history for that matter. This latest stunt was going to be all about keeping her face on the front page and on the TV screen. I shuddered at the thought.

'It would be good publicity though,' said Lisa, seemingly still not taking on board the implications for everyone else.

'But for who?' I snapped.

Candice would get plenty, I was sure, but Luke neither wanted it nor needed it.

'And what would be the point in it? It isn't as if Luke's planning to open the place up to the public, is it?'

'Who knows,' Lisa shrugged. 'But from here on in I reckon that what Luke wants might not matter if Candice has anything to do with it.'

It was a horrid thought, but she was right.

The second I closed the front door behind my friend I raced back to the kitchen and snatched the calendar from its hook on the wall next to the sink. My heart was hammering as I realised I wasn't just a couple of days late; I had now more than missed my period. I had made an appointment to have a health check-up but thoughts of a potential pregnancy hadn't even entered my head. I was 'fertility challenged'. It was practically impossible that I would fall pregnant through properly trying, so a one-night stand resulting in a quick conception had to be an absolute impossibility.

I slumped at the table with my hands in my hair thinking about all the novels I had read, all of the television programmes I had watched where women had ended up pregnant and then acted as if it had taken them completely by surprise. I used to hate scenarios like that. I didn't think anyone could be that naive, or that irresponsible or that stupid, and yet here I was, potentially pregnant and completely and utterly shocked.

I glanced up at the clock. I was catching the train to Peterborough soon, but I still had time to buy a test, or perhaps I should wait until I was back in Wynbridge and do it there, safe in the nurturing embrace of kith and kin, with my mother and Jemma crowding around to see the result before I did and then spending hours quizzing me about the father when it was confirmed that I was with child.

With child . . .

'That'll be seventeen ninety-nine, please,' said the young girl behind the counter in the chemist.

'Thanks,' I said, tapping my card on the screen and bundling my random selection of purchases into my bag.

I don't think I'd ever raced to the shops and back so fast, but now I knew there was a possibility that I was having a baby there was no way I could wait another day to find out. Once inside the bathroom, I tore the cellophane wrapping off the box with shaking hands and skimmed the instructions.

'Pee on the stick,' I muttered to myself. 'One line not pregnant, two lines . . .'

Those two minutes were without doubt the longest of my life. How many lines was I hoping for? That was the fifty-million-dollar question. During the one hundred and twenty seconds I forced myself not to look, I think I talked myself in and out of the pleasures and pitfalls of single parenthood at least fifty million times.

This was not how I had always imagined this moment

would be. When, so long ago, I had been thinking about how I could convince David that starting a family wasn't the nightmare he had it pinned as, I never, not once, imagined that I would be crouching on a bathroom floor, on my own, without a wedding band and feeling . . .

The timer on my phone buzzed and I forced myself to my feet.

I pressed my forehead against the train window and closed my eyes, hoping the cool glass would temper the heat which was coursing through me and making my face look like an overripe tomato.

There had been two lines. Two very distinct, bright pink lines, although the packaging stressed that the 'presence of pink' did not denote the sex of the child, just that I was pregnant.

I was pregnant.

I had the wand wrapped in my handbag and the rest of the test stowed away in my suitcase so I could double check tomorrow. Like I needed to check. There was no way it could be wrong. I glanced around at the faces of my fellow passengers and wondered if any of them could guess just from looking at me. I wondered if any of them were carrying such an enormous secret.

There weren't many things in my life that I was obsessive about, but this had been one of them – I had always clung to the belief (ignoring the ridicule of my neighbours, who alleged that they were my friends in spite of our differences) that falling in love and the things that followed in relationships as a result, were meant to happen in a certain order.

In my head, life had to be neat and tidy and regimented. First, along came Mr or Mrs Right, then love, engagement, marriage, children and the HEA. However, given that I now found myself pregnant by a man I barely knew, in spite of the fact that I had been left challenged in the fertility stakes courtesy of the STD I had contracted from my so-called one true love, I couldn't help thinking that my idealistic theory was actually a little off kilter.

Perhaps Lisa had been right after all. Perhaps I did have to accept that life was a mess and a muddle where things sometimes happened out of order, but that the most important thing was to be happy and celebrate the fact that they had happened at all.

'Tickets, please,' called the guard.

I rifled through my bag for my phone and opened the app, wondering if I was going to have to invest in a car for future trips back to Wynbridge. I didn't think I'd ever seen anyone travelling by train with a tiny baby.

'Thank you,' said the guard, tapping the screen, 'enjoy your journey.'

'Thanks,' I responded, shoving the phone away again.

But how was I going to afford to run a car if I wasn't

working and how was I going to work if I had an infant in tow? I closed my eyes again and tried to block out the questions and scenarios which seemed determined to stamp all over the joyful moment I had waited so long for.

It was late afternoon by the time the train pulled into the station at Peterborough and it was a comfort to see Tom and Ella, my niece, waiting just beyond the platform barrier to welcome me home. I hoped they wouldn't be able to guess my news, or that I wouldn't break down and blurt it out, because I had no intention of telling anyone for a while yet. There were so many things to think about and I knew the announcement would be met with a barrage of questions. Questions I was determined to have answers to before I started picking out names and nursery colour schemes.

'Auntie Kate,' beamed Ella, squeezing me tight. 'It's so good to see you.'

I kissed the top of her head, barely having to bend to do so.

'However much have you grown?' I asked her. 'You weren't this tall when I left you at Christmas.'

Suddenly I remembered the manner of my departure post-Christmas, thanks to Mum's interference, and changed the subject.

'And how are you, Tom?' I asked. 'Still knackered?'

'Better than you by the looks of it,' he teased.

Did I really look that bad?

'No wonder you didn't want to get your face in the paper or on the news.'

'What do you mean?' I frowned.

'That house called Prosperous Place,' Ella gushed. 'Mum said it's just at the end of your road. It's been all over the telly.'

Given everything else I had going on, I had completely forgotten that Wynbridge and Norwich shared the same East Anglian newspaper and television news channels, and that everyone had no doubt seen the Prosperous Place coverage in all its glory.

'And Jemma wants to know why you've never mentioned the owner before,' added Tom meaningfully.

He didn't sound particularly impressed, and I guessed the reports and coverage had caused quite a stir in my home town once the connection to where I lived had been made. I shrugged, trying to convey that the presence of someone like Luke in your life was an ordinary everyday occurrence. Which, I supposed, for the last few months it had been.

I felt myself going hot again as I thought about the very different bombardment of questions I was now going to have to face, along with how on earth Luke was going to react when he found out I was pregnant. He had already had one ready-made family turn up since his arrival and I was fairly certain he wouldn't want another camping out on his doorstep. Was I going to have to leave Nightingale Square and my lovely little home so soon?

'My god,' tutted Tom, snatching at my suitcase and pulling up the handle so he could wheel it out of the station. 'You've gone bright red just thinking about him, Kate. Personally, I can't see what all the fuss is about.'

Ella looked at me and winked mischievously.

'Mum says that's because you're jealous.'

I bit my lip, but was in no position to wind him up. It was a shame because this was just the sort of fodder siblings thrived on as a rule.

'Come on, Auntie Kate,' giggled Ella conspiratorially as she linked her arm through mine. 'Mum told Dad we have to hurry up because she can't wait to hear all about him.'

Chapter 28

The shock of discovering that practically the whole town knew about the presence of famous Luke Lonsdale in our tiny corner of the world was fortunately enough to stave off the nausea which had been plaguing me for longer than I had initially realised.

During the brief journey back to Wynbridge Tom readily accepted my pallor was the result of the neighbourhood sick bug and told me that half the employees in the council department where he worked had succumbed to something similar. I only hoped that Jemma would be so easy to fool, and held my bag with the pregnancy test wand wrapped inside closer to my chest.

'Here she is at last,' she squealed the second I crossed the threshold. 'Neighbour of the most handsome man in the world.'

'Thanks,' said Tom, dumping my case.

'You know what I mean,' Jemma laughed, planting a consolation kiss squarely on his lips.

'Unfortunately, I do,' he said, a smile gently tugging at the corners of his mouth. 'And while you get it off your chest and have a good gossip, I'm going to the pub for a pint.'

'All right,' she beamed, pecking him briefly on the cheek this time. 'Dinner will be ready in a couple of hours.'

'Just make sure you've exhausted the topic by the time I get back,' said my brother as he headed towards the front door, 'and then we can go back to bloody normal around here.'

I sighed and bent to pull off my shoes. I didn't want to have to talk about Luke for two minutes, let alone two hours, but there was a glint in Jemma's eye and an open bottle of wine on the kitchen counter which suggested I wasn't going to have much say in the matter.

'Is it too early?' she asked, pouring herself a small glass. 'I opened this to cook with and thought, why not?'

'It's a bit early for me,' I said lightly, 'especially after that journey.'

'Coffee, then,' she suggested, reaching for the kettle.

I still couldn't face tea or coffee either, but I knew I had to drink something.

'Have you got anything chilled?' I asked. 'My taste buds,' I cleverly added, 'have been all over the place since I've had this bug.'

She found some fruit cordial in the fridge, poured me a

glass and then beckoned me over to the kitchen table where the newspaper was spread out in all its glory.

'I just can't believe this,' she said, pointing at the photograph of Luke, Candice and Jasmine, which Lisa had shown me earlier. 'Why ever didn't you say anything when you came home at Christmas?'

'He wasn't living there then,' I said honestly. 'As far as I knew in December the place had been sold to some development consortium and was going to be ripped apart.'

'No way,' Jemma gasped, looking back at the photograph of the impressive Prosperous Place.

'And you'll laugh at this,' I said, rolling my eyes and deciding that hamming it up might help get me off the hook. 'When he did arrive and I first met him, I didn't even know who he was!'

'You're kidding,' Jemma spluttered, choking on her wine. 'You're not being serious.'

'I am,' I told her. 'Straight up, I didn't have a clue.'

Jemma shook her head.

'It wasn't until he invited us all to dinner on Valentine's Day that—'

'Hang on,' she said, holding up a hand to stop me, 'are you telling me that on Valentine's Day evening, when I was stuck in the pub for the umpteenth year on the trot, you were being wined and dined by Mr Beautiful.'

'It wasn't an intimate meal for two, Jem,' I said, giving the suggestion the tut it deserved. 'I was there along with everyone else from the Square and it was then that some friends realised who he was.'

'Unbelievable,' she laughed, taking another sip of wine and raising her eyebrows. 'And tell me, is he every inch as gorgeous as he looks in the glossy ads?'

'I don't know,' I tutted, banishing all thoughts of how honed his biceps looked covered with a thin sheen of sweat, 'I can't say that I've seen many of the glossy ads.'

'You don't sound all that bothered,' she pouted.

Clearly my reaction to having Luke Lonsdale as a neighbour wasn't living up to my sister-in-law's expectations at all. If only she knew the true story behind the façade. She'd fall over in a dead faint if I gave her all the delicious details.

'I'm not all that bothered to be honest,' I shrugged.

'But still,' she said, flicking through an old copy of *Vogue* until she found what she was looking for. 'You can't tell me that you aren't even a little bit stirred by a sight like that?'

She dropped the magazine on top of the newspaper and together we admired the image in silent awe.

Reclining on a speedboat, amid a sparkling sea, with a cerulean sky above and wearing an almost indecent pair of swimming trunks, was the father of my unborn baby. His dark curls were slicked back from his face, his eyes were smouldering and his flawless physique glistened in the sun.

The tiniest of sighs escaped my lips as I remembered the weight of that body on mine and Jemma pounced.

'I knew it,' she grinned.

'Well, I am only human, I suppose,' I joined in.

What on earth would she say if I told her where I had celebrated Easter and how Luke had laid me down in front of the fire and his sperm had gone off on a very different kind of egg hunt?

'What's so funny?' she asked, turning her attention back to the paper.

'You,' I lied, biting my lip, 'and all this. I can't believe it's such a big deal.'

'I live in a small town,' she shrugged, 'where there's little scandal and even less crumpet.'

'I'm sure my brother would be delighted to hear you say that.'

'You know what I mean,' she nudged.

I wondered how she would feel if Tom had been drooling over some glamorous, glossy goddess.

'And besides,' she added, lifting the lid on the slow cooker and releasing the most delicious smell from the stew within, 'he spent a good long while taking in that Candice's credentials before I got hold of the paper to see what all the fuss was about.'

'Fair enough,' I laughed, secretly pleased that my brother had been doing his bit to maintain equilibrium. 'She is pretty, isn't she?'

'I suppose,' said Jemma, replacing the lid and coming back to the table. 'What's she like? As a person I mean, is she a good match for Luke, do you think?'

'I can't think of anyone less suited,' I told her and I really meant it.

It was bad enough knowing that Candice had once captured Luke's heart and was now poised to pin him down again, but the fact that they seemed to have absolutely nothing in common somehow made it all so much worse. Was she really what Luke wanted? Considering he had declared to me that I was his 'one true love', he hadn't fought particularly hard for me since she'd arrived on the scene.

'But credit to them both,' I sighed, forcing myself to think of the bigger picture, 'they seem determined to do the right thing by their daughter.'

'That's something, then,' Jemma smiled.

'Mmm,' I agreed. 'That little girl is an absolute sweetheart. She's the one who really matters in all this.'

'And how did David get in on the act?' Jemma asked, her tone changing as she shook her head and pointed out a photograph which had him highlighted in the background. 'Did you ask him to track down this painting Luke was so keen to get back?'

'Certainly not,' I insisted, skim-reading the paragraph which identified David as the magician who had conjured the portrait.

I didn't tell Jemma that I believed the painting was a fake and I was grateful that my name had been kept out of the newsprint.

'I got in touch with an old friend on Luke's behalf,' I explained because I felt I had to say something. The likelihood of David popping up without me having had anything to do with it at all would have been too unbelievable a coincidence. 'He was a mutual friend of mine and David's and in spite of my best efforts,' I sighed, 'word got back to him and he couldn't resist sticking his oar in.'

'To impress you,' Jemma asked, 'or undermine you?'

'From what I could gather the underlying motivation was to try and win me back,' I told her.

'He's determined not to give up, isn't he?'

'Well, he was,' I said, my eyes roving over the impostor portrait again, 'but I think we can safely say we've seen the last of him now.'

'Well, I hope so,' she said, giving my arm a squeeze, 'and I'm sorry I didn't stop your mum from asking him to visit at Christmas.'

'It's all right,' I said, squeezing her back, 'I know it was all done with the best of intentions.'

'So, what did you say or do to finally be shot of him?'

'I threatened to set my new best friend on him,' I said, with laughter on my lips.

'Oh, really?'

'Yep, and she's the sort who enjoys frying the balls of meandering men.'

'Is she now?' Jemma laughed. 'I think I'd get on well with this new friend of yours. I think I'd get on with her very well indeed.'

I was dead on my feet by the time we'd finished tidying away after dinner and excused myself early on the pretence of needing a good night's sleep before I faced Mum the following day.

'She can't wait to see you,' Tom had told me after he had bumped into Dad, who was also propping up the bar in The Mermaid pub. 'In fact, she was all set on calling round, but Dad went home and told her not to.'

I bet she had loved that, but nonetheless, she hadn't turned up and I was grateful for a few more hours on my own in which to get used to the idea that I was going to have a baby. I didn't know how I was going to manage looking after a baby, how I was going to afford a baby or even how I was going to explain the arrival of a baby, but I hoped with all my heart that I wasn't going to have to leave Nightingale Square. Lisa and Heather were the only friends I had who would be capable of supplying exactly the sort of no-fuss support network I was going to need to help me through it all.

*

'How did you sleep, Auntie Kate?' asked Noah, my nephew, at breakfast the following morning.

'I've had better nights,' I told him as I stifled the first yawn of the day and thanked my lucky stars that I wasn't stuck in the bathroom with my head down the toilet bowl. 'What about you, Noah?'

'I didn't catch a wink,' he told me.

On closer inspection he did look rather tired.

'Did you not?'

'Nope,' he said, slipping off his chair and leaving his bowl of cereal practically untouched.

'Come back and finish your breakfast,' Tom called after him, but Noah carried on up the stairs.

'Where's Jemma?'

'At the café.'

'And what's up with Noah?'

'Swimming,' said Ella, who had finally looked up from her phone. 'It's his class's turn to go swimming again and he hates it.'

'No phones at the table,' rumbled Tom.

Ella rolled her eyes behind his back and slipped the contraband device into the waistband of her jersey shorts.

'And why aren't you dressed yet?'

Moodily she followed her brother back up the stairs, banging her bedroom door for good measure.

'What's all this about swimming?' I asked, turning my attention back to Noah's problem.

I hated the thought of him dreading it so much. I had felt exactly the same when it came to cross-country and remembered all too well how that one hour of games used to mar the entire school day, along with the night's sleep before it.

'It's nothing,' grumbled Tom. 'He's just acting up.'

'Well, from the look on his face it didn't look like nothing to me,' I shot back.

'Well, you talk to him then,' my brother snapped. 'He can swim fine so I don't see what the problem is.'

'Maybe it's not the actual swimming that's the problem,' I snapped back.

I was determined that he was going to deal with the situation, even if he did have to get off to work.

'What are you getting at?'

'Which lesson did you hate above all others when you were at school, Tom?'

'French.'

He said it straightaway with no hesitation.

'And why did you hate it?'

'It wasn't the language,' he said, leaning against the work-top and abandoning the packed lunches as he thought back to his high-school days. 'It was the two-foot-tall Gestapo teacher who had it in for me.'

'Exactly,' I said, hoping he would make the connection and get the point.

'That bastard made my life hell,' he reminisced. 'It didn't matter what I did, or how hard I tried, he always put me down in front of the rest of the class.'

I raised my eyebrows and nodded in encouragement to try and make him think faster.

'So, what's your point?' he asked.

'My point is,' I said gently, 'that I wanted to remind you of the power something like that can have. Just because it doesn't seem like a big deal to anyone else it can have a massive impact on the person involved.'

'In this case my boy, Noah,' he nodded.

'Exactly,' I sighed, relieved that he'd finally got there. 'It's probably a clash with the teacher, or some low-level bullying in the changing rooms, but it's clearly ruining his opportunity to swim at school.'

'I'll deal with it,' Tom promised, wrapping his arms around me and kissing the top of my head. 'I'll make it my number one priority for today.'

'Good,' I said into his chest.

I was pleased I had been able to help.

'One day,' he said, holding me further away and looking right at me, 'you're going to make someone a great mum, do you know that, sis?'

The words felt like a bolt out of the blue. I shook my head and swallowed hard to stave off the inevitable tears I could feel building.

'Well, I don't know about that,' I croaked, 'but I do like to think I'm a pretty cool aunt.'

I had agreed to meet Mum at the Cherry Tree Café for mid-morning coffee (assuming I could stomach it), and a long overdue catch-up. She had wanted me to call at the house, but I had told her there was plenty of time for that as I was staying for a few days and that my priority for now was making sure I was around to help Jemma and Tom. The real thinking behind the public rendezvous of course was that it was neutral territory and would ensure my annoyance over what she had done at Christmas wouldn't get the better of me.

'Kate,' she cried, rushing across the café when I arrived and enveloping me in a long hug, 'you're here!'

She had already secured a table and ordered us a drink. Jemma cannily switched my latte for lemonade and disconcertingly winked as she decanted the crockery on to the table.

'No coffee?' Mum asked, noticing the change.

'You know Kate's had the bug from hell,' Jemma said breezily, 'her taste buds are totally up the spout.'

That glossed over the unsettling moment nicely as far as Mum was concerned, but I wasn't so sure about my sister-in-law.

'Have you seen the papers?' asked Lizzie, as she appeared from the kitchen with a tray of toasted teacakes.

'Yes,' I groaned. I was well and truly bored with the subject now and hoped my tone would put her off pursuing it. 'Jemma showed me yesterday and yes, I do live within spitting distance of the lovely Luke Lonsdale.'

'There's no need to be so base,' Mum tutted as she took two of the plates from Lizzie's tray.

'I'm not talking about the local paper,' said Lizzie, her red curls bouncing behind her vintage headscarf. 'According to Angela, he's all over the red-tops today.'

Chapter 29

Luke was indeed 'all over the red-tops' as Lizzie had so succinctly put it and he continued to be for the next few days. Lisa and Heather were keeping me abreast of what they could fathom was *really* going on via multiple texts from 'the eye of the storm' as they called it, and to be honest, I was pleased to be out of the way, even if I was missing the sanctuary and peace of my own four walls.

From what I could decipher from my combined sources of information, David had denied all knowledge of the portrait of Edward being a fake and was insisting that he had been as duped as everyone else by the seller in the US. So far everyone seemed to be buying his unlikely story, but had they known what Charlie had discovered, along with what Luke and I had learned from the letters I had found in the secret cupboard in my bedroom, I was sure they would soon change their minds.

I was surprised I hadn't heard directly from David. I thought he would be keen to ensure my silence. Perhaps he had assumed, given our history, that I would keep schtum out of loyalty. If that was the case then he couldn't have been more wrong. I was keeping quiet because I didn't want my name, face or reputation anywhere near the column inches that were suddenly devoted to the life and loves of a model turned 'property mogul'. My silence was nothing to do with protecting my sneaky ex at all.

However, the provenance of the portrait paled into insignificance in light of what happened next. When interest finally seemed to be waning, Candice set about cunningly using every trick in the book to keep the journalists attracted to her and Luke's story. Given the explicit details of the numerous outrageous tales she had 'let slip' about Luke, and the kind of life he used to lead, it sounded far from likely that she was really planning her own happy ever after with him. Had it been me at the centre of the frenzy I would have gone out of my way to keep it all under wraps, but she seemed to be revelling in the revelations and the extra column inches they afforded her.

I knew better now than to judge Luke on the basis of the life he had led; none of us had blameless pasts after all, but even if just one tenth of what had been written about him turned out to be true then I hoped the little life I was carrying inside me never decided to follow in his or her father's footsteps.

'So, is he the father then?'

I practically jumped out of my skin as Jemma threw yet more newspapers down on the kitchen table.

'What?' I croaked. 'What are you talking about?'

There had been other signs that Jemma knew there was more to my aversion to hot caffeinated drinks than the knowing wink in the Cherry Tree. Or at least my paranoia was making me think there had. The longer I stayed in Wynbridge the harder I was finding it to keep the lid on my secret. My nausea had made a comeback and I was going to have to buy new bras soon as my breasts weren't at all comfortable in the confines of such a restrictive cup. It felt inevitable that Jemma would suss me out soon. Having a daughter of Ella's age had made her adept at sniffing out secrets.

'This little girl, Jasmine,' she continued. 'You've seen her and Luke together, haven't you?'

'Yes,' I said, my lungs re-inflating when I realised I hadn't been rumbled.

'So, what do you reckon?' she quizzed. 'Is he the daddy?'

I didn't give two hoots about Candice or why, in this latest twist to their tale, she had decided to now imply that Luke might not be Jasmine's dad after all. I was more concerned about how the vulnerable little girl at the heart of all this mess was coping. I was certain Luke would be trying to shield her from the brunt of it all, but with a mother like Candice it must have been an uphill struggle.

'I don't know,' I said crossly, 'and to tell you the truth—'

I was going to say that I didn't care; but I did actually. Whether or not Luke was Jasmine's dad, and what he and Candice decided they were going to do after the media decamped, would almost certainly have some bearing on my future. I didn't expect or want anything from Luke, but I would have to tell him my own news soon. That thought alone was enough to crank my nausea up another notch.

'What?' Jemma urged when I didn't add anything else.

'I just hope it's all sorted soon, that's all.'

'Me too,' she said, flopping into a chair and kicking off her shoes. 'Can you imagine the damage all this is doing to that dear little girl?'

I felt my temperature rise as I realised I had made the mistake of lumping Jemma's interest in the story in with that of the gossiping masses. I should have known better than that.

'She looks about school age to me,' she added, peering at the page again and shaking her head. 'And the sooner her mother gets her act together and settles down, the better. Not that it's anything to do with me, of course.'

'Or me,' I said.

But it was quite a lot to do with me now, wasn't it? There was every chance, in spite of what Candice was trying to suggest, that Jasmine was the half-sister of the baby I was carrying. I hadn't thought about that before.

*

Things seemed to be coming to a head over the next couple of days and the media was full of rumours that Candice was going to be breaking into television soon.

'So much for you coming here to get away from it all for a couple of weeks,' Tom tutted, as he tossed aside another well-thumbed weekly magazine.

'What makes you think I have anything to get away from?' I asked him.

As far as I was concerned my trip back to Wynbridge was focused on building bridges with Mum and spending some quality time with my family.

'I just get the feeling that there might be more to you being here than a desire to sort out Noah's changing-room dilemma and curbing Ella's obsession with her phone.'

'Well, there isn't,' I shrugged, looking over at Ella, who was still glued to her screen.

Tom tutted and shook his head.

'I just wanted to spend some time with you guys,' I insisted, 'without the pressure of having to play nice because it's Christmas hanging over our heads.'

Tom laughed and I realised it was a sound I hadn't heard often enough recently.

'Fair enough,' he yawned, 'but at least, thanks to you, Noah can now enjoy his time in the pool safe in the knowledge that his bag and shoes won't have been dumped in the showers by the time he gets back to the changing room.'

I was pleased to have played a part in having sorted that out and Noah was over the moon and happily back to his mischievous self.

'That's true,' I smiled.

'Anyway,' Tom continued, 'the point I was really getting at is that it seems a bit odd that the unobtrusive little place you moved to, in the hope of enjoying a few quiet months, has turned out to be the hotbed of all this celebrity goss that the world has become obsessed with.'

'Yes,' I agreed, 'ironic, isn't it? I'm just grateful that I'm not there to have to witness it for myself.'

'And none of it is really anything to do with you?'

'Of course not,' I laughed. 'What a ridiculous thing to even think, let alone say!'

I shuddered to think what the world's press would make of the story I could sell them. I certainly wouldn't be worrying about how I was going to afford to buy a car with the money I could have banked from that particular headline.

'Fair enough,' said Tom, eyeing me astutely. 'And it's probably just as well you're not there.'

'Now that,' I told him, 'you are right about.'

The latest texts from Lisa and Heather were decidedly downbeat and I could tell they were getting sick of having to fight their way in and out of the gates just to water the tomatoes; Lisa had told me John was ready to thump the next person who blocked their drive and stopped him getting his van out for work at a decent hour. She had also hinted that David seemed to be spending quite a lot of time holed up in the house with Candice, but I wasn't much interested in that.

'Well,' said Tom, 'the media madness can't last for much longer. Tomorrow's D Day after all.'

'Don't you mean DNA day,' Ella muttered in the background, referring to the fact that Luke had insisted very publicly on taking a test to shut the speculators up.

'See,' said Tom as he pointed an accusing finger at the newspaper. 'Even my daughter is talking about it.'

'The sooner it's all over the better,' I agreed.

And I wasn't just thinking for Jasmine's sake either.

I was up early the next morning, keen to distance myself from both the newspapers and my phone which, even when switched off, was proving hard to ignore. I planned to leave it in my room until the evening, avoid the papers at all costs, work like a trooper for Jemma and catch up with things after dinner. By then the DNA result would be common knowledge and hopefully the first flush of interest in it would have died down. I had no doubt that Luke was Jasmine's dad, but it was tricky not getting caught up in the drama that had been created. Carole must have been wetting herself in excitement.

My stint in the kitchen had barely begun before I was catching snippets of conversations from folk who were engrossed in the saga.

'I'm shocked,' I heard a girl telling her friend as she waited in line for her first skinny latte of the day. 'It's not what I was expecting at all.'

'Well, I'm not surprised,' her friend forthrightly announced with a purposeful sniff, 'I had a feeling that this was going to happen all along.'

'How could you possibly have known that?'

'Why else would she have made such a fuss?' her friend went on in a sing-song voice which carried wide and far. 'Why would she go and say all those things about him if she was really planning to spend the rest of her life with him?'

'What do you mean?'

By the time I had dried my hands and poked my head out of the kitchen door they were headed for the market square, taking their opinions with them.

'Are you sure you're all right to be here, Kate?' Jemma asked when the early morning pre-work queue had died down.

The tables were already beginning to fill up with the elderly early risers who still shopped daily and made a stop at the café during a trip into town a priority. Looking around I knew I wouldn't have time for an attack of the vapours before the second wave of orders were lined up on the counter top. It was hardly surprising Jemma and her team were tired all the time.

'She still looks a bit peaky to me,' Lizzie chipped in from where she was setting out materials for one of her crafting classes which would be happening later in the day. 'You're working her too hard, Jemma. The poor girl's supposed to be here for a break.'

'I'm fine,' I insisted. 'My bug's gone and this is the first time I've been behind the counter since I got here.'

Jemma eyed me intently.

'Honestly, Jem,' I assured her, 'I'm fine and Angela will be here to help soon.'

She didn't have time to contradict me as the bell above the door rang out and I slipped back to my station at the multi-slotted toaster, ready to fill the inevitable requests for granary and white.

An hour or so, and many loaves later, things had slowed up a little and I was just thinking I might risk a hot drink when the bell tinkled again and I heard Jemma gasp. I had hoped it was Angela, the third member of the café team, who had called to say she was running late, but given my sister-in-law's reaction I guessed not.

'Please don't let it be a coach party,' I muttered, preparing to clear the decks and forcing myself not to speculate on what I had heard the two latte girls talking about earlier.

At least being so busy was helping to keep my mind mostly occupied and at this rate the day was going to fly by.

'Are you who I think you are?' I heard Jemma ask in a voice which didn't resemble her own at all.

She also sounded rather breathless and my ears pricked up to hear the response to her question.

'I suppose that would very much depend on who you think I am, wouldn't it?'

It couldn't be, could it?

'I think you might be Luke Lonsdale,' she said, sounding all a-flutter.

'Then in that case,' he confirmed, 'yes, I am who you think I am.'

'Luke,' I said, stepping out from the kitchen and wiping my hands down my apron. 'What on earth are you doing here?'

'Looking for you,' he said. 'I need to talk to you, Kate.'

He looked dog-tired and nothing like the glossy, groomed icon draped across the aftershave advert in the *Vogue* magazine Jemma had back at the house, but I didn't care. It was just so lovely to see him in the flesh, rather than staring out from the pages of a newspaper.

'We both do,' he added, bending down and standing back up with Jasmine in his arms. 'Don't we, poppet?'

The pretty little thing nodded then buried her face in his neck. She looked every bit as tired as he did, but then given everything that had been happening in her life during the last few weeks that was hardly surprising.

'Hello, Jasmine,' I smiled.

She turned to look at me for a second before going back into hiding. I wasn't at all surprised that she wasn't in the mood for small talk.

'Take my keys and go home,' Jemma insisted, as she fumbled about for them down the side of the till.

'But . . .' I stammered.

'No buts,' she insisted. 'I can't imagine that Luke Lonsdale, of all people, has travelled all this way to have a friendly chat with someone who purports to be just a neighbour.'

Luke and I looked at one another.

'I haven't said anything about us,' I told him quickly. 'Not to anyone.'

I didn't want him to think I was no better than Candice, sharing with one and all the intimate details of our fireside encounter.

'I thought you said there was no us,' he smiled, hoisting Jasmine a little higher.

'Just go home,' Jemma said again, finally tearing her eyes away from Luke. 'There's no one there and you'll be able to talk properly, in private.'

'But you'll be busy in here again in a minute,' I told her as she spun me around, untied my apron and ushered me towards the door.

'And Angela will be here to help,' she said. 'Seriously, just go before someone recognises you, Luke. We can manage here just fine.'

Back at the house Luke settled Jasmine on the sofa and snuggled her under a blanket while I made us both a drink. I was going to risk a weak shot of caffeine whatever the consequences.

'Is she OK?' I asked as he pulled out a chair and sat opposite me at the table.

'Out like a light,' he nodded, 'and she slept all the way here. She's exhausted.'

His car was now parked outside and I hoped no one would recognise it. Not that that was very likely.

'And is she actually, you know, not yours?'

'Of course she's mine,' he said, shaking his head. 'I've never thought any different.'

'So why did you take the test? What made you go through all this?' I frowned, pointing at the stack of newspapers which had grown beyond belief since my arrival.

I wanted to ask why he hadn't confided in me. Didn't he trust me? Probably not, given that I had dismissed even the possibility of there being an 'us' the second he had declared his feelings and suggested there could be.

'Because I didn't want Candice to get the jitters and disappear with her,' he said. 'I've known since she was born that Jas was my daughter, but it wasn't until Dad died, and I got

406

my act together, that I realised what it meant to be a father. Suddenly sending Candice money for her wasn't enough. I was failing my little girl and I wanted that to change.'

'I see.'

So he hadn't been completely shirking his responsibilities as Candice had told David.

'I searched everywhere for them, even when I went away before Easter to think about us, I was still looking.'

'And then she turned up of her own accord anyway.'

'Yes, it turns out Candice had got word of me buying Prosperous Place and thought she'd struck gold, but I've only ever been interested in Jasmine and as far as the papers were concerned,' he went on, 'I tolerated them because they gave her mother enough rope to prove that she isn't fit to own a dog, let alone take care of a child.'

'So, you just went along with it all to show Candice up for what she really is.'

'Yes.'

'Right.'

This was a lot to take in.

'And I couldn't risk telling anyone,' he said, looking back at Jasmine. 'There was too much at stake.'

That answered my question about trust and rather than continuing to feel hurt, I felt touched that he was prepared to put Jasmine's welfare above everything and everyone else; even himself.

'I'm sure you've seen what's been said about me in the papers,' he went on when I didn't say anything.

'I've seen some of it,' I told him, 'but when I got the gist of the depths she was prepared to sink to I made a conscious effort to avoid as much as I could.'

'I'm pleased,' he said, turning red. 'More than half of it wasn't true anyway.'

That meant that almost half of it was. I didn't like to speculate which half that might be.

'So, what was her motive?' I frowned. 'What was Candice really hoping to get out of the situation?'

'More money,' he said without hesitating. 'And when she realised I'd sunk most of what I had into the house she went to the papers to further her profile and give her media career a boost.'

'Crikey. How . . . resourceful.'

I couldn't believe anyone could be that calculating. I had soon worked out that Candice was manipulative, but this took her scheming to a whole new level.

'I can't believe you put up with it all for so long,' I sighed, 'she was set to ruin your reputation just to make a name for herself.'

Luke shrugged.

'I don't care about that,' he said, looking embarrassed, 'but I'm sorry for how she spoke to you.'

'You don't need to apologise for her,' I told him.

'I know I don't,' he said, 'but she'd never think to do it herself and I couldn't bear it if you thought I had accepted her for no good reason. I was just going along with it all because I was trying to protect Jas. If I'd started picking Candice up on everything she'd have sussed me out in a heartbeat. If she knew I was on to her she would have vanished again, taking my little girl with her and that was the last thing I wanted to happen.'

'So where is she now?' I asked. 'Candice, I mean.'

Luke reached across the table and grasped my hand.

'I hope you'll forgive Lisa for telling me,' he shocked me by saying, 'but having explained to me what a shit that ex of yours has been in the past it came as no surprise to me that—'

'He and Candice have disappeared,' I guessed.

Given what Lisa had said about the pair of them spending so much time together I wasn't surprised.

'Correct.'

'You mean they've gone off together.'

'Exactly.'

I squeezed his hand and then let go.

'I'd rather Lisa hadn't talked to you about my relationship with David,' I sniffed.

I felt more perturbed about that than my ex's behaviour. I wondered just how much she had said. Did Luke now know about the chlamydia crisis as well as the infidelity? My pregnancy announcement would come as even more of a shock if he did. Not that I was about to make it any time soon.

'Please don't blame Lisa for that,' Luke said. 'She didn't want to talk to me at all.'

'So why did she then?'

'To stop me being angry,' he said, raking a hand through his hair. 'With you.'

'With me?' I laughed. 'Why were you angry with me?'

'Because I needed you,' he said. 'I wanted you by my side at Prosperous Place and you left. You told me there was no us, that the portrait was a fake and then buggered off.'

'Well, I'm very sorry,' I began, my annoyance growing before he had had a chance to finish.

'But when Lisa explained about everything you'd been through with David I began to understand.'

'That was considerate of you.'

'I could see that you wouldn't want to stick around to support a man who'd allegedly shirked his parental responsibilities,' he went on in spite of my interruption, 'and who in the past had supposedly had more women on the go than Hugh Heffner.'

I couldn't help but smile.

'Not as many as Heff,' I said, 'surely?'

'I did say supposedly and I'm trying to be serious,' he said. 'I soon realised that you weren't going to stick around to get hurt all over again and I vowed that as soon as this whole charade was over, I'd find you and explain.'

'But you still haven't told me why Jasmine is with you.'

'OK,' he said, dragging in a deep breath. 'Well, Candice has left with David, and the portrait.'

'And the portrait?'

This was getting more bizarre by the second.

'Yes,' he said. 'Let's just say I didn't want it in my sight. You were right about it being a fake and when I discovered he'd gone out of his way to procure it to try and win you back I banished him, and it, from the house, grounds, every-where I could think of.'

'Right,' I said, trying not to smile again. 'I see.'

That was one sight I would have liked to have witnessed.

'Anyway,' he went on, 'David and Candice left together.'

'Without Jasmine?' I gasped, the realisation only just dawning.

Her mother didn't want her. Luke nodded.

'Candice didn't want her tagging along,' he said, echoing my thoughts. 'Jas is just an inconvenience now she's got this whole new media-slash-reality-show-host career on the horizon. Obviously, she won't be filming a show about Prosperous Place any longer, but there have been plenty of other offers.'

'You aren't telling me she's really left her little girl behind?' I gulped, my eyes filling with tears at the thought.

Luke nodded again.

'But that's what I wanted,' he said. 'This is the outcome

I've been hoping for all along. I can give my daughter a far more settled home life than Candice ever could.'

'But Jasmine hardly knows you.'

'Don't worry about Jas,' Luke smiled. 'She's the most adaptable kid I know and don't forget, I am her father. We're both looking forward to getting stuck into the catching up we've got to do.'

Chapter 30

Dinner that evening was an interesting affair.

'You should feel honoured, mate,' Tom told Luke with a wink as he helped Jemma gather the post-meal dishes together. 'She doesn't bring out the Denby service and crystal glasses for just anyone, you know.'

Jemma flushed scarlet and whipped the back of Tom's legs with the tea towel she had draped over her shoulder.

'Feel free to ignore my brother,' I told her, trying to save her blushes. 'He's just jealous because no one has ever paid him an extraordinary amount of money to lay half-naked across a speedboat in Venice.'

'I'll have you know,' laughed Tom, 'that we're thinking of doing one of those naked calendar things at the council next year to raise funds for the new leisure centre.'

'That'll set the project back another few years then,' I shot back, sticking my tongue out and ducking out of the way before his hand had time to cuff the back of my head.

'Are they always like this?' Luke asked Jemma as he handed her his empty wine glass.

'Pretty much,' she said, with a sigh. 'They seem to regress after they've shared a bottle of red. Not that Kate has drunk any tonight,' she caught my attention by saying.

'Tom,' I interrupted, 'why don't you take Luke for a drink down the pub? Introduce him to the delights of Wynbridge and a few of the locals.'

'Because I'd never hear the last of it,' Tom told me. 'And besides, I'm sure Luke would prefer an evening where there wasn't a chance of his face popping up in the papers the next day and that he'd rather stay here with Jasmine, isn't that right, mate?'

'I would, yes,' Luke said, 'but only as long as we're not intruding.'

'Of course you're not,' said Jemma. 'Our sofa is at your disposal for as long as you want it.'

'And Jasmine can sleep on the futon in my room,' Ella kindly offered as she wandered in with the uncanny knack of one who could telepathically tell when the clearing up was done. 'But only if she wants to.'

'I'm sure she'd love that,' said Luke, this time making my niece colour, 'thank you, Ella and thank you for keeping her amused this evening.'

Once the children were finally settled for the night, Luke and I took a walk around the garden.

'Jasmine certainly seems to be taking everything in her stride,' I told him as I looked back towards the house.

Out of the three youngsters, she was the one who had gone to bed with the least amount of fuss.

'Like I said earlier, she's the most adaptable kid I know,' he sighed. 'But with a mother like she's had to put up with, always dragging her from pillar to post and moving her to a new home every other week, she's had to be.'

'I hadn't thought of it like that,' I said, slipping my arm through his. 'She's very lucky to be with you, Luke.'

'Do you really think so?'

'Absolutely,' I said. 'She'll be starting school soon and she needs some stability and security to make that transition.'

'She needs to be around kids her own age rather than adults all the time,' he said, nodding back to the house. 'She needs this.'

'What do you mean?'

'Family,' he said. 'She needs family and kids her own age to play and laugh with.'

Having watched her playing with Noah and giggling with Ella like I'd never heard her giggle before, I knew he was right.

'I know from what Lisa told me that you have some very fixed ideas about how life and love should be, Kate,' he smiled.

'They're not quite as fixed as they used to be,' I gently corrected him.

'Well, that's good,' he said. 'Because life and love can get pretty messy sometimes.'

I inadvertently pressed my hand to my stomach, thinking he was telling me nothing I hadn't now worked out for myself, but I didn't say as much.

'And I'm hoping that you'll change your mind about there being no us, Kate, because I would love it if your family became my family. If you became my family, mine and Jas's.'

'Really?' I asked, looking up at him.

'Really,' he said, staring deep into my eyes. 'I want there to be an us, Kate. I've always wanted there to be an us, right from the moment I bumped into you in the street and then caught you sneaking around my garden.'

I laughed as I remembered how he had ended up carrying Carole after she twisted her ankle and how I had later assumed he was just some flashy sod with no depth and even less soul. It all felt like years rather than months ago. So much had happened in such a short amount of time.

'I suppose,' I told him, still locked into his gaze, 'that if nothing else, the history between our two homes just goes to prove that there should be an us, doesn't it?'

'Exactly,' he said, pulling me into his chest.

I didn't resist and wrapped my arms around his back.

'Come away with us tomorrow,' he whispered, kissing the

top of my head. 'Let's disappear, the three of us and learn how to become the family I want us to be.'

It wasn't anything like how I had always imagined my 2.4 little unit would be, but it sounded good to me.

'All right,' I told him. 'If that's what you want, I will.'

'It is,' he sighed, 'but is it what you want?'

'Yes,' I said. 'It is. I can't think of anything better, as long as you're really sure? I'd hate to make more of a muddle for Jasmine if things didn't work out.'

'Things will work out.'

The thought of eventually returning to Nightingale Square and my home and friends and Prosperous Place, with Luke and Jasmine, filled my heart with joy.

As I stood, content and safe in Luke's embrace part of me was thinking this was the perfect opportunity to tell him about the baby, but I just couldn't bring myself to do it. I still needed to live with the news a little longer myself before I shared it with anyone else, even him.

'Things will work out,' he said again.

'In that case,' I told him, 'we'll leave first thing tomorrow, and I'll help you track down Edward's portrait if it's the last thing I do.'

When we'd gone back into the house that evening and explained to Jemma and Tom that we would be leaving together the next morning, my brother was quick to point out that we had nowhere to stay and that wherever we went, Luke was bound to be recognised.

'I know where they can go,' Jemma had announced, leaping up and grabbing her phone.

Ever resourceful she had telephoned her friend Amber from Skylark Farm and booked us a week in their little vintage-themed holiday bungalow. It was tucked away on the farm boundary and Luke, Jasmine and I spent a week there together, enjoying the glorious weather, playing games and building the foundations of a solid relationship. Jasmine was every bit as adaptable as Luke had suggested and hadn't forgotten how I had set her up with a little garden of her own.

'When we get home,' I told her, 'you can have another one.'

'With real plants?' she asked, wide eyed.

'And real flowers.'

She jumped up and threw her arms around my neck and I knew that life with my little ready-made family was going to work out just fine. Luke had tried to scotch my concerns that things between us were moving rather fast for folk who had only known one another for a few months, but it was Jasmine's unreserved affection that finally allayed my fears.

During that week I had planned to tell him about the baby every day, but I hadn't. Not sharing a bedroom ensured he hadn't the opportunity to notice the change in my figure, and watching him relax and focus on Jasmine, I didn't think it would be fair to divert his attention back to me. It was still early days, so there was plenty of time for him to get used to the idea.

It was exhilarating travelling back to Norwich in Luke's car with Jasmine strapped in the back, playing with the dolls Ella had kindly given her when they all turned up at the cottage to wave us off. As we raced along the A47 my mind drifted and it was thrilling to think that we were a little unit, just like millions of others, heading home after a catch-up with family and friends.

It was what I had always dreamed of, even though the child in the back wasn't my daughter, the man next to me wasn't my husband and the homes we were going back to were separated by a road and a communal patch of grass. It certainly wasn't the fairy tale I had spent my adult life chasing, but, I amazed myself by thinking, it was perfect nonetheless and it was real and it was mine.

I let out a contented sigh as we pulled back into the Square. Everything looked so different. The grass was longer, the trees were fuller and the soft warm breeze which wove around my legs when I opened the car door made me think that summer had arrived early in our cosy city patch of Norfolk.

'Do you want to come in?' I asked Luke once we had offloaded my bags in the hallway.

'Better not,' he said, with a nod back to the car where Jasmine was now fast asleep, the dolls still clutched to her chest. 'I should get her home and check Violet and Dash have been behaving for Carole.'

I imagined my nosy but well-meaning neighbour had been thrilled to be asked to undertake the task of house-sitting while Luke came to find me in Wynbridge. He had literally given her the keys to the castle.

'All right,' I nodded. 'Perhaps I'll see you tomorrow.'

'You'll definitely see me tomorrow,' he grinned, kissing me on the cheek and making my knees wobble in the process, 'and the day after that and the day after that.'

He was still saying it as he pulled away and I bent to pick the post off the mat, laughing at his silly performance. Once I had opened all the windows and made myself a small mug of tea – I could still only manage hot drinks in small doses – I sat in the back garden, ignoring the weeds and the grass which was in need of a trim and looked through the letters, bills and inevitable recycling which had arrived in my absence.

A letter from David proved the most entertaining. He apologised profusely for the fiasco over the portrait and begged me not to confront Charlie because it would be bad for future business to lose 'this most useful contact'. And all this time I had been labouring under the illusion that he was Charlie's friend. Was there no end to my ex's conning? I felt extremely grateful that I had finally managed to throw off the rose-tinted specs, and consequently barely skimmed the part of the letter in which he explained why he had done a bunk with Candice. I was more amused that he thought I would care and had felt obliged to offer an explanation.

When I had finished with it, I set the letter and envelope to one side, not even bothering to screw it up, and slowly drank my tea. Finally, I felt completely free of David and my marriage. I had thought moving from London the previous October and accepting singledom would have helped me shed the shackles, but Lisa was right. I wasn't the sort of person who could be happily single. It had taken falling in love again to truly set me free. So engrossed in this amazing thought, I didn't hear the doorbell and only looked up when approaching footsteps drew my attention.

'You're back!' smiled Heather. 'Finally!'

'Heather,' I said, jumping up to give her a hug. 'I've missed you so much. Where's Lisa?'

'Loitering in the house somewhere,' she tutted. 'Waiting to see if she's welcome.'

'What?' I said, looking over her shoulder because I thought she was joking, but there was no sign of the third musketeer.

'She didn't want to come at all,' said Heather, rolling her eyes. 'She thinks that because you haven't been in touch since Luke set off to find you, she's in the doghouse.'

'Is she really worried that I'm cross that she told Luke about David?'

Heather nodded and I shook my head.

'Get your butt out here, Mrs!' I called.

Lisa's solemn face quickly appeared around the side of the house. I'd never seen her looking vulnerable and sheepish before. It didn't suit her and I rushed to give her a hug so she knew that all was forgiven.

'You're not going to knock my block off, then,' she said tearfully when I finally released her, 'or poison my tea.'

'No,' I told her. 'But if you're that worried you can make your own tea.'

Behind us Heather laughed.

'I only told Luke because he was in such a state,' Lisa carried on, smoothing out a large envelope she was carrying and which my enthusiastic welcome had crumpled. 'He thought he'd lost you for good, especially when you didn't call or text. I thought if I explained to him about what you had been through with David then that would make him understand why you had disappeared . . .'

Her voice trailed off and I wondered what she would say and do if she knew the whole reason why I had headed home for a break. Not that I'd had much of a rest.

'What?' she asked, when she realised I had tuned out.

'It's nothing,' I said, shaking my head. The first person I had to tell about the baby was Luke. 'Everything's fine.'

'And are you and Luke actually a couple now?' Heather quizzed. 'Have you been together all this week?'

'Yes,' I sighed dreamily, 'we're a couple now. A very happy couple, and yes, we've been together since the day he left here.'

Heather clapped her hands and Lisa let out a long, slow breath, her eyes shining with tears.

'Now come on,' I said, 'let me make us all a drink, minus the poison, and then you can show me what you've got in that envelope.'

Because whatever it was that Lisa had brought with her, it was clearly important.

'So,' I said, bumping the tray on the garden table and handing round mugs and biscuits. 'What have you got in there, then?'

Lisa's face flushed and Heather let out a little squeal and clapped her hands together again.

'Are you sure we're OK?' Lisa asked.

She was deadly serious and I felt suitably guilty that I hadn't messaged her to help smooth the way before I came back.

'Honestly, it's all fine,' I told her, then added with a wink, 'but don't forget to drink all of your tea.'

She smiled and nodded, while Heather peeped cautiously over the rim.

'Now come on,' I insisted, brushing the moment off, 'what's with the paperwork?'

'Well,' Lisa began, sitting up straighter and carefully

pulling out a small pile of A4. 'You know I've been thinking about looking for a job?'

'Yes,' I said, trying to read the upside-down writing at the top of the first page. 'Have you found one?'

'Possibly,' she said, 'but it might not be what you're expecting.'

This was all very cryptic. I looked at Heather who was still grinning like a loon.

'And you know John told her to follow her heart,' she blurted out. 'Sorry, sorry,' she giggled, clapping her hand over her mouth so she literally couldn't say another word.

'Yes,' I said, thinking back. 'He did say something along those lines the day he helped me move some furniture.'

Heather impatiently tapped her free hand on the table, encouraging Lisa to get to the point before she burst.

'OK,' said Lisa, 'don't laugh.'

I shook my head. I had no intention of laughing at her.

'I've always wanted to be a writer,' she said in a rush.

I could see her face getting redder by the second and realised that this wasn't something she had said out loud very often before. In fact, given the way her voice was shaking, I imagined that what she was telling me was a long-held, but very secret, desire.

'I've got dozens of notebooks at home,' she continued, 'packed full of story ideas and snippets of conversations.'

'I've seen some of them,' Heather burst out again.

'And when I told John I was going to look for a job in a supermarket or something he said that I needed to give writing a proper shot first. He said I should send something I had written to a magazine or a competition.'

'OK,' I said, shuffling closer to the edge of my seat to get a proper look at the papers she was half hiding.

'So I did,' she said, a smile spreading across her face. 'I picked up a copy of one of the celebrity magazines a few weeks ago ...'

'Its was one of the ones with Candice on the cover,' Heather embellished. 'She'd been brewing her media campaign for a while before she turned up here, apparently.'

'And there just happened to be a short story competition in there,' Lisa continued, cutting her off. 'It was ridiculously close to the deadline, but I had something that I thought they might like so I thought what the hell and sent it in.'

'And?' I asked, urging her on.

'I've only made the bloody shortlist!' she squealed, her excitement finally matching Heather's as she shoved a print-out of the confirmation email under my nose.

'Oh my god, Lisa!' I squealed back. 'That's phenomenal.'

'Tell her what first prize is,' Heather said, shaking her head.

'The top three stories are all going to be published in the magazine,' Lisa told me, her eyes shining. 'But the winner gets an e-book contract with a top publishing house.'

I didn't know what to say. The whole situation had literally knocked the breath out of my body. Lisa looked at me and knew exactly how I was feeling.

'I know,' she said. 'It's nuts, isn't it? Even if I don't get any further, the story is going to be published in the magazine.'

'You'll get plenty further,' Heather nudged her. 'You're going to win it, Lisa, I just know it.'

'John's been telling me for years that I shouldn't give up on my dream, but what with the kids and everything I just never had the time to make it a priority.'

'I don't know what to say,' I told her. 'This is all so amazing.'

'I know,' she sniffed, tears coursing down her face. 'I told you I'd be the next one of us to cry all over the place, didn't I?'

'I think this calls for something fizzier than tea,' Heather sniffed along with her.

'I agree,' I said.

It wasn't until I'd said it that I realised that the fizziest thing I'd be drinking over the next year or so was lemonade.

'I can't, obviously,' Heather said, stroking her gently rounded bump, 'but you two can.'

'No,' I said recovering quickly. 'Let's not. Let's save it until the day Lisa is announced as the winner.'

By that time I would hopefully have had a chance to tell everyone about the baby.

'You're optimistic, aren't you?' Lisa sighed, looking long-ingly at the email.

Suddenly she didn't sound quite so excited.

'Well,' I said, reaching across the table for her hand, 'you know how much I've always loved a fairy-tale ending.'

Chapter 31

Lisa's amazing news was the cherry on the top of my home-coming and when I ventured over to the garden the next day it was a pleasure to see that everything was very rosy on that side of the road as well.

'Kate,' said Mark, dropping the watering can and rushing over when I walked through the gate. 'We thought you were gone for good.'

He gave me a hug then took a step back.

'I've only been gone a couple of weeks and besides, how could I possibly stay away?' I laughed, 'just look at this place. It's amazing.'

'Some of the sweet peas are ready for picking already,' he told me. 'And they smell exquisite. Graham says they've grown so well because the walls hold the warmth at the end of the day. The extra heat has brought everything on a treat.'

'I can see that,' I sighed happily.

The place really did look like paradise. Even a grand walled garden in the grounds of a country house such as Wynthorpe Hall back home would have been hard pushed to match our efforts. Everything was looking lush and healthy and that extended to the people as well as the plants. There had been lots of national initiatives recently to encourage people to get out in the fresh air and move a bit more and, if there were any doubters about the benefits of either suggestion, then a trip to our little patch and a look at the faces of the folk involved would be enough to crush any misgivings.

'Anyway,' Mark frowned. 'Are you all right?'

'Couldn't be better,' I told him.

I'd managed a cup of coffee earlier in the day and was feeling much more like my old self.

'Only you look different,' he went on, staring at me more intently.

'Different,' I laughed, turning away a little. 'How do you mean?'

'I don't know,' he shrugged, 'I can't put my finger on it, just different, especially around your eyes.'

'It's relief,' said Luke.

I hadn't heard him walk in behind me.

'Things are finally settling to how they're meant to be,' he added.

'That could be it,' I agreed.

'I know that's it,' Luke smiled. 'After everything we've

all been through in the last few weeks, this peace and tranquillity feels like heaven on earth. This is pretty much how I dreamt things would be when you guys told me you wanted a growing space of your own and it dawned on me that I could make it happen.'

Right on cue Molly, Jasmine and Rob's boys came tearing through the gate, squirting each other with super-soaker water pistols and squealing with laughter.

'Is it?' I asked Luke above the sudden din. 'Is this really what you had in mind?'

'Well,' he smiled, 'almost.'

Our eyes met, just for a second, and I wondered if he thought I looked any different. I wondered how he was going to react when I told him about the baby.

'I'd better get back to my own watering,' said Mark. 'And making sure the kids don't get carried away and squirt the hens. It was a close-run thing yesterday!'

I couldn't help but laugh.

'We can't have them put off their laying,' he added mischievously. 'It's really good to have you home, Kate.'

'Did you hear that?' I asked Luke as Mark walked away.

'What?'

'Mark,' I said. 'He thinks of this place as home already.'

'Good,' grinned Luke. 'That's how I want the residents of Nightingale Square to feel. I know that's how Dad would have wanted them to feel too, had he made it this far.'

'Your dad would be proud of you, Luke,' I told him. 'You've more than answered the questions he wasn't given the time to.'

'Thank you, Kate.' He smiled, looking around him again. 'I think even Charles Wentworth would be happy with this set-up, don't you? What he created in this part of the city was his gift to the world, or those living nearby and working for him at least, and now it's my time and my turn to share what's left of his legacy with the community.'

There was that word again. For some reason 'gifts' kept popping into my head.

'Are you all right?' Luke asked.

'Yes,' I said, 'I'm fine.'

Recently my mind had flitted back to the letters that had gone back and forth between Luke's home and mine and the mention of 'gifts' made me wonder where the other things that we thought might have passed between the two properties had disappeared to, assuming there had really been some, of course.

'Jasmine!' Luke called to his daughter. 'Come and tell Kate where we've been today.'

She abandoned her water pistol and, quickly drying her hands on her dress, ran over.

'We've been to school,' she told me enthusiastically.

'School?' I laughed.

'Yes,' she nodded. 'The one that's just up the road. I'm

going to be going there after the summer, but the lady said I can go in the mornings now if I want to. So I can get used to it.'

'And do you want to?' I asked, hoping she was going to say yes.

'Of course I do,' she told me as if I was asking the most ridiculous question in the world. 'They have a water table *and* a sand table in the classroom!'

Luke looked at me and grinned.

'That was the clincher,' he told me.

'I'm not surprised,' I said seriously. 'A water table and a sand table, that's too good to miss.'

'That's what I said,' Jasmine laughed, slipping her hand into mine. 'Will you come with us in the morning, Kate?'

'Oh,' I said, the word catching in my throat. 'I'm not sure.'

'Please,' she said. 'I want you and Luke to both take me.'

I looked at Luke for some indication as to what my answer should be.

'She's got her heart set on it,' he said huskily. 'She's been asking ever since we got back and like I told you at the farm, there's no point wasting time now we've found our way back to each other.'

'In that case,' I smiled, squatting down to look at her, 'I would be honoured to come with you.'

Without a moment's hesitation she flung herself into my arms and kissed my cheek.

'Thank you, Kate,' she beamed, before rushing off again to retrieve the water pistol, which was almost as big as she was.

'That's your second biggest fan, right there,' said Luke, gently pulling me to my feet.

'Do you reckon?'

'Without a doubt,' he said. 'And please don't worry about things moving too fast, Kate, you know there's always been that special bond between your house and mine.'

'Indeed I do,' I smiled. 'Now come on, Mark promised me sweet peas.'

No matter how hard I tried to put it out of my head, I couldn't stop thinking about the 'gifts' and that 'special bond' between Prosperous Place and my little house in Nightingale Square, but no matter which direction I came at the conundrum from I couldn't puzzle out the answer as to what had happened to the missing portrait. So, to save my sanity, I decided to distract myself by carrying on with my home improvements, starting with ripping up the migraine-inducing dining room carpet.

'Wait for me to come over,' Lisa had said, when I told her of my plans. 'I'll give you a hand and if John's around, I'll rope him in as well.'

Despite Lisa's orders, I decided to forge ahead without them, determined to banish the swirls from sight as soon as possible. To my surprise and relief, the carpet came up with reasonably good grace and beneath it, to my amazement, I discovered what looked like a trap door. There had been no mention of cellars or basements when I bought the house but there was definitely something going on below ground.

I hesitated, just for a second (Tom had made me watch one too many gory films when we were growing up and they always led to an underground and bloody end) before kneeling down to see what I might need to lever the door free.

Eventually, ably assisted by a large metal serving spoon from the kitchen, the wood gave way with an ear-splitting, horror-film-worthy creak and steep stone steps leading down into the darkness were revealed. Against my better judgement, which was telling me to wait for my friends, and guided by the torch on my phone, I gingerly made my way down.

A furtive scrabbling from somewhere deep below made me squeal and I momentarily lost my footing and dropped the garden cane I had wrapped a duster around in lieu of a cobweb brush. My hand flew to my chest as I took a moment to steady my nerves, along with my heart rate, and resolved to climb back up into the light and explore the gloomy place when back-up arrived. I turned to haul myself up the steps, which were far deeper than I had expected, when the beam from my phone caught something bright in the corner fur-thest away.

'Lisa?' I shouted back up to the dining room, in the hope that she would answer, but there was no response. 'John?'

Cautiously I pressed on. I twitched my phone around the space, shining the light into every corner, just to make sure there weren't any nasties waiting to leap out and get me. I don't know what I would have done if there had been of course, but the search settled my silly nerves a little nonetheless.

Beyond a small table with a broken leg and some stacked wood there didn't appear to be much to see, but what there was was covered in clinging cobwebs and a deep layer of dust. I didn't really want to touch or move anything as I knew I'd start coughing and my echoing footsteps were spooky enough without adding my choking to the eerie, musty atmosphere.

I took a deep, brave breath and shuffled away from the relative sanctuary of my escape route, towards whatever it was that had caught my attention.

'Well, I'll be . . .' I muttered as I discovered a tin, a much larger one than the one in the bedroom cupboard, along with something covered in a cloth propped against the wall.

I carefully pulled the fabric away. It was thin and fragile and tore where it was caught against the edges which were pressed against the wall, but I wasn't too concerned about damaging an old tablecloth. I was more interested in what was encased underneath it.

Carefully I knelt on the dusty ground and, with my phone next to me I tried to manoeuvre the frames of what could only be paintings into the limited light so I could get a better look. It was difficult trying to move them around, but I could just about make out through the grime of the protective casings that there was a painting of Prosperous Place, another of the Square, featuring the factory and terraced houses and, joy of joys, a portrait of a young and handsome man with a familiar head of dark curls.

'Oh, yes,' I squeaked, trying not to breathe in the dusty air my movements had stirred up. 'Yes, yes, yes.'

For a moment I forgot I was alone in the grubby cellar and in my mind's eye I imagined all three of the portraits, cleaned, restored and hanging in their rightful positions back in Prosperous Place. This man, I knew as I peered closer, was Edward, it was definitely him, but I only had seconds to admire the likeness between him and my beloved before the torch on my phone turned itself off.

'Shit,' I swallowed, reaching to give it a little shake and trying to press what I thought was the button on the side which would turn it back on again. 'Shit.'

I sat just long enough for the situation to begin to scare me and then decided to move before my nerves completely got the better of me and I became rooted to the spot and trapped for good. I carefully felt my way to leaning the paintings back against the wall much as I had found them and, tucking my useless phone in my pocket, scrabbled to my feet.

I put my hands out in front of me, even though I knew there was nothing I could possibly walk into, and made my way slowly back towards the steps. It seemed to take forever, but my hands finally touched the stairs and I could see the light from the dining room above.

'Lisa!' I called again, but there was still no answer.

I lifted my foot to begin the ascent and felt something furry brush my hand and heard a definite squeak around my feet. Where were Violet and Dash when I needed them? I clapped my hands together to scare away the mouse and its friends and ignored the voice in my head that said it was more likely to be a rat, a whole host of them, all waiting to feast on some unsuspecting person who had entered their private domain.

I clapped harder and, in my growing panic, tried to take the steps two at a time but failed and fell with a yelp, landing at the bottom again with a heavy bump. I sat in a heap, dizzy and dazed, terrified that the fall would have hurt the baby.

'Kate!'

It was Lisa.

'I'm down here,' I tried to shout back, but my voice didn't seem to be carrying.

There was noise in the dining room, then feet on the stairs.

'She's down here,' I was sure that was John. 'It's OK,'

he said, sounding suddenly closer as I began to feel faint. 'I've got you.'

As my eyes blinked reluctantly open I scowled against the brightness and took a moment to weigh up the outcome of what might have happened before closing them again. Either I was dead and these were the bright lights of heaven or I was in hospital, safe and sound and being looked after in a far earthier place.

But what about the baby?

'But what about the baby?'

Had I said that out loud? And if I had, what had happened to my voice? Had I had a sex change?

'Don't worry, Mr Lonsdale,' came the reply, 'we're sure the baby is fine and so is Mum, but just to be on the safe side we've arranged an ultrasound for later.'

'OK, thank you.'

I felt pressure on the bed next to me and when I opened my eyes again, Luke was sitting in a chair with his head resting on the blankets. I lifted my hand, which felt like it weighed a ton and stroked his messy curls. He shot straight up.

'Hey,' he said. 'You're awake.'

He moved from the chair to the bed and took my hand in his.

'What happened?' I croaked.

My lips and throat felt dry, as if I hadn't had a drink for a month.

'You passed out,' he said softly, 'in your cellar.'

'Did I hit my head?' I gasped, my hands rushing to my tummy.

'No,' Luke smiled, 'John caught you, but you took a while to come round and then passed out again, so you're in here as a precaution.'

'OK,' I said, letting out a long, slow breath.

'We can't have anything happening to you or the baby,' he smiled. 'Can we?'

'How do you know about the baby?' I whispered. 'I haven't told anyone.'

I couldn't believe he knew. This wasn't how I had planned to break the news to him at all, obviously, but at least he was smiling.

'Lisa,' he said.

I shook my head.

'I haven't told Lisa.'

'She grabbed your bag to bring to the hospital.'

I still didn't understand.

'Are you sure I didn't hit my head?' I asked, 'because none of this is making any sense to me.'

'She was looking inside for your phone,' he explained. 'So you would have it here with you when you woke up again.'

I remembered I had taken it down into the depths with me.

'It was in my pocket,' I said, shaking my head.

'But there was a pregnancy test wrapped up in your bag,' he said, 'a positive pregnancy test.'

Of course. As unsavoury as it might sound, I hadn't been able to bring myself to throw it away. It was the only tangible proof I had that there really was a baby.

'I had it all figured out,' I sniffed, tears threatening to get the better of me. 'I'd finally worked out how I was going to tell you.'

Luke nodded. He was still smiling and holding my hand.

'And it certainly wasn't like this.'

This ridiculous situation was yet another lesson from the 'life doesn't always turn out how you expect it to' curriculum that I had been grappling with ever since I'd arrived in Nightingale Square. It was another mess in what was turning out to be a rather long line.

'I'm sure it wasn't,' Luke laughed, squeezing my hand harder. 'But just for the record, in case you were wondering, I'm absolutely over the moon.'

'Are you?' I asked. 'Are you really?'

Another mess with a positive outcome then. Lisa would be delighted.

'Of course I am, and before you say anything else, Lisa has already explained to me just how slim the odds were of you ever falling pregnant.'

I felt the colour come back to my face as I realised that he knew all about the legacy David's fling had left behind.

'So,' he added, glossing over what could have been an awkward moment, 'this just goes to prove that you and I are meant to be together, Kate.'

'As if we needed more proof,' I smiled shyly.

My certainty about our relationship had been building and strengthening from the moment I saw him standing in the Cherry Tree Café with Jasmine in his arms, and his reaction to finding out about the baby left me in no doubt of the strength of his feelings for me and mine for him. Feelings that I had once believed I had exhausted on David and that could never be replenished. Thank goodness I had been wrong.

'I know I practically pinched that avocado from you the day we first met and that for a while you thought I was just some shallow idiot who didn't have the brains to match the brawn.'

'I wouldn't go that far,' I interrupted.

'But I love you, Kate,' he carried on, pinning me with his beautiful deep brown gaze. 'I've been falling for you since Valentine's Day.'

He had, I remembered, been a little lost for words when I took my coat off that evening. Was that the moment cupid had struck?

'And I love you too,' I told him.

'And at the end of the day,' he said, kissing my hands and then my face, 'who could possibly want more out of life than to be loved?'

Epilogue

Given everything that had happened in, around and because of the wonderful garden at Prosperous Place, it was only fitting that this year's summer party should take place within its walls, instead of on the green. Everyone, my Wynbridge family included, was invited along to take part. The celebrations kicked off in the early afternoon with everyone crowding into the upstairs room for the second – but this time, without a shadow of a doubt, genuine –portrait-hanging.

'It's almost like looking in a mirror,' Luke had told me when Edward, along with the other two paintings, had been returned from the restorers where they had been cleaned and some minor damage to the frames repaired. 'Even I can see the resemblance is uncanny now.'

'Only our love story is destined to have a far happier ending than Edward and Abigail's,' I reminded him.

'That's true,' he said, folding me into his embrace and breathing deeply.

'But I don't suppose we'll ever really find out how or why the portrait came to be hiding out in my old cellar,' I sighed.

The other tin that had been found along with the artwork hadn't turned up any clues and Harold had given Luke everything he had been hanging on to, but there was nothing extra there either.

'We may yet,' said Luke, kissing the top of my head. 'I'm certain it was something to do with Doris or perhaps her parents, and you never know, this place might still be holding on to a few secrets.'

'Well,' I said with a little shudder, 'don't even think about asking me to look in the cellars. I've had my fill of going underground for the time being, thank you very much.'

Edward looked exceedingly proud to finally be home and we all raised a glass in his honour before heading back outside. As exciting as the moment was, I couldn't stop my thoughts being tinged with a hint of sadness as I thought of Charles and his wife and how devastated they must have been to see the charitable empire they had worked so hard to create crumble. It was a timely reminder, not that I needed another one, that no matter how well you planned, no matter how straight and organised you had things, when life threw you a curveball there was no setting it back on course.

It was amazing to think that a little less than a year ago I had moved into the Square expecting to embrace singledom and resign myself to the fact that my happy ever after was lost forever, and now I was madly in love, having a baby, had moved in to and was working as property manager of the building whose history had tempted me here in the first place.

'Are you all right?' Luke asked. 'Do you need to have a lie down or a rest? You've been rushed off your feet getting everything ready for today.'

'We all have,' I reminded him with a smile. 'But no, don't worry. I'm fine. I'm looking forward to the party.'

Everyone was gathered around the table in the garden, much as they had been at Easter, only now there seemed to be far more people and the table was adorned with jars full of fragrant sweet peas which we had all had a hand in growing.

'I know,' Lisa began, sounding unusually nervous as she kicked off the speeches, 'that only a couple of you here will know what I'm talking about, but—' she stopped and took a deep breath while Heather and I exchanged glances, 'I won!'

'The competition?' Heather squealed.

'Yes,' Lisa grinned, clapping her hands together, 'I won!'

The applause, whoops and cheers that echoed around the walls were a wonderful testament to just how much my friend was loved, but she looked a little confused as everyone joined in.

'We all know!' Luke shouted across the table at her. 'John told us.'

She turned to face her husband.

'I told you to keep it a secret,' she scolded, but all the while laughing. 'I didn't want anyone to know in case I didn't get it.'

John picked her up and spun her round.

'I was never in any doubt that you would win once you told me you'd made the shortlist,' he laughed back. 'I've been telling you to get on with it for years.'

'He has, Mum,' Tamsin butted in, 'and every year Santa buys you a new notebook, so it isn't as if you haven't had anything to write in.'

Lisa shook her head.

'So what happens now?' I asked her.

'I'm going down to London next week,' she blushed, 'for a champagne reception and presentation and to sign the contract. I can't believe it! I've got nothing to wear!'

I promised her we would go shopping at the weekend and then it was Heather's turn to share her news. Glen jiggled Evie on his lap and looked fondly up at his wife who patiently waited for the furore to die down a little.

'If you're going to tell us you're expecting,' Mark called out, 'we've already guessed that.'

Heather poked her tongue out, making Archie and Jasmine giggle, and ran a hand over her pronounced bump.

'I'm well aware that you know that I'm expecting, thank you, Mark,' she said, 'but what you don't know, and we haven't told you all before because we've been getting used to the idea ourselves, is that we're expecting twins.'

It took a moment for her words to sink in and then the clapping started again.

'We have absolutely no idea how we're going to cope,' said Glen, shaking his head.

'Especially now our babysitter across the road is about to embark upon her career as a world-famous novelist.'

'But I'm sure we'll get by,' Glen added nervously.

'Well, I know I come across as a bit of a pain sometimes,' said Carole, rushing to set their minds at rest, 'but I'm only next door and I really would be happy to help when your mum can't come over.'

Having watched her keep the little ones amused in the garden I reckoned that Carole would have liked to have had children of her own. I'd never felt it was appropriate to ask why she hadn't, but was pleased to see Heather give her a hug and I smiled as Glen handed Evie over to her for a cuddle.

Rob then shared the news that he and the boys would soon be moving in with his partner Sarah and her son, who had joined us for the first time today (and out of Carole's match-making clutches, he added later in an aside to me). This announcement was met with astonishment initially and then much laughter as he explained that he had kept her a secret for so long for fear that we would scare her off.

Once the giggling had died down, Neil announced that he was leaving his firm and starting up his own business. Determined not to be outdone, Harold then shocked us all by telling us he had formed a romantic attachment to a woman called Gladys whom he had met at the Day Centre. He caused a further stir by explaining that he would be accompanying her on the Golden Oldies weekend away to Great Yarmouth.

'You old dog,' laughed Mark, raising his glass.

Harold winked and took such a big swig of his own fizz that he started to cough in response.

It was wonderful to look at the sea of smiling faces around the table. Aside from my relatives, less than a year ago I hadn't known a single one of them and now, here I was, an integral part of the group of friends I loved so much they felt more like family.

Along with a lot of things I had learned about myself during the last few months I had discovered that my world wouldn't fall apart if I didn't achieve things in the expected order, or even if I didn't achieve them at all. Life could be a muddle and messy and out of sync with the traditional fairy tale, but that didn't necessarily mean you weren't living a version of it.

'And what about you, Kate?' Lisa called across the table.

'And you, Luke?' joined in Heather, 'haven't either of you got any news you'd like to share?'

'Is there anything we have to say?' Luke asked me, his eyes sparkling with excitement.

Jasmine buried her head in the skirt of my dress and started giggling. She had loved knowing what the others didn't and felt extra-special as a result. And she certainly deserved to.

'Oh yes,' I said. 'How could we possibly forget?'

Jasmine giggled again.

'Let's head over to the green for a minute,' I suggested.

'Come on everyone,' said Luke, scooping Jasmine up in his arms.

We made our way out of the garden and across the road to the little patch of grass. It felt fitting to make our final announcement here, right where my Nightingale Square adventure had started. I looked over at number four and the 'to let' board in the front garden.

'Kate,' said Poppy, who had joined the party, keen to get in on the home-grown produce for her recipes, 'if you have a minute later on, could I talk to you about your house?'

'Yes,' I told her, 'of course.'

I hoped she was interested in renting it; she would be a very welcome addition to the Square.

'So,' said Lisa impatiently, 'out with it.'

Luke came to stand by me, with Jasmine still in his arms, and held my hand.

'Come on, you two,' encouraged Heather. 'Tell us! Boy or girl?'

Luke looked at me and nodded and for a second I lost myself in his eyes. I had never felt happier or more complete than I did in that moment. What an exciting future stretched ahead of me and my new family.

'It's a girl,' I announced, my eyes brimming with the happiest of tears, 'and we're going to call her Abigail.'

Acknowledgements

It never ceases to amaze me, how quickly the months roll by and I find myself sitting down to say thank you to the wonderful collection of family, colleagues and friends who have helped make birthing another book as pain-free as possible. However, I'm not going to make any secret of the fact that writing this, my sixth, has been in many ways the scariest so far. Allow me to explain why ...

Practically since the first day *The Cherry Tree Café* was published, you wonderful readers have been sending messages, tweets and emails telling me just how much you love the little Fenland town of Wynbridge and the fab folk who live there, so deciding to move away has been quite a leap. Fortunately, there were some wonderful neighbours waiting to welcome Kate to Nightingale Square and they have made the transition from country to city really rather fun, so I hope you have enjoyed getting to know them.

Now, back to the huge and heartfelt thank you list.

The family are of course completely used to having me home full-time now and are still saying all the right things in all the right places (cat included), as I talk myself through and around various plot knots, however I still want to say thanks because I'm sure it can't be easy putting up with me wittering on day in, day out.

Next up of course, is the utterly wonderful Emma Capron (aka editor extraordinaire) and standing right beside her, Amanda Preston (aka indispensable agent), both of whom make my life so much easier. Thank you for the encouragement, support, nudges and vision to assist me in writing the very best books I possibly can.

Beautiful bloggers are waiting in the wings for hugs and kisses next. You guys never cease to amaze me. Your support, generosity and cheerleading really knows no bounds and I am certain you have all played a part in turning me into a *Sunday Times* bestselling author. Thank you so, so much for helping make that very special dream come true.

And finally, a massive thank you and an extra bouquet of blooms to you wonderful, wonderful readers who not only take the books to your hearts, you then review them, spread the word, send me wonderful messages and generally make me feel ten feet tall. Which is no easy accomplishment given I'm only five foot nothing! You guys give me the opportunity to get out of bed every single day and do the thing I love most, tell a story. Thank you.

May your bookshelves, be they virtual or real, always be filled with fabulous fiction!

H x

Curl up with Heidi Swain for cupcakes, crafting and love at *The Cherry Tree Café*.

Lizzie Dixon's life feels as though it's fallen apart. Instead of the marriage proposal she was hoping for from her boyfriend, she is unceremoniously dumped, and her job is about to go the same way. So, there's only one option: to go back home to the village she grew up in and try to start again.

Her best friend Jemma is delighted Lizzie has come back home. She has just bought a little café and needs help in getting it ready for the grand opening. And Lizzie's sewing skills are just what she needs.

With a new venture and a new home, things are looking much brighter for Lizzie. But can she get over her broken heart, and will an old flame reignite a love from long ago . . .?

'Fans of Jenny Colgan and Carole Matthews will enjoy this warm and funny story' Katie Oliver, author of the bestselling 'Marrying Mr Darcy' series

Available now in paperback and eBook

Christmas has arrived in the town of Wynbridge and it promises mince pies, mistletoe and a whole host of seasonal joy.

Ruby has finished with university and is heading home for the holidays. She takes on a stall at the local market, and sets about making it the best Christmas market stall ever. There'll be bunting and mistletoe and maybe even a bit of mulled wine.

But with a new retail park just opened, the market is under threat. So together with all the other stallholders, Ruby devises a plan to make sure the market is the first port of call for everyone's Christmas shopping needs.

The only thing standing in her way is her ex, Steve. It's pretty hard to concentrate when he works on the stall opposite, especially when she realises that her feelings are still there ...

This Christmas make time for some winter sparkle – and see who might be under the mistletoe this year ...

Mince Pies and Mistletoe at the Christmas Market

Out now in paperback and eBook

**Curl up with this glorious summer treat
of glamping, vintage tearooms and love . . .**

When Lottie Foster's grandmother's
best friend Gwen dies, she leaves Lottie her
lovely home, Cuckoo Cottage.

Lottie loves the cottage but Matt, a charming local
builder, points out that beneath its charm it is falling
apart. Luckily he is always on hand to help with the
problems that somehow seem to keep cropping up.
But is he just a bit too good to be true? Certainly
Will, Lottie's closest neighbour, seems to think so.

Lottie plans to set up her own business renovating
vintage caravans. She hasn't told anyone about the
project she has cooked up with Jemma from
The Cherry Tree Café to repurpose Gwen's old
caravan and turn it into a gorgeous tearoom.

But before she can finally enjoy living with her
legacy she must uncover who she can trust, and
who to avoid. And with two men vying for
her attention, will she also find love?

Coming Home to Cuckoo Cottage

Available now in paperback and eBook

The *Sunday Times* Christmas bestseller!

When Anna takes on the role of companion to
the owner of Wynthorpe Hall, on the outskirts of
Wynbridge, she has no idea that her life is
set to change beyond all recognition.

A confirmed 'bah humbug' when it comes
to Christmas, Anna is amazed to find herself
quickly immersed in the eccentric household, and
when youngest son Jamie unexpectedly arrives
home it soon becomes obvious that her personal
feelings are going all out to compromise her
professional persona.

Jamie, struggling to come to terms with life back in
the Fens, makes a pact with Anna – she has
to teach him to fall back in love with
Wynthorpe Hall, while he helps her fall
back in love with Christmas. But will it all
prove too much for Anna, or can the family of
Wynthorpe Hall warm her heart once and for all . . . ?

Sleigh Rides and Silver Bells at the Christmas Fair

Available in paperback and eBook